D0934852

ENCHANTING THE ELVEN MAGE

Kingdoms of Lore Book One

ALISHA KLAPHEKE

Cover by Storywrappers

Edited by Laura Josephson

Map by Ren

❀ Created with Vellum

Once upon a time, a witch with hair as bright as summer ivy cursed an infant princess. The king and queen of Lore hid their child at the fae court, and to this day, few know the secrets surrounding the princess and her betrothal.

CHAPTER 1

There were only two good things about the winter solstice celebration at the fae court. Wine and wine.

Aury didn't long for the drink overmuch herself, but it was definitely her ally. Wine turned watchful eyes blurry and slowed cruel, pinching fingers.

Wishing she were still in the barn with the horses, she gripped a rough crystal goblet of spiced red and forced a smile as her aunt, the Fae Queen, strolled through the great hall in a trailing gown the color of pine needles. The queen's hair had been braided artfully around her twisting amethyst-and-ink-hued horns. Though she was a nightmare crafted of snide remarks and cold looks, Aury had to admit the lady was gorgeous.

The queen's gaze flicked away, focusing on her glittering court, and Aury slid out of the hall and into the corridor.

Her fine slippers were nearly silent on the mosaic tiles, but pureblood fae had far better hearing than her half-fae, half-human ears, so she kept the wine as some sort of excuse to be wandering. She crept onward, stealing down the passageway on the sides of her feet and holding her breath. She only needed a peek at the queen's court itinerary to see why in the world she was to be sent on a mysterious journey in the morning.

Nearly to the door now...

A mewling sounded, and Aury's heart jumped. She turned to see a calico ball of fluff climbing the curtains.

"Oh, no. You can't be here, little love." She set her wine on the floor, then detached the kitten from the silken drapes. It was the runt from the barn cat's last litter. "The servants will beat you with a broom if they see these claw marks."

Doing her best to keep quiet and silently praying to the Source the kitten's mews weren't heard, she hurried to the nearest window on the outer wall of the palace. Unlatching the locks, she gently deposited the kitten on the pebble path that led to the stables and the gardens beyond.

"Go find your mother, little love. Hurry now!"

The kitten mewed once more, then ran clumsily toward the barn.

Aury exhaled, closing the window and going back to her wine and her mission to discover where the queen was sending her tomorrow.

In the near dark of the corridor, her foot caught on something. Knee hitting the floor, she lost hold of the goblet and the wine flew, splattering red like blood over the stone walls.

"Oh, sorry!" Bathilda said, even though she was never sorry. "I didn't mean to trip you like that." Her lip curled as she looked down her nose at Aury. "Let me help you up, half-breed."

Ducking out of Bathilda's reach and away from her sharp nails, Aury grabbed her slightly cracked goblet, then shot to her feet. "I'm fine, but thanks ever so much."

But the pureblood wasn't to be thwarted. Bathilda snatched her arm roughly and pulled her toward the great hall. "Your presence is required, Aurora."

Bathilda thrust Aury into the great hall, then grabbed a servant. "Take that hideous necklace off of the half-breed," she said to the servant.

The servant tore Aury's necklace, sending the tiny, flame-colored pearls of the dragon goddess Nix rolling across the tiles. Tears burned Aury's eyes, and her neck throbbed where the broken chain had bit into her skin. Nix was the goddess of fire and festivity, and Aury had always loved the hilarious tales her cousin told of the long-ago dragon shifter.

Bathilda pointed a finger at Aury's face. "Don't even start to tell me that your dear cousin Werian bought you that necklace. I don't believe he cares for a half-breed like you. You lie and lie, a deceit only those with human blood can manage. You're disgusting, and you're a thief."

Werian had indeed given Aury the necklace, and she'd treasured it as a symbol of the one individual who actually seemed to care for her. "I've never stolen a thing in my entire life," she said, meeting Bathilda's glare with one of her own.

"Save your breath. I don't believe you. I'll make certain you're punished for stealing tomorrow."

"But tomorrow, I'm leaving. The queen told me so herself."

Bathilda shrugged. "You'll be back. And I'll be waiting in the shadows." Her cruel smile sent chills down Aury's back. Bathilda crooked a finger at the servant, who had quietly stepped away. "Fetch a washing bowl. Aurora has stable mud under her fingernails."

Aury glared. "Better than the blood of innocents."

Bathilda laughed coldly. "What do you know of innocence? I saw you sneaking toward the queen's rooms."

"At least I don't sneak toward her consort."

Bathilda raised a hand to slap her. Aury fought the urge to flinch, and somehow, she managed it. Bathilda noticed the queen's wandering gaze and relaxed her arm.

The servant took Aury's goblet, then shoved a bowl of water into her hands as Bathilda sauntered away to join in the festivities.

A buzz traveled through Aury as she shook off her encounter with Bathilda, a blend of curiosity and joy. Tomorrow, she was leaving the fae court for the second time in her entire life. Finally, she'd have a break from this place and see more of the human regions of Lore.

As she pulled her hands out of the wash bowl, a deep, golden light passed through the uneven lines of the water's reflection. She paused, lingering over the basin. A cool tingling spread over her body, down her arms, then into the tips of her fingers as a quiet, rushing sound echoed in her ears. It was a sound like the waves she'd heard at the Sea's Claw during her only visit to the ocean. The reflection in the bowl of water showed her face—that of a nineteen-year-old with pointed ears, blue eyes, and silver hair.

But her features faded away. Another face appeared.

Her stomach lifted like she'd jumped from the balcony of the Agate Palace. "What in the name of Nix's Fire..."

It was a man—handsome, with a slightly crooked nose, as if he'd been in a few fights. She couldn't see his ears. He could have been human, fae, or elf. His storm-gray eyes flashed below jet-black eyebrows. Wind Aury couldn't feel or hear tousled the man's dark hair. His image tugged at her, demanding attention. The vision in the ripples was hazy, but stubble showed on his strong chin, and his lips were surprisingly soft-looking and full for such a man.

The vision expanded to reveal that he was holding an axe and pacing around a much larger fellow. Through the inconsistent haze of the golden light on the water, the black-haired man's mouth curved into a grin shaped like his opponent's mountain saber—sharp, dangerous.

The handsome man lifted an eyebrow. The axe slashed through the image.

Aury gasped, heart drumming in her ears alongside that strange rushing sound. The Fae Queen glanced her way, her cold eyes filled with a level of disdain only pureblood fae could manage.

The servants took the bowl away and left Aury standing with her refilled wine goblet, frozen and panicked. Did the queen sense the puzzling inside her head? Was she going mad? It was certainly within the realm of possible outcomes.

Horns sounded, and Aury jumped, nearly spilling her wine on Werian, who had just approached.

"Do we truly need to bring down the skies for every announcement?" she asked him, tugging a length of silver tinsel from his black horns and hoping he didn't notice the absence of the dragon goddess necklace. She didn't want to make him angry on her behalf. Not tonight.

His eyes held mischief, the same look he used to have when he sketched human villages and ships for her when they were young. The Fae Queen had never approved. "You know how my mother loves her drama."

"The king and queen of Lore!" the herald shouted.

Aury looked to Werian in question, but he just shrugged, his gaze skirting away. "This should be interesting," she murmured.

The Fae Queen approached the royal retinue with open arms, as though the king and queen of Lore were friends, but everyone knew the Fae Queen had no friends. She had allies. Entertainers. Kin. The human rulers weren't the last two, so they must have been the first. Allies to the fae court.

"What do they do to make her smile like that?" Aury asked Werian.

"They control the farmland and vineyards. My mother may like rubies and intrigue most," Werian said, "but she also enjoys a nice braid of light bread and spiced red wine. You two have that in common at least." He raised an eyebrow at her empty goblet.

She elbowed him. "I can't put up with you pure types without proper intoxication."

He placed a hand on his chest and shut his eyes briefly. "I understand." His gaze flicked to where the king and two queens were chatting it up. "If it weren't for the human army of Lore, we fae would've been ground into dust by our enemies."

"Why are the human rulers here?" This was the first she'd seen of them. They didn't come around here, supposedly because of an old grievance with the Matchweaver Witch that had happened around the time when Aury was born.

In his youth, the human king had probably been a fine-looking man with flaxen hair, but now his beard looked stained, as if he smoked a pipe a little too often. He held a water mage staff that was covered in runes.

The human queen's eyes were soft, but her mouth had the hard lines of someone who did more frowning than smiling.

"I don't like them," Aury said.

Werian's gaze landed hard on her face.

"Do I have something in my teeth?" She looked around for a pitcher to fill her goblet.

Werian didn't answer; he only crossed his arms and watched his mother talk with the human rulers. "I have loved you, Aury," he finally said, his voice a whisper. "You are my dearest cousin. And a friend. Remember that."

A cold finger of dread dragged across Aury's neck. "Are you drunk?" Of course she knew he cared for her. She loved him too. But to say it like that, with that sadness... Her stomach clenched. "What are you not telling me?" she hissed.

"I was bound to keep the secret, Aury. Remember that, as well."

"What?"

Werian stepped back as the human rulers approached. She hadn't realized they were walking toward her, and now,

ALISHA KLAPHEKE

here they were, and she felt unsteady, for once wishing she
hadn't had all that wine.

She bowed clumsily. The Fae Queen, standing behind
the retinue, looked skyward and sighed as if Aury's
manners were the worst sort of torture.

The king took Aury's chin between his thumb and
finger and studied her face. The urge to whinny like a
bought horse nearly overcame her good sense. "You are a
lovely woman, Aurora Rose."

Rose? She'd never been called Rose. That was...

The human queen smiled, her perfume rolling in like
fog. "You have my second name, my dear."

"Why would I be named for you?" Aury asked. "With
respect, of course."

The human king and queen traded a look and laughed
like only royal people can. Aury forced a smile. What was
happening? She looked for Werian. He stood beside his
mother, his head lowered as he spoke to a servant.

The king took Aury's arm and looped it through his.
"Let's take a walk through the gardens, Aurora Rose. We
have much to discuss."

She let him fairly drag her across the great hall with the
two queens trailing. Unless this king fellow had something
to say about horses, pain-in-the-arse fae, fig tarts, or wine,
they had absolutely nothing to discuss. "I'm sorry, but what
are we talking about?"

"The two greatest forces, my dear. Magic and marriage.
Specifically...yours."

And suddenly, the emptiness of Aury's goblet became
the least of her worries.

CHAPTER 2

Filip slashed the wooden training sword across the younger warrior's leathers, then came down with an overhand strike between head and shoulder. The younger warrior dropped to his knees, but he was grinning like he'd won instead of lost the sparring match. Filip tossed the sword to the side and offered a hand up.

"Prince Filip! That was astounding. You're incredibly fast."

After slicking his sweat-dampened black hair out of his face, Filip yanked the trainee to his feet as snow began to fall in thick waves. "You did well."

The gathered crowd of fellow mountain elves, there for the entertainment of the Frostlight Tournament, shouted Filip's nickname, Hatchet. More people walked the distant path, leaving the highest elevations to celebrate in the relatively flat land where his ancestors had made their home. Already, woolen tents covered the expanse of rocky land from the castle to the cliffs that overlooked the Kingdom of Lore.

Filip strode out of the ice-crusted sparring ring and looked around for his friend Costel while the crowd began to break up and the judges called out the winners of the day's fights.

"Will you have a drink with us, Prince Filip?" Two red-haired women he'd never met gestured toward the tavern and the outdoor tables set among the large, copper bowls of fire.

"You do remember I'm the younger prince?" He grinned, already assuming they had set their sights on him with aspirations of nobility. His elder brother, Dorin—heir to the mountain kingdom throne—was heading up a scouting mission in the highest peaks. Dragons had been spotted recently, and Filip's father the king was determined to record their numbers and protect their young from poachers.

The taller of the red-haired women stretched like a cat, showing off her body, which Filip duly appreciated. "But you are the prince who moves like a mountain lion. A perfect face and the keys to a kingdom say nothing of how a man is behind closed doors."

Filip chuckled. "You're brave to speak to a prince like that. Of course I'll meet you. Perhaps at the bonfires tonight?"

Nodding, they murmured something complimentary about his arms. Knocking the worst of the ring's mud from his boots against the fence, he pretended not to hear.

A whimper sounded through the noise of laughter, conversation, and horses nickering. At one of the tables near the pie seller's cart, Filip's cousin, Ivan, grabbed the front of a young woman's dress. The man was a beast in size and manners, and Filip had hated him since they were forced to play together in childhood.

Ivan shoved her forward, and she slid in the mud, nearly falling before catching herself. "Get me more mead, wench, and be quick."

Without thinking, Filip approached his disgusting cousin. "I see you're spreading the joy of solstice Frostlight."

Ivan grunted and drank the rest of his ale. "Shove it, princeling."

"Seems to me you're the one doing the shoving." Filip looked pointedly at the woman he'd mistreated. She grabbed a pitcher from a nearby table, sloshing the contents.

"None of your business."

Filip held up a finger. "That's where you're mistaken. This is my family's kingdom, and she is one of my subjects. If you insist on acting like a wild boar, you're going to have to go away. Far, far away."

Ivan stood and upturned the table. Filip lurched back to avoid the falling trenchers and mugs. "Fight me, Prince," Ivan sneered. "To the death. I refuse to live another day in a world where you breathe."

Filip clapped. "You just strung together more words than I've heard you say in all your life. You must have taken up reading. What tomes have you been poring over, wise cousin?"

A very large fist swung at Filip's head. He ducked, chuckling.

"I'm serious, Filip. Fight me." Ivan smiled, his eyes bright with bloodlust.

Filip wiped a hand over the stubble on his chin and sighed. "I was really looking forward to a bath in the hot springs, but I guess..."

He took out his hatchet—the weapon that had given him his nickname—flipped it, then hit Ivan in the temple with the butt. Ivan took a swaying step, blinked, then drew his curved saber.

Heat rose in Filip's chest and along his arms, and all trepidation of what he was about to do fled his mind. Ivan really was going to try to slay him right here in the road. "Kill me then, Cousin." He whipped the hatchet around, its handle as familiar as his palm. "Do your worst. I've been spoiling for a fight with you since we shared a nanny."

Like a bear drunk on brazenberries, Ivan lunged and slashed his blade through the air. Suddenly Filip was dodging expert strikes and stabs with his heart drumming in his ears. He blocked a heavy blow. The impact numbed his arm.

"I'll kill you, Prince! I'll find you in your sleep and bash your ugly face." Ivan laughed.

Tasting metal on his tongue, Filip came up behind the cruel beast. With a quick foot to the back of the knee, he had Ivan bending backward and the hatchet's handle laid against the side of his cousin's throat. The big man began to slump in his grip, the blood cut off from Ivan's head by the hold.

"Good rest, Cousin. Remember, you brought this on yourself." He lowered the unconscious idiot to the ground.

The crowd chanted, "Hatchet! Hatchet!"

Shaking, Filip gave them a grin and wiped spittle from his cheek as he walked away.

At the bend in the road, Ivan's voice echoed. Filip spun to see him sitting up, a hand on the overturned table. "We will see what our fathers say of this, Cousin."

Filip gave him a big smile. "Just keep your hands off my subjects and we'll be fine!" *You pig.*

Ivan's father would want revenge for this embarrassment. Filip adjusted the royal family's seal ring on his finger. The heavy thing boasted a detailed constellation, symbolic of the elven god Rigel and the goddess Ursea who first brought elves to this sharply beautiful place. Filip's parents would understand about the fight, surely.

At the lane leading up to the castle, Filip's friend Costel slipped through the small space between the new blacksmith's forge and the tavern. Though he was the same age as Filip, Costel still had the rawboned look of a youth. "Filip! Your parents are requesting your presence." The man's light hair fell over his eyes.

"Word travels fast."

Costel's eyebrows knitted. "News?"

"Aren't they wanting to know why I put Ivan down for a little nap?"

"You did what?"

Filip pushed past Costel. "He asked for it."

"Oh, gods. The earl will have you whipped."

"He was being a boar. As usual. I won't be taken."

"You will. That man is nearly as bad as his son."

"All the more reason for my parents not to listen to his rambling."

"But that's not what they want to talk to you about."

Filip glanced at Costel as they strode toward the inner bailey and the keep. "Do I have time to wash first?"

Costel's lips bunched. "Your mother is pacing."

"So, no."

"Not if you want to keep your ears." Costel flicked one of Filip's pointed ears, and Filip punched him lightly in the stomach. Costel made an *oomph* sound but laughed and came up with an elbow aimed at Filip's chin. Filip caught Costel's arm and shoved him away, grinning.

"Think Ioana will meet me at the bonfires tonight?" Costel asked.

Filip poked at his ribs. "Not if she has anything better to do."

"Eh! I've bulked up this past fortnight, haven't I? I've eaten nearly as much as you."

"Sure, Costel. You're gaining muscle. Well done. I was only teasing." The guards held their swords back as Filip and Costel strolled through the inner bailey's archway. "She'll be there, and she'll beg you to marry her," Filip said.

Costel looked at the ground, his crooked teeth showing as he smiled widely. "You think so?"

"Aye. You have a unique look, friend. And the ear of the prince." Filip winked. "Unless my dear mother lops it off during this audience."

Costel chuckled, then gripped Filip's arm, stopping him just inside the keep's doors. "All your news distracted me. There's a messenger from Lore. That's what the king and queen want to talk to you about."

Valets and servants bustled through the corridor, bumping one another into the furs that lined the walls and whispering excitedly under the glowing oil lamps. Normally, Filip's home was quiet, but at Frostlight, everyone had a job and the wish to see it done quickly so they wouldn't miss out on the fun.

Filip swung around, aiming for the hallway that led to his chambers.

"Where are you going?" Costel hurried to catch up.

"If it's news from Lore, it can wait until I've washed. Those spoiled humans never have anything important to say." He paused and met Costel's wide eyes. "Unless the messenger is a water mage."

"I don't think so."

Filip nodded, shrugging. "Too bad. Those mages did fine work in the war. I never did get the chance to speak with one."

Most humans were simple folk like him, lacking magic —although his speed, strength, and longer life gave him an edge as an elf.

But some incredibly rare humans held powerful magic.

Human witches were blessed by the Sacred Oak and given wands by trees near their place of birth. Witches could enact their will on the world to a certain degree, depending on how much of the goddess Lyra's strength flowed in their veins.

The other type of humans that held magic were water mages. The blood of the ancient race of sea folk, the power of goddess Lilia, showed up in their ability to make water flood and freeze.

Costel grabbed him and turned him around. "You have to go to the throne room now or I'll be in it, Filip."

Sighing, Filip looked to the painted stars on the keep's

ceiling. "All right. I wouldn't want your Ioana to miss out on your brawny presence tonight."

"Shut it," Costel said, grinning.

Filip and Costel wove through the frenzy of servants and finally entered the throne room. Queen Sorina and King Mihai were both pacing. When they spotted Filip, they stopped.

Filip spoke out of the side of his mouth. "Costel, you should go. Now."

"I will never leave your side."

"This isn't an army. This is my parents." Much worse. When they were like this, anything could happen. "Remember Marius's donkey?"

Their friend Marius had been caught sneaking a ride on Sorina's best mare. When Sorina had found out, he'd been forced to ride a donkey to his own wedding.

"Oh, the donkey. Gods in the sky, that bray—"

"If you don't mind!" Sorina's voice pounded across the stone floor, and Filip and Costel clapped their mouths shut.

"Son," Mihai started, "we need to discuss your wife."

Despite the roaring fires blazing from the two hearths, Filip's skin went cold. "I don't have a wife."

Sorina sat on her throne, her silver crown catching the candlelight and her hands folded in her lap. "You do now."

CHAPTER 3

S tomach twisting with worry, Aury let the human king and queen lead her past the giant map on the wall with its colored landscapes and illustrated dragons. The painted cerulean and emerald scales reflected the candlelight beautifully.

The main part of the map showed the verdant kingdom of Lore and the mountain kingdom of Balaur, the elven realm. The humans ruled Lore, including the fae court that lived inside the kingdom's Forest of Illumahrah. Witches had abodes in both Lore and Balaur, wild creatures that they were. Sadly, dragons no longer lived among the other races, nor did they shift into human form as the goddess Nix once had. Dragons were rare, and Aury had only seen one in her entire life.

In the gardens beside the great hall, the Frostlight moon shone down through the canopy of skeletal tree limbs and snow-dusted pines. Dark ivy curled around the ruins of the original palace, leaves grasping well-worn stone pillars where the winter jasmine slept in the falling snow. A tidy labyrinth paved with small, round stones looped a still pool.

Aury had seen a face in the washing water. Would she see something else if she got too close now?

The human queen stared, and Aury picked at her gown, nervous under the human ruler's expectant look.

Dropping Aury's arm, the king faced her, his crown shimmering in the broken moonlight as his gaze flicked to her ear. Strange man. "Aurora Rose, you are not half fae as you have been led to believe."

She couldn't understand what he was saying. The sounds formed words, but they made no sense.

He cocked his head and watched her like a scar wolf eyeing a hare. "You are fully human and most likely a water mage."

"No," she said, touching the pointed ear he'd been focusing on.

"Here. I can help with that," the Fae Queen's voice murmured from the door behind Aury. A tingling spread over her head, and the tips on her ears smoothed into soft curves.

Her heart stuttered. "But... Why would I be human? I'm the queen's niece. Her sister was my mother. The queen didn't love me, but—"

The king tucked his lips inside his stained beard and shook his head. "I'm afraid you have it all wrong."

The human queen gripped Aury's arms, then spun her around. Those wide eyes looked ready to swallow her. "You are our daughter and the heir to the throne."

The garden spun, and Aury let the human queen hold

her upright. She shook off the dizziness. "You're my parents."

"We are," the queen said, smiling.

"And that's not all." The king spun his water mage staff. "You most likely hold a fraction of my power."

"I'm a water mage?"

"Most likely. You showed a few signs even as an infant."

"Why did you give me to the fae?"

"That's a long story," the queen said.

The king tucked his staff under an arm. "When you were born, we betrothed you to a prince. The Matchweaver wasn't pleased that we chose without her advice."

"You did what?"

The queen sniffed. "The witch grows too haughty. She must remember who rules this kingdom."

"She cursed you, Aurora," the king said. "We had to hide you here in the fae court where you would be safe."

"This is too much. Who has wine?" Aury looked around, but there was no help in sight. Water mage. Royal heir. Curses. Her fingers dug into her gown, and she tried to slow her breathing and stop the world from spinning.

"The Matchweaver's curse... Well, she said that because we betrothed you without consulting her and her magic loom, you would prick your finger on a spinning wheel and die."

"Why didn't she just kill me herself?"

The Fae Queen piped up. "Because she is a witch. They adore dramatics."

And the fae didn't? Ha. More likely the Matchweaver

couldn't get direct access to Aury without ending up dead herself.

"Why are you telling me all of this now?" Aury's blood began to simmer. She'd been kept in the dark about everything for her entire life. "You could have at least told me. I haven't been a child in years. Why lie?"

"I never lied," the Fae Queen said.

After clearing his throat, the king said, "Look, Aurora. We couldn't risk someone finding out who you were and telling the witch where you were hiding. The fewer who knew, the better. I don't want to have to slay a woman that my people believe is nigh on being a goddess. The Matchweaver didn't find you. You're old enough now to avoid spinning wheels. Enough arguing. You will train at Darkfleot to receive your staff and hone your water magic. But before any of that, you will marry Prince Filip of the Mountain Kingdom. We have waited your entire life for this marriage alliance."

Her lungs collapsed. Werian appeared with a small stool and helped her sit without falling over. Once seated, she looked up at him. Her chest burned with the splinters of a broken heart. "Liar," she hissed.

Werian winced but didn't argue his case like the others.

"Wait." She held up a finger. "Do you mean the prince of the mountain elves?" Surely not.

"Indeed," the human queen said, looking pale. "The second-born of King Mihai and Queen Sorina."

A mountain elf. A being who knew nothing of kindness or learned discussion or anything besides war and breeding. Aury's simmering blood heated to a full boil. She stood and pointed a finger in the king's face. "You expect me to wed a vicious, bloodthirsty, filthy mountain elf? Well, let me tell you something, Father," she said, pushing her hurt and anger into the word. He was not a father to her in any way. "You have another thing coming. You are a liar, and you didn't care a whit about how I was treated here, how I was mocked for all my days. If my life depended on it, I wouldn't marry someone you picked!" She'd backed him against the palace's wall.

"Calm down, Daughter. There's no reason to be afraid and angry."

He didn't believe her about how she'd been treated. Of course he didn't. They were strangers. "Just try to make me marry him and you'll see what real anger looks like."

His face went blank. "Now see here, girl. I am king of Lore, and I will not be barked at by you. You will marry Prince Filip, and I don't care whether he has fangs the size of daggers or a taste for the blood of babies. We must have his elven warriors to keep the Wylfen at bay. They've ransacked our cities for years. They've brought war to my kingdom once and will do it again. My spies have seen campfire smoke, and they say a contingent of Wylfen forces will march on Dragon Wing Pass sometime during the next moon."

The Fae Queen gasped.

The king nodded. "We don't know how they've managed to make their way through the mountains this time of year."

The bluster went out of Aury, and she stood, her arms limp at her sides. "The Wylfen." Memories of the war on fae grounds pierced her mind—trained scar wolves, burning trees, children's screams, and weeks with nothing more to eat than stale nuts and a few berries. The Wylfen were human, but they fought like demons. "So you need the elven army."

The human queen touched her back, then Aury moved out of reach. "We do," the queen said. "We must have a powerful weapon to fight them. We've lost so many soldiers and mages. We can't fight them and win. Not again."

Aury turned to see Werian watching her, his eyes pinched with what looked like worry. She stared at the ground and moved the small, round stones of the pathway with her slipper. Her bones shook inside her skin. She felt as if her body were remaking itself by trembling, soaking in the truth of who and what she really was. A human. A ruler's heir. A mage. Bound to marry a monster.

Lightning shot through her. She faced the king. "If I am your daughter—"

"You are."

"Then I should have powerful magic as a water mage, yes?"

"Perhaps."

She knew of the Mage Trials, the evaluations by the Masters of the Order, the greatest mages in Lore. Normally, water mage recruits studied for a full year or more before taking them. She'd read the information in numerous scrolls during her tutoring.

"And water mages must train and pass the Trials to earn their place in the army," Aury said. "You don't want me, the princess of Lore, to be coddled, do you?"

"No," the king stammered. "I..."

"I must earn my place and thus the respect of the people."

"Yes, but..."

"How can I focus on training in the middle of wedding plans? Wait to wed me to the elf until I have passed the Mage Trials."

The human queen laughed nervously. "There's only a slim chance you will pass, Aurora Rose. The Trials are incredibly difficult. Few women earn a ranking."

"Maybe because they lack support," Aury snapped.

The queen flinched, then cleared her face of emotion. "We can't risk losing an army of a thousand vicious fighters who have experience with the Wylfen. They're already mobilizing, but to slight them—"

"But what if I become the most powerful mage the kingdom has ever seen? I don't shy away from work. I can learn." The face she'd seen in the water rolled through her mind. "And just today, I saw a battle in a bowl of water."

The Fae Queen traded a look with Werian, who only shrugged. The king and queen narrowed their eyes.

"What did you see?" the king asked.

"A face. A saber. Do water mages scry?"

"They can," the queen said. "Strong ones do."

"See? I'm going to amaze you." *You complete turd piles of lies and apathy.* "You don't care about me yet, but in time..."

"We do! We just wanted to protect you." The queen pulled her cloak more tightly around her shoulders.

"You grew strong in spirit here, at least," the king muttered.

Aury waved a hand to quiet them. "No, you don't care about me. But you will. I go to the Order's castle at dawn.

Promise me you will give me time to train before you marry me off."

"We can't do that," the king said. "Absolutely not. There is no time. And besides that, Prince Filip is most likely on the road to Loreton Palace right now."

Aury's skin felt stretched too thin. "Just give me until the Mage Trials. You don't have to tell the elf a thing. Simply put him off for a while." She would figure out what to do once she had more time.

Werian stepped forward, the purple strands in his black hair shimmering lightly. "The Mage Trials are scheduled for three weeks from today."

The king scowled and shook his head, but the queen tugged at his cloak. "It's only three weeks. Filip can wait three weeks," she said. Then she faced Aury. "The moment the Trials are complete, the wedding will take place at Loreton. You will marry the prince with no argument."

"But if I'm so powerful that we can fight the Wylfen without the elven army—"

"Aurora..."

"Fine. After the Trials, I marry the bloodthirsty elf." She'd figure out another plan. This was all happening so quickly. She needed to stall, to find time to think.

The king whispered something to his wife, and she patted his shoulder and sniffed.

"Agreed," the king said, his stare flat and his shoulders stiff. "We will dine at Loreton Palace soon and meet your future husband."

"My never-to-be husband."

"Enough." The king raised a hand, and Aury stood her ground, setting her jaw, daring him.

"Go ahead, Father. Show me how much you care."

"Ach." He threw up his hands and barged his way through the group and back into the great hall with the queen on his heels.

The Fae Queen stayed in the garden. "You must remain in your rooms tonight and tell no one of this. If you do, you will find yourself dead of some mysterious poison."

"Sounds about right."

"What was that?"

"Nothing, Auntie."

The Fae Queen returned to her feast, and Aury was left with Werian.

He didn't try to hug her or console her, but he stood nearby, tossing rocks into the pool. "Did you really see a face in the water?"

"I did." Tears burned at the edges of her eyes. No way she was crying. "Will you come with me to Loreton Palace? Just for a while?" She hated the desperation in her voice, but she couldn't manage to hide it.

"I can't. My mother would never allow it. Not now. Later, I will visit you, Princess Aurora."

"Please don't call me that."

The calico kitten appeared at Aury's feet. "Back to the barn, kitty," she whispered as she set it on the path again. "I'd flee with you if I could."

"I do have another introduction to make," Werian said, taking Aury's attention from the kitten's shadow as it disappeared into the hole near the stable wall where the cats often slept.

Werian clapped three times, and three fae women walked out of the deeper parts of the garden.

The first two were tall and slim with golden eyes like a cat's. The third one was short, dark-eyed, and curvy. Their tattoos said all three of them had fought in the last war with the Wylfen. The inkings snaking up their arms told of all three's bravery in battle, quick-thinking, and great power in healing.

Werian gave them a nod. "I asked these three to escort you when you leave here."

"Who are you?" She'd seen them around the palace, she was almost sure, but didn't have any idea of their positions.

The shorter one spoke up with a voice like a bell. "I'm Eawynn. We were there when the Matchweaver showed up to your birth feast and betrothal. We altered the curse."

One of the slim women, the second tallest, took out a folded bit of parchment. "And I am Gytha. We have been bound to you since then." With fingers tattooed in thorn patterns, she opened the parchment to show a tiny clip of silver hair. "It's yours. From the day of your birth feast."

Aury touched the hair. "In what way did you alter the curse?"

The tallest woman removed her crushed velvet cloak and slung it around Aury's frozen shoulders. The warmth was welcome. "I am Hilda. We made it so that if you did touch a spinning wheel," she said, a smile ghosting across her prim lips, "you would only sleep forever instead of dying."

The shorter one—Eawynn—grinned, her plump cheeks dimpling prettily. "Yes! And only your true love could wake you."

Typical fae. The ones strong enough to twist a witch's

magic usually had eccentric thoughts on what was best in any given situation.

Werian hugged Aury then, and a tear slid from her eye. She wiped it quickly.

"Eawynn, Hilda, and Gytha," Werian said, "have kept an eye on you since birth. They were told not to interfere unless your life was truly in danger. Now, they can aid you as you train."

Hilda adjusted the cloak she'd given Aury, moving the clasp so that it held more tightly. "We will see that those who hurt you suffer. Not today. But someday. Don't worry."

"You are frightening."

Hilda laughed. "Yes. I am fae."

"But you seem so kind," Aury said. "Unlike all the others."

The cheery, plump Eawynn crossed her arms. "Only because you're our charge."

"I accept your offer to help. I'll need it." Aury hugged Werian one last time. "Thank you. For everything."

"We are kindred spirits, you and I. More than you know."

Gytha clasped her thorn-tattooed hands and gave Aury a sad smile.

"You're still keeping things from me?" Aury asked Werian.

"I'll tell you all about me," he answered. "Someday. For now, you have enough secrets to feast on."

Aury slapped his chest lightly and started to walk inside the palace. "I'll drink to that."

CHAPTER 4

Filip took a step backward. "I'm sorry. Did you just say I have a wife?" A slightly hysterical laugh escaped him.

Sorina pressed her lips into a line, and Mihai answered instead, smoothing his gray hair behind his pointed ears. "Yes, well, you *will*."

"Huh. I would've thought I'd know a thing like that."

Costel laughed but covered it with a cough.

Mihai exhaled sharply. "When you were a child, we brought you to Loreton Palace, and you were betrothed to Princess Aurora."

"Princess who? The king and queen don't have a daughter."

Sorina stood and swept down the three stairs of the dais. She took Filip's hands. Mother's hands were always cool and soft despite the rough weather of their kingdom. "Aurora was hidden in the fae court until now. The

28

Matchweaver wasn't consulted in your match, and she cursed the princess."

"I assume she survived since she is still set to be my bride? I think even King Athellore would stop at using his kin after death."

Sorina almost smiled. "She is well, as this Lore messenger has told us."

A richly robed man stood to the side of the dais. The man's Loreton livery—a ruby red stag on a field of deep cerulean water—stretched over his ample belly, and Filip gritted his teeth. Spoiled humans and their vast stretches of hunting grounds and farmlands...

Filip tried to figure out how he felt about this development, but right now, everything in him was as numb as his arm had been after blocking Ivan's blade.

"And the curse..." he started. How could he wed a woman from Lore? Her people hoarded their wealth and knew nothing of lean winters... She would never understand him, or the close friendships he'd built with Costel, Drago, and Stefan as they'd shivered by the fire in the palace, getting drunk on fruit brandy because the food had run out. He wouldn't have to leave them, surely. His heart stilled, fear gripping him with lightning fingers. No, they would attend him as they always had.

Mihai coughed, then cleared his throat. The ague was coming on him like it always did at Frostlight. "The curse states that Aurora will prick her finger on a spinning wheel and die. The fae at the birth feast used their talents to fight the curse. They attempted to get rid of the curse entirely but could only lessen it. They settled for an eternal slumber rather than death."

Filip rolled his eyes. Who would choose such a horrible fate? He'd rather die than lie on a bed motionless until time crumbled away his body and mind. "Fae," he muttered, the word loaded with what he knew of them. They may have pointed ears like mountain elves, but they were so incredibly different with their odd fancies and chilly demeanor. He'd met a dozen or so over the years, members of the court who enjoyed a trip to the mountains during peacetime. Prince Werian wasn't so bad.

"Since she is grown now, they believe the curse is no longer a threat," Mihai said, joining them, studying Filip like he always did, like he didn't understand what made Filip tick. They got along fine, but they were so different. Father acted slowly, and because of that, he missed many opportunities to expand the kingdom and make beneficial treaties. This betrothal would've been Mother's idea. Queen Gwinnith's pregnancy was just the sort of information Sorina gleaned from informants. She would've jumped at the chance to use the development to their kingdom's benefit.

"Why did you think I would agree to this, and why haven't you told me?"

"We thought the betrothal was voided after the curse," Sorina said. "The king and queen led us to believe the union was not to be...for the safety of their daughter, which we can understand. But now, this messenger has told us the opportunity remains there for the taking."

"What do we get in exchange for my lifetime of servitude?"

"It's not like that, Son," Mihai said. "After seeing her mother, she is most likely a beauty." Sorina raised an eyebrow. He cleared his throat, then glanced at the messenger. "You'll live in a fine palace in a warm kingdom. What's not to love?"

Sorina nodded. "And we will have all the farmland at the foothills in Lore."

Filip jolted. "All of it?" He traded a look with Costel.

Both his parents smiled. "Yes," Sorina whispered, her grin fading. "It's a good thing. Our stores are nearly depleted. If the storms come as they did last early spring, our people will starve. We're already rationing."

"You are?"

Mihai motioned to a servant. The man brought a scroll and a small table. Mihai spread the scroll, which showed a map of the Kingdom of Lore. The palace—where they expected Filip to live at least half of the rest of his life—sat beside the powerful Silver River, a waterway that stretched across the land in all directions and gave life to Darkfleot, where the water mages trained for military action under the Order.

Pointing to the dark scribbles that denoted the water mage fortress, Mihai explained how Filip would become a leader in the Lore forces, training both water mages and those without magic to fight like mountain elves.

"They believe we're mages," Costel whispered, smiling and coming out of the shadows.

Sorina touched Filip's ring. "They do," she whispered. "And we'll keep it that way, Son. They don't need to know it is simply our inborn speed and agility that makes us the finest warriors."

Finally, the reality of what Filip had to do for his people

broke through the ice of shock. A weight pressed into his chest, and his feet felt nailed to the floor.

He met his parents' eyes. "I will marry the spoiled Princess Aurora and leave my beautiful homeland. But first, I will enjoy tonight like it is my last night alive."

A shout rose in the corridor, then the earl, Ivan's father, burst through the doors. "I demand justice!"

Filip's uncle had spittle on his dark beard, and his face was as red as Ivan's had been. "He shamed Ivan!"

Mihai and Sorina stared at Filip, mouths open.

Filip held out his hands. "I knocked him out near the sparring rings. He is fine. Ask Costel." Of course, his friend hadn't been there, but Costel always backed up Filip.

"I don't trust your lap dog!" The earl sneered at Costel, then marched up to Mihai. "Brother, Filip must be whipped. Privately, yes, but it must be done. We cannot allow him to go around beating people on a whim!"

Mihai closed his eyes briefly, then glared at his brother. "I would bet all that Ivan was acting less than civilized." Then Mihai looked to Filip. "Did he raise a hand to you first?"

"Yes."

"Ten lashes," the earl said, his voice like the barbed end of a whip. "I know well how you envy him. You must keep your power in check, boy."

Sorina gasped. "Do not call him *boy*."

Filip snorted. "What do I envy exactly, dear Uncle? The way your son beats innocent women and animals, or the way he can't hold his drink?"

The earl howled and flew at Filip, but Costel bumped his way between them, and the earl took Costel down with a flurry of sloppy punches. Filip and Mihai grabbed the back of the earl's doublet and yanked him away from Costel even as the man shrieked obscenities.

"You will stand down, brother," Mihai ordered, releasing him as Filip did.

The earl's chest heaved as he fought to control his rage. Finally, he ran a hand through his damp hair and bowed shallowly.

"Accept my judgment on this, Earl," Mihai said.

The earl turned his head to glance at Filip. The look he gave him was pure hatred. "Fine," he said straightening. "I accept." He tugged his doublet back into place and started for the door. "But know, Prince Filip, that you have made yourself an enemy in your homeland. I will not forgive this."

Sorina pointed a finger. "Nor will you act on your anger. Swear it."

The earl huffed and heaved another breath. Was he going to lunge at Filip again?

"Swear it." Sorina's voice was an axe on a chopping block.

"I swear it." With a feeble excuse for a bow, the earl strode out of the throne room.

Mihai sighed. "Filip, Ivan is a monster, but did you truly have to shame him in front of the crowds?"

"It was him or an innocent subject beaten. He needed a reminder of who rules here."

Sorina took Filip's hand. "Such acts show a confidence one needs to rule."

Mihai turned his attention back to the map of Lore.

"It's acts like these that show you need a steadying influence in your life."

"You think a princess of Lore will help me rule someday? The lowlanders know nothing of suffering, of sacrifice."

"They suffered at the hand of the Wylfen too," Sorina said.

"Mother. Not like us."

"No, not as we did. But still, she will know the horrors of war."

"How? Because she had to skip dinner once at Loreton Palace?"

"She was raised at the fae court. They lost many to the invaders. She will have lost someone."

Filip shoved his tangled black hair out of his face and studied the map. "Perhaps." He turned to face the Lore messenger, who was acting like he hadn't heard or seen a thing. "Stop pretending you're deaf, man. What is your Princess Aurora like? What is my fate with this marriage?"

The messenger shuffled his feet. "I...I haven't met the princess."

"But surely you've heard talk."

"No, your majesty. Nothing at all. We at the palace didn't know of her existence until now. The head cook told me all the others there the day the Matchweaver cursed her were sent away to the far reaches of the kingdom so the secret would be kept."

"It was a frightful day." Sorina fidgeted with the gold loop in her ear. "Poor little babe."

Mihai kissed her temple.

"If she's like our queen," the messenger said, "she'll be practical and even tempered."

"See?" Mihai said. "That will do nicely for you. Perhaps she'll calm that hot head of yours."

A grin tugged at Filip's lips, and the spark of a challenge warmed his blood. "We'll see if she can tame me, then. I doubt it." If marriage was non-negotiable, he might as well have a good time with the courting.

"Son..." Sorina narrowed her eyes. "You will behave."

Filip smiled and bowed. "As always."

CHAPTER 5

The next morning, the riding party of Aury, her parents, and the royal guard left the enchanted forest of Illumahrah with little difficulty. But they clomped onward and into the countryside at a snail's pace, stopping for water and rest every few hours and sleeping far too long when they found inns each night.

According to the map Hilda had shown Aury, they weren't far from the meadows that led to the Silver River. Lifting herself in her stirrups, she craned her neck, trying to see past the crowns, banners—the endless parade of ridiculousness. Absolutely boiling with the need to get to the Order's castle, Darkfleot, and find out just what it meant to be a water mage, she nudged the lovely, golden mare the horrible king and queen had given her. She wouldn't be swayed, all for a gift, into forgetting years upon years of torment at the fae court while they pretended she didn't exist. But that didn't mean she couldn't enjoy the fine horse. The mare took off at a nice canter, and Aury urged her to veer around all the guards and her parents.

Gods above, it was madness to think that King Athellore and Queen Gwinnith were her parents!

Ignoring their shouts of caution, Aury leaned close to the mare's ear, its pale mane tickling her face. "Let's have some fun, shall we?" The mare took off down the king's road, stirring up the snowy mud. "You don't actually like the name Flower, do you?" Aury winced, and the horse nickered, obviously agreeing that it was sadly bereft of any honor. "How about Goldheart?"

The mare galloped faster, which Aury took as a *yes*.

The only time Aury had seen a water mage with her own eyes was during the war when the fighting had come to Illumahrah. Five Wylfen and their trained scar wolves had torn a path in the forest, heading for the Agate Palace and the Fae Queen's treasure.

When the alarm call had gone up from the sentries, Aury had trailed Werian outside, where he quickly joined his fellow purebloods in battle with bow and arrow. Werian was a master marksman, but the Wylfen's wolves ripped into the fae, the arrows not slowing them much.

Just when Aury had begun to lose hope, a single rider had crashed through the trees, raised his staff, and swung it around his head. The water mage's movements brought the dew off the leaves of every plant in the garden, every tree in the wood, then froze the droplets and shot them like shards of glass. Wylfen fell to their knees, clawing at their shredded eyes and desperate to escape the ice that cut them as well as a thousand tiny knives.

Using every bit of his inborn magical energy, he'd saved

the fae court, Werian and Aury included, and then slid from his horse and slumped to the ground unconscious. The Fae Queen had housed him until he recovered his strength and gave the mage a feast when he woke.

Would Aury someday be capable of magic so powerful? Her blood raced at the idea. Yes, she would. Somehow. Some way.

Snowy hills spread out beyond the Forest of Illumahrah, and Aury urged Goldheart down a steep incline and into the wide meadows that housed the Silver River. Past the meadows, dark mountains supported the amethyst snow clouds.

That was where her betrothed lived, somewhere up there with his bloodthirsty kin. He was probably murdering people right now and drinking their blood. She shivered and set her jaw. She wouldn't be afraid of him. Never. She would be polite but would simply let him know that the marriage wasn't to be. Athellore had told her his people were to gain farmland from the union of the two kingdoms. She'd simply let this Prince Filip know that even though they weren't going to marry, when she was crowned queen of Lore, she'd make certain his people had that land as agreed. No marriage needed to take place, surely. They would have a secret verbal agreement, binding through her royal blood as she'd seen Prince Werian do behind his mother's back once. Prince Filip could just march right back up to his mountain abode and stay there for eternity, or however long mountain elves lived.

Aside from the fact that they longed for bloodshed and quite possibly ate their enemies, her knowledge about elves was muddled. They didn't have the healing power of their fae cousins, but they could run like the wind and fight like no other beings. That much she was aware of. According to her royal parents, if there were more mountain elves, they could probably have destroyed the Wylfen long ago.

Goldheart stumbled, and something flashed in the sunlight. She'd thrown a shoe. Snarling at the delay, Aury dismounted and gave the mare a pat. "We'll get you taken care of, darling." She inhaled the sweet scent of horse and let herself forget about the evil elven mage who would become her husband if she didn't figure out a plan. If she were a strong enough water mage, she could surely put the wedding off indefinitely, right?

Fatigued from travel, they entered a middling village filled with curious children and the sound of a blacksmith, which was welcome. While the smith aided Goldheart, Aury walked to the market with Hilda, Gytha, and Eawynn in tow. And about three dozen human villagers who had probably never seen a fae or a princess.

The villagers tentatively peppered the fae with questions that Eawynn answered before Hilda or Gytha had the chance. Aury stepped on a stone and stopped to examine a hole in her boot.

She removed it and held it up. "Looks like I need a shoe as well. I should be wearing stouter boots than these anyway. Children?"

A bevy of rosy-cheeked faces were immediately staring up at her. It was cute but also a tiny bit creepy how fast they moved. There hadn't been many young ones at the fae court, but it seemed the humans—*my kind,* Aury corrected herself—bred as often as the fae brushed their fine hair.

"Anyone know where I can have my boot mended?"

The children took her hands. Based on how her parents had acted when they'd stopped at a trading outpost bursting with the merchant's little ones, they would have a fit if they saw this. Aury grinned and let the children drag her down the snowy road, all of them talking at once.

"The cobbler is ill."

"But another cobbler sent his niece, and she's lovely."

Aury raised an eyebrow. "Looks probably have nothing to do with the ability to make solid footwear."

A little girl glared. "You don't know."

A boy punched the girl's arm, and she howled before Aury pulled them apart.

The boy took Aury's hand and held it like she was Dragon Queen Elixane's treasure from the ancient stories. "She is a princess. She knows everything."

Flinching at the use of her title, she silently cursed the king and queen for not having her trained to be the person they now expected her to be. "Thank you, but I assure you I do not," Aury corrected. Thank the Source, she'd had Werian around to learn from.

Hilda, Gytha, and Eawynn trailed along, whispering about the sky and what looked like a coming snowstorm.

The cobbler's shop squatted between a tailor and a chandler. Sure enough, inside, the cobbler himself lay on a pallet, his face pale, while a pretty woman a few years younger than Aury worked at a table covered in strips of leather, varying sizes of nails, and small tools. The cobbler's replacement—the niece of a master cobbler from three villages away, as the children told it—pried a shoe apart with a metal clamping tool, the name of which Aury was ignorant.

The little boy at Aury's side gripped her fingers and gasped. "She's sinister-handed!"

The cobbler looked up, her eyes glazed from long focus. "Oh, hello. May I help you? I'm Rhianne." She didn't seem to have heard the boy, but he was right. The cobbler's niece was indeed left-handed.

A little girl ran from the shop, bumping into Hilda and Gytha, who fussed at her in their uptight fae manner.

The boy tugged at Aury's fingers. "Come, Princess Aurora. She is evil."

A foolish superstition. "I seriously doubt it, lad. Go on, if your courage fails you, but I'll stay and get my boot mended."

The cobbler—Rhianne, she had called herself—smiled, eyes shining. "Thank you for staying. I hoped this village would be less superstitious than my own. I guess I'm to be the outcast no matter where I go. Oh! Oh, I should have..." She worked her way around the table and gave a curtsey. "Your Majesty. I must confess, I didn't know we had a princess. But I don't see many heralds in my small village."

Aury set her boot on the table. "I just found out about the whole thing myself, so don't worry."

"Really?" Rhianne took the boot and examined the torn sole. "Do you care to tell the tale?"

"My parents hid me at the fae court until now. To protect me from a curse set on my head at my infant betrothal."

Rhianne's eyes bulged. "So the story of the Matchweaver's curse is true?"

And every human seemed to know the story. Every human except the one the curse had affected most. Nice.

"I suppose. My parents betrothed me without asking the Witch, and she wasn't best pleased."

"I suppose not. Why on earth would they not ask her and her loom about their own daughter's match?"

Aury shrugged, not sure how much she should be talking about this. "Politics."

"The guards are coming," Hilda said quietly from the doorway.

Aury nodded. "Can you fix this quickly? Please? I have gold." She popped a small bag of coin on the table.

Rhianne swallowed and touched the bag. She wore no wedding band. "That's too much."

"We single women should stick together. Take it." Aury shoved the bag closer to the cobbler, wondering why Rhianne hadn't found her own love by visiting the Matchweaver. Perhaps it had to do with being an outcast.

Finally, Rhianne sighed and pocketed the coins. She got to work, fingers moving swiftly. The guards barged into the shop just as Rhianne finished up on the new sole.

"Thank you," Aury said, slipping the shoe on. "It's perfect."

Rhianne curtseyed. "Thank you for not thinking I'm evil."

"Anytime." Aury gave her a smile.

As newly shod Aury and Goldheart led the party down the king's road, the storm that Gytha had mentioned rolled in, sweeping the sun from the sky and powdering them in fresh snow. Two majestic structures appeared in the distance. The nearest had to be Loreton Palace with its old curtain wall and the shining palace of stone inside, boasting peaked roofs and newer architecture. To the east and farther away, the square towers and hulking darkness of Darkfleot loomed over the Silver River.

A shiver ran through her, shaking off the fatigue and tickling her stomach. There, she would become who she was born to be. Not a lie on the lips of the fae court. Not cattle to be traded by her uncaring parents. A ruler and a water mage, powerful enough to defend her kingdom and decide whom she would and would not wed. The idea felt impossible, but nothing about Aury's life had been typical. Perhaps this time, fate would lend her a hand.

Hilda, Gytha, and Eawynn caught up to Aury, each on their own mounts from the fae stables, black stallions that only listened to them.

"That's Darkfleot." Hilda adjusted her grip on the reins, shaking her wrist and making the bells tied to her bracelet jingle. Her stallion slowed to a walk.

Aury pulled back gently on Goldheart's reins, and the horse rumbled out of a trot and into a walk. "It's perfect."

Eawynn chuckled. "It's frightening."

"Exactly."

Hilda nodded approvingly. "The Masters of the Order are away at the Sea's Claw now, so you'll begin your training without them breathing down your neck at least. They won't be back until the Trials."

"I like that. I wish I could go there now instead of having to put up with yet another Frostlight feast."

Eawynn gasped. "But your betrothed will be at the feast!"

"That's exactly what I was hoping to avoid."

"He might already be at Loreton," Gytha said quietly, glancing back at the king and queen. "They invited him before coming for you."

Aury gripped the reins until her knuckles nearly burst. "Lovely. It's fabulous to know how important my opinion is to my dear mum and da."

Gytha chuckled. "You'd best watch your tongue, girl. They are old, but they still hold an army in their wrinkled hands."

Aury groaned and kicked Goldheart into a run. Since she was going to be forced to attend a slew of incredibly dull events, she was going to first feel the freedom of a gallop across the open land. She tore her ribbon headdress from her hair and let her silver tresses fly behind her as she and Goldheart coursed through the biting winter air.

Thoughts of Filip passed through her mind. As an elf, he'd have pointed ears similar to the fae ones she grew up with. It was so strange that it had been a glamour. And he'd have those storm-gray eyes the mountain elves had, frightening in their intensity and able to see much farther than her human eyes. He'd probably smell like a pigsty and have far more muscle than brains.

As the entire party rode onto the grounds of Loreton Palace, Aury didn't bother to hide her longing for Darkfleot, so close but so far.

The stable master greeted them, and a slew of boys took the horses, while servants ran up to hand out cups of wine and water.

Aury stared at the palace walls, wishing she could see through them. She couldn't believe she was the princess here, that this was to be her home.

Athellore strode past her brusquely. "You will mind your manners when you meet Prince Filip tonight, Daughter. Or you will learn what kind of father I plan to be."

"Good day, Your Majesties." An old man they introduced only as Alfred took their cloaks.

Aury's muscles tensed as she watched the king disappear through the palace's jewel-encrusted doors with his water staff. As soon as she had one of those beauties, he'd be the one watching his manners.

CHAPTER 6

Filip stood in his stirrups. "Hah!" he shouted, urging his spotted gray mare, Lavina, through the snowy flats. Her name meant *avalanche*, and she'd certainly earned the label, crashing down the steepest of slopes like an unstoppable force of nature during the years they'd trained together. "You'll get an entire bucket of oats and a full scoop of alfalfa when we're settled, gorgeous. Loreton Palace is known for spoiling their horses." He rubbed her neck and hoped the warmer climate wouldn't wear her down.

Filip's retinue rode just behind, and they were at the gates of Loreton before the sun set. The palace was more formidable than he'd guessed it would look, but it was nothing compared to the power the water mage training castle held in its form. They'd passed Darkfleot earlier, and its rough form was still visible in the distance.

He couldn't wait to talk to one of the Order Masters, to

the ones who'd helped his own people drive the Wylfen back with sheets of jagged ice and by flooding the river at Dragon Wing Pass. It had been amazing to watch from afar. He couldn't imagine how wild it would be to see such magic up close. And he wondered if water mages really did have fins hiding on their otherwise human bodies. Fascinating.

The snow was having a fine time driving them into the gates where the human guards with their knobby noses and clumsy movements welcomed them. He tried very hard not to think about how his bride would resemble them.

Inside the courtyard, tall oaks slept in circles, their boughs decorated with blue ribbons—presumably for Frostlight. Candles danced in cones of what had to be waxed parchment, lighting the varied paths into the palace. A crowd of what Filip assumed were servants poured from a side door, led by a man dressed in gold-trimmed finery.

"This way, Prince Filip. Welcome to Loreton. I'm Alfred, and I will make sure all your needs are met. We're drawing baths for each of your party now." The nasal-voiced servant led Filip, Costel, Drago, Stefan, and their manservants down a corridor decorated with brightly colored tapestries. The threads wove together to show the ancient Lapis and Jade dragons flying in a storm-streaked sky above a man with blue-green hair and a woman holding his hand. The subject was straight out of the legends of the first water mages.

"But you do have Prince Filip's all-important tea? He is obsessed." Drago blinked his one eye and laughed, elbowing Filip.

"Yes!" Stefan ducked as they walked under an archway. "He may look like a strapping young prince, but he has an awful lot in common with my grandmother."

Filip grinned and punched Stefan in the stomach. "Tea is a miracle, you tasteless pig."

Stefan coughed a laugh, holding his middle. "Maybe your betrothed will get a glimpse of you in your precious evening cup."

Drago looked from Costel to Filip. "Can water mages do that?"

"The princess isn't a water mage," Filip said.

The servant Alfred cleared his throat. "Excuse the interruption, but Princess Aurora most certainly is a water mage. And quite possibly a very powerful one at that. She is the first in ages who has the ability to do as you say, to see visions in water. It is called scrying, though I doubt tea would do the trick."

Filip's heart jumped over a beat. He grabbed Alfred's tunic. "No one told me."

"Apologies, Prince Filip."

Filip smoothed the man's tunic and began following him again as the cold dread hanging on him warmed. He was going to marry a water mage. "You would think someone would've mentioned it. But of course, I just now found out I was be to married, so I suppose not. How did you hear about it, Stefan?"

Stefan raised his large, slim hands. "Don't badger me. Costel, you told me, right?"

"No." Costel shook his head of frizzy hair. "I had no idea."

Shrugging, Stefan clapped Filip on the back. "Well, you

know how gossip works."

"I do," Filip said. "It works as quickly as you did on those two redheads at the bonfires."

The men laughed.

"Sorry, my prince," Stefan said. "You arrived late. Was I supposed to leave them all alone for so long?"

Alfred led them into a series of chambers. Each room boasted a wide bed swathed in furs and velvets, and the rooms were connected by wooden doors decorated in carved stags and river fish.

A fire crackled in the room Alfred gave to Filip. Once Alfred bowed and left, Filip stood in front of the flames and allowed the palace manservants to remove his snow-crusted cloak, muddied boots, and road-stained clothing.

A water mage. His bride-to-be had magic. Would the surprises ever stop?

Once he'd bathed and wrapped himself in a linen bath sheet, he went back to the fire, hoping to find the black tea he'd requested. But there was only wine. He needed to wake up for the feast, not grow sluggish. He had a water mage bride to win. She might be hideous as many of the humans were, but at least she wouldn't be dull.

He threw open his doors. "Alfred!"

But there was no elderly servant waiting in the corridor. Instead, a hooded figure bore the brunt of his shout. Light eyes stared from the darkness of a midnight blue cloak, and the scent of sage rose in the air.

"Sorry to disappoint you," a voice made of velvet said, "but if you prefer old men, I'd be happy to inform the kingdom that the deal is off."

Filip leaned closer. "What? I...who are you?"

The woman spun away and strode down the corridor with the air of someone with important duties to attend. She raised a hand and waved to him. "No one. Carry on with your habits. I won't judge."

CHAPTER 7

Aury rushed down the corridor, longing to run but not wanting him to see her desperation to get away. It was him. Prince Filip was the man she'd seen in the water bowl at the fae court.

She pushed past the guards. "I'll be right back. I'm staying in the courtyard," she muttered, hurrying toward the candlelit walkway and the ribbon-festooned trees. Under the solstice moon, she closed her eyes. Inhaling slowly, she tried to burn the image of Prince Filip's bare chest and striking eyes from her mind. He was all muscle and scar, and though his face wasn't one's typical handsome, it demanded attention somehow, just as it had in the water vision.

She hadn't intended on meeting him. She'd only taken the circuitous route to the front entrance to avoid Gwinnith and her frightening unit of hairdressers. And now, she couldn't seem to catch her breath.

What was he doing here already, shouting for old

Alfred? She'd thought he would be another hour yet. They'd put the feast off to wait for him, and the tables were just now being set with glazed venison.

Filip was nothing like what she'd imagined. He had such a kind, deep voice and that lovely scent of sandalwood and leather. The scent was familiar... She'd expected him to smell of blood and steel. Yet he was brutal-looking with all those scars and those murderous mountain elf eyes. The water vision hadn't shown her his ears, but she'd seen them tonight beneath his damp hair. They were more pointed than the fae's, more animal, wilder than her glamoured ones had been. How many screams had he heard with those ears? How many lives had he taken with those strong-looking hands of his? She wrapped her arms around herself and fought a shiver. He'd never be kind or gentle with a wife. He'd order her around like she was one of his warriors.

Well, he'd try to order her around.

He would fail.

But none of that mattered. She returned to the palace, carefully choosing a route to the great hall that avoided the west-facing rooms. She wouldn't be marrying him anyway.

Hilda, Gytha, and Eawynn descended on her as she walked into the great hall.

"Where were you?" Hilda demanded, shoving a cup of wine into her hand.

Aury raised it in a toast, then took three good gulps.

"You look terrible." Gytha pointed at the mud on the hem of Aury's ice-white gown.

"The prince might not like you if are a mess like this," Eawynn said.

Hmm. An idea flitted through Aury's mind. "Come with me. I have a plan." Using a side door, she left the hall and its bustling array of servants, the fae protectors trailing her like ghosts of a past life.

"You three are pretty powerful, right? You twisted my curse, and most fae can't do that much magic." She led them into a room filled with brooms and folded linens. The linen that had stretched across Filip's waist and clung to every curve and line of his body blinked across her memory, and she pushed it away with a growl.

"What's wrong?" Eawynn put a hand to Aury's forehead. "You feel hot. Are you fevered? Oh, no. We can't have you fevered when your water mage training is set to begin tomorrow."

Aury drew away from Eawynn, her cheeks now blazing with the memory that refused to stay gone. "I'm fine. Now, what I want to know is can you three glamour me to look hideous?"

Hilda gasped, and Gytha let out a quiet, low laugh as she crossed her arms. Her thorn tattoos were on display in her sleeveless gown.

Eawynn looked from Aury to her fellow fae. "I'm lost."

Hilda slammed the door shut and whirled on Aury, her hair slipping from its tidy bun. "Look here, Princess. We are here to serve you, not to condemn you to the dungeons. Just what do you think King Athellore would do if you showed up to the feast looking like a hag? And what do you think Queen Gwinnith would do to us for our part in the plot?"

Gytha shrugged. "Maybe it can be slight. Athellore

can't see well, and neither can his wife. We could ugly Aurora up just a bit. Here and there."

Aury put a hand on Gytha's shoulder. "Yes! Exactly that. Glamour me enough that Filip is disgusted but the king and queen don't notice why. I'll make a quiet deal with Filip, written in blood, that he will gain his lands for his people in exchange for his army with only a promise of friendship between us. If I get that from him, the king and queen will surely agree to it."

It was desperation talking. She had no real idea if that would work as it had for Werian at the fae court that one time, but there was no other way around this marriage that she could think of.

"What about everyone else in the crowd?" Hilda asked. "Not all the nobles will have age marring their vision."

"But none of them have met me. There are no paintings of me because my parents," Aury said, allowing her hatred of them and what they'd done to her seep into her words, "never once spoke of me, visited me, or cared to act as though I existed. And now, that little plot of theirs will work in my plan's favor. None of the nobles will say, 'Ah, Athel, my friend, your daughter is quite the dog-faced nightmare, isn't she?'"

Gytha bent double, laughing, but Hilda's glare remained firmly in place.

"Look," Aury said. "This is not simply a game for my entertainment. This is my life we're dealing with. I can't marry a warrior elf. No one even knows for sure if they have magic and what it can do. What if he magics me into believing getting a beating from him every night is my favorite way to exist? What if he eats humans to increase his strength?"

Eawynn turned a pale shade of green. "We truly don't know."

Hilda looked at the door, her shoulders dropping.

Aury pushed her advantage. "See? You can't argue, because I'm right. There is no way to know what horrors this elf will foist on me after our wedding. He might try to drag me back to his ice-crusted kingdom and share me with his friends. We don't know. And I'm not risking it when I could potentially become a powerful mage who can protect Lore alongside the Order. Or I could negotiate a deal between Lore and Balaur that doesn't involve forced marriage. It's archaic. Help me save myself. Please."

CHAPTER 8

With his men at his side, Filip attempted to smooth his hair from his face as he entered the great hall at Loreton Palace. The woman in the corridor had been Princess Aurora. Had to have been. No one else here would have been strolling the palace wearing a cloak that rich and sporting such an attitude toward him. He'd seen only a flicker of reflection from her eyes, but she'd still made an impression on him of someone lovely, dangerous.

"Eh, Filip. Look there." Drago pointed down the way toward a group of women speeding past one of the great hall's arched doorways. "That's her, right?"

Stefan whistled quietly beside Filip. "She's a looker, all right."

Filip's blood rose at the sight of her swaying hips, the twist of her head as she glanced over her shoulder, the silver of her impossibly long hair, and the bold, beautiful lines of her features. "Yes. That's her." A shiver of anticipation traveled the full length of his body.

"Where's she going with her fae ladies? She's supposed to be here, isn't she?" Drago asked as a servant passed with a tray of ale and slices of what looked like cranberry-covered goat cheese.

Taking a serving of cheese, Filip ignored them, his mind filled with Aurora, the sage-scent of her, her lovely voice and quick wit, accusing him of an intimate relationship with old Alfred. He coughed to cover a laugh, shaking his head. She was unpredictable, exciting.

Costel took a mug of ale and drank a noisy swallow. "She'll be here. As the bride-to-be, she is to arrive as the last guest. Loreton tradition."

Stefan and Drago chuckled. "Did you make Ioana swoon with your Lore trivia?" Drago asked.

Costel drank another gulp. "I do think she enjoyed our talk."

Stefan took his own mug of ale from a second servant and eyed the courtiers. "Not as much as your—"

Filip reached up and flicked his friend's pointed ear. "We're here to impress. Watch your tongue."

The nobles buzzed like bees in brocade around King Athellore and Queen Gwinnith. Courts were basically the same wherever one went, he supposed. Dull and full of arse-kissers.

The king moved through the crowd and waved Filip over. Filip approached, hoping he didn't have cheese breath, and ended the trip with a bow in the Balaur style—extending his leg as he bent at the waist.

A tittering laugh escaped the queen's fair face, and Filip

suppressed the retort that rose in his mind. Lore folk thought it humorous to see vicious mountain elves bow so artfully. Costel had told him so, and he'd not believed it until this moment. Now, it was all Filip could do to keep himself from drawing his hatchet just to prove how dangerous his kind could truly be.

But of course, he'd learned to control his temper long ago under the thumb of his mother and father. He straightened as the king announced him to the court.

"Welcome to Loreton, Prince Filip of Balaur."

Filip turned toward Costel, who had retrieved two amphorae of fruit brandy. "I have a gift for you, King Athellore and Queen Gwinnith. Plum brandy. We make this powerful spirit from black plums, then soak blueberries and sour cherries to create this special drink. Please let's share a cup before the feasting to open our appetites."

That codger Alfred appeared out of nowhere and directed the servants in pouring out a serving to everyone in the room.

"To our upcoming union!" Filip raised his cup, then drank the spirit down. The familiar burn warmed him to his toes.

Aurora still hadn't arrived when they all took their seats. Was she simply going to ignore his existence until her parents forced her to show up? He leaned forward in his seat, ignoring the nobles beside him and pouring another cup of plum brandy. This was his first test. Should he make a joke of her absence or demand her presence? Should he act offended when she arrived or ignore her? He downed the brandy and smiled as he glimpsed her cloaked form coming from the shadows of the archway. He'd ignore her behavior. He wanted to see what she would do with that.

"The game is on, *amant*," he whispered.

"What does *amant* mean?" the nobleman next to him asked.

Filip grinned. "Lover."

CHAPTER 9

Aury kept her cloak over her head as she found her place at the feasting table. She'd been given a seat on the dais across from Filip and between two noblewomen from the eastern province. Filip didn't look up as she approached. Instead, he chatted with the nobleman to his left.

The king pushed away from the table and held out a hand. "I present to the court our daughter, Princess Aurora Rose. I'm certain you have so many questions to ask her, but let us please have a quiet feast together and refrain from talk of curses that will no longer smite our darling girl."

Aury shook her head. "How do you know the curse won't strike me down?"

Athellore laughed stiffly. "You are grown now. You know better than to prick your finger on the spindle of a great wheel, don't you?"

The court laughed good-naturedly, and Aury forced a

smile. Before she could argue further, everyone raised their glasses and drank.

A servant pulled out her chair. Filip still didn't meet her eyes, even as he drank to her health. He looked everywhere else—at the Sacred Oak painted on the ceiling, the cerulean ribbons fluttering from the high beams, the king and queen.

Aury reached for her own drink and took a fortifying sip.

Then Filip returned to his chat with the nobleman. "I fight with both sword and small axe," Filip said in an accented version of the common tongue.

His voice rumbled deep in his chest. That chest she'd seen bare just an hour ago. She swallowed and untied her cloak. She'd seen a few male chests in her day, but none as fine as his.

"And your nickname is Bard, yes?" the nobleman asked.

Aury let her cloak and hood fall onto the back of her chair, the heat of a challenge rising in her chest. She'd said this was no game, but it felt like one. One she must win. "Bard? Are you a singer, then, Prince Filip?"

Filip's gaze pinned her down, but he didn't recoil at her glamour or even twitch. She felt as though he stared right into her soul, and the white flash of lightning seemed to storm across his gray eyes though she knew it was merely a reflection of the candlelight. He traced the edge of his cup with a thumb, and his lips parted. Heat speared her body. "*Bárda* means something different in my tongue. But I can make my steel sing if it pleases you, my lady."

Invisible flames licked up Aury's body. Was he threatening her or seducing her? Definitely threatening. He couldn't want to seduce this face she'd had the fae glamour up. Only the caster of the glamour could see through it. Her nose was abnormally pointed now and boasted a nice little wart. They'd puffed her jawline to give her the first hint of jowls. And her eyes were bloodshot like she hadn't slept in ages.

The nobleman laughed, the sound grating. "In the elven language it means *hatchet*."

Filip studied her face, and she smiled at him wanly, taking a serving of venison and chewing it with her mouth wide open. His dark eyebrow twitched, but he returned her smile. She could hardly keep from laughing. He had to be horrified. *See what happens when you try to control me?* she longed to shout. She was done with the control the fae had lorded over her at the Agate Palace. Never again. She would live as she wanted to live. But instead of shouting, which would do nothing for her, she forced her frustration down, only talking quietly with the noblewoman to her right and ignoring Filip as the servants brought in dessert.

"Queen Gwinnith tells me you hail from the eastern provinces. How are grape prices from the islands these days?" Aury asked the woman.

"I'm Lady Ethel, and yes, the queen speaks the truth. The price of grapes grows steadily higher due to the piracy near Sea's Claw."

"Pirates?" Aury hadn't seen anything of that when she'd gone there with Werian.

"It's a new problem and one I don't see us solving soon. They are crafty and quick."

"Are the pirates from Wylfenden or..." Lady Ethel glanced at Filip—all but an accusation in her gaze.

Filip's gaze was flat. His jaw muscles bulged, and he looked to the table, taking a breath before responding. "We are not sailors, my lady."

Aury spotted the dessert now sitting on the table, a perfect subject change. "Chocolate scorchpeppers?" She reached for one, her mouth already watering for the spicy-sweet taste.

The king leaned forward. "I heard you like them, Daughter."

Aury set the dipped pepper onto her pewter plate, a heaviness in her chest. "Thank you, my king."

Her initials had been pressed into the chocolate, and she traced the R for Rose, her mind humming with a feeling she couldn't name.

Filip bit into a pepper, then whistled. "Hot. I can see why you like them."

No one else had tried their dessert, and it was no surprise. The peppers could peel the paint off the walls. Filip finished his and licked his fingers. He leaned his chair back and winked at her.

Aury pushed away from the table, frustration rising at Filip's acceptance of her glamoured looks and her horrible parents' sad excuse for pretending to care about what she liked. They couldn't buy her with dessert. She was a grown woman.

"Apologies. I must take some fresh air with my ladies. It's been a chaotic few days," she said, leaving the table. Kind murmurs of understanding flowed from the guests.

He had winked! He was flirting with her despite the horror that was her face. The nerve!

Hilda, Gytha, and Eawynn stood on the outer edges of

the room with the guards. She gestured to them as she hurried past.

"Is he able to eat?" Eawynn clapped her hands and for once actually looked a bit wicked.

"He winked at me." Aury dragged them into the broom closet again. "You have to make me more hideous. It's not working."

Hilda shook her head. "Any more and the king and queen will notice. We can't risk it. If you defy Athellore, he'll lock you up, and you'll never get your chance at Darkfleot."

"How old are you? How do you know so much about him and what he'll do to me?"

"Older than I'm going to share, thanks very much," Hilda snapped. "Trust me."

"Why should I? You knew the truth about everything, and you never told me even though you were supposed to protect me."

Gytha snorted. "Aury. We were under a binding. If we had uttered even a word, the Fae Queen would've taken our tongues. And you know that for truth."

Aury sighed. "All right. I get it. You aren't the enemies here. My father and mother are. And Filip." She still didn't trust a single one of them.

Eawynn spun in a circle, looking more like a lovesick youth than an old fae female. "He's stunning!"

"No." Aury gripped Eawynn's arms and stared into the fae's brown eyes. "He is not stunning. You do not get to think that when you're playing on my team here."

Eawynn stuck out her lower lip. "But he is as spicy as those scorchpeppers you love!"

"Nope. He's not spicy. He's a killer. And he'll treat me like a slave." She'd read a scroll about mountain elves and their slaves during the century war with the islands of Khem, a land across the sea. During that long ago war, the elves had taken on hundreds of human slaves to build the fortresses in the higher elevations. "Prince Filip is an obstacle blocking my path to ruling as a princess, and someday a queen, in the way I see fit. That's the only version of freedom I see in my future, and I will have it."

Eawynn shrugged and pointed a finger at Aury's face. "I made your nose longer."

"Good. I'll try to belch more, too." Sure, it was childish. But she'd seen baser plots work at the fae court. In some matters, males were males, no matter where they were raised. "I'm headed back." She swung the broom closet door open. "You hang back. I don't want my parents to guess what we've been up to. Return to the guards after you've given me a few moments to go on ahead."

As she rounded the corner, she slammed into Filip.

Aury's heart careened into her throat as he caught her arms and helped her step back. His sharp gaze went to her hand, and he squinted like he was trying to see something there. She yanked away from his hold and tried to summon a belch.

Filip leaned against the doorframe, the hall growing loud behind him as the king and queen announced the end of the feast. "Has King Athellore promised me a madwoman as a wife?" He raised his eyebrows. "Or are you acting strange because you just found out your life wasn't what you thought it was?"

"You don't know anything about me."

"I know very little, true," Filip said. "But what's to know? I need you, and you need me. The rest can be worked out later."

"Ha."

He cocked his head. "Ha?"

"Yes, ha. You're truly a wit. My life can be worked out *later*. I *need you*. All hilarious."

He unhitched himself from the wall, and his stormy eyes seemed to darken. "The Wylfen will come again. My army can help you."

"I do need your army," she said. "But I don't need you. No offense."

"Plenty taken."

She went on like he hadn't spoken. "We don't need to wed to make this happen. I'll make a promise in blood that the farmlands in the foothills will go to Balaur if you swear the elven army will continue mobilizing near Dragon Wing Pass and fight with us. No marriage needs to occur."

He looked at her hands. "Am I that hideous to you?"

"No. I just don't... Do you agree?" she asked, praying it might be this simple. "I'll have my ladies set up the agreement, and they'll bring it to your rooms."

"I can't do that." His full lips pressed into a line.

"Why?"

"Because my father already signed and sealed such an agreement with your father."

Aury's throat tightened, and she pulled against the ties of her gown. "I'll figure it out. I'm going to train to be a water mage. They think I might have some significant power, and with that, I'll have more influence."

"I'm surprised King Athellore and Queen Gwinnith are

all right with you risking your life to train at Darkfleot and eventually fight," Filip said.

She met his eyes, not flinching from their lightning flash of... What was it? Ferocity. That felt right. "Though we don't always win," she said, "Lore is built on courage. To deny me the chance to train would be naming our family as cowards."

"I see." He rubbed the stubble on his chin. "So it's a reputation issue. They will risk you and this alliance to uphold their reputation as brave warriors and leaders. I can understand that. My people are much the same way."

"Why do you keep staring at my hands?"

He bit his lip, one very sharp incisor showing. A heady blend of curiosity and strange desire ran down Aury's back.

"I heard water mages have webbed fingers," he said.

"I...uh..." She lifted her hand toward the oil lamp hanging from the wall. Light passed through the thin skin between her thumb and forefinger. She froze.

"You never noticed this?" He took her fingers gently and studied them, running his fingertip over her knuckle. "It *is* incredibly subtle..."

A delightful tingle danced down her arm, so she pulled her hand back. Warmth pricked the place where his hand had touched hers, and her chest went tight again. She forced a slow, deliberate breath, firmly ignoring the way his own chest rose and fell not an inch away.

"It's nothing."

"It's the sea folk blood. From one of your ancestors. That's why you can do water magic."

"You make me sound like a project your tutor gave you."

He shrugged, then leaned close suddenly, moving faster than a human could. His breath was warm on her neck, and she was near to panting. "I'd study you, Princess."

The word broke the spell or whatever had been working there. "I wasn't raised to be a princess, to do as the royal family sees fit. There will be no wedding, I'm afraid. I'll see to it that your people get the lands they need to farm, but we will never, ever be husband and wife. Somehow. Count on it. Now, if you'll excuse me, I don't want to miss the moon singing. It's my last night at Loreton Palace. Tomorrow I go to Darkfleot to train, and I ask that you refrain from following me. Forever."

CHAPTER 10

Filip fell against the doorframe as Aurora strode away, her dress fluttering behind her like waves. With whatever glamour the fae had put on her, she was as ugly as a lie, but she kicked everything else out of his mind when she spoke with that velvet voice, smelling of sage, and using that sharp tongue to mock him.

A grin tugged at his mouth. She was awful. But she wasn't dull, that was certain, and he'd take awful over dull any day of the week. He'd have great fun flirting with her and annoying her to the point of violence against him. It wasn't as if she could actually deny him, could she? It was too bad that his men had been seated so far and missed the entertainment of that magicked nose.

He joined the last of the crowd heading out the front doors into the courtyard only to have Costel grab his arm.

"King Athellore asked if you would do the moon singing in our tongue."

"Ugh. I'd rather spar."

"You can't say no."

"All right. Singing it is." He walked with Costel toward the king and queen, who stood beneath a grand oak festooned in ribbons and surrounded by children holding flickering candles.

Where was Aurora? She wasn't beside her parents or anywhere in the crowd.

He and Costel bowed to the king and queen.

"I heard she went back to her chambers," Costel whispered out of the corner of his mouth.

Filip straightened, rubbing the back of his neck.

"You'll sing for us, Prince Filip?" Queen Gwinnith's frail form was ghostly in the full, solstice moon. "We've sent Alfred to find the princess so she doesn't miss it."

"Of course, Your Majesty."

The king's watery gaze touched on the hatchet and sword Filip wore on his wide, leather belt. "I've never heard the moon singing in the Balaur tongue."

The crowd took turns lighting their own small candles using a candelabra near the dormant fountain beside the trees.

Filip walked closer to the king and queen. "King Athellore, Queen Gwinnith, may I ask an indelicate question?" he said quietly.

"Speak freely," the king replied. "You are to be our son-by-law soon enough."

Filip inclined his head in thanks. "Princess Aurora doesn't seem pleased about our marriage. Do you have any suggestions on how I might win her?"

While the king's face went red with rage, his lips a tight line, the queen smiled broadly and touched Filip's sleeve. "So kind of you to ask. She will wed you no matter what she wants. She is obedient."

Were they talking about the same woman? "There is talk that if she can wield her water magic on level with the Order, she won't accept my hand." They didn't need to know Aurora was the one who'd told him. By the Source, it seemed like they had plenty of family drama already and didn't need him stirring the flames further.

The queen traded a look with the king, then Athellore spoke, his eyes cold. "Once she fails the Mage Trials in three weeks, she will marry you."

"I'm the consolation prize."

"Yes, I mean, no, of course not." The king cleared his throat. "You are her future, and your union is the future of Lore. Please don't worry yourself about the princess's...idiosyncrasies."

By that did he mean the fact that she might a little bit want to murder him? Because that was the sense he'd had from her just moments ago. He had to laugh. What a strange life he had.

"What is it?" the queen asked, watching him closely.

"Nothing, Your Majesty. Nothing at all. I will try not to worry myself and listen to your counsel. Thank you. I suppose I'm to sing now, yes?"

The last courtier's candle was lit, and the crowd lifted their flames skyward.

Drago and Stefan gave him encouraging raised fists, and though he hated singing in public, Filip prepared to do his best to honor the solstice with song. Perhaps the princess would be listening from some dark alcove and see that he could indeed be a bard as she had thought, and he wasn't simply a man with blade and blood on his mind.

CHAPTER 11

In the back corridor near the great hall, Aury jerked her arm away from Alfred. "Look, I'm not a child. If I want to spend time with my darling parents and their bloodthirsty, dragon-killing choice of son-by-law, then I will. If not, well, walk on, good sir, because I won't."

"You will." Alfred raised his nose not unlike the southern nobles had at the fae court. "Because the king outranks you, and he has commanded it. You will also instruct your fae nannies to wipe this ridiculous glamour from your lovely face and cease embarrassing the royal court."

The tingle of magic flurried across her face like snowflakes, and she turned to see Eawynn wiggling her fingers, a puff of amethyst smoke curling from her palm.

"Sorry, but I don't want to live in a dungeon," she squeaked.

Aury blasted past them all and stormed through the

palace. "Fine. One more day." Soon she'd be gone and glad to be rid of every single person here.

The snow descended lightly in the courtyard, and a deep, gorgeous voice echoed off the stone walls, singing words she couldn't quite make out. She found a spot beside the king and queen, then looked past them to see who was singing.

A gasp left her, too loud during a break in the song. She clapped her hands over her mouth. It was Prince Filip, performing the moon singing in Balaur. He'd closed his eyes, and his head fell back, the knot in his throat bobbing. His hands on the hilt of his sword and hatchet, he sang, and the words were longing made into sound; her heart ached with every note. This whole performance didn't fit who he was—a murderous elf with frightening, lightning-touched eyes and possibly cannibalistic tendencies. He looked...beautiful. He sang a higher note, and a pleasant shiver danced down her back as he started the second round.

"*Adu lumina la care râvnim,*
Canta, cântecul lunii,
Flācāri dansatoare,
Gheata strālucitoare,
Ore de adunare," he sang, the crowd joining him for a stanza.

Aury twisted, keeping her head down. "Hilda, he is casting a spell. I can feel it."

Hilda adjusted Aury's hood. "I've already told you," she whispered. "Elves have no magic. They live longer than you humans, move faster, are stronger, but that's it."

"That is magic," Aury argued as his mellow voice stilled the crowd once more.

Gytha poked her side. "That is allure."

Aury wanted to argue, but it was too quiet to do it discreetly now with only Filip singing. It wasn't allure. Before she'd grown properly immune to the fae, she'd fallen in love with two courtiers and the Fae Queen's blacksmith. Well, perhaps not in love. Romantic love aside, the only real affection she'd ever felt toward anyone was for Werian. And he had betrayed her. Love, in all its forms, was a myth.

Her breath left her. Tears rose to her eyes, but she blinked and refused to let them fall.

Werian had known everything. She didn't want to think about his betrayal. He wasn't even her cousin. She hugged herself and looked up, letting snowflakes fall cold on her cheeks and chin. No, she knew nothing of love. Werian had lied. Her real parents wished to use her. Hilda, Gytha, and Eawynn only helped her because they'd been commanded to by the Fae Queen. The Fae Queen, who had pretended to be Aury's kin, had simply wanted grain and wine.

Of course, Aury knew she wasn't as important as an army Lore could use to defend themselves from the Wylfen, but a tiny part of her—a part she would squash because it served no one, including her—truly wished her parents had considered her equally as important as their royal responsibilities. It was childish. Yes, that part of her had to be crushed and forgotten. There was no love in her world. All was strategy and striving; nothing else proved true.

"Primāvara v-a venii,

Cânta-ti numele lunii,
Si ascultă răspunsul ei venind cu vântul.
Cu vântul,
Cu vântul
Cu vântul."

As Filip's song came to a close, Hilda nudged her from the back. "Your mouth is hanging open, my lady."

The prince looked at Aury, a knowing glint in his eye and a smirk playing with the edges of his full lips.

She gritted her teeth. "Rat."

The queen inhaled and gripped her gown. "Where?"

Aury rolled her eyes and patted the woman's arm. Her mother's arm. She shook her head. She'd never get used to that. She didn't want to, if she were being honest. "It's fine. I was just...never mind."

Gwinnith stared into her face. "Are you feeling all right? Someone told me you looked strange at dinner."

She laughed. "No, I'm fine. Really. Now, if we are done here, I'd like to have a moment to myself. Tomorrow I go to Darkfleot." *Just try to stop me.*

Gwinnith blinked and fussed with the red and blue velvet ribbons woven through her skirts. "As agreed."

"As agreed." Gritting her teeth, Aury nodded toward Athellore.

Enough of this. Sure, Filip could sing. That didn't matter one little bit. It only meant he was good at hiding his vicious nature. A wolf in sheep's wool and all that. She was no fool. She wouldn't be wooed by sweet songs and fiery glances. She had some magic to learn and a kingdom to run. And by Nix's fire, she'd do it all on her own.

"I'm going to the stables," she said to the fae and her

royal parents, pressure building in her chest. "Don't follow me."

"You'll mind that tongue," Athellore said, "or Lore will have itself a mute princess."

She gave him a simpering curtsey, then spun to leave.

THE STABLES ENVELOPED AURY WITH THE FAMILIAR scent of alfalfa and manure, leather and horse. Moonlight drifted through the slats in the high ceiling, and she found Goldheart knocking a hoof against her stall door. Aury cupped a handful of oats from a bucket near the tack room, then held out her palm to the golden horse who had carried her away from the Fae Queen and Werian and all the lies. Aury leaned against Goldheart's warm neck as the horse snuffled soft lips across her fingers.

Animals were so much better than people. They had no agenda outside basic needs. They didn't lie. If a horse hated a person, said individual knew it quickly. There was no art of falsehoods or betrayal.

She took a deep breath, and Goldheart echoed the lengthy exhale, making Aury smile into the horse's pale mane. And with the wind tossing the ends of her cloak against her legs and the solid presence of a good creature holding her up, Aury at last allowed herself to weep.

CHAPTER 12

Before the rising sun dissolved the night, Filip knocked on Aurora's chamber door. The fae named Gytha answered, already dressed in a deep green tunic and tall boots. "The princess is asleep, my lord. She should be up soon though. She's anxious to leave."

"Actually, it's you whom I need at the moment."

The auburn-haired fae frowned but slipped out the door and followed him from the palace. "What's this about?"

The winter air bit the pointed tips of Filip's ears as he led the fae out of the palace walls and into the spot where his men had gathered for the short ride to Darkfleot. "It's about what we have in here." He pointed at the wagon, where a massive wooden crate hid beneath a woolen blanket. Snarls ripped through the quiet morning, and Gytha stilled. The pink in her cheeks bled away.

"I know that sound."

Filip put a gentle hand on her tattooed arm. "Yes. But

it's caged and slightly drugged with seasleep." The sea tuber was a powerful plant that could kill if the wrong amount of it was used for dosing.

Trembling, Gytha approached the wagon. "You want me to speak to it."

"If you will. We are running very low on seasleep, and I'd rather not have to kill it. It's not the animal's fault the Wylfen got ahold of him. We need him to understand that he won't be killed today, that this is training. I need to use him for a demonstration."

The fae's throat moved in a swallow. "All right. I'll try. But firstly, this is a complicated concept for such a beast. Secondly, you know the Wylfen-tainted ones don't usually listen to fae voices. Not like the others."

"I'm hoping it'll work because we've cared for him for nearly a year."

Gytha nodded and began to whisper, her hand not quite touching the woolen blanket over the crate. The language was just the common tongue, but she spoke with the accent of the fae of Illumahrah, and the magic in her blood, her direct tie to the twin sons of the god Arcturus, Lord of Air, and the goddess Vahly, Lady of Earth, gave power to her words. A chill spread over Filip, raising the hairs on his arms and the back of his neck.

The snarling quieted, and a bump sounded inside the crate.

Drago lifted the end of the blanket and peered through the slats. "He's asleep. Nice work, Gytha." He gave her a smile. "I'm glad I won't have to fight him down the road."

The horses hitched to the wagon whinnied quietly, tossing black manes in Gytha's general direction.

"I'm guessing they say thank you too," Filip said.

Gytha smiled, her color returning. "Glad I could help. I can't wait to hear how your demonstration goes. You know there is a captain there who is raising arguments against your upcoming training."

Filip had heard, but he kept quiet to see if she knew more than he did.

"Captain Godwin is not too keen on your arrival in Lore. He claims you will turn his upstanding warriors into fighters no better than their enemies."

"I'll be sure to keep my growling, swearing, and slobbering to a minimum."

Gytha barked a laugh, then looked toward the dark silhouette of the military grounds. "I'm sorry that my countrymen are so close-minded about you and yours. Good luck today."

The urge to ask about Aurora pushed at Filip's lips, but he didn't want Aurora getting too comfortable with the idea that he was pursuing her. A woman like that needed a challenge.

"Well, thank you. And good luck with your charge as well." Filip winked.

The fae shook her head, smiling, and left them to their preparations.

Shooing the palace stable boys off, Filip helped Stefan replace his mount's bit. The one he'd been using was too large for his new horse. Costel appeared from the palace gates carrying two large satchels. Filip took them, the scent of fresh bread sifting from the load, and tied them to his saddle.

Back at the wagon, Filip checked to see if Drago was ready.

Drago crossed his thick arms. "I wish I'd had that fae around during that Source-cursed trip down the mountain with this beast. Eh, what did she ask in return for her work?"

A slight panic pinched Filip's stomach. Too late he recalled Costel's warning yesterday about owing the fae a payment. "I forgot about offering her the coin. She'll ask for a reward at the worst moment, won't she?"

"Most likely. They are a tricky bunch over there in Illumahrah."

"But maybe that's a generalized assumption just like the one Lore folk have about us."

"It's not," a velvet voice said. On horseback, Aurora approached from behind.

Filip stepped back. "Eavesdropping, are we?"

Goddess Nix in the skies, Aurora was the image of feminine power and beauty up there on that golden horse of hers. The winter wind lifted her hair like a banner, and the sunrise glowed over her bold cheekbones and pert chin. Her cloak had bunched beneath her thigh to show the strong curve there, and he imagined running a hand along her leg and behind her knee, making her breath catch, and... A surge of desire coursed through him.

"I would travel with you, of course," she said, her tone telling him that she had no plans whatsoever to do such a thing, "but I must be off. I'm to receive my staff first thing today. Good day."

She kicked her heels into her horse's sides gently and took off, barely dodging the wagon and startling his group's mounts. Her fae ladies rode by, galloping to catch up with her.

Costel squeezed Filip's shoulder. "I'm glad it's you and not me. She'd eat me alive."

Filip didn't say it aloud, but he wasn't so sure he would avoid that fate.

CHAPTER 13

Aury pulled Goldheart to a stop. A group of twenty horseback-riding knights wearing her family's livery made a wall between her and the drawbridge of Darkfleot.

"What is this about?"

A man with a shaved head grimaced and nudged his black gelding forward. "I am Captain Godwin, and I'm here to escort you onto the training grounds. As soon as you cross that bridge, you are no longer the princess. You are my soldier."

On a bay mare beside Aury, Gytha snorted. "What a darling."

"Can't wait to cozy up to him," Aury whispered back.

Godwin waved a hand, and the knights surrounded Aury and the fae, practically pushing them across the drawbridge and under the teeth of the portcullis.

The scent of fresh water, baking bread, and woodsmoke

welcomed Aury as Goldheart's hooves crunched across the small pebbles covering the courtyard of Darkfleot.

Five men in leathers laughed from an alcove before walking into the sun with wooden training swords. Two women and a man stood around a large fountain in the center of a circle of oak trees. The shortest of the women held a water mage staff. She pointed the staff at the fountain, and a hand of glistening, clear water rose into the air. With a smile, she twitched the end of her staff, and the hand shot for the man's wrist. He leapt back, shouting encouragement.

A falcon soared over the courtyard, its shadow bleeding over the merlons on the battlements and guiding the way to the largest of the archways that obviously led to the main section of the square castle.

Ignoring Captain Arseface, Aury dismounted and led Goldheart to a young girl who came running for the reins, a bevy of stable lads on her trail.

Aury gave Goldheart one last pet along her sleek neck, then turned to see a tall, thin woman in Order robes standing at the large archway.

"Good morn, Mage Mildred," Godwin said from behind Aury. "I have brought you your newest recruit."

Aury gave Mage Mildred a respectful nod. "I came here of my own will, my lady. The captain's escort was entirely unnecessary."

Mildred's slightly wrinkled lips drew into a tight line, and she clasped her staff, her knuckles going white. "I'm sure it was positively delightful," she murmured to Aury. "And thank you ever so much, Captain Godwin. As usual, you are everywhere I look."

Aury turned to see Eawynn and Gytha snickering beside a chiding Hilda. Aury thought maybe she was going to like this Mildred.

"Come," the woman said smartly, spinning and hurrying into the dark interior.

For a moment, not a thing was visible except for the tiniest glint of reflection off the tight bun on Mildred's head, and then the corridor opened into a cavernous foyer.

Banners fluttered from the ceiling beams in four shades of blue—cyan, cerulean, midnight, and one with variations in hue that made Aury think of ice in sunlight. The walls were dark stone, and the floor matched, though covered in ruby-colored rugs with silver tassels. Sconces as tall as her stood along the walls, and buttery light melted over the stones. Despite the powerful cold following the party in from the large double doors, the place was almost warm.

"We will get you changed, Aurora. Your ceremony begins at half past. This is quite extraordinary, Darkfleot accepting a new recruit in the winter. Aside from the timing of this ceremony and the bedchamber you'll have to yourself, there will be no differences between your training and that of a common-born water mage."

"I understand. I only now found out that I am a princess, and I certainly don't feel like one."

Mildred glanced over her shoulder and gave a quick, sympathetic smile. Aury hoped she might say something about what the king and queen had done, how they'd kept Aury hidden way, cloaked in lies, all her life. But the woman kept a bruising pace through the foyer, then up a winding set of stone stairs.

Five sets of similar staircases crowded the foyer's back

wall, leading to arched hallways hung with tapestries. The corridor they walked ended in a stained-glass window that depicted a waterfall cascading from a mountain covered in dark pines. The rising sun lit the gray water, and Aury thought the color was nearly the same as Filip's eyes.

She gritted her teeth and shoved the thought away. "Will there be others at this ceremony?"

"Yes. The entire castle will be in attendance. That is normal procedure. Usually the Order's Masters would be there as well, but I'm sure you've heard they are securing the border."

"Yes, Mage Mildred."

"Good. I will have to do."

Mildred led her into a room with wall-to-wall cabinetry and a small washroom. A thin girl in a dark blue tunic bumped past the fae and Aury to hand Mage Mildred a stack of clothing and a pair of tall, black boots just like the ones both women wore.

"As you asked, Mage Mildred," the girl said, her voice strong and loud.

"See to it that the bells are rung. Our new recruit will be there promptly."

When the girl left, Mildred handed the items to Aury. "Now...a few rules you must follow. When you receive your staff, do not attempt any magic. You have no training, and you've seen little of water mage's work. Is that right?"

"Yes. Only once. During the war."

Mage Mildred's features collapsed for a moment, then she seemed to gather herself. "Of course. Do not think hard about what you would like to do with the water, with any water around. Keep your thoughts disciplined. Do not speak any demands while holding your staff near a water source. Even your wash basin can become dangerous once you have the runed staff. The coral inside it will call to the thread of sea folk blood flowing through your veins, and it will turn your words, your will, into truth." She tilted her head, considering. "Well, depending on how powerful you end up being. We shall see. Regardless, carry the staff as you would a new type of sword, one with which you've never had instruction. Remember it has its own version of deadly sharp edges that will cut you and those near to you down if you break these rules. Now, dress quickly. You are expected quite soon, and we do not tolerate tardiness. You will hear the bells when you are expected to enter. There may be a slight delay because of Prince Filip's arrival and the assembly of the non-magical army on the grounds, but it shouldn't delay us too much."

Aury's mood darkened. He was going to dog her every step, wasn't he? "Can't the non-magical army train away from Darkfleot?" She'd focus so much better if Filip were far, far away.

A flicker of frustration tightened Mage Mildred's features. "This is the training fortress for all of our military forces. We must work close by to have strong and consistent communication between the two branches, mage and non-mage. Now, as I was saying, you must simply walk straight into the great hall and meet me on the dais. Entering on your own without your retinue will show the other mages you are here on the level with the rest of them and have thrown off most of your royal trappings."

Her brow knitted as she looked at the fae congesting the doorway. "And you three will be shown to Aurora's chamber. You may serve her there as you wish, but you are not to follow her during training. You must stay back and as much out of sight as is possible. I will admit that I don't want you here, mucking up the Order with whatever fussing you see fit for the princess, but the king has spoken, and his is the final word here. Stay out of the way, ladies, or I will petition for your removal more seriously. Aurora must work hard here, or she will drown."

Hilda widened her stance and cocked her head. "Metaphorically, of course. Under the strain of her training..."

"No, I mean that quite literally, and I'll thank you not to muddle my words. If Aurora is seen as weak by her instructors, they will do everything in their considerable power to drown her so that she won't be the cause of further death on the battlefield."

A ball of ice formed in Aury's stomach. "I understand."

Mage Mildred whirled around and pointed her staff at Aury. The fae started to move, but Aury held out a hand to keep them where they were.

"Do you?" Mage Mildred snapped. "Because this isn't a game like they play at the fae court. This is not a young woman's distraction or a way to play hard-to-get with one's future husband. This is a military facility, and if you fail during your first courses here, you will be punished. If you do not learn quickly and work to the best of your ability, focusing on your training and your training alone, your staff will be taken and broken, and you will be removed from the premises. And they," she jerked a thumb at the fae, "will not be able to protect you."

The ice in Aury's stomach remained, but she met Mage Mildred's gaze. "I understand."

Mage Mildred exhaled and lowered her staff. "Good. Now, change quickly, and don't forget to put all that wild hair up and out of your face." She left in a rush, and Aury had the urge to collapse to the floor in relief.

"She's something." Aury set her new boots near the first cabinet and put her uniform on a nearby bench. She sat to remove her boots and begin changing.

"I think we should leave." Hilda was still looking down the corridor like Mage Mildred would be right back to wallop them all across the head with that staff of hers.

"I agree," Eawynn said as she helped Aury into her new tunic. "You don't need us here. What good are we against water mages even if we do want to protect you from them?"

Gytha flicked the back of Eawynn's head. "Our magic worked against the Matchweaver's curse. We have to stay and keep our eyes peeled for more of that witch's nonsense."

The tunic was looser than the gown and comfortable. "Murdering me is nonsense? I'm not sure I would've used that word. More like evil plotting."

Gytha waved Aury off. "Yes, yes. Evil nonsense. And we were ordered by the Fae Queen and the human king and queen to remain by your side in case she strikes again."

"So you're staying." Aury tightened the belt that went with her uniform, then ran a hand over the pin positioned at the shoulder. The metal, warm against her fingers, had been crafted to form a D for Darkfleot and a border of undulating lines she could only guess were meant to be rippling waves.

"Indeed," Hilda answered.

Aury almost felt grateful, but then she remembered how these three had also been privy to the truth, and they'd never once even shown themselves to her, let alone told her anything. She raised her chin. She didn't need anyone. She was about to become a water mage.

Without another word to them, she left the room and retraced Mage Mildred's path to the foyer for the ceremony.

Would they accept her? Or was she about to make a fool of herself?

The only way to know was to get it over with.

Hearing the murmured conversation of a multitude of voices, she pushed through another set of tall, double doors to find the entire population of Darkfleot staring.

CHAPTER 14

In the training yard, Filip faced row upon row of Lore warriors. His stomach turned. None of them looked gaunt, their bellies all full and their skin flush with health. Such a stark difference between his troops and these men and women. But the marriage would change all of that. His warriors would be just as hale and hearty as these next year after the farmlands were handed over and the harvests brought in. Teaching his army's secrets to this force was the right choice.

"Greetings, army of Lore!" Filip paced the small hill above the men-at-arms. The soldiers remained silent, but perhaps that was their habit. "As you know, I'm Prince Filip of Balaur and King Athellore and Queen Gwinnith have welcomed me here to show you what I know of fighting."

Still no sound. Shrugging it off, Filip continued.

"Most of you were in the war and witnessed our three basic types of attacks. First, the archers thin the enemy's front lines. Then, the foot soldiers head in with hatchets, shields, and short swords. Lastly, when a space is made, our warriors on horseback enter the fray to break the enemy apart with sword and axe. A few of ours are skilled enough with small recurve bows to pick off the outer circle of the enemy's force from horseback as well, although trees good enough for such bows are difficult to find in our forests. I would like to work today on the long bow and how it might help all our peoples drive off the Wylfen more quickly and avoid greater loss within the ranks."

With a nod from Filip, Stefan and Costel directed a group of pre-supplied servants to hand out long bows to the first line of warriors.

"Take a moment to pull it back. You'll notice how difficult it is compared to your typical bows. It will take quite a bit of strength to wield these properly, but I know you can manage it with some practice." Humans had far less strength than Filip's people, but they would grow stronger with time.

Once the soldiers held the long bows, the very bald, very arrogant Captain Godwin raised his hand where he stood at the front, just to the right of the gathered troops. The man had been polite when they'd been introduced. Too polite. Filip knew enough of Lore to know when fine manners covered extreme disapproval. What was he up to?

Godwin's hand dropped like an axe on a neck.

The men and women dropped the bows to the snowy ground, and Godwin crossed his arms. "We do not use archery in Lore. It is a coward's weapon."

Filip's head began to pound. He wanted to say, 'Oh really? Then you'll die like brave fools once again when the enemy comes roaring through Dragon Wing Pass.' But he forced himself to take a breath and rework his response. "Long ago, many would have deemed a long-shield a coward's tool. But we all use them now, and there is no shame in it. Only wisdom. We must adapt our fighting techniques or die. There is no honor in flooding the ground with our blood while we stand on old prejudices."

Godwin dropped his hands to his sides, then fisted his fingers. The soldiers stepped onto the bows as if to break them with their boots.

Filip looked skyward and whirled around only to have Costel grip his arm. "Show them the wolf," Costel said.

"But they'll surely hate me then. They'll kill me. I truly think they might. And then where will our lands be? Still in Lore hands."

"No. Try it. You'll shock them, and Godwin won't have an arranged strategy for this. He knows nothing about our little surprise." Costel's grin was deadly.

Filip nodded and spun to face the crowd once more. He ignored the bows lying dark on the white-shrouded ground. "What is it about the Wylfen we fear the most?" he called out as the sun's early rays broke over the distant northern mountains to fall into the flatlands.

"They are unrelenting!" a foot soldier in the second unit shouted.

"True. But why? Why don't they fear us as they might?"

"The wolves," a few new voices murmured, as if saying the word too loudly might summon the trained scar wolves of the Wylfen. The beasts that tore out throats and lapped the blood of Wylfen enemies.

"Indeed. They seem unstoppable. The fae cannot speak to them as they do the scar wolves in Illumahrah. Our arrows and blades don't push them back unless we maim them beyond the ability to strike, and even then, they fight with whatever they have left, never quitting."

Heads turned as the warriors whispered to one another of lost battles and the horrors of the last war and their slim victory. Filip could hear their conversation. Fatigue. Hopelessness. Raw fear.

"Drago!" Filip watched as his men drove the wagon up and over the hill so the troops could see the covered crate and hear the snarling.

Captain Godwin drew his sword and started forward, teeth bared. "What are you doing, elf?"

"Fool!" A thickly bearded man who had stood near Godwin looked around like he might see Wylfen suddenly surrounding them.

Filip held out his hands. "Men. Please, stop. I assure you I have this under control."

"Like flames, you do!" Godwin strode up to the wagon, but the scar wolf inside growled, and he jumped back a step. "What in goddess Vahly's name are you up to, elf?"

Costel walked up to Godwin. "His name is Prince Filip, Captain Godwin, and if you continue to disrespect my prince—"

Filip put a hand on Costel's chest. "Ah. We are fine here, men." Filip turned to face the crowd. "During a border skirmish shortly after the Wylfen's autumn retreat, we managed to capture one of their trained scar wolves."

Godwin looked like he might vomit. Filip truly hoped he would.

"The animal, of course, didn't respond to our attempts at calming him. We have trained wild dogs and even one mountain cat, if you will believe it, so we, as a people, have experience with such things. But the animal here has been beaten repeatedly over the course of its life. The name of scar no longer simply details the stripe down its wide back, but the signs of the Wylfen's cruelty."

Whispers hissed through the ranks, and Stefan and Filip exchanged a wearied glance. Filip was well aware the Lore soldiers believed Balaur sometimes captured dragons and treated them in the same manner. It was wildly untrue. Not only were dragons incredibly rare and one would have to be insane to go against them, but the vast majority of Filip's people would never think to hurt a creature just for sick joy. Of course, there were always criminals in every population, those twisted and unwell in the head. But the ideas that Lore folk had about Balaur and dragons were completely untrue, an explosion of gossip that could most likely be traced to the story of some poacher.

"We did, however," Filip continued as Drago pulled the blanket fully away from the crate, "discover what reward the Wylfen give the wolves during training. Yes, they do indeed reward as well as punish. Costel?"

Costel gave up his glaring contest with Godwin and approached, his hand going to his cloak. He carefully removed a wrapped length of dried orangebranch. Filip took the plant and raised it high, turning so all could see.

"This is orangebranch, a plant that grows in the western mountains and nowhere else." Filip took a small bite, and the salty taste burst over his tongue. "It tastes like bacon, and the Wylfen use it in sparing amounts to encourage the wolves." He went to the crate and pulled the three pins holding the side shut. Drago, Costel, and Stefan came close, swords drawn.

"We tried every kind of edible distraction on the wolves during the wars. You can't possibly—" Godwin started, but Filip interrupted him.

"Watch closely."

The wolf's golden eyes shone as it warily stepped from the crate. Godwin flinched, and the wolf lunged, but Filip crushed the orangebranch and flung it to his own feet. The wolf jerked like it was on a lead and landed at Filip's boots, licking the ground, the orangebranch gone before even Filip's elven eyes could see it eaten. Then the wolf sat and looked up at him as if awaiting orders.

The troops gasped and threw out quiet questions.

"How did you find the plant?"

"Did you learn about this through your spies?"

"How much of the plant does the Balaur hold?"

Filip eyed the animal, its musky scent sending shivers down his back. "Stand."

The wolf obeyed, lifting its snout as if for inspection.

"We did learn this from a spy, yes. And we have very little in Balaur, so it would be wise to send a group to gather more in the western mountains. It dries well and keeps fine in a wrapped bit of cloth. I think if we have enough on hand during the next war, we will turn the tide more quickly and drive the Wylfen back."

Cheers lifted from the ranks, and a smile pulled at Filip's mouth. Not even Godwin could help but nod in reluctant agreement.

CHAPTER 15

Taking a breath, Aury walked calmly into the castle's great hall. This hall was by far rougher than the fae's pillared monstrosity or the smooth-walled room at Loreton. This was a fortress's feasting hall, not merely a place for noble festivities. Ancient tapestries showing battles of flying shards of ice and fanged men—who looked far too much like Aury's husband-*not*-to-be-thank-you-very-much—covered most of the walls, but where the stone was bare, gouges lined the rock as if some of these fights had occurred here.

Behind the rows of gray-haired instructors, every trainee present wore the same uniform as Aury, but that was where the similarities ended. Some were skinny and hardly looked ready for a walk across the room, let alone waging a war, while others were quite bulky, and it surprised her considering most had come from noble families and weren't exactly digging ditches before they'd come here. She might fit in since she was somewhere in the middle, size-wise. They all seemed to be around her age as well, nineteen, maybe twenty. Sadly, she was the only cursed princess, and that would cause some gossip.

The mages here would be on the front lines when the Wylfen attacked.

She missed a step and stumbled.

She would also be on the front lines.

Her gaze caught on a crossed pair of staves hung above a tapestry and cloaked in a black length of linen. It was a tribute to their fallen. Suddenly, this venture of hers was all too real—fighting for Lore, and most likely dying for Lore.

Swallowing her fear, she walked more quickly now, determined to go bravely into this new stage of her life. She'd lost so much of her true life, years and years spent worthlessly entangled in the lies of others, hidden away at the fae court. So what if she died? The risk was worth experiencing her true life as a water mage.

Mage Mildred stood on a dais at the end of the room beneath a cluster of leaded glass windows. Below the windows, a statue of goddess Lilia—who'd supposedly lived under the ocean ages ago and wielded all the power of a water mage and so much more—seemed to burst from the wall with stone fins down her arms and a pitted staff of coral in her outstretched hand. Another statue peered from the wall under goddess Lilia. It was the Spirit of the River, her form being simply three concentric circles and quite familiar from Aury's days with her history tutor.

"Welcome to Darkfleot, Recruit Aurora," Mage Mildred said, her voice carrying across the tables lit with thick, cream-colored candles.

Every step of Aury's boots sounded insanely loud on

the flagstone floor. She reached the front and gave Mage Mildred a respectful nod, completely unsure what the tradition was here. It would have been nice if someone had told her even one thing about how to act. They all seemed to forget she'd been raised by fae and knew next to nothing about the human world and the kingdom she was meant to reign after her parents.

"Thank you, Mage Mildred."

Mildred nodded and almost smiled, pursing her lips before turning to the gathered recruits. "Ladies. Sirs. Please stand for the presentation of the staff," she said loudly as she guided Aury with a firm hand on the shoulder. They walked toward a stone basin set in the wall below goddess Lilia and the Spirit of the River. The basin was filled with fresh water, and it rippled ominously as Aury peered over the edge.

Mildred walked to the far side of the dais, leaving Aury by the basin. The woman lifted the lid of a massive trunk and removed something wrapped in blue velvet.

A tingling danced across Aury's fingers and palms.

"As temporary Master of the Order of Darkfleot, I, Mage Mildred, present your staff, Mage Aurora Rose of Lore." She flipped the edge of the velvet to show a length of polished white oak, then held the staff out for Aury to accept.

The distant sound of the ocean whispered in Aury's ears as she wrapped her hand around the staff and brought it close. A twisted knot of wood at the end had been hollowed out and expertly carved to show what lay inside —a branch of sunset orange coral.

She'd never been given anything so lovely unless one

counted Goldheart. But horses were not gifts; they were friends or enemies. "It's beautiful."

"Pass your staff over the water," Mildred said.

Heart jumping, Aury stretched the staff slowly over the basin. The rippling grew stronger, as did the ocean sound in her ears. The shushing of non-existent waves wasn't loud enough to bar her from hearing anything else; the sound seemed to exist in a place separate from other noises, as if she had a second pair of ears made to hear her magic. Ridiculous thought, but it was the only way she could wrap her mind around what she was experiencing. She longed to ask what was meant to happen now and if she was doing it all wrong, but she held her tongue, not wanting to look as green as she knew she was.

"Prince Filip!" Mildred called out.

Aury jerked in surprise, and chilly magic rushed through the staff to buzz along her fingers. Water blasted out of the basin, soared over the open-mouthed crowd, and crashed over Filip.

Begging all gods and goddesses, even the Source, to make the floor inhale her, Aury watched Filip slick water from his chiseled features and sling his wet hair back from his face.

Silence dropped over the room. Everyone was probably wondering if Aury had just started a war with the elves.

Heat rising in her chest and cheeks, Aury glared at Filip, just daring him to show anger. It was his fault for barging in here during the ceremony, a ceremony he wasn't invited to. Filip's eyes met her gaze, and she could swear his lips twitched like he wanted to laugh.

Aury gritted her teeth. She was going to murder him. Repeatedly.

Mildred cleared her throat, obviously waiting for the royal pair to say something and lead the reaction of the mages.

Aury had no idea what to say. She just hoped Mildred wouldn't have her kicked out of Darkfleot.

Nix's Fire, she could see every line of Filip's muscled chest and stomach through his tunic. Her rebellious mind wondered how those powerful arms would feel wrapped around her. Why did the evil elf have to be so handsome?

"Sorry for the interruption," he said across the hall. "It's been...interesting." He bowed and pushed the doors open to leave.

"Arrogant horse's arse," she hissed under her breath.

He paused, then left.

There's no way he could have heard her whisper from that far away, right? Eh, even if he did, what did she care? Maybe he'd give up more quickly.

Aury turned to face Mildred, whose nostrils were flared so widely that they were all in danger of being sucked inside.

"Does that happen often?" Aury asked.

Exhaling, Mildred bent her head. After another breath, she raised her chin. "Powerful magic can be unpredictable." She turned to face the crowd, obviously deciding to act like nothing had happened. "Mages, join me in saluting our newest recruit, Mage Aurora."

Was she just being nice until later? Once everyone had left, Mildred would kick Aury's clumsy arse from Darkfleot and reclaim the staff.

Everyone in the hall stood as one and raised their staves. "Mage Aurora!"

Aury smiled at the instructors' shouts of congratulations and encouragement. The trainees swamped her with cheers and friendly claps on the back. It should've been a lovely moment, but the acceptance and kindness didn't seem real. How could they be? She'd done nothing to earn their goodwill. Not yet. No, this was merely protocol and nothing sincere. Yes, that made sense.

She let herself smile more fully then. It was a pleasant way to start training, and that was enough; that was real and true. And she would earn this welcome. She would prove her worth to them and to the kingdom. No matter how much Filip messed with her fate.

CHAPTER 16

I n his chamber in the western wing of Darkfleot, Filip
shucked off his wet tunic as Drago, Stefan, and
Costel belly laughed.

"I can't believe she doused you!" Drago slapped Filip on
the shoulder, then bent double laughing again.

"What can I say?" Filip removed his boots and poured
water from them onto the stone floor. "I have a strong
effect on the princess."

He had to chuckle, but he did feel bad about disrupting
Aurora's ceremony. *Aury*, he silently corrected himself.
He'd noticed she liked being called Aury. Regardless, he felt
terrible about the interruption. He'd only been curious to
see her receive a water mage staff. The troops had been
busy working on a cavalry technique he'd taught them, so
he'd had a moment. He'd had no idea the great hall would
be in total silence and that his entry would so fully distract
everyone.

And he'd heard what she'd called him on his way out.

He had to think of something that would make her possibly hate him less.

"What are you lot doing here, anyway? I'm fairly certain I assigned you each a calvary technique to practice with Godwin's units."

Stefan lifted his hands. "Arc's Light, save us from that man. I can't stand to look at his face for another minute."

"Agreed." Drago flicked a knife from his belt and turned it to catch the light from the window. "Godwin reminds me how long it's been since I stabbed someone."

Costel sighed heavily. "Come, all. We've checked on our lord. They'll be missing us on the training grounds."

Once he was in a proper set of leathers again, Filip trailed his men back outside to deal with Godwin, the scar wolf, and the new fighting techniques.

THE DAY WENT BY IN A BLUR OF SHOUTS. THOUGH Godwin had the air of a fool, he was quite good at twisting Filip's words so that the Lore soldiers thought ill of Filip. Filip bathed and dressed, the water turning his mind to Aury. He had to think of a way to please her. She wouldn't let him close. Not yet. So he'd have to be creative with his seduction. He could just imagine how she'd roll those gorgeous blue eyes at a posey of hothouse blooms, and she'd have some kind of bladed remark if he tried to woo her with a compliment. She seemed to love horses—the talk was that she liked animals more than people, which he completely understood considering her background. But he couldn't gift her a new mount. Not here. The feast at Loreton Palace came to mind, along with her reaction to the scorchpeppers. The woman loved food as much as he did and had leapt on those peppers like a starving man.

In the common area between their chambers, Costel sat beside Drago and Stefan, who were sharing a bottle of fruit brandy. A sudden memory flicked through Filip's mind.

He lightly smacked Costel on the arm. "Eh, didn't we pass a thorny bramble thick with scorchpepper plants on our way here?"

Costel scratched his skinny face. "I think so. Was it near that oak grove?"

"Aye, that's the one."

Aury had shown a love for scorchpeppers, though not when her parents gave them to her, for reasons he could easily grasp. They'd been trying to sweeten her mood after lying to her for her entire life. Even if the lying had been done to protect her, she remained hurt. But maybe from him...

"Where are you going?" Costel grabbed for his sleeve but missed.

Drago and Stefan set down their bottle and stood to follow Filip.

"I'm going to pick some of the leaves," Filip said. "For the princess. I've heard you can use them for cooking. They'd go well in a chocolate custard, I'd think." Maybe she wouldn't turn away the peppers he gave to her. After all, Filip was only doing as he was told by coming here to meet her, to marry her. Surely the spicy treat would shuck some of the ill will she held for him. "You get some rest," he said to Drago and Stefan. "I'm pretty sure I can handle a patch of woodland on my own."

"You're sure that she wants scorchpepper leaves from you?" Costel studied Filip's face like he thought he'd gone mad.

"I'm not losing my mind. I just know she likes them. I'm trying to woo her, remember? To save our people from starvation? She likes spice."

Drago snorted. "I doubt that's the spice she wants from her elven warrior."

Filip glared. "The princess is my business. Go on, now. Enjoy your beds while you can. You know Godwin will have us up before dawn."

Drago moaned. "Gods, he is a creature from the darkest caves of misery."

Costel stood. "Straight out of the legends of the galtzagorri tunnels. So, my prince, we will leave you to your peppers." He bowed.

Filip pretended to lunge—a thing they'd done since they were boys—and Costel flicked a finger at him as Drago and Stefan returned to their drink by the fire.

"Just watch out for errant puddles," Stefan called out, making Drago guffaw.

THE GROVE WAS CLOSE ENOUGH FOR WALKING, AND FILIP welcomed the bitter chill as he made his way toward the brambles through the cloudy night. The cold helped him think more clearly, kept him alert. It was good to get away from the castle and his men for a bit, too, for some peace and quiet.

He found the thorny area easily enough. The scorchpepper plants with their evergreen leaves grew through the tangled web of brambles and threaded into the pitch dark of the grove. His elven eyes picked up the shine of the palm-shaped leaves, and he set to plucking.

The brambles stirred.

Filip froze, holding his breath to listen and feeling his ears twitch.

A very particular scent rose into the winter night. Charcoal and citrus. A chill slithered down his spine. *May Arc's Light be with me...*

Dragon.

The plants and thorny bushes shuffled, then a puff of hot breath caressed his cheek. His gaze slid left to see a pair of glinting, golden eyes.

Slowly, every movement a study in careful grace, he went to his knees and lowered his hands to the ground. His elder brother, Dorin, was the one who had the obsession with dragons and the experience with them. This was the first time Filip had been this close to one of the wild, rare creatures.

And in the dark, he could honestly say they were the most frightening things in the world.

The dragon huffed, and the heat of its breath warmed Filip's back uncomfortably. He swallowed. What now?

A quiet growl rumbled from what he guessed was the dragon's throat. It wasn't a massive beast like the other three he'd glimpsed from afar throughout his life. This was a youngling—slim, less muscled, and only the size of two horses stacked one on top of the other. Something moved beside Filip's hand, and his small finger twitched. He felt the hard texture of a talon as the dragon dug into the snowy ground. A moan shuddered through the air, and

Filip bit his tongue to keep from shouting out in surprise. He looked up to see the youngling dragon lifting its broad head, or rather, trying to do so. Thorned vines had the creature trapped, and the dragon tossed its snout, moaning in pain again. Besides being stuck fast, it was injured too, from the sound of it. Spikes along the dragon's head reflected the dim, inconsistent light of the stars, and the scent of blood mixed with the smell of dragon fire. He would have to cut it free and pray to the Source, as well as every god and goddess, that the dragon would think him friend and not foe.

CHAPTER 17

Aury's bedchamber was a dream. A four-poster bed curtained in midnight blue velvet stood beside a nightstand that had carved images of curling clouds and rippling streams. Frost had turned the windows to lace, but a snapping fire in the far wall chased the chill away. The place smelled of beeswax and was so blessedly quiet—the chatter of other mages shut out as well as the hum of gossip that had trailed her up the tower stairs to where all the north wing bedchambers sat. She fell onto the bed and shut her eyes. This was suddenly the best place in the entire world.

Still in her Darkfleot tunic and boots, she woke to the watery light of near dawn slipping through the windows. Energy drummed through Aury, and suddenly she couldn't bear the thought of staying here and waiting for the day to begin. After checking that Hilda, Gytha, and Eawynn slept soundly on their three trundle beds positioned in the antechamber, Aury splashed her face with clean water in the basin on the side table. Once dressed in clean clothing, she donned her mage baldric, which could hold her staff at an angle and facilitate riding or running. She took up her staff, which sent a zip of power through her arm, then crept out of the tower.

At the castle gates, the guards saluted her and let her pass without a word. She grinned and gripped her staff tightly. The benefits of being more than just the Fae Queen's tainted niece or a human princess were already showing, and she was glad of it. This was how she was meant to live. On her own terms. Making her own decisions of when to leave and what to do with her time.

She crunched across the snow, the feeling of freedom as fresh and exhilarating as the cold. The stars and moon still hung in the sky, not yet chased away by the sun. Once she cleared the rise and knew the guards wouldn't be able to see her, she pointed her staff at a snow drift. Not knowing the first thing about how to make it do anything, she simply imagined the snow lifting into the air and twining around itself.

A crack sounded from her staff. Snow and dirt blasted from the ground, and she stumbled back a step. Chunks of ice and earth rained down on her head. "Nix's weighted dice," she swore, standing quickly and shaking off the debris.

A laugh preceded the appearance of Gytha, Hilda, and Eawynn.

"Might want to wait until you've had your tutoring, my girl," Gytha said, snickers breaking her words.

"You shouldn't have done that," Hilda snapped.

"Anyone could be out here, just waiting to kidnap the princess for a ransom."

Eawynn shuddered and eyed the wood beyond them. "It's true. You should have asked us to come along. You know the king and queen and the Fae Queen too would've flayed us alive if you went missing."

Aury opened her mouth to argue that a kidnapping was unlikely so near the army's fortress, but movement at the line of trees stopped her. "What's that? Can you see?" The fae had better eyes than her. Elves did too.

Eawynn grabbed Aury's sleeve and tried to pull her back toward the castle. "Let's go. It could be a bear."

Aury patted Eawynn's hand, then not-so-gently jerked away. A strange moan threaded through the breeze, and Aury stiffened. She'd heard that sound once. One dark night during the trip to Sea's Claw, a similar moan had broken the noise of insects and Werian's jokes.

"Dragon," Werian had said with a tone of awe and respect in his voice. "And hopefully, one that doesn't crave my delicious blood."

"Your blood is delicious?" she'd asked.

"Look at me. Of course it is," he'd teased.

The glittering scales and the whipping sound of the creature's wings had dominated Aury's dreams for months after that trip. She'd never been quite sure whether fear or fascination took the lead in her feelings about dragons, but she found herself rushing toward the sound, so her curiosity was obviously winning at the moment.

"Stop!" Hilda called out behind her.

They were following, but that was fine. It would be good to have three quick fae at her back if things went badly. But it would be fine. Aury would simply get a peek through the brambles at the amazing creature, then pop away to the castle without bothering it.

When she reached the tangled growth at the trees, a familiar voice spoke quietly from a cluster of scorchpepper plants.

"Don't come closer."

Aury's heart jumped and not only because she knew there was a dragon somewhere in the shadows. The voice was Filip's.

The rising sun glinted off a raised hatchet.

"No!" She tore around the side of the thicket, thorns ripping at her arms and clothing. "Don't hurt her!"

The vicious, horrible elf was probably already butchering the dragon for its teeth and spikes as his people were known to do.

"I swear by Lilia and the River Spirit, I'll see your head on the end of my staff if you so much as—"

She cleared the thorns to see Filip's hatchet back on his belt and his hand cradling the dragon's chin. Blood ran down both of them, along Filip's hands and cheeks, down the dragon's snout and flank. Chopped thorn branches lay in piles around them. Filip had cut the creature free and was cooing to it like it was his favorite barn cat.

"Shh, *mica bijuterie a cerului. Nu voi lasa pe nimeni sa îti faca rau.*"

He spoke in the Balaur language, so Aury had no idea what he was saying, but he wasn't killing the dragon. He was helping it. But what if he was only calming it before he cut its throat?

"If you hurt it..."

Filip's stormy glare cut through the nearing dawn's pale

light. "I don't hurt dragons. Only the criminals in both our lands do. Drop your preconceived ideas about me and my people, Princess Aurora. Prejudice doesn't suit you."

The dragon's lip curled, revealing a set of teeth that Aury would never, ever argue with.

"Hey, beastie," Aury said. "We're going to help you."

"We are?" Filip's eyebrow quirked, but then he raised his nose and sniffed. "Ah, your fae ladies are here."

"Yes. They'll be able to heal her."

The anger finally left Filip's features, and Aury hated how much it pleased her. "Over here," he called quietly as the fae leapt one by one over the brambles, wind catching in their hair.

With the way they could jump, the fae almost seemed to fly. It brought a question about Filip and other mountain elves to Aury's mind, but she pushed it away as the fae approached with graceful steps and cautious gazes.

Filip and Aury moved a few steps away to give them room. The fae set their hands on the skittish dragon youngling and began to send glowing, healing magic into the creature's torn body. The dragon shuddered and purred, nuzzling Gytha, who smiled but remained nearly still. If they startled the dragon, it could very easily roast them all in one or two breaths.

"Can elves really fly?" Aury asked Filip quietly. "Simpletons believe they have air magic like the old elven gods of Illumahrah, but the fae are just grand at leaping."

Filip's gaze remained trained on the dragon, his hand on his hatchet and a muscle in his jaw tensing like he was ready to move if things went sideways. "We can't fly either, but many humans think we have magic of that sort."

"What sort do you have?"

His brow knitted, then a sly smile stretched his full lips. He turned to face her and leaned a fraction closer, crossing his arms, muscles rolling under the tight fabric of his tunic. The heat of his body and his scent—steel and woodsmoke—curled around her. "Curious about me?"

Breaking through the trees, the rising sun illuminated his thick eyelashes and highlighted the ring of darker gray around his irises. His smooth, elven skin was perfect aside from the scars of battle.

"I suppose. Isn't everyone?" Her body hummed like it was ready to run or fight or argue.

He looked away, sniffing a small laugh. "Yes. Especially Captain Godwin."

"Oh, that man is a rat-faced boar."

He laughed, covering his mouth to muffle the sound, gaze on the dragon as it stretched one pale blue wing over the thicket. "Isn't calling him a boar insult enough? They aren't pretty. Why add the rat?"

Aury found herself smiling. "Less threatening. No rat is going to ruin my plans."

"Your plans to win all during the Mage Trials and deny my hand." He didn't sound upset by it. With his hands loosely clasped behind his back, he watched the fae work with an impassive gaze. She'd forgotten for a moment that he probably ate babies for breakfast.

"As I said, you will get your lands as long as you provide an army. Marriage has nothing to do with it."

"The king disagrees."

"The king can shove off."

Filip's eyebrows shot up, and he pursed his lips, trying to hide a chuckle that shook his broad shoulders.

Aury was suddenly itchy and too cold and insanely hungry. She couldn't stand here another moment. She leaned her staff against a tree and knotted her hair at her neck, feeling flushed and frustrated. "You don't want to marry me."

"Oh, no?" His gaze slid up her arm and into her hair, and she shivered like she could feel his warm touch, his fingers brushing the base of her neck.

"Certainly, you'd be better off with one of your own people," she said.

"So we can bathe in blood together?"

A bitter taste hit the back of Aury's tongue, and Filip touched her arm. "Eh," he whispered, "we don't actually do that, you know."

"You're a mountain elf. Of course you do. It's why you're so good in battle. You are heartless. Vicious. Blood-wild."

Filip cocked his head, considering. His pointed ears showed through his tangled black hair. "We can go blood-wild, but do you truly believe I'm heartless?"

Cracking branches, the dragon lifted itself onto two legs, and the fae fell back. Spreading its wings, the dragon roared and blew fire in a rippling banner of orange and blue flame over their heads. The heat pressed on Aury's head, and she ducked even as she peeked up at the creature. She wasn't going to miss any of this.

The dawn's light passed through the membrane of the dragon's wings, turning the blue to a pale amethyst. The crystal spikes on its head and back were like icicles, fracturing the light and painting the surrounding trees in rainbows. The beast turned, and its golden eyes focused on Filip. It lowered its snout.

Filip took a step. "Enchanted to meet you. Fly well, new friend."

To call a dragon a friend...

The creature burst from the brush and flew from the trees, taking Aury's breath. It soared out of sight.

"Do you think the stories are true?" Filip asked.

"About the dragons once having a human form? No. That's too much. But I believe they could communicate with us once upon a time."

"They do seem highly intelligent."

"Smarter than Captain Rat-Faced Boar."

"Agreed." Filip snatched Aury's hand before she knew what he was up to, and his lips touched her knuckles, soft as down.

She swallowed and pulled her hand away.

"I will see you later, Princess." He gave the fae a courtly bow, then left the wood with a quick pace.

Aury took up her staff and started off behind him, feeling incredibly agitated. He was so tricky, that elf. Acting all nice and charming and mysterious. Ugh. She had to be firmer with him in the future. He wasn't taking her rejection seriously at all.

"I don't like that look," Hilda said.

"What look?" Aury hurried toward the castle grounds. The sky was fully light now, and she needed food before training began.

"The look that says you're working up to something truly evil." Gytha grinned. "Do tell."

"I have to show Filip that I'm not playing hard-to-get, that I'm serious about my rejection of this marriage. I'm worried the king and queen will back out on our deal if Filip pushes the marriage. Why does he even want to marry me? I told him he could have the lands for his people."

"He knows as well as we all do that your father will have the final say in giving up farmland," Hilda said. "Prince Filip is merely playing his role."

"You have a lovely face," Eawynn chirped. "He is smitten with you, Princess."

Gytha pinched Aury's backside. "He isn't only in this for land. He is a man."

"He is an elf," Aury said.

"And all the more reason to believe he wants you in his bed," Gytha said as Hilda tsked.

Aury crossed the drawbridge and the guards saluted. "What do you mean?"

Gytha linked her arm in Aury's. "Elves are known for their skill in the art of love."

Aury tripped, and Gytha caught her. Before Aury could ask further questions or argue that such a vicious folk couldn't possibly have such a reputation, the horns for breakfast sounded.

CHAPTER 18

In her bedchamber's washroom at Darkfleot, Aury squeezed lavender-scented water from her clean hair, then dressed in a fresh set of Order clothing.

The image of Filip's wry smile couldn't be scrubbed from her mind. She waffled between wishing she could punch the grin off his mouth and wondering what his lips would taste like. He'd been warm and so very tall standing there beside her in the first hints of dawn as they watched the dragon take off. He'd seemed kind to the animal and even pleasant to talk to.

But she was being stupid.

If she hadn't discovered him, he would have killed the dragon and taken its teeth and spikes. Years ago, the Fae Queen had told the whole court about two mountain elves caught by King Athellore—*Source above, she could not think of him being her father*—and punished for selling dragon scales. That, she knew was true because the Fae Queen had no reason to lie about elves.

Filip had every reason to lie. She had to crush the base urge to kiss him, the desire to press her body against his just to feel his solid presence. Her breath caught, and she cleared her throat. She was here to train. There would be no wedding, especially with an elf who lied so well. No, it would be much better if she reigned on her own after her parents gave up the throne in their old age. That way, the only focus she would have would be her people and her people alone.

Outside the washroom, Gytha polished Aury's tall boots. Eawynn and Hilda argued over ribbons and brushes at the vanity table.

"Hurry!" Hilda barked, waving Aury over to the stool in front of the round mirror.

"Just plait it." The candle burning against the silver sconce that marked the hours showed that it was nearly time. "I don't want to be late." She'd downed a trencher of eggs and a mug of watered wine in the hall before rushing here to ready for her first day of training.

Hilda and Eawynn worked in unison, their nimble fae fingers firm and quick in Aury's hair. Soon enough, she had a long silver braid running down her head and over one shoulder with wine-colored ribbons threaded throughout.

"Don't you think it's a little much?" She plucked at one silken tail.

Hilda smacked her hand. "It's fine. Here's this." She handed her a wooden box.

On the lid, a carved stag reared over a rippling river—the symbol of the royal family. Aury flipped it open to see a ring of gold, pressed with the same image. A weight settled onto her shoulders, something like a heavy cloak.

She slid the ring onto her pointer finger and found it felt right.

She could continue to fight who she was, but where would that lead people like Rhianne, the cobbler from that small town? What would happen if Aury continued to deny the fact that she was born to rule and another had to take the throne? She knew so little of the Lore nobles. Maybe there was someone who would serve Lore well, but perhaps there wasn't.

"What happens when there is no heir?" She kept her voice to a whisper.

Hilda shifted her skirts, her throat moving in a swallow and her gaze going to the flagstone floor. "The Witan would decide the next ruler."

Eawynn rushed to Aury and knelt, gripping her skirts. "The Earl of Cynuit runs the Witan. He's awful, Aurora. You must not give him the chance to take your place."

"How do you know this? You were at the fae court with me for all those years, right?"

Gytha crossed her arms and looked down at them. "We were told what we needed to know. My sister married a human, and she lives on the earl's holdings. He isn't the sort of fellow one likes to bring up in decent company."

The glint in Gytha's eyes told Aury enough. If she refused the throne, Lore would be gripped by a foul man, and the people would suffer. Aury flexed her hand, attempting to get used to the feel of the heavy, golden ring.

Gytha helped her with her boots, and Aury gave her a grateful smile. "It's nice to have a hand getting ready, but you know none of this is necessary. It's not as if you were preparing me for feasts at the fae court."

Gytha's lip curled. "We wanted to. We were bound, remember? I've been over this. And we begged the Fae Queen to allow it because of who you are and all you dealt with at the hands of others. But she refused us."

Eawynn nodded, wrapping her arms around herself. "She threatened to lop off my fingers if I found a way around the magical binding. She said you were only to be kept alive. That was it. And that no human girl was going to have pureblood treatment at the Agate Palace."

"Horse's arse," Aury muttered as she grabbed her staff and felt that now familiar zing of power shoot up her arm. It was like the staff was saying *hello*.

"Good luck!" the fae called out as she tromped down the spiral, stone staircase.

She nearly thanked them again, but the memory of Werian and his betrayal stopped her. A cage of protective ice seemed to form around her heart—cold but strong and good. She couldn't trust her fae ladies. They would betray her like everyone did.

How awful was it that her parents insisted on her marrying the very man who had caused all of the problems in her life? Of course, Filip had been a toddler at the time, so it wasn't his fault, but still. The Matchweaver had been against the betrothal between her and Filip because the witch hadn't first seen the match in her magical loom. That made sense if one considered the goddess witch's nature. And everyone knew the Matchweaver was a mercurial sort with a tendency for grand drama. Cursing an infant to spite a king and queen who had slighted her also fell into line with what Aury knew of the Matchweaver.

Was the Matchweaver at her castle in Illumahrah right

now, stewing over the wedding she thought would come to pass? Was she thinking up ways to break her banishment and get revenge on the king and queen, and maybe even Aury, again?

Perhaps Aury should send the Matchweaver a message, telling the witch that she had no intention of marrying a mountain elf and that Aury was completely open to suggestions from the magical loom? Although of course, Aury had no plans to wed. Ever. Freedom would be her only mate. But the witch didn't need to know that. She could pretend to be interested in the Matchweaver's suggestions.

Regardless of whatever came to pass, Aury wouldn't be getting near any spinning wheels if she saw them. What a strange curse...

Deciding to send a well-crafted message to the witch as soon as she had a moment, she climbed yet another winding stretch of stairs before she could take the steps leading down to the ground floor. Well, even if her magic didn't pan out, she'd have legs like a plow horse by the end of her stint at Darkfleot. That was one thing anyway.

The ground floor was crowded with other mages who gave her a wide berth, their gaze flicking from the ribbons in her hair to her face and back again. Her stomach knotted as she walked the length of the main foyer and into a candlelit corridor. The smell of fresh water permeated the air as she hurried toward the door where everyone seemed to be going. Again, other recruits moved away.

She stopped just before entering. "I don't have the plague!"

The room was dark despite the three windows on the western side. Shadows extended black fingers away from the corners, shading a tapestry that showed a battle between the Wylfen and the water mages. The artist had given the Wylfen horns, and though Aury knew that was a lie, the addition of horns served to communicate the demon-like fury with which they fought.

Standing beside a man with red hair and a massive sword and a woman with impressively muscular arms, Aury eyed the stone troughs of water placed along the far wall. How was this going to work? A shiver of anticipation traveled through her. She turned her sigil ring around her knuckle, the gold warming under her touch and the stag's antlers catching at her fingertip.

"Hello," a timid but bright voice said.

Aury looked up to see a blonde woman with one green eye and one blue. Her uniform was perfectly tidy—unlike Aury's that had somehow adopted cat hairs even though there weren't any cats in the castle that she could see. The woman wore jade earrings, which were hard to come by.

Werian's lessons on trade came to mind, and Aury's stomach twisted thinking of him. At some point, she'd have to write to him.

"I'm Sunniva." The blonde stuck out a hand, and Aury tentatively shook it. "I'm a merchant's wife from the Eastern Province. I'm going to train here until I can serve Lore at the borders." She mumbled something about how many miles it was from here to the Eastern Province and from there to the border in the mountains. Numbers had never been Aury's strength. They buzzed around her like annoying gnats, so she mentally shooed them away and focused on the other bits of the woman's greeting.

"Your husband is fine with this?"

Aury wasn't too proud to glean marriage information from a stranger. If she did get caught—which by Nix's great tail she would NOT—it wouldn't hurt to know a bit about the way of things. Marriages at the fae court most likely weren't the same as human unions. Of course, if she were forced to wed an elf, it wasn't as if that relationship would follow human rules. She pinched the bridge of her nose. She was already so done with everyone having their hands in her life.

"He travels all over to find new things to sell, so we're hardly together anyway. We meet up when we can, when the markets coincide with my training." She wilted, her two-colored eyes softening. "I'm sorry you must wed an... an elf to help our kingdom," she whispered, looking toward the windows like Filip might bash into the room with a bloody hatchet and demand a human sacrifice. For all Aury knew, he would.

Fear cut at her confidence, but she ignored the sensation. "All will proceed as it must," she said. That could be taken in two ways. Growing up at the fae court had taught her much about diplomatic talk, saying much and saying nothing at all.

Sunniva smiled in sympathy, and it made Aury's stomach turn. "Did the Matchweaver give you his name?" Aury asked, changing the subject.

"She did," Sunniva said tentatively. "I'm sorry for all she did to you, or tried to do. But I have to say I am incredibly grateful. You see, my husband has no desire for children outside orphans we might end up taking in, and I have no longing for what one must do to create children."

"None?"

"Kisses and cuddles are lovely. But nothing more. Never have felt that longing."

Aury felt loads of it. "Interesting. You probably wouldn't have found a man like your husband without the goddess witch, then, hmm?"

"People like him and me are incredibly rare," Sunniva said. "Like those golden unicorns in the old Illumahrah stories."

Aury couldn't completely loathe the Matchweaver because of situations just like this. The witch did indeed keep true love going in Lore, and sometimes, beyond. "How long have you been here?"

"Since harvest."

It was a good thing this Sunniva had ended up at Darkfleot. With those mismatched eyes, she'd probably suffered from superstitious attacks in the smaller villages like the cobbler's niece, Rhianne, had for being left-handed.

A tall, older man with a glare as hot as a fire poker strode into the room and slammed a rune book onto a small, wooden table. He wasn't bad-looking for an old fellow. His staff was dark and flecked with silver etchings, and it had Aury wondering at how the Order decided who received what type of staff and why.

"Shut it, animals," the instructor bellowed.

Aury covered a laugh with a cough.

The man glared. "I'm Mage Finn. Tell me what stopped the Wylfen at Dragon Wing Pass last year."

Sunniva's smile looked like a threat, and Aury started to like her more. "The Red Letters of Grogan state that the Wylfen travel in units of one hundred seventy-nine. It's a lucky number to them. They attacked last year with eight hundred ninety-five over the course of two months. Three hundred forty-one died while Lore lost eight hundred ninety-nine. Only flooding managed to stop the enemy and end the war," Sunniva said.

"Very good," Mage Finn said as he pointed his staff at the trough of water by the window. He whispered something under his breath, the whiskers on his beard twitching.

The scent of the water grew stronger—greener, somehow. As if the whole room had suddenly been plunged beneath the Silver River and watercress was about to bloom from their very heads.

The water shivered, then began to bubble.

CHAPTER 19

Filip had fallen into bed and woken only because of Costel's threat of a letter to Filip's mother, Queen Sorina. With just three hours of shut-eye, he was back on the training grounds, his body moving in the familiar steps of warfare. Stance, reach, strike. Slip, shield block, slash, slash.

From experience, he knew well he could do this with far fewer hours of sleep, but it didn't make the day feel any better. Not with Godwin making snide remarks about Filip being the youngest of the royal elven family. For some strange reason, the man thought that fact was a thorn in Filip's side. It wasn't. Filip had never longed for the level of responsibility that Dorin shouldered as eldest and heir to the throne of Balaur. Honestly, anyone who knew how ruling a kingdom actually went from day to day would never be envious of such a position. Only fools who thirsted for power they weren't born to wield had such silly dreams.

"Wouldn't it be better if you created an arrow-shaped force with the shieldmen? I've seen your brother, Prince Dorin, use such a strategy with great effect."

The wind rose and pushed at Filip's back. "It's a useful attack, and I've said as much. The warriors of Lore should learn more than one type of formation from my men and me. They must be nimble, quick-thinking, and capable to defeat the Wylfen."

"As quick as elves," Godwin said cuttingly. "How could we ever be as quick as elves?"

"You can't!" Stefan called out as he slashed at two humans, then spun to knock down two more with a leg sweep and a well-placed shoulder.

"Stefan!" Filip tried to sound angry but could hardly contain his grin. "Captain Godwin, how about you help the fourth learn how to hold a hatchet instead of pouring vinegar all over my training over here."

"You would like that, wouldn't you, elf?"

"Prince Filip, you meant, correct? Surely you wouldn't insult a royal guest of King Athellore."

Godwin jerked the reins of his ill-used mount and hurried away.

Aury was dead right on that man. Rat-faced boar.

Filip dodged a strike, then dealt an overhand blow to his sparring partner, brushing past the woman's head.

"Nice one, Prince," she said, panting and heading off for water.

Filip tossed his training shield into the pile and splashed his face with water, Aury coming to mind. "Don't forget to keep your shield up, soldier."

"Will do!" The soldier saluted him in the Lore style of

touching a hand to where a sheathed sword would hang from a belt even though she wasn't currently wearing one.

These Lore warriors were skilled and fast for humans. They'd give the Wylfen a good fight if it came to it again. Especially now that some of them would have dried orangebranch in their baldrics, ready to toss at the scar wolves to distract them. Victory wasn't assured, but it was much more of a possibility now, and Filip felt proud of that fact.

Aury needed to know more about the training. She'd eventually be the queen of this kingdom. Her old-fashioned father had shown he wasn't forthcoming with information, and he'd want Filip to handle the war side of ruling. Aury wasn't the type to be on board with Filip handling anything in her lands without her having a say. He liked that about her and hoped they could discuss it further over the scorchpepper dessert he would have the kitchen prep for the upcoming feast.

The mages and the warriors had a regular feast once a fortnight to improve relations between the divisions. Tomorrow night, they'd all come together in the great hall for long talks, rich foods, and dancing. And if she saw him dance, she'd know exactly how skilled he was physically.

He'd woo her from all directions. She didn't stand a chance.

"Prince Filip!" Godwin beckoned.

Source save him, this day would never end.

He jogged over to see the warriors in that unit training as directed with shield and hatchet, learning one of the various Balaur techniques of close fighting. Godwin was still mounted, his face gone red under the winter sun.

"One of the recruits, Elis of Damerham, said you found a dragon in the grove beyond the drawbridge."

"Aye." He hadn't wanted this man to know, but he supposed it did no harm. The dragon was gone, hopefully back to its kin and safe from idiots.

"He ran off to try to see if it left any tracks. We need you to fetch him back and tell him to quit being so foolhardy."

"Me?" Filip wasn't above helping out wherever he could, but this was odd.

"Only you know where the dragon was seen. Osberth there tried to find him, but I think he looked in the wrong place. Would you mind too much? I realize princes rarely need to aid lower ranks like this, but you know where the dragon landed, and this was due to your actions... Young Elis could be mauled if the dragon returns. With your experience, you're the only one fit for checking on him."

Filip tapped his sigil ring against the hatchet at his belt and glanced at Costel, Drago, and Stefan, who had mounted up and were deep in training, showing three other units the ways to strike a shielded warrior from horseback.

"If Young Elis hasn't shown up by tomorrow at the end of training," he said quietly to Godwin. "I'll go on the search."

Godwin looked a little too pleased with his acceptance. Yes, something was definitely off, but Filip wasn't about to call him out and play the coward. He could handle whatever Godwin had set out for him. A group of masked men charged with ambushing him? He would make quick work of the humans. An injured man that Godwin would claim Filip had beaten down off training grounds? Athellore wouldn't care. The agreement between them meant too much to Lore. What could Godwin possibly do to Filip to truly hinder or hurt him? Nothing that Filip could think of, and honestly, he was curious to see what the rat-faced boar would attempt.

CHAPTER 20

In her chamber washroom, Aury pointed her staff at her water basin and whispered, "Grow and spill over. Grow and spill over. Multiply. Multiply."

Her head pounded, and her jaw ached from hours of gritting her teeth. The water did nothing. She tossed her staff into the corner and splashed a hand across the silvery surface of her reflection. When Mage Finn had doubled the water in the trough this morning, her heart had stilled. Her world had shifted. The mage had filled the entire room with ankle-deep water before demanding it recede back to the confines of the trough.

Seeing his magic from so close, hearing the power behind his words and knowing she was capable of such a feat—it had weakened her knees more than any man. Filip's steely gaze cut into her memory, and she nearly snarled. Well, more than almost any man.

She washed the day's grime from her face.

"Towel?" Eawynn held the cloth out with a tentative hand.

Aury ripped the towel out of the fae's hand. "I'm fine."

"I didn't ask." Eawynn frowned and turned to go back to Gytha and Hilda, who stood by the fire.

Aury took up her staff again and sighed. "Fae."

Gytha stretched and yawned, her war tattoos like thorny branches piercing her arms. "Are you steamy because of your failed magic attempts or because you long to have someone other than us fae ladies in your chamber?"

Aury's jaw cracked, and she set a glare on Gytha. "Mind your own business."

Gytha crossed her arms. "You are our business."

The bed was soft, and Aury was done with this day of nightmares. "Go away. Grab that handsome guard Mildred set at my door and find some new business."

Gytha barked a laugh, but Hilda tsked. "You need that warrior at your door. The moon is dusky tonight. There is ill will here."

Great Nix in the morning. Would she never be free of fae superstition? "Isn't the same moon shining over the entire kingdom? Why would the ill will be right here?"

"Believe what you want, Princess, but you mark my words." Hilda gathered up a shift she'd been embroidering and ushered Gytha and Eawynn toward the door. "This night brings trouble."

"I can feel it in my bones." Eawynn shivered and hugged herself as they disappeared from the chamber into their own room beyond.

Aury tucked her staff into a nook between her bed and her nightstand, blew out the candle, then crawled under the covers. While the fire cast sunsets over her walls and bed hangings, she pictured Filip and what he might be doing right now. Aside from wondering if she was the failure everyone was surely saying she was from here all the way to his kingdom in Balaur.

Great mage, *ha*. She hadn't even managed to beat sweet-faced Sunniva in their training today. At least Sunniva had been able to make water bubble and to frost the surface of a basin. Aury hadn't even managed a single wobble of the waters, not a shiver of a drop. Nothing.

She was an absolute failure, and everyone in this castle knew it.

Including Filip. He had to. He'd probably think she was easy pickings now that she'd shown such a lack in magical ability. He'd be in her face at breakfast most likely, telling her about how their wedding day would go.

She rolled viciously to her side, untucking the coverlet and shoving her feet free from the blankets.

Tomorrow would be better. It had to be.

Her dreams threw her into Loreton Palace, where the walls slowly crept closer and closer. The grinding sound of their movement tore at her nerves. She sat on a throne of melting ice, listening to supplicants, tenant farmers, and merchants, but when she tried to answer, her mouth wouldn't open. Her subjects kept asking her questions and going on and on about how great her elven warrior mage husband was, and she couldn't tell them he wasn't even a mage and that she had answers. Her lips refused to crack open no matter how hard she tried to force her jaw to work. She shrank in size until she was a tiny, black dot in a giant puddle that had once been the throne of ice. Voices spoke above her, one deep and mellow—Filip's. He was searching for her, but she remained lost forever. Unseen. Unremarkable. Useless.

EAWYNN WOKE AURY, AND THE DAY BEGAN IN A WHIRL of rushing up and down stone steps, shoving food into her face, and dealing with gut-wrenching hope that she could rectify yesterday's mistakes and really shine.

First up was Flooding.

Mage Finn had moved all the water troughs to the back of the room. He stood at the front beside a new crockery bowl the size of that dragon Filip had found. "Who would like to try to move all the water from those troughs into this bowl? You must fill it exactly to the rim. If you do, you earn a free day. If you fail, you earn mopping duties in the great hall. Duties that will begin right after the Staff and Steel Feast tonight."

Aury leaned over to Sunniva. "The what and what?"

"I'm sure you've noticed the non-mage army eats at different times, yes? Well, once a fortnight we dine together to forge a better bond between the two groups. It's called the Staff and Steel Feast."

"Ah. As long as I get to eat, I'm all for it."

No one had yet volunteered to attempt to move the water.

Aury took a step forward. "I'll probably make a fool of myself yet again, but at least you'll have some entertainment."

She gritted her teeth as her fellow trainees laughed nervously. She wanted to tell them to go ahead and have a nice guffaw on her behalf and to stop holding back because she was the princess, but what did she know? The king or queen might very well hear about it and relieve them of their laughing heads for insulting her. She'd certainly caught more than a few gossiping about how horrible it would be to have to suffer a marriage to a bloodthirsty, uncivilized elf, their talk going quiet as she passed by.

Now, with her staff pointed at the troughs, Aury willed the water to crawl out of its containers and slither over the floor toward Mage Finn.

Absolutely nothing happened.

Finn gave her a gruff, "Good try," and she stormed back to the group. Wishing with everything that she was a witch and not a broken water mage, she tried to disappear, slipping into the room's dark shadows and pulling up her cloak's hood. Disappearing would have been delightful. Or igniting into flames and taking the entire castle with her. Either one. She wasn't picky.

Training couldn't be over soon enough, and by the end, her temper had risen to a fever-pitch, her blood absolutely boiling. She strode out of the room with Sunniva's encouragement trailing her like gnats.

Perhaps the next class would be better. It had to be. This couldn't be a repeat of her first day. No. She refused that outcome. Not happening.

The Ice Room on the second floor had wall-to-wall windows that let the late morning light slide over the drains set into the floor. Aury heard that pipes there brought spilled water all the way back to the Silver River. A fountain gurgled in the center of the chamber. A very talented witch had magicked the fountain, or so Sunniva said.

Though the room was the coldest in the castle, Aury threw her cloak onto a hook by the door. Frustration and embarrassment gave her all the heat she could stand.

Mildred rushed in and stood in front of the group, staff already raised for a demonstration. Everyone went quiet, well aware of Mildred's reputation for being as coldly dangerous as the subject she taught.

"Center your mind." Mildred shut her eyes, her mouth pinched.

Aury was wedged between Sunniva and some arrogant fool named Cuthbert who had a truly obnoxious habit of roaming the grounds giving everyone nicknames they didn't ask for. Sunniva's two-toned gaze kept drifting to the door.

"Are you waiting for someone?" Aury asked.

Sunniva shrugged. "I was hoping that northern lord would end up on our schedule. They switched some of the units' training timetables."

"What northern lord? Why?"

"I met him at the Harvest Ball. He was so quiet, but when I finally talked to him, he had so much interesting information about dragons, like how many pounds of meat they need to live and how far they can fly…"

"I saw one."

Sunniva's jaw dropped. "What? Where?"

Mildred cleared her throat. Aury straightened and held her staff upright.

"If we're finished gossiping," Mildred said, "then I'd like to get on with training."

"Sorry, Mage Mildred," Sunniva said.

Mildred nodded and pointed at the fountain with her staff. "I am imagining the smallest units of water to come together, to solidify, to join. I work the words around my mind, infusing them with what I know will happen. Magic works on the power in your blood and your will. If you truly believe water will do as you demand, and if you have the power in your veins, the water will obey you."

A quiet crackling broke the silence as a sheen of frost danced across the fountain's bowl. The bubbling cascade went still, like a man shot through the heart. The water froze solid.

Mildred's shoulders fell as she exhaled and lowered her staff. The circles that every old woman had under their eyes grew a shade darker on her pale skin.

"You may come forward," Mildred said, "and check the surface yourself. It is ice. It is now ready to become your weapon. But know this, even with great amounts of sea folk blood in your veins, the power of that lost race, magic drains a mage in a manner similar to running a long race. You can only do what you can do. Keep healthy. Get your sleep. You'll have the ability to accomplish far more if you have a strong body as well as a strong mind."

Mildred set a piercing gaze on Aury, who hated the agitation currently rising in her chest. She refused to fail again.

"Mage Aurora, please attempt to crack the ice. That is the first step in creating a weapon to use against Lore's enemies."

Aury swallowed and stood as the other trainees halted

their study of the new ice and moved away. With a deep breath, she raised her staff.

Break, she thought. Water particles, snap, and break from one another. She imagined the shards of ice that had flown through the Forest of Illumahrah, right outside the Agate Palace.

A pop sounded in the fountain.

CHAPTER 21

S till attempting to break the frozen surface into shards, Aury shook. The memory of that battle rose bright and burning in her mind. Shards of ice tore across the battlefield to chase the Wylfen warriors and their wolves. Werian shouted for help. He'd be killed. He couldn't fight this many. He'd be one of the corpses by the time help arrived. No, that wasn't the order in which things had occurred. Aury's head pounded, and suddenly there was an arm gripping her, shaking her.

Mildred stared into her face. "Mage Aurora. Are you unwell?"

The fountain behind her was in pieces, and water covered the floor as everyone spoke at once.

Sunniva took Aury's other arm gently. "Aury?"

She shook the memory away. "I'm fine. Sorry. I am fine."

The hands and the questions jabbed, and her heart raced, her mind still hazy from the bloody memory, the fear, and the new betrayal that painted the whole scene in oppressive grays.

Pushing away from Mildred and Sunniva and what felt like one thousand fingers, she muttered, "Please." They didn't really care. They were trying to get something from her, like the fae had done her entire life.

She broke free and ran.

Down stairs. Around a winding corridor. Past a dark set of doors. And then she was at a set of windows in a tall corridor of stone. She looked out, breathing heavily, sweating.

"I've lost my mind," she muttered. "Gaping out the window and trying to forget the past like I'm eighty instead of nineteen."

But her mind needed a moment of something outside the castle and her failures with magic.

Simple warriors simply fighting was a reprieve of sorts.

And then Filip moved into view, swinging a practice sword.

Though snow mixed with the muddy ground, he had removed his shirt. Perhaps his elven blood kept him warm, that and the fighting. His arms and legs moved like a dancer's—graceful, lithe. The muscles and tendons along his back, all the way to his narrow waist, tugged and rolled. His wide shoulders bunched as he drove an overhead strike down onto a training opponent, the blow hitting bluntly, not full strength. Even at this speed, with this fierce and deadly ability, Filip was careful with his sparring partners. He swung again, and his partner fell back. He tilted his head back in a laugh, and she squinted to see him better. She was maybe one floor up, so she saw

him clearly. Joy glittered in his eyes as he helped his
partner up.

Was it joy at the idea of war? If someone had asked her
a few days ago, she would've said yes. But at this moment,
it seemed his joy bloomed with interaction with his fellow
warriors, with the camaraderie.

He looked up, as if searching for something with those
lightning eyes.

Then his gaze met hers.

A jolt went through her. She gasped, and power rushed
across her chest and down her arms. The snow at Filip's
feet and piled beside him rose into the air, then spun a
cocoon around him. She watched in horror as his eyes
widened inside the small storm.

Pressing her staff against the window, she tried to will
the snow to settle, but it spun faster and faster.

Then, just as suddenly as the snow had leapt to life, it
quieted, sparkling, unassuming at Filip's feet. His half-
lidded gaze found her in the window again. He winked.

A flush of heat sped through her body and into her
cheeks, and she glared, not totally certain why she was
angry, but angry all the same. She spun and strode back the
way she'd come. How dare he wink at her? Everyone on the
training grounds had seen him do it. They'd be whispering
about the royal couple. It was her private business whom
she loved and whom she hated. And she'd be dead before
she accepted Filip like an obedient girl doing as she was
told, loving as she was pressured to do by the people.

"Never," she hissed. He wouldn't control her. Neither
would her parents. No matter how fantastic Filip looked
without a shirt or how kind he was to sparring partners.

How quick and caring he'd been with the injured dragon. She'd tried to believe he was a monster, but he was proving to be a good person.

When she returned to the Ice room, the place was nearly empty, the session obviously over.

"Mage Mildred." She walked slowly toward the woman. Mildred stood by the windows in a way reminiscent of Aury's recent post. "I apologize for leaving so abruptly."

"You cracked the ice."

"And the fountain. Oh, and I melted the ice too."

Mildred turned for a moment, and there was that brief smile she'd had on Aury's first day. "You did." She took one more long look out the window, then faced Aury fully. "Your magic is wild, Mage Aurora. It isn't a lack of power that inhibits you. It is what you have suffered in the past that makes your water work so unpredictably. You must deal with the hurt, or your magic will rule you instead of the other way around."

"But I didn't fight in the war. I didn't lose anyone. What have I suffered?"

"One cannot compare hurts. Injuries of the heart refuse measurement. It is enough that you suffered in your own true way. You must come to terms with the fear you experienced and the one who hurt you."

How could she know so much from one class and one destroyed fountain? The image of Filip's face in the water basin blinked through Aury's mind. "You scried my past." The knowledge pinched. It wasn't betrayal, but Mildred certainly hadn't asked permission to delve into Aury's life.

"I am the one who owes an apology," Mildred said. "You are correct. I can scry as well as you."

"I only did it once. By accident."

"And so it will happen again. And again. Throughout your life. It is a curse, more than anything." Mildred's hands shifted on her staff. "I didn't scry Prince Werian of the Agate Court on purpose. I had no wish to see the day you watched the fae nearly die. The scenes came to me without any choice on my part." She blinked and raised her pointed chin. "It's good I know, Mage. I can now push you to seek closure. Do you have writing materials?"

"I do. I sent a letter already."

"You did? May I ask to whom?"

"The Matchweaver."

Mildred nearly dropped her staff. "Against the king's orders?"

"I never heard any orders about letters. She needs to know I don't plan to marry Prince Filip. That I respect her role in Lore and I don't seek to fight her loom and whom she sees as my future mate. Of course, I also don't plan to wed anyone, but she doesn't need to know that."

Why was she telling Mildred this? Maybe because Mildred would have every reason to keep all of this to herself. If Aury's actions, done under Mildred's care at Darkfleot, would anger the king, then the woman had every reason to stay quiet on the topics at hand.

Mildred was staring out the windows again, visibly trembling. "What have you done, child?"

"I'm no child, and this is my life. No one else's. I will deal with the repercussions as they arise. I'm quite tired of being kept in the dark about the Matchweaver's role in my life. I'd rather face her head-on and find out what the threat may or may not be instead of blindly going along with my father's plans, plans that most likely will anger her once again."

Mildred faced Aury and raised an eyebrow. "I can see the wisdom, though it is wildly dangerous. I suppose one of your fae ladies delivered the letter."

Gytha was on the road at this very moment. "I'd rather keep the details to myself, with all respect, Mage Mildred."

"A queen already," she muttered, brushing past Aury. Mildred stopped though and set a hand on Aury's shoulder. "I am sorry for the pain you suffered at the fae's hands. Please know your parents didn't know of the Fae Queen turning a blind eye to your treatment. I don't know how, but I will see she is punished for that."

"I'd rather you didn't fight my battles for me, but thank you."

Mildred huffed. "Hasn't anyone told you that you now have a full army at hand? One of warriors and mages?" She grinned, and the young lady she had once been peered through the wrinkles. "Your battles are our battles now, Princess Aurora." Mildred took Aury's hand and kissed her sigil ring.

The woman was gone before Aury could think of what to say. Was Mildred being kind, offering to stand up against the Fae Queen, because she'd been ordered to support Aury as princess? Or was it something else? From where did her loyalty spring?

"Aury!" Sunniva ran into the Ice room. "Eat this." She shoved a small round of bread into Aury's hands. "You missed luncheon. It's time for striking, and you have to do better today than yesterday or they'll be asking the king and queen for a new princess."

Aury's mouth fell open.

Sunniva laughed and smacked her arm. "Just teasing. Come on though! We'll be late."

An argument touched Aury's tongue, but she swallowed it down. Sunniva didn't need to know about Aury's dilemmas. It'd be best to focus on training. Tonight, she could think on everything. And pray that Gytha was on her way back with a message from the witch who had cursed Aury and started this entire mess of a life.

CHAPTER 22

F ilip felt ten feet tall. Aury could argue all she liked, but she reacted to him. Sure, it could've been because she loathed his very presence, but was he really someone she hated that much? She had said the forced marriage wasn't his doing, so she didn't blame him for their situation. If she didn't hate him, then she felt something else as strong as hate. Lust, maybe? He hoped for more, but that was a grand start.

Once the training was through for the day and the men were off to wash and prep for the Staff and Steel feast, he started toward the outer gates of Darkfleot. They wouldn't be a problem. Godwin had sent out a search party for the missing warrior, Elis, but, of course, they hadn't found him. Filip snorted. This was definitely a ruse.

A hand stopped him. "Where are you going without us?" Sweat ran down Costel's flushed face, and the cold had turned the end of his nose red.

"Godwin has some sort of mischief set up for me. Or

there might actually be a young warrior who went missing where I found that dragon. Either way, I'd rather take a walk into a possible ambush than deal with the man's mouth for another hour of the dial."

"I did hear that the spearman with the long hair was missing."

"Elis of Damerham. Perhaps Godwin is telling the truth, then."

"How do you already know everyone's names?"

"I pay attention. These are to be my men after I'm married. My men and Aurora's. I need to know them well."

Bowing his head with respect, Costel said, "I listen when they're introduced, but I can't hold their birthplaces in my head. These Lore towns are difficult to remember."

"Ah, for once, your large brain is challenged!"

Costel smiled. "Indeed. A new experience."

Filip bumped him with an elbow. "Show off. Now, go on and get ready for the feast. I'll be fine on my own."

"We are coming with you." Costel turned and waved a hand at Drago and Stefan, who were handing off their horses.

"No, stay here."

"Sorry, my prince, but you're being a fool."

Filip chuckled. "All right. It'll be an adventure. Who knows? We might glimpse the dragon youngling."

Drago and Stefan loped over, joining Filip and Costel as they were waved on by the castle guards. Their boots knocked along the drawbridge, and the river flowing below was black and deep.

"Why do they call this the Silver River?" Filip asked.

Costel picked a rock from the bottom of his boot, then

lobbed it into the water. "It was named in the old scrolls. Back when dragons flying high above named most of the geographical features. It would appear silver when the sun glinted off the surface."

Drago shook his head. "You know everything written in scrolls, don't you?"

"Maybe if we wrote down every Lore name and town on a scroll and had a witch coat it in dust and dragon feces, you'd have better luck learning them all," Filip said, unable to keep from teasing Costel.

Costel dodged a lazy punch from Stefan as the wind blew hard. Dried leaves and tiny bits of ice lashed across their path toward the hill beyond the king's road.

Stefan pulled up the hood of the short chaperon he wore over his padded doublet. "Nice evening you chose to go for a walk, my friend."

"Godwin chose this, so that fits, eh?" Filip said, watching the sky.

Drago stopped and held up his hands. "He's the reason we're out here in weather that's worse than what we deal with in the mountains?"

Filip frowned. "I figured Costel told you earlier."

"No. No time. Sorry," Costel said. "You were leaving, and you needed your men."

"Godwin told me a man was missing," Filip said, "a man who went to see the brambles where I saw the dragon. He said it was my responsibility to find the man. I don't disagree if that's the truth, but this is Godwin we're talking about. We might be walking into an ambush. You should all know that. Or we're going to be blamed for whatever happened to Elis of Damerham."

The men unsheathed their weapons as Filip whistled casually and strode into the grove.

"Lost Lore warrior? Are you here? I do hope my dragon adventure didn't cause you to lose your head. You won't find a clutch of younglings here to harvest, you sick thing," he muttered. "And if you did, I'd off you before you could so much as touch a scale."

The ground fell away, and Filip's world went dark.

He woke to a voice saying his name, the sound weak and broken.

"Filip. Are you alive? I am. I think. Not sure."

"He'd better be alive so I can beat him senseless for this."

It was Costel and Drago. Their voices were muffled, but close, as if they were in a small room. The scent of freshly turned dirt filled Filip's nose. He tried to speak, but his tongue stuck to the roof of his mouth.

"This is all Godwin's doing," Stefan said. "I'll see him dead. I swear it." A cough and a hiss of pain stole the last word.

Filip wanted to shout out in agreement about Godwin, but his mouth still wasn't functioning. His legs didn't want to work either. He tried to look for his friends' faces, but all he could see was a strip of stars and the pattern of a pine branch.

"Filip, please say something. They set a fall trap for us, but we'll get you out as soon as we untangle ourselves." Costel's voice was reedy and drawn down with fear and worry. "My prince. Please." No teasing ran through the title this time, only devotion, kinship.

Drago growled and swore, and the shuffling sounds of someone slowly moving carried through the darkness. "My leg is ruined."

The numbness in Filip's body fled and opened the door to pain. He gasped with the power of it, then the stars blinked out.

CHAPTER 23

After training in striking on the grounds—all the while receiving a full list of how many steps it would take to climb Jade Mount if one were Mage Finn's height versus Sunniva's, courtesy of the woman's continued obsession with numbers—Aury hurried back to her chamber for a bath.

"How did you do?" Hilda asked as she took Aury's snow-wet tunic and muddied trousers.

"Fine." She didn't want to talk about how good she was at turning the more sensitive parts of her body away from a hit. The fae at the Agate Palace had accidentally taught her that skill. "I am better at striking back than I thought I would be."

"Did Prince Werian teach you how to use a staff in fighting?"

"No. But I had some anger built up, and rage does pretty well in making up for skill."

Hilda flinched slightly. "Of course. Again, I'm sorry for

what you suffered." An inner flame lit her eyes, and Aury was reminded of the Fae Queen. "I will see you avenged on that count."

She'd believe it when she saw it.

Eawynn hurried into the small chamber off the bedroom and stoked the charcoal in the burner before adding more water. Pipes ran under the tub, and the steam heated the water where Aury washed. It was a marvel of a design.

"When do you think Gytha will return?" Aury scrubbed at a smear of dirt on her forearm while Eawynn poured water over her hair.

Hilda uncorked a glass vial with a pop, then drizzled Aury's hair with a rose-scented elixir. "Tonight, I'd guess."

It was completely strange to have these women bathing her, but Aury was too tired to argue about it. Every muscle in her body was tight from striking and blocking and dodging. And from climbing all the gods-forsaken stairs in this place.

"Can I have a minute?" she asked, wanting some quiet time to think.

Hilda and Eawynn left as the bubbles from the elixir gathered across the top of the bathwater. Sunlight from the windows touched the little domes of pink and green. It was oddly mesmerizing.

The three bubbles nearest her hand popped and created a circle of flat, clear water.

An image took shape. A room in another castle and a loom strung with rainbow-dyed wool. An old woman with ivy-green hair and wrinkled fingers on the shuttle.

Lightheaded, Aury stared.

She was scrying, and this was the Matchweaver.

The walls of the castle were wispy and chilling. Aury knew long ago mages had instilled the castle with powers to protect the Matchweaver from wolves, bears, and any attacks on her life. The goddess witch passed the shuttle through the yarn, a strand of bright pink catching the light from a cracked door. She was working the Mageloom, the loom that showed her strong matches between lovers.

The Matchweaver stopped, turned. "Who is there? I feel your eyes on me, water mage."

Aury sucked a breath but held still, curiosity keeping her gaze steady on the vision.

Setting down her shuttle, the witch stood. She walked the length of what appeared to be a great hall. The Mageloom was far larger than Aury would've guessed. It took up most of the massive room.

The Witch picked up a piece of parchment and held it above her head. "It's you, isn't it, Princess Aurora?"

Aury's heart hammered against her teeth. She had to keep still and learn what she could. This was what she had wanted, after all, to face the witch and deal with what her parents had done to insult the Matchweaver.

"It is," Aury whispered. Would she hear her? She had no idea how this worked. She should've asked Mildred. "And I can see you quite clearly. That is my letter, yes?"

"Oh, you're a pompous one, aren't you? Just like Athellore and Gwinnith."

"I'm nothing like them. Did they take time to inform you of their choices? No. But you hold in your hand the evidence that I do care for your position in the kingdom."

The witch snorted and threw the parchment to the

ground. She whipped out a wand and pointed it at the letter. Bright flames devoured the ivory square.

Aury gritted her teeth. She longed to leap into the vision and take the witch on.

"It doesn't matter what you say, little princess," the witch hissed. "Athellore and Gwinnith should have kept you hidden. Such fools." She stared toward the ceiling, past the hand-hewn beams of the old castle, and she seemed to be gazing directly into Aury's eyes. "I will see your curse come to fruition. I swore it would be so, and so it shall be. You, fair princess, and your elven prince, will sleep by my will forever."

In a haze, Aury dressed for rune training. The vision had blinked out like the witch was in control, and she didn't recall climbing out of the tub. The rage in the witch goddess' eyes had felt like a blow to the head.

"I can't believe you scried her." Hilda sounded pleased and angry all at once as she squeezed water from Aury's hair with a bath sheet. "She had to have been incredibly surprised. No one scries the Matchweaver."

Eawynn chewed her lip. "I don't like this. You didn't see Gytha?"

"No. I don't...I don't think so. Only the witch, the Mageloom, and the great hall in the enchanted castle. But she had my letter, so Gytha succeeded. Why did we let her go alone? Stupid."

"She'll make it back." Hilda didn't sound like she believed herself.

. . .

ON THE HIGHEST FLOOR OF THE CASTLE, AURY RAN A finger over the runes on her staff, wishing she could read them. She'd already noticed the slanted lines and angled slashes varied from staff to staff.

Mage Edgar's creepy voice slid into the peaked ceiling before falling on her ears. "Mage Aurora." He was tall but very slight. He looked like one of the hollow-bellied cats at the fae court who had taken up the bad habit of eating faeberries. "Show us your runes."

She held it aloft.

"You can see," Edgar said, "she has laguz for water as you all do. That's this one that looks like a hook. The vast majority of you also have this rune—the kenaz, the beacon for awakening, creativity. She also has the algiz elk for protection. Who here has that one as well?"

All but one woman in the back murmured that they did have that rune on their staves.

"But Mage Aurora has two rare runes. Uruz, the auroch for brute strength, and Isa, or ice, for blocks, stasis, and the potential for great talent with freezing and weaponizing ice. This mage will be a fearsome warrior if she can harness her power. Mage Sunniva, your staff."

He faced Sunniva, who handed hers over.

"Where Mage Aurora has strength and ice, Mage Sunniva has been given ehwaz, the horse and the symbol of stability. A key element in war. One must have consistency and reliability in battle."

"Why wouldn't the Order Masters give all of us every rune so we'd all be strong and stable?" Aury asked.

The group chuckled like she'd told a joke, then Edgar

frowned. "You do know where the Order receives the staves for water mages, right?"

"I don't."

He thrust Sunniva's staff back into her hands. "Fools," he muttered. Was he talking about Aury or her parents or the fae who raised her? Any way he meant it, he wasn't wrong.

"The Masters receive the staves for water mages at the Sacred Oak in Illumahrah. Once a year they travel there to wait beyond the oak's shadow. Staves drop from the tree, already carved and set with a piece of coral. The oak knows the hearts and minds of all mages."

"What?" Aury blinked. How in Nix's name...

"It's a miracle, to be sure. The old stories say a sea folk seer joined with the Sacred Oak and together, their spirits bestow magic on our world. The oak also gives witches their wands, although wands tend to show up when a witch first needs them no matter where they are at that moment. The Sacred Oak knows what staff you were born to possess. We have inborn traits which can be shaped, honed. The way we work together is a large component of being a mage. Without our differences, we wouldn't explore new strategies. Challenges encourage growth. I believe if we were each born to have every rune, we'd have been conquered long ago. It is in our coming together to deal with challenges that we find victory."

Interesting perspective. If he was right, Aury needed Sunniva as much as she needed Aury and so forth. "How do you know which staff goes with which mage?"

"It's an acquired skill. Mage Mildred is quite good at it."

Sunniva nodded. "She told me once that a staff will warm up as its mage approaches. There is a certain energy to the air when they are first united. Mage Mildred said she sees the staves and their mages in the water more often than not."

"This should've been part of my introductory tour," Aury snapped. There was so much she had to learn. In fact, she was aware of so little that she didn't even know what to ask.

Edgar continued the training, discussing how mages without an ice rune, for instance, could still become proficient with freezing. "When a mage has an ice rune, it simply means they will be far more skilled, more deadly."

Aury turned her staff over in her fingers, the wood warm and buzzing lightly. She could almost smell the sun-warmed meadow where the Sacred Oak stood and the seawater in which the coral piece had once lived. She was tied to the land, to Lore, to old magic. The blood of sea folk ran through her veins. Despite her cluelessness on all things mage, she did indeed belong here with these men and women. She looked around at them, at her fellow mages, and a true smile stretched her lips. This was home.

CHAPTER 24

Filip remained in the darkness, his body numb. His mind floating. Where was he? What had happened?

A voice whispered in his mind. The voice was unfamiliar and sounded as old as the hills.

"Go, Filip," the voice cooed. "Embrace the sleep of those who are finished. You don't want to face the light again. The dark is so easy. So soft and lovely. Sleep. Rest forever, sweet prince." A foul note of sick joy echoed through the last phrase.

This voice didn't like him for some reason. But why? He didn't know this voice.

"Rest. Rest. Rest."

But the voice was right. The darkness was lovely. He let go of his musings and plummeted into its arms once more.

CHAPTER 25

T he conversation and the clinking of horn and
pewter mugs that filled the great hall at
Darkfleot stopped as Aury walked up the center
of the room.

Filip wasn't here yet, it seemed. What would he say
about her little snowstorm incident? Her cheeks blazed.
She begged goddess Nix to grant her the sharpest
explanation, a story that wouldn't expose her complete lack
of control when it came to the elf. Why did he affect her
magic like that?

She swallowed, feeling too warm in her laced sleeves
and billowing skirts. She longed for the simple Darkfleot
tunic, but alas, Hilda and Eawynn had insisted she dress as
a princess tonight. They'd gone so far as to place a golden
circlet in her elaborately plaited hair. Everyone had worn
their best, so it seemed the fae had been right to guide
Aury this way. But still, her skin itched under the silken

underdress and warmed uncomfortably beneath the layers of blue velvet.

Gytha hadn't returned yet from her mission to deliver Aury's letter to the Matchweaver. Aury wished now that she hadn't allowed Gytha to travel alone. The fae had vowed she'd done far more dangerous things during the wars, so Aury had relented, but now...Aury should've insisted Gytha bring a unit of soldiers. Would the Matchweaver find a way to take revenge on Gytha for being one of the fae who had twisted the curse on Aury? There had been no spinning wheel, so it hadn't mattered in the end, but surely the witch would be angry for the attempt at thwarting her magic. Hopefully, Gytha had glamoured herself fully and placed the message into the hands of one of the Matchweaver's castle workers before the witch had known anything was afoot. Hopefully.

In front of the dais where King Athellore and Queen Gwinnith sat with Mildred, Finn, Godwin, and the other Darkfleot instructors, Aury curtseyed to her parents.

"It's lovely to see you, Daughter." Gwinnith's approving gaze tore at Aury's fake smile. Aury longed to turn around and raise her bum at her cold mother just to see if she'd react like a real person.

"And you as well, Queen Gwinnith." Over her dead and rotting corpse would she call the woman Mother in front of all these people. They should know the truth—that Aury had been ignored by these two entirely, beaten in dark corridors by fae, and treated like an unwanted stepchild at the Agate Palace for her entire life. And it was their fault.

Gwinnith's hands fisted on the tabletop, but that was

the only frustration she showed at Aury's more formal address. It was a small victory, and Aury felt her lips quirk into a grin.

"I've heard you made great progress in your mage training," Athellore said, sounding like any proud father.

"Not really, King Athellore. I'm a bit of a disaster." The room seemed to implode, but Aury ignored it and continued on her merry way to committing a crime that would be punishable by death to any other Lore inhabitant. "You're wrong." A rush of reckless, vicious joy spread through her. "It's quite possible I'll either be snuffed out in my attempts to raise water magic, or I'll flood the entire castle. But thank you for your sudden interest in my life." She dipped a curtsey so low that she nearly keeled over. Then she spun and found a seat beside Sunniva.

The room remained silent, everyone's eyes wide, their mouths agape. Aury wished Filip had been here to see this, to realize how far Aury would go to show that no one would bend her to their will.

Gwinnith let out a shrill laugh and clapped her hands. "What a wit we have, my darling king! She takes after your side of the family!"

Athellore's face had gone a raging red, but his chest rose in a controlled breath. He smiled. "Indeed! Our Aurora never stops surprising us with her jests. Now, enjoy the feasting, everyone!"

The lutes and drums started up, and the sounds of drinking and gossiping swallowed the dangerous feeling in the air.

Aury inhaled deeply, and the tang of lemons mixed with rosemary. "Yum. What kind of chicken dish is that?" she asked Sunniva as servants brought steaming trays to each long table. She placed her staff in one of the open double hooks on the wall.

Sunniva just stared.

"Hello?" Aury waved a hand in front of her face. "Are you unwell?"

Sunniva sputtered and gripped Aury's hand. "I can't believe they didn't order your punishment on the spot," she whispered between piles of chicken and bowls of roasted potatoes.

Aury's anger shot through her blood. "I would love to see them try." She jammed her eating knife into a chicken thigh and threw it onto her trencher.

Holding a hand to her chest, Sunniva shook her head. "Goddess Amona, give me wisdom." She tugged an Amona necklace from under her tunic and kissed the lapis lazuli stone in the center of the dragon eye pendant.

"What kind of chicken is this?" Aury asked around a mouthful.

"In my province, we call it Southers Fowl. Only the southern province can get lemons regularly enough to have this dish as a traditional part of their winter feasting."

"And royalty," Aury said wryly as she glanced at the dais to see Athellore and Gwinnith. They were talking to Godwin, who laughed loudly, a piece of chicken on his chin.

Aury glanced at the double doors. Filip was still nowhere to be seen. His men weren't here either. Not that she cared.

"Darkfleot enjoys some nice perks while training you." Sunniva raised her chicken leg like a salute then tucked in.

The meal went on with music, a cold vegetable soup course that reached new heights in disgusting, and even a round of dancing that the king and queen led between the dais and the first of the feasting tables. Still, no Filip. Where was he?

But then the great hall doors swung open to show a guest she hadn't been expecting at all.

A servant called out, "We welcome Prince Werian of the Agate Court!"

The hall broke into applause and whispers as Werian threw her a tentative smile and walked up to Athellore and Gwinnith to pay his respects. His horns, such a normal thing at the Fae Court, were incredibly out of place here. Many of the mages shrank back from him as he passed, their eyes wide at his strange dress and stranger hair color.

"I can't believe he's here."

"I guess you saw him during your time at the Fae Court?" Sunniva asked.

"I thought he was my cousin. We grew up together. I love him like a cousin. Well, I did before I learned he'd been lying to me my entire life."

Werian left the dais and approached. "Greetings, Cousin!" He held out his arms like she might embrace him.

She kept her seat. "Hello."

Nodding like he had halfway expected this, he begged a spot between Osberth and Cuthbert on the opposite side of the table from Aury and Sunniva. The men gawked at his horns, their forks paused halfway to their mouths.

"How is the training coming along?" Werian accepted a goblet of wine from a servant.

"It's been great aside from the complete failure."

"It's not that bad," Sunniva said, her gaze darting nervously between Aury and Werian.

Aury finished her wine and leaned forward on her elbows. "Now, do tell. Why are you here?"

"Firstly, this." He opened his hand to show her dragon goddess necklace with its fiery-hued pearls, the very necklace that Bathilda had ordered ripped from Aury's neck. "I found the parts scattered around the floor of the court and had it repaired."

She took it from him, her heart melting a little as she put it on. Goddess Nix had always been her favorite and still was despite the fact that she should have preferred goddess Lilia.

"Also," Werian said, "I discovered something of interest in a scroll detailing the water mages of old."

"I'm currently in a castle with hundreds of them. I am one of them. Why would I need a history lesson on what's happening around my very ears? My very round ears?" She flicked her fingers at her ear but meant the rude gesture for Werian. It wouldn't do to flick him off in front of the entire hall, not with the royal parents here.

His eyebrows lifted. He had received the message. "You loathe me. I understand. I loathe myself at times. But I think you'll want to hear about what I've learned."

The surrounding mages had scooted well away from Werian, Aury, and Sunniva, so Aury waved him on. "Give it to us then, Prince of the Agate Court, Liar of all Liars, Deceiver with the Divine Visage."

"Although I appreciate you recognizing my fine looks, I could do without the venom. Remember, I was ordered to keep your identity a secret, Aury," he said, eyes softening.

He leaned forward so that his face was near hers. "I am so sorry. But I did believe it was for your safety. I couldn't risk telling you and being the one who might have caused your death. I love you, Cousin." She started to argue that they weren't related at all, but he held up a hand. "In my heart and soul, you will always be my cousin. I don't care what blood says."

He reached for her hand, hope light in his dark eyes. Her heart shook, afraid, but she took his fingers in hers. "I love you too, Cousin."

Exhaling and relaxing his shoulders, he smiled widely, making Sunniva sigh in appreciation. He really was a fine-looking fae.

Aury poked Sunniva in the side. "I thought you didn't feel such things."

"I still enjoy a lovely view." She grinned and went back to her trencher of chicken.

"The scroll spoke of a ranking that hasn't been seen in the Lore army for at least a century. Magelord. If you get top marks in the Mage Trials, earn a top ranking as a captain, then you are in the running."

"What does that mean?"

"If you become Magelord, you earn your own piece of land, which of course you don't need as the princess, but—"

"Get to the point, Werian. Please."

"As a Magelord, you have the choice to live exactly as you please," he whispered below the sound of the lutes starting up and the bubbling conversation in the hall. "Magelords can marry whomever they choose. Or not marry. Or divorce their current partner. They are not bound to their family's demands or the king's."

Aury gripped her eating knife. "That's exactly what I'll do, then. Somehow." She refused to give in to the feeling of defeat the two days of training thus far pressed on her shoulders.

"But," Werian said, holding up a finger, "you must prove yourself in battle. Another captain must acknowledge your battle prowess, make a sacrifice of his or her own on your behalf, and then you will be declared a Magelord."

Aury sank into the bench. "I don't even know if they'll let me fight in the upcoming battle at Dragon Wing. I'll be shoved into my parents' version of my life long before I can possibly perform some amazing feat against the Wylfen."

Werian's mouth tucked to one side, and he reached across the table to pat her shoulder. "Don't give up. Not yet. You've proven that you can break the odds. No one else has survived a direct attack from the Matchweaver."

"I just have to work harder. Get my magic working. And demand that my father allow me to fight in the upcoming battle."

"That's the spirit!" Werian looked past Aury, so she turned.

A kitchen worker with hair escaping from a white bonnet rushed to her side.

"Princess." The worker curtseyed, her eyes flicking to Werian. "I'm the Darkfleot pastry chef."

"Nice to meet you," Aury said, giving a smile and now smelling the familiar zing of scorchpeppers in the chocolate.

"Prince Filip supplied scorchpepper leaves, which we

tried to muddle and include in a chocolate custard, but the custard curdled under the spicy oil, so he suggested melted chocolate for the oil and that we dip the flatbread triangles into the chocolate to form a sort of dragon wing." She indicated the nearest tray of the dessert. "I present to you Mage Aurora's Dragon Wings."

"Ooo la," Werian cooed. "You do have him by the teeth now, don't you?" He was joking for the benefit of those listening, but the worry showed in the pinch of his eyes.

A lightness lifted Aury's heart even as she gritted her teeth at the attention she was getting from others. "Thank you so much, Chef." She took a bite, and the chocolate burned its way over her tongue, smooth and hot. "Oh, it's perfect."

The chef dipped another curtsey, then hurried away.

King Athellore stood and called for Werian. "I'll be right back," he said before leaving.

"You are so lucky, Aury." Sunniva nibbled at her dragon wing, then gulped half a carafe of watered wine. She waved her hand in front of her open mouth. "To have someone who thinks of you so often. He must have known you like hot foods."

"He does. But I'm not lucky." She leaned forward, her mind full of the illustrations in the scrolls at the fae court. The scrolls had shown the elves' hands slicked with blood and their teeth sharpened to needlelike points. "You wouldn't marry a mountain elf, would you?"

Sunniva coughed and drank more. She wiped her mouth on her linen napkin. "I am not a princess."

"What you refuse to say is loud enough. I grew up at the fae court. You know that, right?"

"I do. Everyone does."

"The fae talked about how vicious the elves were during the war. How they bathed in blood and ate meat that...that could've been human."

Sunniva raised an eyebrow. "Whatever it takes to beat back the Wylfen, it's fine by me."

"You sound like my...like King Athellore."

Sunniva barked a laugh, her blonde hair slipping from its pins. "Never thought I'd hear that."

Aury laughed too, imagining her father overhearing this conversation and the pompous expression that he wore like a traveling actor, slipping the frown on and raising his chin as if kings had to show complete disdain for all the world.

"But you've seen Prince Filip now." Sunniva took a slice of dried apple from a tray. "Does he fit what you learned about the elves?"

"His teeth are almost like ours. No fangs really, although his incisors are much sharper." A vision of Filip dragging those fangs lightly over Aury's neck made her shift in her seat. She grabbed a fresh drinking horn and downed three large swallows of sweet, light wine. The drink went straight to her head, and her body warmed, her mind indulging in more thoughts about Filip's mouth.

Clearing her throat, she raised a hand to signal a servant. A man with a scar across his chin rushed over and bowed. "Is there any word about Prince Filip and his men? Why aren't they in attendance?"

"Ah, yes." The servant glanced toward the dais, then back again. "Prince Filip was seriously injured. He is being tended by the Darkfleot healers now."

"We have three healers at the castle, with two serving as apprentices," Sunniva said quickly.

Aury pulled at her collar, her chest tight. "What? Why wasn't I told?"

"I...uh..." the servant stammered, "the king instructed us to keep to pleasant talk this evening and that the prince would be fine."

With scorchpepper chocolate still on her tongue, Aury was up and gone before she thought about why she did indeed care very much.

CHAPTER 26

A ury found Filip's chamber and rapped on the door. His man, Costel, answered, shadows marking his large eyes and his red hair flat against his head.

"Princess Aurora." He bowed, stumbling a bit, then stepped back to allow her to enter. "The healers of Darkfleot are attending Prince Filip. There was an accident in the grove."

"What happened?"

Five men in hats with tassels crowded around what she assumed was Filip's bed. The curtains had been drawn on all but one side, so she couldn't see him around the men. The metallic scent of blood hung in the air.

"Someone," Costel said, his tone implying he knew precisely who but couldn't declare the truth outright, "dug a very large hole in the grove, then lined it with sharpened sticks that were partly buried to stand upright. Captain

Godwin sent Prince Filip looking for Elis of Damerham, who'd gone off to see if he could find the dragon."

"Captain Godwin. I see." They traded a knowing look before Costel's eyes went serious again.

"One of the sharpened lengths of wood pierced Prince Filip's side. He also broke a rib and a leg."

She felt as though Costel had just punched her in the stomach. Pushing past the healers who bowed and murmured respectful niceties, she made it to Filip's bedside.

Blood-soaked linen wrapped his torso, and he wore only his small clothes on his lower body. His leg had been splinted, and a pine-scented poultice darkened his wrapped ankle. With his eyes shut, lying so still and pale, he looked like a statue carved of stone. The tips of his ears peeked through his jet hair, and his lips were parted, his breathing uneven.

She swallowed. "He is not doing well."

"No," a healer said quietly. "He lost too much blood."

Aury shivered and hugged herself, hating the way the blood continued to spread across the linen at his side. "Where are the fae who live here?"

A healer with two deep wrinkles between his eyes cocked his head. "Fae? We need no fae. We use advanced science at Darkfleot. We have no fae healers."

"Nix's ample rump, you don't."

She stormed out of the room and headed for her own chambers. Hilda and Eawynn could do loads more than those fools. "Poultices and wraps. Pfft. What he needs is air magic from fae hands," she muttered as she wound up the stairs and blasted into her chamber.

Gytha sat on a stool between Hilda and Eawynn. Gytha's hand was black. "She cursed me too, the old bat."

"Oh, gods, I'm so sorry. I shouldn't have allowed you to go alone. That was a stupid move on all our parts."

"It was," Hilda said as Eawynn nodded and wrung her hands.

"Here. This is her answer." Gytha held out a slip of parchment, slightly singed along one edge.

Aury took it, but the memory of Filip's pale face and stillness won the moment. "I need you all to come with me. Prince Filip is on his deathbed."

They rushed through the castle and were back in Filip's chamber before the bells rang at midnight.

CHAPTER 27

A velvet voice stirred the darkness that wrapped Filip's mind. His heart beat hard once, twice. Aury was here. He tried to open his eyes, but weights pressed them shut. It was impossible.

"Move aside," Aury said above Filip's head. Her demands were followed by protests from male voices. "Save your pretentious behavior for my parents," she snapped. "It won't work with me. Move. That is a royal order. I will see Prince Filip of Balaur healed by my fae ladies, or each and every one of you will voluntarily serve as targets during the Mage Trials."

After a short silence, a prickling warmth eased through Filip's side, leg, and chest.

"Can you do it?" It was Aury's voice again. "Please tell me you can do it. And I demand that Captain Godwin be brought to Mage Mildred for questioning. Now. Someone, go. Yes, you. I don't care if it's the middle of the end of the world. Now. Hilda, can you heal him? Is it too late?"

"I'm not sure, Princess Aurora. We gave so much to the youngling dragon. Prince Filip's injuries are deep, and he's lost a large amount of blood."

A lighter voice, possibly Eawynn's, spoke. "Healing blood loss takes great energy, and we've not had enough time to heal ourselves since the dragon. Gytha, what should we do?"

"Call on Prince Werian," the raspy-voiced Gytha said, speaking of the Fae Queen's son. "He'll come. He's powerful."

"Of course!" Aury shouted.

The prickling warmth disappeared, and the darkness took Filip into its arms once more.

A CHILL SPREAD OVER FILIP'S CHEST, AND HE OPENED HIS eyes to see Aury's silver hair. Her bright gaze was focused on the window, and aside from Eawynn standing at the door between his chamber and Drago's, they were alone.

He was alive. "Miss me?"

Aury gasped, and water flew from a basin on the nightstand. The liquid shifted into a disc of bladed ice and spun toward Filip's neck. Aury held up her staff and said, "Stop."

The ice halted right before hiting his chest, then it rolled off the bed and shattered on the floor, making Eawynn yelp.

Aury set her staff against the bed and stood, hands hovering over his body like she wanted to do something but didn't know what to try. "Great Nix, I'm so sorry, Filip."

Brushing water from his neck where the ice had nearly beheaded him, he laughed. Pain lanced through his torso. "No problem. You should've let the ice do its work and finish the job Godwin started." He tried to laugh again but winced as the ache in his side pulsed in time with his heartbeat.

Her gaze had snagged on his mostly bare chest. "Don't you own a tunic? You're always half clothed."

"Did you order me murdered so I would distract you less? If so, my thoughts are with you as you come to terms with your failure to end me."

She rolled her eyes. "Watch it, elven prince. I can call up that ice blade again." Her shoulders dropped, and she glanced from him to the floor. "Actually, no, I can't. I have no control at all over my magic."

A memory of the night before Filip's first battle flickered through his mind. His father, King Mihai, had explained how the fear floods a warrior's body and soul, tying him up or throwing him into reckless behavior. "*You must center your thoughts, my son. Focus on one goal, one enemy. Once you have dealt with him, you move to a second enemy. Don't try to see the whole battlefield at once. Not as one warrior on one horse. That is the job of seasoned generals, kings, queens,*" Father had said.

Filip took Aury's hand in his, and a spark of heat blazed where their skin met. His mouth went dry. Surprised she didn't immediately yank her fingers away from his touch or curse him in some colorful manner, he held on lightly. Her sigil ring was smaller than his but gold as well. The skin around the ring was pink, as if she wasn't used to wearing it. *Of course, she wasn't, you dolt*, he chided himself silently.

"When I first began fighting," he said, finding it difficult to concentrate with her leg almost brushing his hip and the pain pulling at him. "I had to learn to focus on one task at a time. One fight with one enemy soldier. If I tried to take in all that was expected of me or all that could happen on the field or where my friends might be and what was riding on the battle, I lost my will to raise my hatchet. Maybe you can try that when you attempt your magic? I know nothing of magic, so ignore me as you will with my best wishes, but that is what helped me first hone my fighting skills. I see your water power as your talent for war."

Arc's Blessed Light, she was beautiful. It hurt to look at her for too long, knowing what he might have with her and guessing it might never happen. He'd take the pain if only for the chance at being hers.

Aury's rosy lips bunched, and she nodded. "That makes sense, but I'm not really a one-thing-at-a-time kind of girl." She grinned sheepishly, her cheeks pinking.

"Why don't you try it, here, now?"

"No, no. Even I have my limits on how many times I try to murder you in a day." She leaned forward, a mountain lion's glint in her eye. "Let's talk about Godwin." Her lips twisted into an evil smile that did dangerous things to his state of mind.

She was so close. One slight move, and his mouth would be on hers. What would her lips taste like? Spice, no doubt. And perhaps wine. He imagined sliding his hand around the back of her neck and pressing a kiss to the soft place just below her jaw, how she would gasp and soften in his arms, her body warm against his. She'd probably quickly have the upper hand. The thought made him grin.

"I'm fairly certain he had his men dig the trap," he said, clearing his throat and shifting his blankets. "He certainly was the reason we were out there. Did anyone find Elis of Damerham?"

"I don't know, but I'll find out. He's an innocent in this, you think?"

Filip shrugged, then hissed with pain that jabbed nails into his side.

Aury's eyes softened. "Prince Werian was here for the feast. He did most of the healing, and my ladies will return to heal you further as soon as they've rested. We will have you on your feet with steel in hand in no time."

"Thank you, Aury."

She flinched at his use of her name but said nothing against it. Another win.

"I ordered Godwin sent to Mildred and Finn to be questioned. Ordering him about was the first time being a princess felt rather lovely."

"What about when you had a dessert named after you?"

She laughed whole and loud then. "Ah. I did enjoy that. Thank you very much. The Dragon Wings were delicious. I hope that if your scaled youngling friend was flying overhead during the feast, he realized we were munching on chocolate and not his kin."

"I doubt dragons care at all what we small ones have to say."

Aury touched his arm. "Small ones." She raised an eyebrow. "You are not so small, Prince Filip."

Ah, if he weren't injured...

He raised his arm and tucked it behind his head to better display the musculature. It had the intended effect of making her cheeks go pink again. "Alas, I am no dragon. If I were, Godwin might not mess with me."

"Godwin is going to suffer for this. Mark my words."

"Careful. I still have one more jug of water in here."

Her mouth fell open. "Brat." She started to pinch him, but instead gently tucked the wrap around his injury so the end wasn't sticking out. She stood, and it took everything in him not to beg her to stay a little longer. Knotting her silver hair away from her face, she said something to Eawynn, then looked at him again. "I'll see about Elis and Godwin. Tomorrow, send Costel to my chambers."

"I'd rather be the one in your chambers, my lady."

She gave him a withering look. "Focus on one task, you said."

"Oh, that's for beginners. I'm experienced."

Throwing up her hands, she left the room, Eawynn clucking and following in her wake.

For the remainder of the night, Filip dreamed of shimmering hair like the river itself, strange knots of scarlet thread, and the scent of sage.

CHAPTER 28

The moment Aury was back in her chamber, Hilda, Gytha, and Eawynn gathered to read the Matchweaver's note.

"Be careful unrolling it," Hilda said.

Eawynn nodded so hard that her hair slid from its pins. "It could be stuffed with foul magic."

"She is very powerful," Gytha whispered.

Too tired to be properly frightened, Aury stood by the candle on her nightstand and spread the slip of parchment in her palm.

In the water, I told you. I tell you again. Your curse remains and will remain. The king and queen sealed your fate when they shamed me, the greatest of all, in front of the entire kingdom. They have dealt true love a blow, and they will feel its pain. You will sleep forever, and the blame sits on their crowned heads.

A sliver of ice chilled Aury's stomach, but she snorted

and wiggled the note. "That's it? Same threat. I think she's full of hot air."

Hilda snatched the note. "Watch out!" She held it with only her fingertips, tilting the letter in the candlelight.

A shadowy image moved behind the inked words.

"It's a spinning wheel." Eawynn gripped Aury's arm.

The sharp point of the great wheel's spindle winked in the light. Aury stepped back, shaking.

Hilda threw the note into the crackling fireplace. The parchment screamed and went a dark purple. "If you had touched the right spot on that note, the curse would've come to call this very night."

Aury let Eawynn and Gytha tuck her into bed like she was a child. "Stop with the fussing."

Gytha glared. "You're trembling like a sick fawn. This is what we're here for, Aury. Let us do our job."

Rolling her eyes, Aury lay back and laced her shaking fingers on top of the duvet. "Thank you. If the witch's curse did put me to sleep, what then?"

Eawynn squeezed her eyes shut. "I don't want to think about it."

Gytha clapped Eawynn on the back encouragingly. "We would do our best to wake you. The entire kingdom would come together."

Hilda blew out Aury's candle. "Yes. We would be at war, every resource aimed at waking Lore's powerful princess."

Aury wanted to roll her eyes again, to hold her heart back from the well of gratitude and hope Gytha's and Hilda's words gave. But fatigue dissolved her hard shell and left her smiling weakly. "Gytha, how is your hand? You never explained the curse and what we are going to do to help you."

Earlier, Gytha had waved away all Aury's questions about her blackened fingers.

"It happens sometimes when magic collides." Gytha held up her fingers and studied them in the firelight. "The Matchweaver threw a spell at me, trying to confuse me, but I twisted the spell like I did with the curse she cast on you. The power tangled midair. An altered version of her spell and mine retreated into my hands. It's not bad. I just need to go to the forest to get the trees to help me heal. The land's soul will fix it in no time."

Hilda nodded, then began pushing Eawynn and Gytha toward the door. "You need healthy sleep now, Princess."

"Aury."

"Aury. You need your rest. You don't have much time before the Masters return and you must face the Mage Trials."

Aury groaned and put her pillow on her face. "I will attempt to be less of a complete failure tomorrow," she mumbled through the goose down and silk.

Gytha was the last to leave. She gripped the edge of the door, peering around and meeting Aury's eyes. "You are at war already. Don't forget that. You will succeed, and you will dominate. Believe it, and watch it happen." Her smile was a flash of bone-white in the dark.

"Thanks." Aury rolled over. "I'm really sorry about your hand."

"Bigger, badder things than this have tried to take me down. This won't be my end."

"I wish I had your confidence."

"You did when you first arrived here."

"Reality has a way of tarnishing the brightest hope."

Gytha laughed. "You'll find a way, vicious princess mage. I know it." She raised a fist, then disappeared into the outer chamber.

Aury stared at the fire. She wished she could've said goodbye to Werian and solidified their peace. She wasn't mad at him anymore. He was the same old Werian, mischievous and good to the core.

A very different but also handsome face flickered through Aury's mind—Filip with his flirtatious smile. Her body hummed at the thought of his comments at his bedside, how he wished to be in her chamber. What would it be like to have him here beside her? Sure, he'd shown kindness and honor. But he'd also shown a dangerous side. What kind of husband could he be?

She shook off the thought. It was no business of hers. She wasn't going to marry him. And even if they forced her into it, she'd find a way to untangle herself.

Her mind spun around what Werian had said about the Magelords and the sacrifice a fellow captain would have to make in order to give her the title. Her dreams held a blood-stained staff and the Matchweaver and her letter's shadowy spindle.

She woke to Eawynn shaking her like a rag doll.

"I'm up, woman. Stop!"

Eawynn thrust Aury's clothes at her. "Prince Filip is at your door, waiting for you."

Aury scrambled to the washroom. "Why?"

"Mage Mildred has called you both to question Captain Godwin."

"Nix's flaming cider." She dragged a wet cloth over her face, then dressed faster than she'd thought possible.

Hilda shoved Aury's staff into her hand, then Gytha crammed a scone into her mouth.

She was still chewing and blinking when they opened the door to Filip. Though his experience had drawn circles under his eyes, he seemed well enough. He leaned against the doorframe, his large arms straining against his linen sleeves and his narrow hips cocked to one side. His intense gray gaze traveled the length of her, trailing a sizzling heat wherever they went. Her heart knocked against her chest, demanding that she throw him against the wall and have at it.

"Morning." He winked.

Aury coughed around a bite of scone and a bit of cranberry. It was like he knew what she was thinking even though he didn't. Elves didn't have that power. They had no magic, from what he himself had told her. Calling elves mages was simply another form of ignorance. "What is this about? Why do they need me at Godwin's questioning?"

They started down the corridor, taking the first set of winding stairs. His body brushed hers, and she swallowed. Half of her wished she had a glass of water to wash this scone down, but the other half knew it was good she had no water nearby with which to accidentally attack him. He was as hot as a summer day with that fresh grin on his chiseled face and his health mostly back to normal. He did have a slight limp, but it wasn't slowing him down.

"Don't you want to berate Godwin on my behalf?" His lips twitched like he wanted to laugh.

"I wanted to string up the rat-faced boar from day one, but it would have been nice to have a proper breakfast first."

"So in the future," he said, "breakfast then beheadings."

She dusted crumbs from her tunic. "Correct."

"Noted."

Tossing her hair, she sped past him. He was getting far too comfortable with her. "I am glad you're feeling up to this. You're feeling hale due to the healing, I presume."

"Because of the fae's work, and your presence." His voice was close, warm at her ear.

A shiver of pleasure danced down her sides. "Good."

She took a quick right turn and sped down the next set of stairs, leaving him behind. If she spent one more moment that close to him, she was either going to turn the world to ice or erupt in flames from want. She'd never, ever admit it to anyone, but the elven prince drew her in like no one else.

He didn't try to catch up to her, instead taking his time in the descent.

Mildred and Finn stood with Godwin at the doors to a room Aury hadn't yet seen. Godwin's glare was a brand searching for a marking place, but Aury stared him down. She gave him a broad smile, and his eyes widened before going to slits.

"Mage Aurora," Mildred said in greeting. "Is Prince Filip on his way?"

"He is."

"Then let's get started." Mildred led them into the dark room.

Godwin walked behind Aury. It was astounding the difference between his presence and Filip's. A sucking darkness compared to a frustratingly attractive light.

"You should be more careful in a labyrinth place such as Darkfleot, Mage Aurora," Godwin whispered. "Accidents happen."

She whirled. "I'm sorry. Did you say something, Captain Godwin? Hold on, Mage Mildred, Mage Finn. The captain has something to tell us. What do I need to be careful of here at Darkfleot exactly?"

Did she trust Mildred and Finn to always take her side? No. But in this case, the risk of it was worth the wilting look on Godwin's ugly face.

"Please sit, Captain Godwin." Nostrils flaring, Mildred jerked a hand toward a chair facing five other chairs.

Godwin did as instructed as Filip entered the room. Mildred and Finn gave him a curtsey and a bow before sitting beside Aury.

Once they were settled, Filip leaned close to her ear. "Did you poke the boar already, my frosty princess?"

She knocked his forehead with her staff and stared straight ahead, trying not to wish his mouth would stay close, whispering and warm.

Mildred addressed Godwin. "What happened the night of the feast, Captain?"

"Prince Filip kindly offered to search for Elis of Damerham. The young lad had gone off in search of the dragon youngling the prince rescued from the thorns in the grove. Elis was missing for two days. As I heard it, Prince

Filip and his men fell into an old hunting trap. Terribly unfortunate."

Aury gripped her staff, fury rising. The man didn't give away a thing with his blank features and calm demeanor.

Filip stood and sauntered over to Godwin. "Let's get one thing straight..."

"Prince Filip, please wait a moment." Mildred tutted and started forward.

"I may not be your prince," Filip said quietly to Godwin, who was sweating up a storm, "but I am a prince, and I will not have my suspicions doubted." His hatchet was out and at Godwin's neck in the blink of an eye. "You did this, and you will admit it. I didn't come here for deception, but for a request of mercy. I will gladly give mercy when a subject asks. If not, we will let the *bárda* sing its steely song."

Filip's presence was powerful; his way with a blade was fearsome. This was a true ruler with every bit of confidence he needed to run a country.

"Thank me for my kindness in not slaying you right here and now."

"I...but I..." Godwin's face was red as wine.

Filip set his hatchet under the captain's chin and lifted it so they saw eye to eye. "It's very simple. Say it and you might live. Don't, and this is your last moment."

"Prince Filip, you can't just..." Finn had stood and was moving his staff from hand to hand like he wasn't sure what to do. "You can't murder Captain Godwin."

"Oh, but you're wrong there, Mage Finn. I most certainly can. And your king and queen can dish out whatever consequences they see fit. But I'm convinced that they need my army more than they need"—he glanced at Aury—"a rat-faced boar of a captain who binds one of his men, forces him to lie, then attempts to kill an ally to the kingdom in one of the most cowardly manners history has yet seen."

Aury stood, her blood racing for a million reasons. How much she hated Godwin. How she was probably breaking royal rules. How absolutely dangerous Filip looked, and indeed, was.

"You heard Prince Filip," she said with more strength than she felt. Godwin deserved some humble pie and a good thrashing, if not a bloody death. "The captain will beg for mercy. On your knees, brute."

Filip's eyebrows lifted, and he nodded approvingly before tipping his head to her.

Godwin slid from his chair and knelt before Filip and Aury. "Please forgive me."

"For trying to murder me and my men," Filip said.

"For trying to kill you." Sweat rolled down Godwin's face. "And the others."

Filip pressed a knee into Godwin's chest, pressing the man against the edge of the chair's seat. Godwin gasped.

"You swear you will never," Filip said, "as long as you live your miserable life, ever attempt to harm anyone from Balaur ever again."

"I swear it."

"Say it," Aury snapped.

Godwin repeated Filip's suggested oath word for word.

Filip looked to Aury. "What is a medium-level punishment in Lore? We'd take an ear at least." He held the edge of his hatchet to Godwin's head.

The captain struggled to breathe between the chair's edge and Filip's knee. Finn and Mildred had obviously decided to allow the royals to do the job. Undoubtedly, Filip's steel had much to do with that decision.

"An ear. Yes. Sounds good to me." She grinned, righteous fury boiling in her blood. "Get it? Sounds good."

Filip barked a laugh. "Yes. Well done, Mage Aurora. Well done. Or should I call you princess when you are administering royal punishments with me?"

"I'd rather stick with mage, thank you." She gave Mildred and Finn a smile. They looked ready to faint.

"Fine, then," Filip said. "Mage Aurora, Godwin will lose an ear, his rank, if you will it, and begin new duties..."

"In the kitchens."

"The kitchens sound rather nice for such a man," Filip said.

"If he misbehaves there," Aury replied, "he will be on chamber pot duty."

"Ah. Very wise. We must keep him motivated to refrain from murdering folks."

"Yes. Exactly."

"But I," Godwin gasped, "I must ask that King Athellore be told and—"

Aury grabbed the captain's disgusting ear and held it tight. "You lost your chance to ask for anything the moment you began digging that hole in the grove. You're quite lucky we're not using it as your grave."

"There's still time." Filip grinned, showing his elven incisors, so sharp and long in the flickering candlelight.

Godwin's ear was gone in a moment, and Aury looked

away as the man screamed, though she couldn't say she felt an ounce of guilt.

A thought flashed through her mind—being betrothed to a vicious elf had its benefits. Her gaze snagged on his leather trousers, then his wicked grin, and her body jolted with an unnameable heat. Anger? Want? Curiosity?

Fine. They could be betrothed, but that was as far as this feint would go. No wedding. No marriage. She'd pretend her grudging approval of the betrothal, assuage her parents' worry—and therefore hinder any meddling they might have up their fancy sleeves—then continue merrily on the path to freedom and independence when they least expected it. Training would be more pleasant with some eye-sugar riding beside her in this new life. And Filip certainly qualified. But only for a while. Until she figured out how to claim the freedom and power of a Magelord. Then he would leave, and she would stay, and both their kingdoms would be the better for it.

CHAPTER 29

Filip collapsed onto his bed, dizzy from pretending he was completely healed. "Costel, can you send for Gytha? She seems like she can keep a secret. I need her healing if she's well enough to give it. And by the Source, please tell me there is tea."

Costel set what smelled like a mug of mint tea on the nightstand, then untied half of the bed curtains so Filip was partially enclosed in glorious darkness. "I will. If she isn't well enough, do you want another of the fae to come?"

Filip shook his head, then ran a hand through his hair to get it out of his face. "No. I don't want Aury knowing I need more help."

"You nearly died. I hardly think she'd begrudge you another healing session with her ladies. She certainly seemed amenable to staying by your side last night."

A lightness spread through Filip's chest. "She did, didn't she?"

"Does she know about the Balaur ceremony?"

Throat tightening and body suddenly thrumming with anticipation, Filip thought she most likely didn't. The Balaur traditional marriage ceremony was rather intimate... and Aury didn't even want to marry. Yet. "I'll tell her. She should know what she's getting into."

"That'll be after the Mage Trials, won't it?"

"It will. I assume our party will leave the day after, in fact. The Wylfen will be approaching the pass by then."

"What if she tries to call off the wedding?"

"I can't control that, Costel. I'm going to do what I can to woo her. That's all I can manage."

Costel gripped Filip's shoulder and studied him with a wide gaze. "I hope you succeed, friend. I can't imagine things going well for Balaur if you fail."

"Who is failing?" Drago burst into the room, followed by Stefan, who was chomping on a chicken leg.

"Not me." Filip lay back on his pillows and shut his eyes briefly. "The princess and I joined forces to spill Godwin's blood and force his confession."

Stefan clapped, nodding. "Very good. I like to know Lore's future rulers can dole out justice. Tell me he'll be here presently to clean up my chamber pot."

Drago growled and rubbed at the leg injured in the trap. "I'd rather see his dead body hanging outside my window."

"If we were in Balaur," Filip said, "Godwin would be dead. But this is Lore, and they are less bloodthirsty than us elves."

"But you can secure this marriage, right?" Drago asked, leaning against the bedpost. "If you don't..."

Stefan smacked the back of Drago's head. "Arc's teeth, Drago. Stop doubting our devastatingly alluring prince."

Drago flexed the muscles in his right arm. "I'm just saying, if it were me she was considering, the marriage would be in the books already."

Filip took three large swallows of his tea, then tossed the remainder of the contents at Drago's chest. "Shove off, boar," he said, laughing.

Drago pretended the tea was some foul poison and crashed to the ground, choking and gasping. Stefan kicked him in the side.

"Get out, you idiots," Costel said. "Filip needs to rest. Don't you need to be on the training grounds?" He shooed them from the chamber.

"Aye!" Filip said. "Start them on the maneuvers for dealing with the wolves. I'll be out there in a few and release the wolf. We'll see which of them followed my orders to keep the orangebranch in their pockets. I hate that we have to use so much of the plant to train when we don't have enough as it is, but they must have the practice."

Costel shut the door as Drago and Stefan called out, "It will be done, my prince!"

A few minutes later, Costel brought Eawynn—instead of Gytha—who set her hands on Filip's chest and side. The fae's wide eyes glittered as her magic seeped into his body.

"Thank you again," Filip said, finally breathing deeply.

"Gytha can't heal you right now. The Matchweaver cursed her a bit when Princess Aurora sent that message. She'll be right as rain soon enough though. Not to worry."

Filip sat up. "Message to the Matchweaver?"

Eawynn clamped her hands over her mouth. "I shouldn't have said that," she mumbled.

"Well, you did, so now you must ease my fears. Is Gytha truly all right, and what did my lovely princess have to say to the witch goddess?"

Standing and backing away, Eawynn flushed. "Gytha will heal. But as for the message... I can't say, Prince Filip. I'm sorry, but that's my lady's business. She can tell you if she has a mind, although I don't know why she wouldn't want to marry you this very day, Your Highness." Her hand had strayed back to his side, where her fingers danced along his abdominal muscles.

He raised an eyebrow. "Oh, yes?"

She giggled. "Quite a catch, in my humble opinion."

"Even with these?" He flashed his sharp, elven teeth.

"Ooh. Especially with those." She hurried from the room before he could ask her anything else.

Costel leaned over the bed, his face darkening. "What do you think the princess told the Matchweaver?"

"That she has no plans to wed me. It only makes sense. The wedding was what angered the witch in the first place. Of course, it is a good move to assure the powerful lady that we don't want to further incite her ill will."

"But you still believe you can sway the princess?"

"I do."

Filip hoped he wasn't lying to his best friend.

More than that, he hoped when he did succeed in gaining Aury's hand, the witch wouldn't kill them both. They would have to be very careful on the road to Balaur, away from the safety of the castle walls. Though King Athellore had banished the Matchweaver to her castle in

Illumahrah, Filip wasn't fool enough to believe the witch was no longer a threat. She was clever. Dangerous.

Witches could do all sorts of terrible magic.

There was only one witch in Balaur that he knew of, and she could make people see what she wished them to see. Only a sight rune painted in blood on the forehead protected those who walked close to her home in the high peaks.

Perhaps Aury's runed staff would protect them as they traveled through Lore to Balaur for the betrothal ceremony. That and their wits would have to be enough for the trip and for the battle that would shortly follow.

On the training grounds, the ground was a mire of mud, weary horses, and frustrated Lore soldiers.

One young recruit nearly lost his seat. "Prince Filip, how are we supposed to get the horses to draw together like Captain Drago instructed? This isn't right, shoving them together in the mud like this." His mare's ears flicked in agitation, her teeth bared against his asinine grip on his reins.

Feeling much better since Eawynn's visit, Filip nudged Avalanche forward. "First, let your horse do her work. Ease off those reins. As for the mud, well, do you have a witch who can control the weather in your back pocket?"

Stefan barked a laugh and drove his horse sideways, completing the crescent shape of the formation. "It's as dirty as goddess Nix's mind up there at Dragon Wing Pass! Be ready, young warrior!"

Filip grinned, thinking of Aury's Nix necklace and

wondering what exactly drew Aury to that particular goddess.

"Ready!" Drago shouted from the wagon where the scar wolf's crate remained.

"Now!" Filip waved a hand in the signal they'd developed for releasing the wolf.

The wolf shot from the crate, a blur of black and gray fur. The Lore soldiers shouted in surprise, some falling from their horses and others digging in their belts for their orangebranch. The man who'd been snared into Godwin's treachery, Elis of Damerham, was the first to throw a handful of orangebranch. The wolf paused in its pursuit of the nearest horse, then raised its snout, sniffing the air for the bacon-like plant. The wolf lunged toward the treat.

Filip cupped a hand at his mouth. "Circle him. Throw the net."

Elis led the move, tossing the weighted net he'd had loosely tied to his saddle. The net landed on the wolf.

"Wait! Don't pull yet!" Filip called. The wolf had to be in the exact right spot for the net to secure the animal.

The wolf thrashed against the net but went immediately back to snuffling the ground, desperate for more orangebranch.

"Pull!" Filip yelled.

Elis yanked on his end of the net, and the lead weights clicked together, upending the wolf and holding him tight. A shout of "Huzzah!" went up.

Drago quickly ran to the wolf and threw out another small bit of orangebranch that had been dosed with seasleep tubers. The wolf gobbled the concoction and was swaying in moments. Drago and Costel worked the scar wolf back to its crate, where several men helped them cage the animal.

"Why should we net them instead of killing them?" One of Godwin's men, a fellow with two teeth and fists like hams, spoke out, his gaze on Filip like a challenge. Stefan had mentioned that Godwin's men were spreading discontent among the warriors, saying Godwin had been treated unfairly and that they'd see their captain restored once the elves were gone.

"Since you appear older and more experienced than some of our soldiers here, I'm sure you know as well as I do that scar wolves will take five arrows and multiple gaping wounds from a blade before falling. Netting them when we can will save time in the moment of attack. We will put them down when it serves us strategically."

"I think you cuddle up with this one at night," the man muttered. A few snickered around him. "Since you can't seem to get our princess in your bed."

Hot anger burned under Filip's skin, but he gripped the pommel of his saddle and held his seat. "If you're so worried about my talents in the bedroom, perhaps you'd care to join me this evening and try them out yourself?" He blew the arse-head a kiss.

The men and women erupted in laughter, and Filip turned Avalanche around to head toward the stables. The joke worked for now, but soon there would have to be a more serious reckoning for Godwin's men. They thirsted for a fight, and so Filip would give them one.

CHAPTER 30

Nearly a week had passed and still Aury had no control over her magic. It sat inside her like a hibernating bear lately, doing absolutely nothing.

Filip had been busy too, teaching the Lore army more archery techniques and dealing with Godwin's disgruntled men. During striking, Master Dun, or Brute—as Sunniva and Aury deemed him—detailed the various formations they would use during the upcoming battle, and Filip's name came up quite frequently. Master Brute was obviously pleased with what the elves brought to the army. Aury had barely seen Filip in what felt like forever.

Instead of asking around about him like half of her wanted to, she spent her off hours in the stables brushing Goldheart's mane and talking as one only could to a kindly animal. It was just fine that run-ins with Filip had been few and far between. She needed to focus on her training.

She stared at the trough of water in Mage Finn's training room. Her staff shook and warmed in her hand. She had to use this power she'd been given to pass the Trials and then help Lore and Balaur win the upcoming battle with the Wylfen. There was no time left for her failures.

Why couldn't she get it to work when she wanted? It was hers, after all. This made no sense! Her teeth squeaked as she ground them in frustration.

The other mages in the room reminded her of everything she desperately longed to be, the positive significance she wanted to have on her kingdom, the strength she simply had to gain to live the life she'd been born to. This had to work. She had no more time to wait for her power to cooperate. The Masters would return soon, and the Trials would begin. She had to do more than pass. She had to amaze them all, secure her role as ruler, and show her royal parents that she wasn't someone they could push around. They had to give her a position as a captain in the battle if she was even going to have the tiniest of chances to achieve Magelord status so she could rule and live how she thought best instead of how the king and queen thought best.

A conversation with Filip echoed through her memory. *Battle mindset. The enemy in front of you. One fight at a time.* His storm-gray eyes flashed with passion. His lips parted as he spoke quietly, sincerely.

Allowing the memory to fade, she breathed in slowly, focus narrowing to the trembling, black surface of the water. Sunniva's encouraging remarks grew quiet, her percentages on those who had trained and struggled dissolving into silence. Even Finn's appraising gaze dimmed into the background of Aury's awareness.

A rippling sensation ran across her arms and chest, a sweep of cool magic. The taste of fresh spring water danced over her tongue.

It wasn't going to work. She would leave training again today with her stupid bear sleeping worthlessly inside her. Shedding the poor attitude, she closed her eyes.

The image and feel of water flooded her mind, blurring all her longing, her desperation, her fear, her anger. A persistent burbling soothed her and drew her attention in full. The sound of water magic rushed through her ears, somehow so familiar despite its newness. She sank into the sensation, drawing the magic from deep inside and letting it run down her staff and plunge toward the trough.

Soon, the entire chamber was doused in a foot of churning water.

Applause erupted.

Aury blinked, her lips spreading into a wide smile. Finally.

"You did it!" Sunniva gripped her shoulder and smiled. "Incredible."

"Very well done, Mage," Finn said gruffly as he waved his staff and sent the water back into the troughs set about the room.

Shaking the water from their oiled boots, the mages left the room and headed toward the next training session. This one would be with Mildred and the fountain that Aury had shattered. She blew out a breath, praying to the Source she wouldn't annihilate everyone within spell-shot.

"If you can perform the flooding magic that well during

the Trials, you'll get top ranking." Sunniva tucked her staff under her arm and adjusted one of the five copper rings on her long fingers. The woman wore different rings every day. Most were simple. "I didn't hear all of what Prince Werian said to you, but I did hear you talking about becoming a captain."

"That's my goal."

"Does leading the fight scare you or excite you?"

"Oh, I want to lead. As long as I have a strong general who knows strategy, which we do." The generals at Darkfleot visited the striking sessions regularly, Filip among their small number. "I want to help as much as I can." The mages here supported her, and surely there were more good folks like Sunniva throughout the kingdom, people who weren't like the nasty fae she'd had to deal with at the Agate Palace. "I won't lie though. I'm as scared as anyone of the Wylfen." But at least they came at you, face-to-face, instead of stabbing you in the back.

Sunniva shrugged. "You'd be a fool not to fear them."

"Why do you wear so many rings?"

She grinned sheepishly. "It's an old tradition from my home village. They say precious metals help you work your magic. I try new ones every day and keep track of how well my training goes."

"Anything working?"

She slid a copper ring off her thumb and handed it to Aury. "I do think these copper ones help me with my control."

"But you have that rune on your staff." Aury slipped the copper ring over her right thumb. "You're already good at control."

"I want to learn how to hit a single rider with a spear of ice exactly where I aim to strike," Sunniva said.

"That would be amazing. Have you seen anyone do that?"

"Once." The arched entrance to the Ice chamber yawned open and cold. "She took a black bear down the day I arrived." Sunniva looked at Mildred, who was standing beside the mended fountain speaking to another soldier mage. "The thing was foaming at the mouth, and it was so fast. Came straight at me. There was no time to think, to call for help, and suddenly, the bear was on its side, dead, and Mildred stood beside me, her staff trembling in her hand."

"She saved your life."

"Yes."

A few of the men in the back of the group were laughing about something. Mildred sniffed and raised an eyebrow. They immediately went quiet, the gurgling fountain the only sound.

"Sorry, Mage Mildred," a man with long, black braids said.

"I'd love to know what is so entertaining that you feel the need to force our training to wait on your laughter."

The man rubbed the back of his neck. "Talk is that Prince Filip had some trouble from the former Captain Godwin's men. They were taking the piss out of him over his challenges with..."

The man's gaze flew to Aury. She felt her neck grow hot. She held his gaze and dared him to say something about her behavior. She wanted him to ask her why she was holding the prince at arm's length. She would explain it all to these warriors, these fellow mages. Then they would see who she was, a woman who would not be cowed by the king or the queen. A woman strong enough to rule when the time called for it.

But the man didn't prompt her. "Godwin's man made a comment about the elven prince's talents." A demon's grin pulled at his mouth, and everyone tittered, knowing what he was alluding to. Aury rolled her eyes. "And the prince invited the man to his chamber tonight to test them out."

The room erupted in laughs and approving guffaws.

"Wish I could've seen the man's face at that!" a woman said.

"Godwin's men are so uptight," the man stage-whispered.

Mildred shook her head. "Indeed. More tightly wound than the bun atop my head, yes?"

Even Aury had to laugh at that, Sunniva trading a grin with her.

Mildred held up her staff. "All right. Lovely. It's good to know some things never change. I used to instruct the youth. Here I am with adults, but the humor of intimate relations remains top material for entertainment." Mildred's gaze slid to Aury for a moment, and concern shone in their depths.

What would Filip be like behind closed doors? Would his teeth pierce her lips if he tried to kiss her? Would his elven strength break her bones even if he tried to be gentle with her?

A spark lit Aury's belly and burned hotly. She was suddenly breathing too quickly.

"Are you prepared to work your magic, Mage Aurora?" Mildred said.

Aury startled, then cleared her throat. "I...of course."

Sunniva touched her back briefly and gave a supportive smile.

Shutting out the scuffs of boots on the stone floor and thoughts of Filip's dangerous nature, Aury focused on the fountain. She held out her staff and imagined the water going still, the droplets linking up like archers in a firing line, the bubbling quieting to the silence of the pond at the Agate Palace after the new year broke over the festival season. Cold danced across her cheeks and the hand she was using to hold her staff. The fountain froze. The windows snapped like a sudden frost hit them. Aury's breath released in a white-feathered plume of mist.

A woman's whisper, barely audible and tinted with a laugh, slid through her focus.

"The elven mage has himself an ice princess."

Aury glanced away from the fountain to see another mage snickering.

A cold so deep spread from Aury's staff and into her hand. The fountain cracked, and water spilled from the center of the room to flood the chamber, rising so quickly that no one did more than stammer and blink. Then the cold flew from her staff like a vengeful ghost and swept across the crowd.

Aury stepped back, her breath gone.

A coat of solid ice covered every single person in the chamber except Aury.

The silence was death. A shiver jerked her viciously.

"No..." She held out her staff, shaking, thoughts

whirling through her mind, chaotic and useless. "Mildred!" she called, turning toward the powerful mage.

A blue light grew inside Mildred's shell of frozen water.

Then the ice around the older mage blasted away, shards careening across the room and over Aury's head.

Mildred, gasping, held out her staff. The ice around everyone else shivered, then exploded, turning to a heavy rain as it descended. The water sifted into the drains and pipes set up in circles around the room.

The other mages stared at Aury, some of the faces in awe, others with fear.

"She will be a boon to our forces." Mildred said it like she refused to allow anyone to say otherwise. "Mage Aurora, you will spend the rest of the day with me. Mage Sunniva, please remain also. I think you two could be a strong team. The rest of you, go on to the great hall. That's enough for today."

Aury leaned over to Sunniva. "Um. Sorry about that."

Sunniva exhaled and patted her on the arm. "I'm just glad you're on our side."

The rest of the crowd filtered out of the room.

"Mage Aurora," Mildred started, then she collapsed to the floor.

They ran to her, and Aury shook her arm to try to wake her. "Mildred! I'm so sorry. Mildred!"

Sunniva ran a hand down the older woman's face. "Aury, just let her rest for a moment. She'll be all right. Sometimes after a powerful spell, you lose consciousness. It takes a vast amount of energy to work magic like that."

Aury only felt the beginnings of fatigue. Was that a good thing? It had to be. "I feel so bad. Mildred, I'm seriously so, so sorry." She looked up at Sunniva. "Should I get Hilda and Eawynn?" Gytha still wasn't quite herself even though she'd gone off to the grove one night to heal among the trees.

Before Sunniva could answer, Mildred's eyelids fluttered. "Ah. Thank you, Mages."

They helped her to sit in a chair, Aury continuing to apologize.

Mildred waved her words away and smoothed her tunic. "We all lived, and now we know that your power is ready to work with you. You've developed a proper mindset. May I ask what helped you gain such focus?"

"It was Prince Filip, actually. We were talking about battle mindset and dealing with one enemy at a time during a fight."

"I like seeing you give credit where it's due, despite your...situation."

Did she mean the whole Aury-refused-to-marry-him situation? How much gossip was there really about her and him? Probably cartloads. One could probably fill the great hall with the gossip were it a physical commodity. Aury closed her eyes for a moment.

Mildred's voice was closer. "I see that someone has given you a ring." Her words were soft like she was talking to a panicked horse. The wisdom of Mildred's approach wasn't lost on Aury. Who knew if she would spook and freeze them again?

"I did." Sunniva stepped forward. "I hope that isn't against regulations."

Mildred cocked her head. "It's unusual. Some of the Masters wouldn't like to see it. But I find that old wives' tales often hold a kernel of truth." Her smile was there and gone before Aury could figure out how real it was. She reached for Aury's hand, her gaze asking permission.

Aury set her hand in Mildred's, bracing for a strike like she would've received from a fae noble in the dark corridors of the palace. But Mildred's touch was soft and sure, and Aury found herself relaxing.

Locking her gaze on Aury, Mildred said, "You must learn to set up walls for your magic. Barriers that are quite similar to the ones you've put on your heart."

Aury jerked her hand away. "What do you mean?"

"You know what I mean, child."

Aury's feet itched to move, to run, to flee. She longed to shove the old woman back and hurry from the room, but she couldn't. She had to learn this. She had to succeed with her magic, or she'd be stuck doing her parents' bidding all her life. Her kingdom would see her as a failure, a disappointment. Aury couldn't allow that, so she stood her ground and forced the child inside her to at least try to trust Mildred.

"How do I build barriers for magic?"

"Feel the magic in your mind."

Aury sensed the cool ripple of water, smelled the scent of rivers and streams and oceans, heard the rush of waves and waterfalls in her ears.

"Yes," Mildred said. "Very good."

"I can feel her magic," Sunniva whispered. "Amazing."

"She is incredibly powerful," Mildred said, a note of warning in her words.

"I make my walls of water," Sunniva said. "In my head. Currents to drive the direction of the magic."

"Ah, yes," Mildred said approvingly. "A good plan. Why don't you visualize that, Mage Aurora?"

Aury imagined flowing rivers on either side of the sensations at the sides of her body and head.

"Now, try to create ice with the currents of control in place." Mildred pointed to the fountain. It had magically reformed itself, obviously another effect of the magic cast upon it during its creation.

Aury raised her staff, let the magic rise up inside her. The imagined currents struggled to hold in the freezing flow of power she was directing at the fountain. Shaking with the effort, sweat streaming down her cheeks, she focused on that gurgling source of water, pressing the droplets together, urging the cold into the ripples...

Ice power snapped through the walls of control. Mildred shouted, and Sunniva hit Aury's staff, driving it from her hand. The weapon skidded across the flagstones as Aury staggered back into Sunniva's hold.

"You're all right," Sunniva said. "Everything is fine."

Aury straightened and gave Sunniva a quick squeeze on the arm before facing Mildred.

"Maybe you need ice to hold ice," Mildred said as Sunniva handed the staff back to Aury. "Let's practice again. You'll sleep well tonight, Mage Aurora, you and me both." She huffed a laugh.

Aury hoped she wouldn't kill the two people here who were truly on her side.

CHAPTER 31

B eyond Darkfleot's grounds near the river and the forested foothills, the land sloped into a mostly cleared area where the bustling city of Loreton had grown. Three-story shops leaned toward one another over narrow roads where knots of men argued, overly rouged women waved to passersby, and merchants sold false scarbane. Filip had seen numerous attempts at this forgery, and every new appearance of the scam increased his anger two-fold.

On their way to the Jade Folly, Loreton's most popular tavern, Filip and his men stopped at one particularly vocal merchant. Filip plucked the corked, glass vial from the merchant's grasp and held it to the light of the candle flickering in the tavern's window. "What do you tell people is in this if they ask?"

"Why, sir," he said, looking Filip up and down, gaze touching the pointed ears and the hatchet, "who are you to ask?"

Drago lurched forward and grasped the lying merchant's cloak. "This is Prince Filip of Balaur."

Filip untangled Drago's fingers from the man's clothing. "Cool down, Drago." All of them were on edge. Godwin's men had been a constant irritation, and the air was practically on fire with an impending fight between those who supported Filip and those who held no love for elves. Filip faced the merchant. "Now, tell me. How do you make fools believe that anything in this concoction of yours will ward off scar wolves?"

"It was my father's recipe. He used it in the old war."

Uncorking the vial, Filip took a whiff. "Mountain mint. Cloves. Tallow. And...anise. Is that about it? Are you attempting to make the people attractive to the wolves? Because that scent is alluring if you ignore the tallow."

Costel shook his head. "Neither humans, elves, nor fae have vomeronasal organs to detect beneficial elements for mating, so there's no way this human merchant could develop such a blend."

"Costel, stop showing off. I only meant it smells nice."

"I'm simply helping you point out this merchant's inability to create a product that will in any way affect scar wolves through warding them off or making them appreciate humans."

Filip threw the vial to the ground and crushed it with the heel of his boot. "Stop scamming the folk of this town, merchant. Use your father's recipe instead to create perfumes. It would be less dangerous to the public at large if you use the lie that your mixtures allure other humans rather than protect them from death by wolves."

The merchant's face went red. "Forgive me, Prince, but you're telling me you prefer one lie to another?"

Stefan patted the merchant's arm. "It's called politics."

Filip chuckled as they left the stammering merchant in the road and walked into the tavern for some much-needed drinks. It was known to all that Aury had gone to meet with her parents. He had a good guess she would try to talk them out of the marriage.

A large fire crackled along the far wall, and barmaids brought drinking horns to long, wooden tables packed with men and women. Two white-beards with folded blacksmith's aprons beside them toasted, their words calling for a short winter. A pair of women who smelled like horses stood by the barkeep's counter laughing and sharing a mazer of pungent cider. A dozen familiar faces showed beside the back door—Godwin's men leaning against the wall, drinking and glaring. Such delightful fellows.

Then everyone began to realize who Filip was. Silence shrouded the room.

A man began to stand to bow, but Filip held up a hand. "I'm not the prince of Balaur tonight, friends. Let me just be another warrior, here for a cold cider, hot fire, and a game of dice."

The crowd mostly cheered pleasantly and raised their cups, but of course, Godwin's men hissed whispers, eyes filled with plotting.

"Think they're talking about our fabulous moves on the training grounds today or the fine shape of my arse?" Drago whistled and held his fresh drink high to them.

"Stop, Drago. I don't want to fight. I just want to have

a game and a laugh." Filip took a horn from Stefan, then headed over to the pair of blacksmiths who had set up some bone dice. "You two care for a third player?"

"And maybe a fourth?" Costel added, eyes already shining from the drink. He never could hold his spirits.

"Aye, we'd love that, Prince Gillip." The old man with the longest beard scooted over on the bench to make room.

"Actually," Costel said.

Filip smacked him lightly. "Prince Gillip at your service, good sir." The old fellow probably couldn't hear. He didn't need Costel further embarrassing him for such an unimportant detail.

The other old man scratched his bulbous nose with a blackened finger. "It'll be Lore rules, all right?"

"I bet you'll trounce me. I haven't played Lore rules in ages."

Costel took a seat beside the large-nosed man. "You play twos are wild and every six is a second roll, yes?"

"Exactly so."

The old men took their turns rolling the dice, everyone placing bets with the lowest coin in the kingdom so as to keep the game friendly.

"We heard you found a way to deal with the Wylfen wolves," the first old man said.

"Orangebranch." Filip threw the dice and managed a strong pair of sevens. "It's a plant the Wylfen use to train and twist the animals' minds. Now, Lore soldiers will have a small supply on them to confuse and throw off the wolves. It's not a perfect solution, but I do believe it will help in the upcoming battle."

"So it's true they will be at Dragon Wing Pass soon?"

"Unfortunately."

"How are they crossing the mountains in this weather?"

"No one knows." Filip watched Costel roll, his mind whirling. How were the Wylfen moving in the snow and ice? They'd always shunned magics of all kinds, burning magic-workers when they found them, but maybe their ideas on such powers had changed? It never made any sense to shun such a strong possible aid to one's army, and surely they had water mages hiding in their forces, afraid of being found out and killed. Witches, of course, never fought in the wars. They were such solitary folk and mercurial to a fault. But if the Wylfen had indeed turned around on their hatred of magic and employed water mages, it was possible they could make their way through the mountains by way of manipulating the ice. Father's scouts would arrive soon for the Balaur wedding and share more information.

Aury's face washed all other thoughts away. For some reason, he couldn't stop thinking about the way her fingers knotted her long, silver hair. Those fingers on his chest, those fingers in his hair...

"Your roll, Prince Gillip," Costel said, smirking.

Filip blinked and grabbed the dice. "Sorry. Yes."

"I suppose you have much on your mind with the Wylfen coming again," the first old man said.

"And with a wedding approaching," the other one replied, nodding and tugging at his bushy, snow-white eyebrows. "How long to go now?"

"Eight days."

Stefan and Drago had come up behind them. "Arc's

Darkness," Stefan hissed. "Only eight sunrises until our kingdoms are united."

One of Godwin's men strolled to the table, hand loosely gripping his sword's hilt. His grin was a slash in his black beard. Filip was fairly certain his name was Leofric. "Some say the union will never happen."

Filip set his hands on the table, willing himself not to slice the man's head off and end this quickly. He'd be doing everyone a service, really. "And why's that, pray tell?"

"Balaur will seize valuable farmlands, and Lore will receive you and your army in return. But some don't believe we need your army."

"You do. And we need yours. We'll have to work together against them. They must have a new advantage. Something they haven't used before now. A formerly shunned magic they are putting to use or perhaps an innovative technique permitting them to travel in winter." Filip still hadn't turned his head to look at Leofric in full, but his muscles were coiled, and he was ready to spring. The man would attack. He could smell it in the air.

CHAPTER 32

Riding Goldheart, Aury felt her nerves flutter in time with the pink and deep red banners now flying along the Silver River.

"They lead the way to Loreton Palace," Hilda said.

Headed toward the forest near Loreton city so that Gytha would heal among the trees, Aury and the three fae ladies rode with two Darkfleot guards. One of the guards was flaxen-haired and named Oswald, and the other—a shorter man simply called Bee—had a scar from temple to neck.

"It's a path to the wedding," Eawynn said, her voice tentative and her gaze on the rippling banners.

Aury closed her eyes and tangled her fingers in Goldheart's soft mane.

Her wedding. It seemed impossible that her parents were trying to force her into spending her entire life with a man they had chosen for her.

Gytha snorted. "They could have at least asked what colors you preferred."

"Whoa, girl," Aury said to Goldheart, who slid to a stop on the ice of the drawbridge. "We're going to Loreton Palace. I need to talk to my parents."

Trading looks, the fae nodded and followed Aury and the guards away from Darkfleot.

Loreton Palace was entirely prepared for the coming wedding. Beyond the beribboned and garland-strewn foyer, Athellore and Gwinnith sat on their thrones, receiving Lore folk who wanted justice in everything from fistfights to stolen horses. A servant announced Aury, and she walked down the length of the room to bow to the two people running her life.

"Greetings, Daughter," Athellore said in a clipped tone. "What brings you here this afternoon?"

Gwinnith glared. Aury guessed her behavior of late hadn't been impressive.

"I must speak with you in private."

The king waved everyone out of the room. "Speak."

Aury cleared her throat. "Because you didn't consult the Matchweaver for my betrothal, she laid a curse on me. And yet, you still want me to marry Filip."

"The Matchweaver can't touch you now. We've been over this."

"I wrote to her."

The king stood, face going red. "You did what?"

"I told her I wasn't going to marry Filip and disrespect her place in Lore."

Athellore stuttered, spittle flying, but Aury held up a hand.

"And she wrote back. After injuring Gytha, one of my fae ladies."

Gwinnith looked ready to slide off her seat. "What did the Witch say?"

"Gytha is fine, thanks so much for asking, Your Royal Kindness. The Witch indicated the curse will indeed come to fruition. I think she'll continually attempt to spell me into an eternal sleep. The only possible solution is for me to refrain from marrying Filip and beg her forgiveness."

Athellore's teeth showed. "We do not beg. Ever. She is banished to her castle and can't reach you."

"That's where you're wrong. She cast some sort of spinning wheel image spell into the letter she sent back with Gytha. I nearly touched the wrong spot, and when Hilda threw it into the fire, the magic there was obvious in the flames. She can reach me beyond her grounds in Illumahrah."

The king marched down the dais steps, then grabbed Aury by the upper arm. "Enough. You will do as I say and as your kingdom demands. You will marry Filip, and this is the last I will need to say it. King Mihai and Queen Sorina will not follow through with the elven army if our kingdoms are not joined by way of wedding and kinship. This is the way things are done and have been done for centuries. Lore has waited nineteen years for this opportunity. Lives have been lost. Your marriage is not up for discussion. Defy us, and you will wish the Matchweaver had her way."

"Athellore." Gwinnith was standing now, but she didn't do anything more than wring her hands.

Aury ripped herself free and strode toward the doors. "Source above, but you are a sweetling. I'm so glad we had this chat."

"One more word," he hissed. "Try it."

Aury bit back another retort. She didn't long for shackles. She'd find another way. After giving him a shallow curtsey, she hurried away.

DURING THE RIDE DOWN TO LORETON TOWN, SHE muttered angrily. "So pigheaded. Do they think I'm making this up like a masquer? Like I'm some fantastic entertainer or that I just live to frustrate them into apoplexy?" She kicked Goldheart gently to urge her into a gallop, welcoming the feel of the cold wind on her face.

They left the horses with a stableman in town and walked to the forest in the foothills of the Jade Mountains.

"It's better to arrive on foot," Gytha said.

"Do these trees here feel the same as those in Illumahrah?" Aury asked as they made their way along the path, feet kicking up the thick piles of pine needles.

"No." Gytha, strolling beside Aury, rubbed her cursed fingers together, her eyes pinched with focus. "But they'll do."

"That's what you said last time you visited," Eawynn said, "but you're still suffering. I think we should get you back to the Agate Palace and find some proper spirit agate. With that, we'd have you healed in moments."

Hilda lifted a branch that had fallen across the path and

tossed it into the dark. The path forked around a small meadow circled in tall pines. "This is a nice enough spot. Let's work here." She sniffed the air. The clouds, lit orange by the sunset, spun like wool. "I do hope we can finish before that snow comes down on our heads."

The wind rose and whispered through the trees. But it was quiet. Too quiet. Even in deep winter like this, there were still redwings and bramblings, red squirrels and foraging deer. The fae and the guards had also noticed the quiet; they glanced from one to another, shifting their weight too often.

In the circle of pines, the fae grasped hands. The swirling sparks and snaking dark smoke of air magic curled from their fingers, then gathered around Gytha's cursed fingertips.

Aury wiggled her freezing toes in her boots and pulled her plain brown cloak tighter around her. The wool was soft but thinner than her Darkfleot cloak and the ones provided by her royal parents. Though she hadn't given up her staff, they'd all dressed in clothing fit for common folk, for less wealthy merchants or tradesfolk, so that they wouldn't be recognized. Remaining unrecognizable made their trip through the city that sat before this wood faster. They hadn't had to stop and say hello to the city mayor or answer questions from well-meaning townsfolk.

Gytha's sigh was the only sound aside from the gentle but sharp-toothed breeze. "Look." She released the others' hands and held up her fingers. "I'm finally free of that wretched witch's curse."

Indeed, her flesh was unmarred, the tattoos of war the only marks on her skin.

But the forest's strange stillness kept Aury from celebrating. "We should go back to town. I don't like the feel out here."

Hilda tsked. "Now who is the one talking of ill omens?"

A screech flattened them all to the snowy ground. Aury's blood froze as a shadow blocked out the sunset's dying light.

"It's the youngling," Hilda whispered, finding her feet. "The dragon."

Oswald unsheathed his sword and scanned the skies.

Shaking, Aury brushed snow from her cheek. "Put the sword away. Don't show aggression. They are incredibly intelligent. More so than us, most likely."

The guard nodded and obeyed.

"Yes, Princess Aurora," the second guard, Bee, said.

The dragon whirled over the pines, and its crystalline spikes twinkled, its wings like silken gowns fluttering as it soared away.

Aury ran down the path, branches snagging her hood and hem along the way. "It's headed for the city. We have to do something."

Gytha hurried past Aury and the rest, her strength obviously back to normal. "With one errant sneeze, that pretty beast could end Loreton."

They broke through the line of trees to see the dragon flying over the city's thatched rooftops and guard tower and through the smoke of the many chimneys.

"Won't the tower guard call out a warning?" Eawynn grabbed her skirts and hurried to catch up to Aury.

"They will, and I'm afraid of what they'll do," she said. "Guard Oswald."

The flaxen-haired man turned briefly. "Yes, Princess?"

"What is the order when a dragon is spotted?"

"There is no official order for dragons. We so rarely see them."

"So the tower guard will make his own judgment on the order to call out to the city guard?"

"Yes, Princess."

Snow blew into the air as they rushed down the now empty roads.

Eawynn pointed toward a sign with pewter lettering spelling out the Jade Folly. "It's circling the tavern!"

And Aury knew why. "Prince Filip is in there." When Filip had cut the dragon free from the thorn patch, he'd cooed at the beast like it was a pet, and the dragon had rubbed its head on him, enamored as Aury was with his deep voice and kindness. "The dragon wants to see its new elven ally."

The snowstorm blew hard, pushing Aury's skirts against her legs and making it difficult to hurry. A crack of lightning snapped across the twilight sky.

Inside the tavern, voices were raised like a fight was about to break out. The crowd of Lore soldiers and townsfolk bumped and jostled Aury and her crew as they entered.

"Eh!" Gytha called out above the din. "A dragon's out there! Eh!"

The arguing coupled with the growing storm slamming a shutter against the window made it so she went unheard.

A break in the crowd showed none other than Filip, arms crossed and leaning against the barkeep's countertop beside his men while five others glared at him. They were Godwin's men.

In the middle of several others shoving and shouting, one of Godwin's men, a fellow with a black beard, stepped closer to Filip. "You should leave Lore now. We don't want you. And Princess Aurora doesn't want you. We will have our princess wed a man of Lore and one we approve of. King Athellore will agree at the next Witan, I'm sure. I've heard talk."

There was no time. The dragon was circling above. Aury began pushing through the crowd.

Filip's eyes widened with recognition, then a sly grin slid over his full lips. Aury swallowed. "Princess Aurora." He bowed deeply, showing a leg. "This man has bet me a gold piece that I can't get you to kiss me without the king's direct order."

"We don't have time for this. Your dragon friend is up there." She pointed at the ceiling. "And I'm guessing dragon fire and thatch don't exactly get on."

Filip let out some elven swear. The crowd parted for them, and they were out in the snow looking up at a dragon in the time it took for Godwin's men to say, "Wait!"

The dragon was lapis lazuli blue but looked black in the snowstorm. A group of twenty men with swords were running toward them. The town guard.

"*Buna, frumoaso,*" Filip shouted into the swirling white. "Land here if you wish, and we will talk."

Aury smacked his arm. "Here? You think those fellows are going to let you have a nice chat?" She pointed to the quickly approaching guards.

"Ah, so now the Lore folk are the danger to the dragon

instead of me, the vicious elf?" He looked very pleased with himself.

"If those men think you drew this dragon here, they won't trust your motivations."

"They would think my grand plan was to lure a dragon into Loreton and watch the town burn?"

"While you laugh and show off your elven fangs."

Shaking his head, Filip called for the dragon again in his language. Then he turned to Aury, snow catching on his black eyelashes. "I would argue that gaining valuable farmland and the hand of a gorgeous, powerful princess are far preferable goals than toasting a city to ash, but it's true that men don't always think before they act."

"Nor do women. But we can discuss philosophy after we save the city, all right?"

The dragon alighted, impossibly graceful, beside him, its nostrils streaming black smoke. The guards skidded to a stop, and the crowd quieted. Filip moved slowly, reaching out a hand toward the dragon's flank.

"Shhh. We should go beyond the city. We can visit there without trouble." He flicked his gaze toward the guards, and the dragon focused on the men's drawn swords, the creature's slitted orange eyes like glowing coals. "The lady and I will follow you there. Near the grove where we met the first time, yes?"

The dragon cocked its head. It definitely understood him. Aury had no doubt. Something in the way its eyes shone...

Filip glanced at her. "Do you think he can follow what I'm saying?"

"I do."

The youngling lowered its head and made a sound like a purr.

Drago approached slowly. "My prince." None of his usual jesting colored his words. "The dragon might be offering himself as a mount."

Spinning to face Drago, Filip said, "Truly?!" The dragon startled.

Aury considered it. "He is showing that docile movement some horses do when preparing for a rider."

Filip walked up to the dragon, who remained still, head and upper body lowered. It extended a wing.

The crowd gasped.

Throwing Aury a wicked grin, Filip held out a hand. "You must come along."

And before she knew it, she was riding a dragon with an elven prince.

With her staff tucked into her mage baldric, Aury sat between one of the dragon's spikes and Filip. The ground drew away, and while the storm had relented somewhat, the snow still bit into her cheeks as the dragon's wings pumped and pulled them into the sky. Her stomach lifted, and she didn't even try to fight the smile stretching her lips. It was amazing. A part of her wished they could fly into the night and leave everything behind.

The city below erupted into movement.

"Stop them!" one of the folk shrieked.

"He's stealing the princess with his elven sorcery!" A town guard waved his sword.

"What are they doing?" Aury shouted into the wind.

The dragon turned and flew low over the tavern's thatched rooftop. Filip's body was warm behind hers, his chest rising and falling against her back. If she hadn't been on the back of a dragon and worried about everything...

"Get the spears!" another town guard shouted.

"Strike now before the beast is too high!"

"No, aim for the elf!"

Filip reached over Aury's leg and ran a hand along the dragon's glittering scales. Aury found she was stupidly jealous of the dragon. "You must fly on to the grove, dragon," he said quietly.

But the dragon wasn't listening or understanding, because it continued whirling around the town. Maybe because it was a youngling or because it didn't care as much for what humans and elves wanted it to do.

A dark shape spun from the city walls and crashed into the dragon's side. The creature lurched and wailed, Filip catching Aury's staff before she dropped it far to the roofs below.

"The trebuchet!" Filip said. "They're readying it again. Fools!" He pointed to the tall, wooden catapult beyond the walls where men ran to and fro, pointing up at them. "Go, dragon. Go to the grove before we're all killed!"

The dragon snarled, and sparks snapped from its mouth. They began to turn.

"I don't think this dragon is a pacifist."

"Arcturus and Vahly's blessing on us," Filip whispered.

The dragon's wings beat the air relentlessly until they hovered over the tavern where the town guards had first attacked. The scent of charcoal grew overwhelming, and then fire poured from the dragon's open maw.

The Jade Folly's roof was now made of flames.

CHAPTER 33

"You can stop this, Aury," Filip said against Aury's head. His heart clanged against his ribs for a thousand reasons. "With your magic."

"I'll accidentally freeze everyone to death. Don't laugh. I've nearly done it. Also, I can't believe any of this is happening. I'm pretty sure I'm dreaming. Pinch me. I'm serious."

The dragon suddenly whirled around, and they gripped the creature's cold spikes to keep from falling. As the dragon aimed for the town guards, a snarl pealed from his throat. The creature was plenty smart enough to know what trouble he was causing, but since the fools on the ground had tried to hurt him, the dragon most likely just wanted a nice dose of vengeance before taking off. But how much?

A bead of sweat ran down the side of Filip's face. They had to get control of this situation. As amazing as it was to ride a dragon with Aury, this could mean death for them as well as the entire town.

"Please, dragon, drop us on that next roof, then go. We'll finish the job you started." He pointed to the counting house beside the Jade Folly, and the dragon flicked its gaze back at him, then at the house. Running a hand along the dragon's scales, he made a promise. "I'll make certain these humans hear the truth about dragons and do my best to teach them to respect your kind. Please spare this town, dragon. Be merciful. As your savior of the thorns, I ask this favor."

Aury kept quiet during his pleas, but she joined in on soothing the lovely beast with a caress.

The dragon lifted its head and roared, the sound shaking its body and its riders. Aury and Filip both gripped the spikes in fear. The creature sailed away from the shouting guards, then soared low over the roof that wasn't yet aflame.

The dragon was listening.

"Hold tight to that staff of yours." Filip grabbed Aury around the middle and fell sideways.

She shrieked, but he ignored her fear for the moment, knowing his elven body could manage to land properly and without much hurt, and they had no time for discussing strategy. He hit the counting house's roof and rolled, holding Aury against him, his arms doing their best to keep her from injury. The heat from the nearby fire reached toward them. The folk in the street, his men and Aury's ladies included, were grabbing buckets and lining up to provide water from the well in the nearby square.

Aury stood, staff in hand and silver hair flying as she watched the fire dancing. "I can use the snow."

"How can I help?"

"Don't let me murder you."

"I'm not sure how to refrain from dying by your magical hand, my lady, but I will endeavor to please you with every action."

She smirked at him, then held her staff high, tipping the end so it was pointed at the flames on the Jade Folly's roof. Closing her eyes, she whispered something to herself.

On the ground, the shouting stopped. Filip looked down to see the snow in the road rising like snow in reverse. He stared, mesmerized, as Aury raised what looked like all the snow from the entire length of the road, then pressed it together into a ribbon of sparkling white, all refuse from horses and humans left below.

Filip started toward Aury, but she held up her free hand. "Not you. I can't handle you being closer right now." Her blue eyes blazed like the base of the hottest fire. She was glorious.

Aury lifted her staff higher. The massive ribbon of snow shot at the roof in a rush of wintry air. That much icy snow would destroy the beams and bring the whole thing down. "Aury!"

She shivered, and her eyes briefly closed as she pulled back on her staff like she was holding a set of reins. The snow shifted and spun, only half of it falling in a great heap on top of the flames. A hiss rose along with the steam of the fire's death, and the dragon roared beyond the city walls.

Source help us and keep that fantastic creature in the wilds.

"Aury, you did it!" He ran to her side, drinking up her smile and the delight in her gaze.

"And you're not dead. Progress!"

A cheer came from the road below, and they leaned over the edge to wave to the people. The roof was still smoking, but with the thatch so wet from the weather, the fire hadn't done too much damage. The owners of the Jade Folly were still in business.

Aury glanced at Leofric. Did she know him? "Eh! About that bet." She whirled, then planted a kiss on Filip's mouth.

A fire hotter than the dragon's flame seared his lips and shot down his body, lighting up every inch of him. His fingers found her waist, and he tugged her to him, ready to return the kiss, but she pulled away gently, her eyes half-lidded.

"I believe Prince Filip is owed a gold piece!" She laughed loud, her eyes sparkling as they stared at Filip.

"I'd give it up gladly for another round of that." His voice was embarrassingly husky, but he found he couldn't care about his pride.

"Another round of dragon riding and fighting fire? I think we've had enough excitement for one night."

He jerked her to him, pressing his body into hers as the crowd let out another cheer. His skin lit up, and his chest tightened as his breath came more quickly. She felt like velvet-wrapped flame in his arms, and he wanted to burn for eternity. Her lips parted as her gaze brushed his mouth, his cheek, his neck. Her throat moved in a swallow, and she too was breathing fast. She could deny it all she liked, but indeed, she wanted him as much as he wanted her. Every one of his elven senses told him so.

A bang preceded the appearance of the top of a ladder and Costel's mop of red hair. "Since your dragon took off, I thought you could use a hand down."

Filip tried to be angry at the interruption, but Costel's kind smile damped the frustration in his body and soul. He broke away from Aury completely and started toward the ladder, throwing an unreadable smile to her over his shoulder. Let her come to him again. "Thank you, Costel. Your timing is impeccable."

Aury coughed a laugh behind him, and the sound warmed Filip's heart.

As he climbed down, he caught a gold coin thrown at him.

"This isn't over, Prince Filip." Leofric gave a curt bow, then turned on his heel and strode down the road, the rest of Godwin's men at his back.

CHAPTER 34

Aury didn't sleep that night and only managed a few hours each night for the next six days. The memory of Filip's body pressed to hers and the brush of his lips... Her face flushed hotly, and she shoved the feelings deep into the dark recesses of her heart and mind. He was not her future. She would determine her own fate. No amount of desire or fun would get in her way.

Hilda pushed back the bed hangings. "They're here."

It was the morning of the Mage Trials.

Gytha opened her palm to reveal a piece of spirit agate blinking in the morning light that pierced the frost on the window. "I forgot I had this sewn into an extra cloak. This will aid you today."

Aury wasn't sure why a piece of fae stone would help a mage, but she'd take all the luck she could get. She climbed stiffly out of bed, sore from the long hours of training in both magic and fighting. The Masters of the Order of

Darkfleot rode through the courtyard below the windows, their horses' hooves loud on the cobblestones.

Today was the day. If she failed to receive top ranking, her dreams of becoming a Magelord would be drowned forever. Not only would she be forced to live married forever to a man she hadn't chosen, but the Matchweaver would attack her again, and if she survived the attack her parents refused to acknowledge would come, Aury still wouldn't have true freedom.

She had to destroy these Trials. She had to devour the competition. She had to rule the fields today or die trying.

After Aury washed her face in cold water and dressed in her Darkfleot tunic, Gytha shoved the spirit agate into her trouser pocket and showed her teeth. The fae's war tattoos were dark under her pale sleeves and highlighted the movement of her fingers as she fisted her hands.

"Give them raging rivers, darling," Gytha said. "Ice that stops them in their tracks. Burn them with your cold and brilliant power."

Aury's heart stirred, and she grasped Gytha awkwardly, hugging her. "Thank you," she whispered. Sweat gathered at the nape of her neck. Despite what she had learned at the fae court, she trusted Gytha. She couldn't help it.

Eawynn joined in on the hug, grabbing Aury in an embrace from the side. "Beat the trousers off them all, Mage Princess!"

Hilda looked on, smiling like a mother in a painting. She reached out a hand, and Aury took it, horrified to realize her eyes were filling with tears.

"Thank you, all," Aury said. "You've been here for me day in and day out since we left the Agate Palace. I can't say I forgive anyone for what happened at the court, but here—here, you have been truly wonderful."

Wiping her eyes, Aury accepted her staff from Hilda. She gave them one last wave, then left to face the day.

PUSHING ERRANT THOUGHTS OF FILIP AWAY EVERY OTHER moment, Aury ate breakfast with Sunniva and Cuthbert, the annoying nickname fellow. The hard-boiled eggs and porridge weren't fancy, but they were filling and would give them strength. Aury reached for a carafe, wanting whatever hot drink they were serving to warm her middle before heading into the cold training field.

Sunniva's green and blue eyes flashed as she leaned over the table. "It's Prince Filip's favorite tea for breakfast drink this morning."

"Source above, I can't get away from him."

Cuthbert's thick forehead bunched. "I'm sorry?"

Maybe it was best not to spill her frustration about personal and royal matters everywhere. "I said, I can't get away from tea. My ladies keep serving it to me, and I loathe tea. I'd rather have hot cider or watered wine."

"Right." Cuthbert went back to eating as Sunniva gave Aury a look that said *I know what you're talking about, but I won't say a thing.*

"Do you like the tea?" Aury asked Sunniva, giving her a grateful smile.

"I do. It's called *dinte de leu ceai.* I have no idea what that means. It tastes slightly bitter, but cleansing."

Aury was curious what it tasted like, but she had to

keep Filip out of her head, so she stuck with the watered wine the servants brought in crockery pitchers.

"It's funny that the vicious Hatchet loves such a calming drink," Sunniva said. "Of course, I did hear about the powerful fruit brandy he brought to the king on his first night here. Were you there, Aury? Of course you were."

Pressing her eyes shut, Aury tried to change the subject. "What is up first for the Trials? I know we're to show off basic skills, but to whom and how exactly?"

"Master Daw." Sunniva sipped her tea.

Cuthbert shivered. "I'm not ashamed to say that man frightens the piss out of me."

Sunniva nodded as they stood to leave. "He is fairly evil to everyone. Except the horses."

"I might get along with him, then," Aury said.

"You do prefer the stables to games in the great hall at night, don't you?"

"I do."

Cuthbert's large form pulled to a stop, and he jerked his chin toward the side doors that led out to the training grounds. "There's Daw now."

The Master mage walked quickly, black eyes unblinking and his hair pulled into a loose knot on top of his head. He had wide-set cheekbones and a wiry, slim build. His staff appeared to be made of the same kind of wood as Aury's— white oak. Daw passed them without so much as a nod, and they continued outside.

The Masters must have ordered all the fields cleared of snow, because only a slim layer of white lay over the mud of the training grounds.

"And there is Master Malle," Sunniva said.

"She's pretty." The woman had light brown skin and large, expressive eyes that seemed to dance as she spoke to Finn and Mildred.

"Aye, well, here's the truth about Malle. Looks sweet. Will destroy you," Sunniva said. "She has failed one hundred twenty-three mages in her career here."

"All right, then. I'll remember that." Aury pushed a fallen lock of hair behind her ear. Her face was damp with perspiration. *Goddess Nix, get me through this,* she silently begged.

The Masters had divided the mages into four groups, and Sunniva and Aury were placed side by side in the first row. Everyone had their staffs and faces that showed everything from determination to desperate fear.

Mildred raised her staff, and all talking ceased. Malle and Daw stood beside her now, their gazes chilling.

"First row, you will start your day here. Good luck to you all. Remember what you have studied, what you have learned thus far. First, you will move the water from the trough before you into the trough between Masters Daw and Malle."

About half of the mages failed to accomplish the task. Sunniva managed it neatly, her ability to calmly control her magic impressive. Aury completed the task, but her second trough was fuller than the first. She'd accidentally multiplied the water, and Malle's sharp gaze said that the Master had taken note of her lack of control. But she had passed.

"One down, two to go, right?" she asked Sunniva.

"Right. This second one will be about freezing and

manipulating water in some wild way they come up with. Something we haven't strictly practiced, no doubt. I hear horror stories about this next one all the time during the games in the evening."

"And that's why I prefer the horses. They don't get me nervous ahead of time."

Sunniva grinned. "It's not a bad strategy, keeping your worries at bay for a while. I bet you've slept more than I have because of it."

Aury seriously doubted that she'd had more sleep than Sunniva. A certain elven prince kept crashing into her dreams and waking her up with feelings she had to work very hard to suppress.

Sweating in full now, Aury followed Sunniva to an adjoining training field where Finn and two other mages stood on a dais talking in hushed tones.

"Ah. There's Master Royse." The woman Sunniva spoke of was powerfully built, dark-skinned, and she held a staff made of a rosy-colored wood. "Everyone loves her. Great tips. Quiet. Kind. She won't let you get away with anything on the field though."

"I wouldn't want her to."

Sunniva agreed. "Beside her is Master Hann."

"He is..."

"Incredibly tall."

"That's not what I was going to say." She wanted to say he could melt the northern ice cliffs with just that body. The man was a joy to gaze at. Only Filip's arms rivaled Hann's in appearance and the look of power. Aury bit her lip. If she allowed herself to appreciate Filip without fear of the consequences, she would have to admit Filip was actually the most attractive man she'd ever seen. Frightening, but altogether knee-weakening.

Hann tugged at his beard, studying the mages streaming into rows for the Trial.

"Well, you might enjoy staring at Master Hann until he barks at you," Sunniva said. "I've heard he is a real bear to please."

"Fabulous."

"Today, you will attempt two forms of water magic." Finn's gruff voice carried over the rows of mages as he gestured toward a massive labyrinth of water flowing through freshly dug and stone-lined canals on the western side of the fields. The Silver River fed the labyrinth's curved roads of water, a wooden irrigation system bridging the distance between the river where it passed beyond the castle and this field. They'd put quite a lot of work into this Trial, and now the sounds of hammering and shouts of workers over the last few days made more sense. She'd thought the Darkfleot staff was only making winter repairs on a part of the castle grounds she had yet to visit.

"First," Finn continued, "you will force the water to burst its boundaries and flood the entire area surrounding the labyrinth."

The dais on which the Masters and Mage Finn stood now made sense. The rest of them were going to be very wet the remainder of this cold, winter day. Aury could push the water from her boots and trousers with magic, but it was a concise and exacting chore, and she needed to conserve her energy. Granted, she had more energy than most, seeing as she hadn't keeled over after freezing the class or any of that. But still. She wouldn't be wasting power on drying herself off unless it was life or death. A little discomfort would—

"There's the prince," a voice whispered behind her.

Aury's heart kicked a rib. What was he doing here? He had to leave. She couldn't work with him standing around. Sure, she'd managed well enough with the dragon's fire, but it had been a tough thing. She'd nearly made everything worse by shooting three cartloads of flying snow and ice into the tavern.

Wearing his black training leathers and his hatchet at his belt, Filip strode across the field like he owned the place—goddess Nix take him—eyes flashing, legs long and well-muscled. The winter breeze tousled his ebony hair as he jogged up the dais steps and spoke to Master Hann. They were about the same height, but Filip had him by an inch. Hann crossed his arms and cocked his head as Filip spoke, Finn leaning close to say something, his arm waving. Royse's mouth moved, and her gaze roved the grounds. Then her gaze landed on Aury.

They were talking about her.

Filip looked so very elven beside the others. In addition to an occasional incredibly quick movement, his flesh had this subtly muted sheen to it, like marble, and his eyes seemed to glitter. He had to leave. Now. Could she speak up, or would they fail her right on the spot for trying to take advantage of her place as princess?

Hann broke away from the conversation and addressed the mages. "Prince Filip has volunteered to stand beyond the labyrinth and do his best to fight through the flood you are able to raise. You will work in groups of ten. Let us thank the prince for serving the Lore mage units in this manner." Hann raised his staff to Filip and bowed his head, the rest of the mages mimicking the gesture.

"No way. I have to get him out of here," Aury hissed under her breath.

"Why?" Sunniva touched Aury's arm gently.

"Because every time he's around, my power goes wild."

"Not every time."

Aury rolled her eyes, exasperated with herself and the entire situation. "Nearly."

Sunniva raised her hand in question to the Masters. "Excuse me?"

"Sunniva! No. Just...don't. I don't want to act like I'm a princess who can get her way in all things."

"But you said—"

"They might fail me," Aury said.

"What is it?" Royse asked, her voice spreading from the dais to where they stood in the front row.

"Nothing. Apologies." Sunniva grinned and shrank back into line.

"Thanks anyway," Aury said.

Finn grouped Sunniva and Aury with Cuthbert and a handful of mages whom Aury had seen doing quite well in striking. She wasn't sure how good they were with magic though, as most of them had varying training regimens from hers.

Filip glanced at Aury and winked before walking purposefully toward the far end of the labyrinth. Aury glared. He was going to ruin this for her. Of course he was. It was in his best interest to keep her ambition quelled so they could marry and he could be a prince of Lore as well as Balaur. Well, he had another thing coming. She wouldn't let him rattle her. She would have him begging for air before this Trial was over.

"You're going to snap your staff in two if you grip it any harder," Cuthbert whispered, eyeing her white-knuckled grip.

"Better than a prince's neck."

"What?"

It was a good thing Cuthbert couldn't hear for shite. "Nothing. I was just saying I don't like the idea of being judged in a group."

She fell into line beside him and Sunniva at the end of the labyrinth. Filip was removing his vest, sleeves, and tunic. Of course he was. The man loved being half naked.

"And why is he disrobing?" Her teeth ground together.

"I assume it's so his entire uniform doesn't suffer from the water?" Sunniva retied the black ribbon holding her knotted hair at her neck.

"Right."

CHAPTER 35

Filip tried to focus on Aury's voice within the mess of noise from the running water and the many humans lined up around the field.

"...he disrobing?"

He chuckled. "To watch color rise to your lovely cheeks, *amant*," he whispered.

Aury's group of mages held their staves aloft, and the ethereal sense of magic sifted through the air. The water bubbled and spilled over the canal walls, spreading in all directions instead of directly in Filip's path. He used the error to stride across the first canal, only wetting his oiled boots to the ankle.

"You'll have to do better than that, mage warriors!" He started toward the next loop of canal work, Aury's focused glare keeping him warm in the cold wind. "Fight me, love. You'll need the strength at the pass. Let that power fly."

She wouldn't hear him, but he couldn't help speaking to her like she was by his side. It was painful how much he wanted her here, not allowing one quip of his to slip by unmatched, tossing her head like a wild mare, her sage scent intoxicating more thoroughly than any brandy.

Aury's head turned, and she shouted something to her fellow mages. The water near the outermost canals slithered across the ground and rushed him.

"Aha!" He grinned, leaping to the right and dashing forward, his movement faster than any human's. It was rather fun showing them up from time to time. Their arrogance was second only to fae and could use a little taking down.

The Masters on the dais shouted a warning, and Aury thrust her staff in Filip's direction. The water rose higher and higher, the tips of the small waves hissing with water magic. Filip drove immediately left, Aury corrected—her magic quite obviously running the show—then he lunged toward the center. The mages' wave crashed to his left, drenching him soundly but not stopping his progress. He ran straight at Aury, unable to stop grinning at the challenge in her eyes. He could see her properly now, and he'd have her in his arms in only a—

Suddenly, water thrust from the canals and swallowed him like a great beast. Choking, he rolled in the wall of water they'd raised under Aury's direction, and he tried to relax, knowing he was well and truly bested and they'd release him shortly.

Still upside down, he sucked a breath as a window opened in the magicked water. Aury stood there, looking incredibly smug, then she pulled back on her staff, and her unit of mages did likewise. The wave fell away slowly until he lay on the ground before her, soaked and defeated. Aury loomed over him, a lock of her silver hair falling over one bright blue eye.

"You lose, elf."

He propped himself on one elbow and didn't for a moment miss the way her gaze lingered over his stomach and waist. "Or did I?"

She huffed and spun to see Master Royse, Master Hann, and Mage Finn arrive to congratulate the team. Hann gave Filip an unnecessary but kind hand up, then patted him on the back.

"Nicely played, Prince Filip."

"It was exciting and a bit humiliating, but I asked for it," Filip said. "I might need a break before resuming my attack."

"Take your time. We have plenty of not-so-willing volunteers." He held out a hand toward the spot where Filip had started. Two guards threw Godwin into place.

Filip laughed. "I like how you think, Hann."

"I'm always trying to get in good with the royals."

Filip gripped the mage's shoulder. "I'd be forever grateful if you'd give me a good word with the princess," he said very quietly while Aury spoke to another mage. "I'm sure she values your opinion as a Master of Darkfleot."

"Consider it done."

Aury's group broke up and moved away from the labyrinth of canals so the second unit could work. Once a servant had retrieved Filip's undershirt and leather vest, Filip jogged to Aury's side.

"You could at least wring me out, Mage Aurora."

She walked faster, her friend Sunniva keeping pace and

eyeing Filip like she might back up Aury if the need arose. Filip gave Sunniva a smile, and she grinned back.

"Fine," he said, tugging his undershirt on. "What happens now?"

"We have a short break," Sunniva said.

"What's next in your Trials?" Filip asked. "Perhaps scrying? I'm headed inside for a hot bath."

Aury's head whipped around, her cheeks pinking. "We don't scry in the Trials."

"Actually, I heard a rumor," Sunniva started, but Aury smacked her not-so-lightly, and she clamped her mouth shut.

"I'll see you soon, then, mages." Filip touched a hand to his belt in the Lore fashion, then walked off, slinging his wet hair back and feeling the hot gaze of Aury on his back.

CHAPTER 36

Betwen the second and third round of the Trials, Mage Mildred had all the testing mages sit for scrying.

Yes, scrying.

"Excuse me, Mage Mildred," Aury said from her stool, determinedly not looking into the copper basin of water in front of her. "Is this the usual order of events at the Mage Trials?" She adjusted her staff in the hook on the table beside her.

Mildred walked over and glanced into Aury's bowl. "It isn't. I suggested it to the Masters upon their arrival. Since you discovered scrying quite accidentally as I did, I thought perhaps it would be wise to discover if anyone else has this affliction, er, skill. It might be of use in the coming battle. Hopefully, others can control their scrying more than you and I."

Aury wanted to ask if Filip had been in the area when Mildred had brought up testing the rare skill, but Mildred had already marched toward Master Daw, who was trying his own hand at the magic over a mazer bowl.

A dried bunch of faegrass and lavender had been tied and tucked between Aury's and Sunniva's bowls, along with a tiny copper cup with a smoking chunk of charcoal.

"Light your faegrass and allow the magic-touched smoke to settle on top of your portion of river water," Mildred instructed.

Sunniva did so first, then handed the faegrass to Aury. "All I'm going to see is how red my nose is from this cold. I hope this isn't part of the true evaluation."

"I'm sure it's not. Mage Mildred said the talent is hardly ever seen." Gritting her teeth, Aury moved the smoking bundle over her bowl. She chanced a look into the reflection there, her hands trembling as she remembered the Matchweaver addressing her the last time she'd scried.

"Focus on the surface of the water, then let your gaze relax as if you've had far too many cups of cider," Mildred said to a few chuckles.

Daw walked behind the mages on Trial, his hands clasped behind his back.

Mildred could scry; she knew this wasn't something one could control. Why were they wasting time on this when, from what everyone claimed, scrying was an incredibly rare ability? Aury glanced at Daw. His lips were a tight line, and his black-blue Masters tunic and cloak whipped in the wind as he went from mage to mage, peering over shoulders, eyes quick as a bird's. She supposed he hoped to glimpse whatever someone might scry even though she'd never heard of such a happening.

They were searching for something. Desperately searching.

Aury breathed deeply, then took up the smoking faegrass from the table, once again drawing the curling tendrils toward her water with her fingertips. The smoke curled on the surface like a sleeping cat. She could see nothing.

"Try whispering to the water," Daw said, earning him a sharp, curious glance from Mildred. "I saw that work for a scryer once during the war."

"Show me what I need to see for my people," Aury said, pushing her quiet words across the smoke.

Sunniva touched her arm and gave her a quiet, "Good luck."

The tendrils slipped to the sides of the bowl to show a dark circle of flat water. The sun's rays blinked through the surface as they had the day she'd seen Filip. She remembered his saber-shaped grin, predatory and alluring. She'd never asked him who he'd been fighting that day.

The surface shimmered, sparkling gold, then cleared to show a shape moving in the dark. A man, maybe? Arms shifted, and the sound of water dripping touched her ears. The vision remained too dark to see properly, but a new sound, incredibly faint, whispered through the air. Voices rumbled somewhere beyond the focus of the vision, but the man in the center was singing.

"'I once met a girl with a bucket,
I found and gave her a locket,
But when she smiled at me,
The chain broke free,
And I was left holding her bucket.'

That doesn't even make sense, Drago! Are you sure you translated it correctly?"

Suddenly, the vision cleared, and there was Filip dousing his hair in the bath, rivulets running over his pointed ears, his face, throat, the corded muscles in his shoulders... Heat poured through Aury's body as he stood to reach for a bathing sheet, water coursing down the length of him. He was beautiful. Powerful. Graceful. A fine elven warrior prince who wanted her as his own.

He paused, hand over the folded length of linen, head tilted, staring into the water, directly at her.

"Aury? Any chance you're there?" He grinned wickedly.

She spun on her stool, her heart skipping. How had he known? He'd somehow heard they were going to scry, but had he sensed her there? Was that possible, or had he only guessed? Either way, she was dying.

"Aury, you all right?" Sunniva asked.

Master Daw hurried over. "What did you see? Mage Mildred told me you have the ability."

She was incredibly glad for the stool underneath her. Her legs would've been far too shaky to hold her upright after seeing Filip like that. He could never know that he had guessed right and that she'd seen him there.

"I...uh...the vision was too dark to see," she said in answer to Daw.

"But something shook you. Please share what you did see with us. Anything might help."

Aury's face couldn't grow any hotter. "It wasn't anything to do with the Wylfen, which is what you want us to glimpse, yes?"

Daw straightened. "Yes, Mage Aurora."

Whispers rose from the mages, but no one else seemed to have seen anything.

"I'll try again," Aury said, tipping the faegrass over the bowl. The smoke sank and spun over the surface. "Maybe now that I know what we need to think on..."

"There have only been twenty-one mages capable of scrying recorded in history. We know so little. The ability is unpredictable."

Aury stared at the water, and Daw's voice faded along with the field and the tables. A new shape flickered between the plumes of smoke. Her stomach twisted as she tried to will it into a clearer form. Jagged lines moved up and down, undulating rows of... She had no idea. Beside the shape, rough triangles of white. "I can't tell what any of this is. Mage Mildred, can you look into my bowl? Does that work?"

Mildred stood behind her with Daw. "No, that's not possible. It comes from your mind and blood connection."

The vision fizzled into an erratic display of wind-rippled water, and then there was nothing.

"I wish I had good news, but I couldn't make a thing out of that mess of a vision."

Sunniva took a cup of hot cider from a servant's tray and handed it to Aury. She took it gratefully and sipped the warm liquid, inhaling its comforting scent of cinnamon and apple.

Mildred and Daw traded a look, then Mildred announced, "Adjourned for one hour. Watch the candles in the great hall for time. The clouds are coming in."

The sun dial in that field was indeed struggling to show

a shadow as Sunniva and Aury left the scrying and headed for the castle's side doors.

"Are you ready for the final Trial?" Sunniva slipped past Aury, then turned to face her.

Aury shook off the flood of Filip-filled images currently drowning her every thought. "I could say I'm not at all ready, seeing as the Masters will surprise us."

"No doubt. They'll want to see our military techniques in action, but they'll put some strange barrier up or add in a consideration that thwarts basic forward aggression," Sunniva said.

Aury set her jaw and stared straight ahead, already visualizing victory. "But I'd rather say I'm going to kick arse all over that field."

Athellore and Gwinnith would be there, and she wanted to show them what she could do. She couldn't quite untangle why. To prove she was powerful and should be permitted to make decisions on her own, yes. To make them worry that she would grow more influential than them in the eyes of the Lore people. Did they remember the old Magelord title and its rewards? Would they guess that was her impossible goal? But there was more to her desire to prove herself in their eyes. She wanted to throw off their grasping hands, the reins they had tied around her just when she'd escaped the awful fae court and its bindings. She wanted there to be no doubt in their minds that she was not the sort of person anyone could control. Maybe that was a juvenile wish, but it was her deepest longing nonetheless.

CHAPTER 37

Filip found Aury standing at the bottom of the wide stairs in the grand foyer, tapping her foot like mad. He wanted to tease her about possibly seeing him in the bath—he'd felt a strange sense that she'd been scrying—but she looked vexed and not in the fun way.

He bowed, extending a leg and sweeping his arm across his middle. "Mage Aurora, may I be of service to you? Are you waiting on Mage Sunniva and Mage Cuthbert?"

She glanced at him but looked away, her cheeks pink. "I'm trying to figure out what I saw in the scrying bowl."

"Now that you mention it..."

She smacked him in the stomach with her staff.

"Oof."

"Focus, Prince Filip. This is serious. Master Daw and Mage Mildred had us scrying in an attempt to see what the Wylfen are up to. My vision in the water was nothing I could untangle. It was too hazy. But just now, I realized the outline of the shapes in the water might have showed the mountains and..."

"Yes?"

"A dragon."

"Our dragon?"

"I don't think it is ours. I believe it's another one. Longer. Leaner."

"Well, my elder brother, Dorin, is higher in the mountains, and he is tracking dragons. There are certainly clutches of the lovely beasts up there. Maybe more than we know."

"But I was focusing on the Wylfen."

Arc's Blessed Light. Filip stumbled back a step. "You think the Wylfen have a dragon at their side."

"I don't know, but if they do... If my horrible guess is right—"

"That's how they are making progress. The dragon is melting the ice and snow when they need it and providing fire for heat. Aury, do you realize what this means?"

"We're on the wrong end of a dragon."

"Is there a right end?"

She laughed and made a weeping sound. "What can we hope to do against a trained dragon, a unit of Wylfen warriors, and only goddess Nix knows how many of their mad scar wolves?"

The room spun for a moment, then Aury took his hand. Sparks flew up his palm and along the underside of his arm. He met her gaze.

"Are you all right?" Her blue eyes were soft, genuine, their usual fire banked in her fear and concern for him. At least, he hoped that was what was happening. The woman confused him at times.

"I'll make it through." He kept a light hold on her fingers, hoping she wouldn't pull away. When had this wooing gone from a duty to his people to a hope in his heart? "We need to meet with the king and queen."

"I knew you were going to say that."

He rubbed a thumb over the back of her hand. "I wish I could have been there for you when you were at the fae court, living a lie. I would have at least worked to make you smile once in a while. I'm glad you had Prince Werian. He's a good sort, isn't he? I met him years ago when he visited Balaur, and then we caught up when he was here to see you."

"He is the only family I have," she said quietly.

Werian, of course, wasn't kin to her, but Filip knew what she meant. It was how he felt about Costel, Drago, and Stefan.

"I can't talk to my evil parents right now though. It's time for the last of the Mage Trials."

He respected that. "I'll go if you wish it. I can relay what you saw."

"Yes, please do. I don't think we should wait to inform them. We must begin plotting a defense right away, some attack against the dragon. Has your brother had any luck when he's come up against a dragon that didn't care to be tracked?"

"I'd love to say yes, but dragons always win."

She exhaled, gently pulled her fingers from his, then ran a hand over her face.

"I'll go. Good luck on your final Trial..." He nearly said

amant. But today, he wasn't going to push her. She had enough to deal with. "I will attempt to be there to cheer you on."

He bowed, then turned to leave, but she grabbed his sleeve. "Wait." She looked as surprised as he was that she'd stopped him. "Thank you for challenging me during the flooding of the labyrinth. You gave me focus. I am loath to admit it, but it's the truth."

Light spread through his chest, and he took her arms gently. "You see? We make an amazing team. Why do you fight our betrothal?" He shocked himself at how very true it was. It was the truest thing he'd ever said. This wasn't simply about saving others—which was of course noble— but it was also about himself. He wanted her, and he wanted her to want him. Her quick wit, her courage...

She pulled away. "I can't marry you, Filip. The Matchweaver reminded me of the curse. She isn't happy to just let it go because I'm grown and the insult to her place in the world was years ago. I scried her, Filip. I saw her, heard her threaten both of us."

Filip's mouth parted, but no words would rise to his lips.

"And you can guess how much power I had over my life at the fae court as they pretended I was some ill-born half fae," Aury said. "I'm not above cleaning and running errands for others, but when I'm ordered around night and day, tripped and scratched *by accident* in dark hallways, creatively lied to in a million ways... I want my life to be my own. Fully. I want to get up in the morning and lead Lore as I see fit. I don't want to have to check with a husband every time I make a decision. I want freedom."

The light in his chest flickered, then went dark. His mind threw every reason they needed to be apart at him like sharp stones. The Matchweaver's anger at her parents —he couldn't endanger her life simply because of the love growing in his heart. Her desire for freedom—he understood that feeling. As a prince, he definitely understood.

He cleared his throat. "No matter what your parents or mine say, I will sign an agreement that the Balaur armies will support Lore against any and all Wylfen attacks on your promise that my country will gain the formerly agreed upon farmland. I will help you argue your case without the marriage," he said. "But considering there is already a signed agreement, I doubt this can work out. Know that if it comes down to my people starving or your freedom, I choose my people."

She gripped her staff. "I...if it comes to that, I choose your people too. I can't have anyone starving for me and my freedoms. Even if the Matchweaver tries to kill us both."

His heart pounded in his ears. He loved her so very much. The ache of it was going to kill him.

CHAPTER 38

Aury wanted to close the distance between them, but she held herself back. It was better this way. This was what it was to be a princess. She felt oddly sure of herself, well aware what decision was to be made here. Stepping closer, unable to help herself, she stared into his lightning gray eyes. "It's nothing against you. I hope you know that."

His hand hovered at her side as if he wanted to touch her. Her body hummed like it could feel his hand's intent.

"You no longer hate the vicious mountain elf?" He grinned, showing a sharp tooth, but a sadness hid under his mirth.

"Men like Godwin and Leofric or whatever his stupid name is are the vicious ones, spreading hate."

His jaw tensed, and he raised his chin, looking down at her. "I've done terrible things in war. I won't lie to you."

"They were necessary. I saw you with that dragon youngling. You wouldn't hurt a creature unless you had to.

I had it all wrong, and so do most of the folk in Lore, unfortunately. Our agreement will shed light on that foul prejudice."

He held out a hand. "Our parents will never agree to this unless you have some magic of negotiation up that sleeve of yours, but I swear to lead the elven army in Lore's defense against the Wylfen if you swear your kingdom will hand over the agreed-upon farmlands."

They needed seals and signatures, but for now, this was binding in its way. She clasped his hand tightly, their sigil rings—his a constellation and hers a stag over water—reflecting the light from the windows. "So agreed."

Turning on his heel, he left, and she felt empty. Hollow. She leaned on the bannister, legs weak.

Pushing the ridiculous feeling away, she looked up to see Eawynn approaching through the main doors of the castle. She handed Aury a slip of parchment. The fae's face was pale as milk.

"What is it?" Aury unfolded the note to see handwriting she didn't recognize.

You will immediately cease arguing with your betrothed in public, Daughter, or you will be pulled from Darkfleot and the wedding will take place tonight rather than on the morrow.

-Your Mother, the Queen

"I guess our antics on the field were noticed." Aury sighed. Gwinnith had witnessed them discussing the scrying and Filip's bath perhaps. She swallowed hard.

"What is it? Can I help?" Eawynn asked. "The messenger was horribly rude when he delivered this to Mage Mildred. I was standing right beside her. Hardly bowed at all. A nod, really. I assume it's from the king and queen?"

"It is." Aury tucked it into the pocket of her trousers and started outside, Eawynn on her heels. She didn't want to talk about it. About anything.

ON THE TRAINING FIELDS, THE MASTERS HAD ORDERED the snow cleared away, but a new round of white flakes cascaded from the steely skies. A series of enormous, water-filled troughs stood around rises of ground. Lore warriors—both water mages and those without magic—stood in units beside the earthworks.

Aury shuddered.

The scene could've been taken from the sketches in the war scrolls she'd studied during tutoring. The field was set up to mimic the way water mages battled on open ground, and now she'd have to prove she could do the same.

A shire horse pulled a trebuchet onto the field while servants ran back and forth from the Masters' dais, relaying information to the captains and warriors. Voices called out orders. Some fighters checked their elven bows and the blunt-tipped arrows they'd been provided. Others brandished their wooden training swords, the weapons as large and nearly as menacing as true Lore broadswords.

Hilda, Gytha, and Eawynn stood beside the dais along with the team of Darkfleot healers, ready for when this Trial grew bloody.

"You know what's not here?" Aury said to Sunniva, who was counting something under her breath.

"What?"

"Anything that can stop a dragon."

Sunniva spun around, her green and blue eyes wide. "No more unclear and frightening comments, Aury."

"I'm fairly certain the Wylfen have a dragon. A big one. In the mountains."

A sigh like a whimper left Sunniva. "You saw this when you were scrying."

"How did you know?" Aury asked.

"Well, first you saw maybe...Prince Filip?" Sunniva said. "Because you turned a shade of red that does your middle name justice."

Aury shut her eyes. "Please stop."

"And then you saw something that made you hold your breath for a count of thirty-two," Sunniva said, "which is wildly unusual. For humans. Elves and fae—well, at least your fae cousin-not-cousin—hold their breath more often."

"You have it right."

"About Prince Filip or scrying the dragon?"

Aury exhaled. "All of it."

A triumphant smile flew over Sunniva's mouth before it fell flat. "This is foul news indeed."

"Quite."

THE FIRST THREE GROUPS THAT FOUGHT SHOWED bravery and cunning, using quick spellwork and physical agility even if they ended up losing the mock battles.

Aury watched Sunniva compete in the fourth group. When Master Malle and Master Hann directed a troop of warriors to loose blunted arrows at the same time they sent twenty-five soldiers with wooden short swords and practice daggers after them, Sunniva and her team threw the water from the troughs into the air. Most of the arrows were dragged off course before hitting anyone. But half the soldiers pushed through the deluge and began striking with the mages on Trial. Sunniva slipped behind a rise of earth and pointed her staff, her lips moving in that way she had when she was counting.

"What are you up to, friend?" Aury whispered.

"I hate to be petty, but this is a bit unfair," Cuthbert said beside her. "You and I are in the last group. We've learned from watching these earlier mages fight, seen what the Masters like to try in an attack."

Aury knew why. She glanced at her royal parents in the stands, their curtained box above the other spectators. They wanted her to show courage and bravery as a princess, but they didn't want her to be seriously injured. Not for a second did she think it was because they loved her. But they needed her for the marriage to Filip, to gain the elven army, and to keep the crown in the family and out of the Witan's hands. Filip's face showed then from the dark recesses of the box. His mouth moved as he surely told them about what Aury had seen in the scrying bowl. Athellore and Gwinnith stood, eyes widening. And yes, there it was—their reaction to the knowledge that death in the form of an enemy-trained dragon would meet them in the upcoming battle. Gwinnith dropped into her seat. Athellore's hands fisted at his sides, and his chin dropped, his eyes closing.

Filip found Aury's gaze, and her heart stuttered. Was he preparing to tell them about his agreement with her, about calling off the wedding?

The crowd gasped, then Sunniva was lifting her staff, and the troughs behind the advancing attackers spilled large globes of spinning water into the air. The spheres of water crashed into the swordsmen and thrust them to the ground. One of Sunniva's teammates froze the water, and the soldiers slipped and fell as they tried to stand. Their practice weapons were trapped in the thin layer of ice.

"Victory!" Master Royse shouted from the dais.

Aury applauded, but even though she was happy for Sunniva and impressed with her tallying of where to throw the water spheres to impact the forces the most, Aury didn't feel the joy like the others seemed to. This was nothing like going up against a dragon and a troop of trained scar wolves. Everything today now felt like an enormous waste of time. They'd be wiped out by fire the moment they arrived with no time for flooding, freezing, or throwing water.

Filip was no longer speaking to the king and queen; in fact, their box was empty. She scanned the crowd only to find them beside the Masters and Filip on this field's Trial dais.

Servants dashed around, gathering weapons and resetting troughs. Healers tended to the bruises and cuts from the fighting.

Master Hann turned away from Athellore, Gwinnith, Filip, and the other Masters to face the crowd. "It's time for the final group to show their proficiency in battle. Time is short. We will begin immediately."

Stomach twisting and hands sweating, Aury took the lead, and the other mages who hadn't yet been tested trailed her into the icy mud of the mock battlefield. It was time to earn her rank as a mage captain or fail miserably. If she didn't win here, she would be forced to bid farewell to her slim chance at becoming a Magelord, at escaping a life of doing exactly what her royal parents decreed. There wasn't enough time for her to attain the rank of captain in the more traditional military process. She had to seize this quick route to a high rank or end up wholly trapped as a powerless princess, just waiting for the crown.

CHAPTER 39

F ilip left the dais to join Costel, Drago, and Stefan, who were gearing up to gather in their assigned units for the Trial battle.

Costel slid a blunted short sword into his belt. "You look like you missed your tea this morning."

"Ha, Costel. No, truly, there is something..." He waved them closer, keeping an eye out for eavesdroppers. His men could know this, but it was up to King Athellore and Queen Gwinnith as to who else learned of the dragon.

He gave them every detail he had.

Drago looked to the skies. "We're well and truly cursed."

His choice of word made Filip wonder if he should have told them more about the Matchweaver and what Aury had said of the curse. But they had enough to deal with right now. Later, he'd tell them. Soon.

Stefan ran a hand through his tangled hair and blew out a breath. "What's the plan? Is there one?"

Filip took a wooden hatchet from one of the armorers. "They've no more idea how to deal with the beast than we do. I wish Dorin were here." Dorin's level head and experience with dragons would be highly valuable. "I'll send one of our retainers to Balaur and see if we can get Dorin out of the higher reaches and back home to help."

He and his men joined the less organized crew ordered to filter through the attacking units aimed at Aury and her mages. His forehead broke into a sweat as she took a position behind one of the middle rises of earthworks. She had to do this, to prove herself to her kingdom—he knew that—but it didn't make it much easier to see her come up against this formidable force. Her fierce eyes blazed as she raised her staff.

And then he had to focus on his role here, driving toward Aury's group, taking out the soldiers who were serving as guard to the mages. Careful to remember this was a practice battle, he struck one large, red-haired man between neck and shoulder with the wooden hatchet, and the man nodded defeat, dropping a mace to the ground and raising his hands. He exited the field as Filip pushed onward.

Beside Costel, who was quick with his wooden short sword, Filip brought down two more men. Costel feinted a high strike, then went low, acting at cutting the backs of two warrior's knees. They were down.

A blow hit Filip's side, the pain minimal. He turned to block a second strike from a bulky woman.

"Filthy elves," she muttered, dodging Filip's wooden hatchet.

"A friend of Godwin, are you?" Filip ducked her swing,

keeping his moves human-speed. It would be good to know what was going through this soldier's head. "The archery has been a grand addition to your country's fighting skills, don't you think? And come now, you must see how simple and smart the orangebranch distraction will be for the wolves."

"Godwin saved my life twice over." She raised her hand, and Filip came up behind her.

"My men have probably already saved your life again with the new techniques you'll bring to Dragon Wing." He hit her spine with the dull edge, and she growled, releasing her weapon. "Now, be a good warrior and apologize for digging that trap for me and my men." It was a guess that she'd been directly involved, but her fervor plus the fact that she'd been with Leofric at the Jade Folly made a solid conjecture.

She spat on the ground, very close to his boots. "I'd do it again."

He flipped the hatchet and hurried off; they were nearing Aury and the mages. They'd have to root these soldiers out of the army. He couldn't go to battle with warriors who would stab him in the back when given the chance. Plus, such behavior as that had to be punished. He was a prince and would be leading troops. He couldn't permit this type of disrespect and expect the rest to follow him.

Whirling, he joined Drago and Stefan to defeat five swordsmen. Judging from the way Filip's boots were sinking into slush, Aury's unit seemed to have escaped the arrows with a similar water wall technique carried out while he was busy fighting. The field was soaked. But the attacking force was on them now, and Aury and her mages needed to do something fast, or this was going to end in failure for them.

A tiny, evil voice inside him said, *if she does, she might be more inclined to wed you.*

He burned that thought from his mind. Aurora Rose was a natural warrior mage if he'd ever seen one, and to wish her failure here would be the same as wanting to see her spirit crushed. He never wanted that. Even if he couldn't have her fierce self as his own.

Three large warriors bore down on her, and she shouted.

Even though this was a Trial and not a real battle, he began to run, panic rising in his chest.

CHAPTER 40

Magic sizzled in Aury's veins, and the sight of Filip's concerned face made her heart beat like a war drum. She willed the scant snow on the muddy field and the flakes trailing from the clouds to lift and hold.

"Together. Together," she whispered, imagining the frozen water to compress more tightly to become ice.

A sword arced toward her head, and another mage blocked it with their staff as three more soldiers lunged. Aury had to release her hold on the water and spin to avoid a blunted slash. She struck the advancing man with her staff, hitting his knee a bit harder than she probably should have, and he tumbled away from the earthworks, face squeezed as he endured the pain. The two others stabbed at her. She avoided the first by dropping low, but the second hit her across the temple.

Filip's voice rose over the din. "Foul! No strikes to the head!"

She struggled to her feet, dizzy from the blow, then raised her staff sideways with both hands and stopped a fresh hit from the same man. She spun away and released one hand's hold on her staff, her hair fluttering free of its ties, and extended her arm to strike the man in the back with her staff's end. The man went down, arms raised to show defeat.

Head pounding, she faced the onslaught. Warriors raised swords and bows against mages who drew water from the wet field to create liquid hands that dragged their opponents to the ground. Surrounded, Aury focused again on the snow, held it in place, then gasped as the snow blinked, shining in the beam of sunlight through the clouds —the flakes had become ice, and they hung in the air, ready to do her bidding.

"Shields!" Filip called out.

The warriors lifted their charges as Aury flung the ice at them just like the mage in the Forest of Illumahrah had during the last war.

The ice hit the shields hard, and shouts of surprise and pain filled the air. Never before had the magic drained her like it had Mildred and the others, but with the head strike and the fighting, she was spent. Her knees hit the ground, and the world went black.

She woke to Filip's face. He was speaking quickly in the elven language, his eyebrows drawn tightly together. His arms held her, warm against the chill of the ground, and his gaze found hers, sending a jolt of gratitude through her. He helped her sit up.

"The Trial's over. You passed," Filip said, smiling now, his eyes glittering. He glanced away, then back at her. "The Masters are approaching. Can you stand?"

She nodded, and he helped her up, Sunniva dashing over to give an arm too. Costel, Drago, and Stefan stood nearby, their eyes wide with shock.

Master Royse grinned widely. "Mage Aurora, that was impressive."

"To say the least!" Master Hann clapped, looking around and nodding as the crowd of onlookers joined in.

In the stands, Athellore and Gwinnith stood in their box applauding.

Master Daw studied her with his dark eyes. "Now, we award ranking. Take a break to clean the mud from yourself," he said to everyone. "Report to the great hall in one hour."

Despite her terrible headache and the nausea stirring her stomach, Aury felt light enough to fly. She had passed and impressed the Masters as well.

And Filip defended you, a voice inside her head whispered. A bubbly feeling rose in her chest, and she squeezed his hand.

"Thank you," she said before she could think better of it and her plan to avoid further entanglements with him and her rebellious heart.

He lifted her fingers and kissed her wrist with soft lips and hot breath. Lovely chills spread across her skin as his gaze met hers. "My pleasure."

AFTER A RUSHED WASHING AND CHANGING WITH HILDA,

Gytha, and Eawynn's help, healing, and cheerful encouragement, Aury hurried back to the great hall for the rankings.

Sunniva had saved her a seat, and Aury slid into place as Master Malle's voice rang across the room.

"Stand, Mages." She held up her hand, her black hair shining in the light from the long, stained glass windows.

The trainees stood as one and stepped away from their tables, staves in hand.

Malle went through the assignations in order of arrival to Darkfleot. Sunniva earned first lieutenant, and Aury cheered her wildly. Malle left Aury's results for last. "Mage Aurora, please approach."

Hilda smiled from the back of the room where she stood next to Gytha and Eawynn, who were whispering furiously. Aury gave them a wave, and all three waved back enthusiastically, the gesture endearing considering the fae's tendency toward coldness. Not that those three had ever fit the stereotype.

Gytha jerked a thumb toward the other side of the room.

Werian stood in the corner near Filip. Aury's chest warmed as Werian gave her a nod and Filip raised a fist, smiling.

Aury's boots sounded too loud on the floor, and sweat gathered along her tunic's collar. The Masters, Mage Mildred, Athellore, and Gwinnith stood on the dais, looking down at her. Her father shifted from one foot to the other while her mother chewed her lip. Mildred gave her a quick grin.

"Mage Aurora," Malle said, "for the feat of commanding

ice shards on the fields as well as scrying and calling water, we name you a captain of the armies of Lore."

Everyone applauded as Athellore came forward to pin a purple-glazed pin onto Aury's tunic. His lips were a line in his yellowed beard. "Welcome to the world of war and rule, Daughter. I hope you feel the full weight of your duty to our people and to our agreement with Balaur." Before she could say a thing, he faced the crowd. "Tomorrow at sunset, you are all invited to the wedding of Mage Aurora and Prince Filip. It is hereby decreed by myself, Queen Gwinnith, King Mihai of Balaur, and Queen Sorina of Balaur. The royal couple will enjoy our Lore traditions here before departing for a ceremony in Balaur in just two days. Three cheers for our princess!"

He almost sounded as if he liked her. Aury raised an eyebrow and gave him a curtsey, following with one for Gwinnith, who was clapping so hard her hands looked ready to fall off.

Holding her head high, Aury tried not to make eye contact with Filip. The wedding was going to happen. She couldn't stop it. But she could still escape the bonds of matrimony if she proved herself in battle somehow. Werian would be there. He could deem her Magelord with a sacrifice. He would, she knew it. She only hoped he wouldn't have to give up anything too costly for her. He'd already done so much.

She managed to keep from looking toward Filip as she rejoined Sunniva, then her fae ladies, and let the crowd carry her from the great hall. She spotted Werian in the happy chaos and waved to him. Thankfully, he wasn't with Filip. The confused feelings she had for him...

"Werian!"

Two grinning women tried to keep him from passing, *accidentally* pressing closer in the crowd. Werian survived their coquettish strategy and slid close to give Aury a chaste kiss on the cheek.

"Hello, Cousin," he said. "So you've managed the first step to becoming a Magelord."

Sunniva was talking noisily to Cuthbert, but she paused and gave Werian a quick curtsey. Cuthbert bowed, then went back to their conversation.

"I have." Aury tapped her fingers along her staff. "Werian, you'll be at the battle, and I was hoping..."

"Of course, I'll sacrifice and speak up for you, darling."

A rush of gratitude rolled over her, and she grabbed him, hugging him tightly. "But please don't sacrifice anything too costly."

"Ah." He patted her back. "Your freedom to choose your mate and your safety from the Matchweaver are worth at least some of my princely treasure."

Aury wasn't so sure that staying clear of Filip would appease the Matchweaver, but she tried to be hopeful like Werian. "Did you hear about what I saw in the water?"

He wiggled his eyebrows. "Filip in the bath. Though I love the ladies, I can imagine that was a fine view indeed."

Going red-faced, she smacked him hard in the stomach. It hurt her hand. "No. I saw...a dragon," she whispered.

His gaze flicked to Sunniva, then to the doors of the hall where Athellore and Gwinnith stood talking to the seasoned captains and Masters. "I did," he said very quietly. "But we must keep that knowledge from the lower ranks until we have a plan in place."

"Agreed. We don't want to strike too much fear into their hearts before the march to Balaur."

"Prince Filip says he and his men will slip away after the wedding at Balaur and attempt to pick off the Wylfen to lessen their numbers and give it their best to find any weaknesses in the dragon. He is going to send for Prince Dorin, who knows a thing or two about the majestic beasts."

They talked all the way to her chamber, where Hilda, Gytha, and Eawynn served them mulled wine and biscuits. Werian wanted to know every detail about her ride on the dragon youngling and the developments in her magic. Thankfully, he seemed to sense that she didn't want to talk about Filip anymore, because he didn't bring him up again. Once the evening was through and they'd eaten their way through a full-sized roast and two pomegranates each, Werian stood to leave, the hearth's light washing across his black horns and purple-tinged ebony hair.

"I'm glad to see you blooming, Aury Rose."

She gave him another hug. "It feels good to grow."

"You do forgive me, yes?" Hope lit his familiar eyes.

"I forgave you the first night you visited."

"You said as much, but I wondered if it was true."

"It is," she said. "I'm still trying to forgive the king and queen, but I don't know if that will ever happen. I went to them about the Matchweaver." She'd told him about the scrying and the letter. "But they refuse to see her as a threat now that I'm of age. It's foolish."

"Completely. I have spies set on the Witch. She hasn't made any movements toward you yet that they have been able to detect, but then again, they didn't know she sent a spelled letter, so perhaps my spies are better at drinking my ill-gotten rum than watching witches from trees."

Aury laughed and walked him into the outer chamber, where Hilda, Gytha, and Eawynn were talking up the handsome guard. Aury swung the door open for Werian.

"You'll make a lovely bride tomorrow even if your heart isn't in it," he said.

Gytha snorted from across the room. "She does look her best when she's angry."

"Shut it," Aury barked, grinning despite herself.

Werian gave her a bow, then walked away. She was glad he would be at the wedding at Loreton Palace's chapel. Sunniva would be too and the fae ladies, of course. She had her people. She could do it.

"Arc's teeth, don't look like you're going to hang on the morrow," Gytha said, dragging Aury to her room. Eawynn shoved a cup of herb-scented tea into her hands while Hilda turned down the bed. "Filip is not so bad even if he is a mountain elf."

"It's not Filip, and you know it." Aury took two sips of the tea, then let them pull off her tunic and help her into a sleeping gown. She was too tired to fight it and decided to just enjoy the perks of being a princess for a moment. "You do know that, right?"

Eawynn and Hilda sat on the bed while Gytha leaned on the bedpost, her tattooed fingers toying with the curtains.

"It's your blessed freedom," Gytha said.

Aury slid between the sheets and wiggled her aching toes. Every inch of her ached despite the healing the fae had given her earlier. She didn't want to ask for more. "Why do you say it with that tone?"

Hilda traded a glance with Gytha. "Freedom is a myth," Hilda said, her voice prim. "One is always following some outer influence. Fear, love, desire..."

"Curiosity," Eawynn added.

Hilda nodded.

"But I simply want to make my own decisions as often as I'm able without doing damage to my people or those I care about."

"It's commendable," Gytha said. "You're seeking to reduce your limitations. But consider what you are sacrificing for these decisions."

"Please stop lecturing me. I'm no child, and I'm certainly not your child." Aury softened her voice. "But thank you for helping me heal tonight and for being here during this training. I don't want to think about how much more difficult it would have been without you three. Truly, thank you."

Gytha kissed her hand, Eawynn gave her a tight hug, and Hilda smiled as she pulled the hangings closed.

"Get your sleep, Mage Captain. Tomorrow you must do your best to smile as a bride."

Aury groaned and shoved her face into her pillow.

CHAPTER 41

T he day of the first wedding, the one in Lore, Filip's requested tailors arrived for the tenth time. They dressed him in the clothing they'd created especially to help him look the part of a Lore royal rather than the vicious elf so many saw him as. He wore a long, loose tunic in the particular ruby red the royal family here preferred. Over that, he had the bulkiest golden belt and ornamental sword in existence.

"How did this custom come about?" he said to Costel in the Balaur tongue so it was less likely to anger the tailors still fussing around him. "It's not as if one would ever or could ever fight with this hunk of metal around their waist."

Costel huffed a laugh. He was already in his groomsman tunic of blue and red stripes. "I don't think they worry about having to fight on their wedding days."

"Lucky Lore folk." He wanted to ask what Aury would be wearing, but it felt like a silly question, so he held his tongue. Instead, he finished a cup of his favorite tea and watched the tailors lay out the rich red cloak he'd wear on his way from his rooms at Darkfleot to Loreton. There was to be a royal parade through the bustling town that crowded the old outer bailey, the walls that stood when Loreton Palace was a true castle and not as lavish as its current form. "I'm going to look like a giant cherry riding about," he said to Costel.

Drago and Stefan wandered in, dressed like Costel, in stripes with their hair slicked back in the Lore style. "And we'll be your jesters, Prince Cherry."

"This hair..." Stefan touched his own head and sighed. "I smell like a field of lavender."

The tailors waved in three new men who held crockery and combs, the scent of flower and tree oils clouding around them.

Filip held up a hand. "No. This is where I draw the line. You're not putting that in my hair. I will succumb to becoming the royal pomegranate, but I refuse to let you slick back my hair. A man must have his limits."

Stefan, Drago, and Costel laughed at the looks on the tailors' and hairdressers' faces. Costel escorted the lot out of the chamber, and Filip was left with his men alone.

"I have a gift for each of you, as is customary here."

"Gifts are a great custom! We should adopt that one in Balaur so I get two instead of the one," Drago said, rubbing his hands together.

"Your greed knows no bounds, my friend." Filip handed them each a wooden box carved with both his sigil and Aury's.

The men opened their boxes to find a chain and coin-like pendant. Drago removed his, eyes glittering as he examined the silver carvings.

"Wear this only if you swear to protect Princess Aurora even above me, your prince. It is your choice, and we won't speak of your decision either way outside this room."

Stefan traded a look with Costel, then came forward and knelt before Filip, holding out the chain. "I swear to protect Princess Aurora with my sword and my life."

Filip slid the chain over Stefan's head. Stefan kissed the pendant, then tucked it inside his undershirt.

When he stood, Costel took his place. "What if the marriage—"

Stopping his words with a hand, Filip said, "Even if something goes awry, I want to protect her to the best of my ability. As I said, you don't need to swear to this. I won't hold it over you. I promise you that, friend."

"I don't want to protect her over you, but I see the love you hold for her. If she dies in battle, you will suffer greatly."

Filip didn't say a word. The truth of Costel's phrase stabbed him as surely as a blade.

Costel held up the chain and repeated the oath, then Drago did as well. Filip set the pendant on them, feeling better by the moment. Soon, they'd be off to Balaur and away from the temporary safety of this kingdom. Aury would be in lands she'd never visited, then she'd be on the battlefield. The idea of it scared him more than he'd ever admit because he knew exactly what it was to fight the relentless Wylfen.

· · ·

THEY RODE OUT OF DARKFLEOT'S WALLS AND MET AURY and her retinue beyond the drawbridge. Unlike Filip, Aury definitely did not look like a cherry or a pomegranate. Atop her golden mare, her midnight blue cloak fluttered around her, the fox furs at the collar brushing the proud line of her jaw. The ruby bodice of her gown fit snugly against her body, and her blue eyes shone like sapphires. A massive crown of gold and silver had been braided into her thick hair. The deep pink light of the sunset glowed across her cheeks and smooth forehead.

He couldn't seem to get his tongue to work.

She raised a silver eyebrow. "Don't you look...rosy."

A laugh burst from him, and he smoothed his tunic. "I heard you enjoyed the cherry scones at this week's breakfasts, so I followed their lead."

A smile spread across her glossy lips, but she didn't meet his eye. "Shall we, then?" Without waiting for him to respond, she nudged Goldheart with her heels and left them all riding to catch up.

Avalanche snorted like he was insulted at their treatment.

Filip rubbed the horse's neck as they broke into a gallop. "It's not you. It's me, my fine fellow."

By the time they reached Loreton and were greeted by countless townsfolk, melancholy had swept over him. The sight of Aury slowing so they could ride side by side in the parade, the sprigs of pine and dried oak leaves showering down from rooftops where her people gathered... He wished this would last, wished this were really a marriage he could fully enjoy, and the ache of his wanting rang through him, deep and powerful as the city bells that announced their arrival.

Children shouted Aury's name as Filip, Aury, and the rest of the wedding party rode along the tight and twisted roads. Aury threw coins, while Gytha and Eawynn tossed small, wrapped packages behind them. Hilda held Aury's staff, the older fae's reproachful gaze on him. He still hadn't spoken to Aury. He didn't trust his voice.

Aury glanced his way, one hand rested lightly on her pommel and the other taking more coins from the pouch tied to her saddle. Her lips parted, but then closed again. She didn't appear unhappy about this, but he knew she was. She'd told him repeatedly. Tonight, they'd have to share a chamber, as was customary, so Costel had informed him. The agreement had to be sealed with an assumed consummation of the marriage. But Filip wouldn't press her, wouldn't do so much as attempt to hold her hand tonight. He was no foul beast. If he were such a criminal and inclined to attempt anything, she'd probably drown him or slice his head from his shoulders with spelled ice.

The parade concluded, and soon the multitude of horses were clomping over Loreton Palace's drawbridge and past the flying ribbons on the wedding poles. Passing the portcullis, the party rode through the courtyard, which smelled of the smithy's forge, then on to the royal chapel that sat beside a cluster of dovecotes.

Aury dismounted before he could offer up a hand in good manners, and then they were entering the room where their doomed marriage would begin, dead before it started.

CHAPTER 42

As she entered the gorgeous chapel and gave the nobles seated in the pews a tentative smile, Aury's heart and mind tangled into an absolute mess. Filip walked beside her down the aisle, still completely silent and thoroughly unknowable.

What was he thinking right now? Did he think her the worst sort? Or did he truly understand that she had to escape this union to be the person she wanted to be? She wished the day felt cold or perhaps dull, but it had been absolutely beautiful riding beside him with the crowd cheering and the feel of Filip's gaze, burning and bright.

At the same time, the whole event thus far had been incredibly uncomfortable. Every time his leg brushed hers, they nearly spoke, but instead fell into strange silence. The people were so excited, and it felt quite wrong to be going through these sacred motions, fully aware she'd do everything in her power to break the upcoming bonds.

But this day could never be deemed cold or dull. Never.

At the end of the aisle, Hilda took her cloak, and Costel removed Filip's. Aury and Filip knelt at the base of the tree carved into the back wall, their knees between the wooden roots scored between the painted green and brown tiles of the decorative floor. The tree had been crafted in the likeness of the Sacred Oak of Illumahrah, and its glazed green oak leaves spread across the wall, reaching toward the black beams of the high ceiling.

A door opened from the trunk of the tree, and a hook-nosed priest emerged. He set a hand each on Aury's and Filip's heads.

"Welcome to the day we have longed to see for so very, very long."

Athellore tapped his staff on the floor lightly, something she'd seen him do to show approval. Gwinnith gave Aury a tight look, mouth pinched and severe.

Filip was focused on the priest, his face devoid of the emotion she'd glimpsed during their ride through Loreton.

She chewed her lip and let the priest's words flow over her, a jumble of phrases about partnership, care, and blessings.

Filip took her hand gently, his gaze flicking to her. His fingers twitched, the tips brushing her wrist and scattering sparks down her arm. Chest lifting in a hurried breath, she watched his full lips part. His gaze burned like the sun.

Athellore handed the priest a small wreath of pine sprigs and twined ivy.

"The Source blessed our lands with the power of the ancients long ago. The earth magic of Vahly, the air magic of Arcturus, the fire magic of Nix, and the water magic of Lilia.

To these gods and goddesses, we give thanks. With this wreath symbolizing goddess Vahly's binding and the Source's will, we join these two souls." The man set the wreath around Aury and Filip's joined hands, and the tingle of magic spread from the pine needles into her skin, a remnant of the old earth magic that had once reigned in Lore, then called Sugarrabota. "Speak your vows," the priest ordered.

"I vow to love and protect until I have no breath," Filip said.

She repeated the traditional words, her heart beating too quickly.

A bird chirruped, and everyone looked up to see it flying lazy circles in and around the beams, its feathers as gray as smoke. The priest hissed a prayer and touched his necklace, no doubt a goddess Vahly pendant with a golden oak leaf and sword.

"It's just a bird," she whispered to Filip, pushing her worry away.

"A bird inside can be a harbinger of doom in Balaur. Perhaps it is here too?"

The priest hurriedly concluded the ceremony, then urged them to stand with a touch on their shoulders. "A kiss to seal the union."

The memory of the kiss on the roof of the Jade Folly ran through her head, and her body grew warm.

Filip studied her face like he was asking permission. She closed the distance and pressed her lips to his, feeling the intake of his breath, his surprise at her initiating the kiss. His chest pressed against hers, and his hand found her lower back, holding her to him. She melted against him, feeling every slope and line of his body, her breath coming faster. She pulled away.

The crowd cheered and threw tiny pine sprigs as they walked back down the aisle to leave. At the arched door, the bird flew in her face, spreading its smoke-black wings wide and letting out a crow like a growl—an unnatural sound. A finger-length of yarn fluttered into her hand. The bird twisted, then soared outside before exploding into a sparkling cloud far above them.

Aury's heart beat in her throat, and her hands shook. "Did you just see that?"

"I did." The whites of Filip's eyes showed all the way around his gray irises. "And that's yarn."

Sweat rolled down her back as he slipped the marriage wreath up his arm and stared at the piece of yarn.

"It has to be a warning from the Matchweaver." She twisted to see where Hilda was with the staff. The fae had been caught up in the crowd behind them.

Filip opened his mouth to say something, but the nobles pushed them merrily into the courtyard, then onward to the palace's great front doors.

She scanned the bustling crowd, searching for threats while Filip whistled, bringing his men close. They didn't draw their blades but kept hands on hilts, ready for whatever the Matchweaver Witch might have in store. Every face—except those of Filip's men—was split wide with smiling or singing, eyes wild with excitement for the wedding.

Fingers reached through the royal guards and Filip's men to try to touch her and Filip, happy townsfolk who wanted a bit of the wedded pair's luck.

Little did they know.

Filip circled her waist and thrust something into her grip. Her staff. "Keep this on you. Just in case," he said.

Hilda must have managed to shove it through the chaos to him. "Thank you." The warm hum of magic helped her fight the press of the people. At last, they were inside the palace, and the royal guard shut the double doors to block out the celebration and any possible threat. Aury leaned against a stone pillar, exhausted.

The doors opened again, and Athellore and Gwinnith entered, pine sprigs in their hair and crowns shining.

"What was that, Prince Filip?" Athellore strode up to Filip, and they all started toward the great hall.

"I called my men close because of the Witch's warning."

Gwinnith spun to look at Aury. "What warning?"

"The bird. It dropped this." She held up the yarn.

Athellore waved it off and hurried ahead. "So it was nesting in the chapel. What of it?"

"The bird exploded in the sky. Exploded, dearest father. That is not exactly normal behavior for a black bird. Wouldn't you agree?"

He glared, stopping at the great hall's entrance, the Loreton sigil banner hanging above his head. "You didn't see that."

"Really? I didn't? Huh."

Gwinnith stood between them. "You are both dazed from the crowd and the wedding magic. That's all..."

Aury shook her head. "I'm done here." She pushed past them and found her chair at the feasting table.

The herald announced the first group of nobles, who were immediately escorted in, cutting off their argument.

How could Athellore and Gwinnith be so blind? Such arrogant fools. They were going to get her and Filip killed.

Filip took the seat across from her. He poured her a glass of wine and handed it over. "Drago, Stefan, and Costel will remain on guard, specifically watching for sign of witchery."

Hilda, Gytha, and Eawynn hurried through the side archways of the hall and dipped curtseys to Aury. "Costel told us what happened. What do you wish us to do, Princess?"

She would never get used to ordering fae around. "Spread out, taking positions between Prince Filip's men," she whispered to Hilda as the nobles chatted and offered congratulations to Filip over the table. "And make certain no messages enter this hall since she's proven she can use parchment to attack."

They rushed away as the hall filled to the brim with richly robed men and women. The Order Masters were notably absent, as they'd left already for Balaur and the armies gathering there for the march to Dragon Wing Pass.

The feasting passed in a blur, and Aury wasn't sure what she had said to half the people who spoke to her.

Athellore stood. "Now for the bride and groom's dance! Music!"

The lutes and pipes started. Filip walked around the table and bowed. "Princess?"

She took his hand and let him take her waist, the touch equal parts thrilling and worrying. The king and queen looked on, their expressions irritatingly approving as she and Filip circled and stepped to the music. The thump of her heart nearly drowned the music and conversation. Fear of the witch, anger at how she was being sold off like a cow, and the confused feelings she had for Filip had spun a storm inside her.

"This is a nightmare," she whispered.

"Happy wedding day to you too," Filip said wryly.

She squeezed his shoulder. "You know what I mean."

"Oh, the fact that the most powerful witch in the world just sent you a message that basically states she remains bent on killing you and possibly me as well?"

"Yes, that's part of it."

"Whatever comes," he said, his mouth now at her ear, sending shivers down her neck, "we face it together."

Her eyes closed as the storm spun and spun and spun around her heart and mind.

What would the end of this day look like?

CHAPTER 43

T he dancing in the great hall of Loreton Palace went from staid and formal with practiced steps and nasal conversations to chaotic circles of stomping feet and slurred voices.

Hands grabbed Filip and Aury, dragging them out of the great hall.

"To the bedchamber for the royal couple!" Several Lore men and women shouted and whooped as they lifted the couple onto their shoulders.

Filip had enjoyed a few cups of strong fruit brandy himself, and so he found a smile easily for the crowd despite all. Aury was rolling her eyes and blushing furiously, which he adored though he was wise enough not to tell her that.

"Aye!" A low voice shouted. "It's time for another type of dance!"

Laughter echoed off the walls of the corridor leading to Aury's chambers. Drago, Stefan, Costel, and the fae ladies kept a close spot in the riotous party, their faces grave and their gazes alert for threats.

The crowd threw open the chamber doors and unceremoniously dumped Filip and Aury both onto the bed, where Aury let out a huff of air, barely catching her staff, which someone had tossed through the air.

Hilda and Costel took the lead on clearing the raucous folk from the room and shutting the doors to leave Filip and Aury alone.

Costel's reedy voice cut through the noise in the corridor. "Go on, you lot! Leave them be!"

"I heard there's another cask of fruit brandy in the courtyard!" Drago shouted.

"Smart man," Filip said, rolling to an elbow as Aury set her staff against the side table. Her hair had fallen out of its braids completely, and the long tresses spread over the duvet like a sheet of pure silver.

Aury swung her legs around but remained seated on the bed.

Filip stood and took an armless chair by the crackling fire. Garland of pine and ivy hung across the mantle amid a slew of candles and ribbons. "I'll sleep here. My men will take watches outside the door so we can rest. I assume your ladies will be there from time to time as well?"

"Indeed." A layer of meaning slid through her tone, but Filip let it go, knowing it was doubtful she'd share whatever it was.

"Good. They will be far better at spotting magical attacks, I'd wager."

Aury went to the frosted windows and pulled the curtains across so only a sliver of the outside was visible.

Moonlight traced her nose and forehead. She looked like the statue of the ancient goddess Vahly, proud and fearless. "I don't know if I can sleep at all. The Matchweaver's attack could come at any second."

"Or in twelve hours. Or not at all. You might as well attempt to rest. Not only do we have a second ceremony upcoming in Balaur, but we have a battle to win."

Her eyes shut briefly. "Tell me what to expect in your kingdom, Filip. My ladies know very little of Balaur, and my mother's instructors were decidedly vague."

Filip reached for the tea service some amazing soul had set out on the table by the fire. He poured a cup and downed its warm contents, trying to get his throat to work properly. "We are a bit more...intimate with our weddings in Balaur. And more primal, I suppose you could say."

Aury's fingers tightened on the curtain, but she kept her gaze on the moon. "I don't think I like where this is headed."

Shrugging, Filip leaned back in the chair. "We are mountain elves. What can I say?"

Leaving her post at the window, Aury reached for the tea pot, but Filip beat her to it, filling her cup and handing it over. She sipped and stood on the far side of the fire, her side to him. "Should I prepare myself for bathing in blood fully naked as the rumors go?"

Tea sputtered from Filip's mouth, and he laughed, that same sting he'd felt when her court had tittered at his Balaur-style bow hitting him again. "Oh, definitely. Lots of blood baths. Loads of them."

She turned, a dimple showing in her right cheek. "Good. I'm feeling a bit violent."

"Toward the Matchweaver or..." He grimaced and pointed at himself.

"Athellore and Gwinnith. It's their stubborn foolishness that has put us both at risk. They'll let me become a captain, but they won't listen to me about a curse that affects just me." Her lip curled as she glanced toward the window.

She wasn't going to get any rest in this mood, and the trip to Balaur would be rigorous. He stood and gestured to the chair. "Please, sit. I won't make any untoward advances despite our doomed nuptials, but I give a deadly shoulder and neck rub. Will you permit it?"

She plopped into the chair in a rather unprincesslike movement. "Sounds great, actually."

He was surprised. He'd half expected her to storm out of the room and go for Athellore's throat. She pulled her hair to the side and scooted forward in the chair. That space behind her was very tempting, but did she want him to sit behind her or did she expect him to stand and awkwardly massage her from above? Shrugging, he slung his leg over the chair and slipped into the seat. She gasped slightly, turning to look at him with those big, blue eyes. Her tongue touched the corner of her mouth. He very much wanted to taste the tea on her lips. His legs pressed against her hips and thighs. This might have been a rather embarrassing error on his part because his body was now rather well pleased at its current position. He closed his eyes for a moment and thought of frozen ponds and incredibly ancient old men.

"You all right back there?" There was a heavy layer of teasing in Aury's voice.

"Just plotting my attack."

"Does the bloodbath begin so soon?" she asked.

He popped his knuckles. "Shoulder rub, then gore."

She almost laughed. He was learning this huff of an exhale was her habit when she was amused but wished she weren't. "Like breakfast, then beheadings?"

He lifted the fine hairs from her neck, enjoying how her skin pebbled at his touch. "Exactly so."

Setting his knuckles against the smooth line of tendon running along the top of her shoulder, he began to knead.

"Dearest Arcturus in the heavens," she moaned.

He chuckled. "Satisfactory thus far?"

"Less talking. More massaging."

A laugh bubbled from his throat as he circled his thumbs down the outside of her shoulders, then smoothed his hands swiftly up her neck.

There was a loud knock at the door, then the oaken entrance swung open to show Gytha, eyes wide. "Oh! Sorry. I thought...I worried. Never mind! Carry on!"

"No, Gytha!" Aury raised a hand. "It's not—"

The fae slammed the door, said something outside, then a cheer went up in the corridor.

"Lovely. Our audience has returned."

"And now they are even more full of brandy."

"I don't care. Just give me a few more moments with your fingers."

Filip froze, eyebrow lifting. "I—"

Aury stilled. "Not one word."

Pressing his lips together to hide his laughter, he began kneading again, rolling his knuckles and thumbs up and down her back. She melted against him.

"That's enough," she said, breathily. "I'm fine now. Thank you."

He slid out of the chair and went to her feet by the snapping fire. Goddess Nix, but she was beautiful with her gown rucked up a bit and the firelight dancing over her legs. She'd set her head against the chair and let her eyes shut. He had her fine, silken slippers unlaced before she noticed what he was doing.

"You don't need to do that," she said sharply.

"I know," he breathed over her ankle. "But I want to."

She opened her mouth to argue, so he quickly ran the heel of his hand under her arch. An unintelligible sound came from her throat.

He paused. "I can stop now, if you wish."

She pointed a finger. "Don't you dare."

Grinning, he worked the stiffness from her slender feet. He was winning this war, and the enemy didn't even realize the battle was on. He slipped a hand up her calf, massaging the muscles there, her gown dusting across his forearm. Dare he go further?

CHAPTER 44

A ury bit her lip, trying to keep from raining more praise on Filip for this foot rub situation. Goddess above, it was amazing. His hand shifted behind her leg, his fingertips brushing the back of her knee. He massaged her calf and looked up at her through his thick, black eyelashes. It was the same look as the one he'd given her before they'd kissed during the wedding. He was asking permission.

She swallowed and stared back, neither giving it nor pushing him away. His hand moved to her knee, and his thumb swept over the skin just above her stockings.

"Would you like me to remove these?" His breath touched her skin, and she shivered.

She couldn't do this. She'd promised herself. Imagine how pleased Athellore and Gwinnith would be if they could see them now. Imagine how angry the Matchweaver would be.

She sat up straight and slid her gown back into place, pulling her leg from Filip's gentle grasp.

He nodded and moved back, crossing his legs and glancing into the fire. "Would you like to use the washroom first?"

The loss of his touch and his gaze made the room colder. She stood. "Yes. Thank you."

When Aury was at last in bed and Filip lay out by the fire on furs, she tried to go to sleep. Every shift in his breathing made her heart jump pathetically with hope that he was about to say something that would solve everything or make her absolutely loathe him and therefore turn refusing him into less of a nightmare. Every inch of her body longed for the touch of those skilled elven hands. She could quite easily imagine how his body might feel wrapped in these sheets alongside her. She blew out a breath and turned over.

A rumbling sounded outside. The room quaked, and the teacups clinked in their saucers.

Filip was at her side, sword drawn. Cold with fear, she grabbed her staff as the palace trembled like the walls were about to fall in.

"It's her." Aury could feel it somehow, that slippery, snaking feel of the Matchweaver's magic. The crone might give love, but she could gift terror just as easily.

"My prince!" Costel's voice carried through the doors.

"We are well enough," Filip called back, remaining beside her. "Do you see anything?"

"No."

"The rest of the fools don't seem to notice," Drago said, his voice gravelly.

"Maybe it's isolated. She's hitting our room specifically," Aury said.

Filip adjusted his grip on his sword, his gaze flicked to her face. "I'm going to check at the window."

"Gytha!" Aury called.

"We are all three here," Gytha answered through the door. "We felt the magic, but it's gone now."

Aury swung the doors open to see her ladies and Filip's men armed and standing watch. "Rouse the palace guards and check the grounds, Hilda, Gytha, and Eawynn."

Aury peered over her shoulder to see Filip looking left and right out the window glass. He shut the curtains, then met her at the doors. "Stefan."

"Aye, my prince?" Stefan's hair was tangled, but his eyes were alert.

"Go with the fae. And make certain old Alfred knows what's amiss if you see him. We don't want them thinking you're on the wrong side of this."

"True. Good plan."

Aury hated that he knew some still saw elves as vicious and foul-minded.

They closed the doors, and Filip barred them with the sideboard. "I'm sleeping beside you, Aury. I won't try a thing, but I need to be close. Who knows what this witch will do?"

Aury set her staff beside the bed again and crawled under the covers. "Fine by me." She was too scared to worry about anything other than surviving this night, a night when she'd crossed the Matchweaver in word and deed.

For his part, Filip remained on his side of the bed. Aury

fell asleep watching the flicker of the fire in his watchful eyes.

A LOUD KNOCKING HAD AURY SHOOTING UPRIGHT IN bed. "Break your fast, lovelies!" Eawynn bustled in followed by three servants bearing trays.

Filip stood by the window, gaze distant and his fingers on the hilt of his sheathed sword. He looked as bright as the sliver of sunlight through the curtains.

"I guess you've been up for a while." Aury swung out of bed and rubbed her face. "You could have woken me."

"You needed your rest." Filip's words weren't flirtatious, but rather serious.

Eawynn's face went as red as the tunic Filip had been forced to wear to the wedding. "Oh, yes. Of course." She removed the lids from the trays to show steaming eggs, a rasher of bacon, and fresh slices of bread with butter. "And you'll need food to restore yourself for the coming ride. They're waiting on you in the courtyard already."

Fighting the urge to grumble, Aury stalked over to the plates set out on the sideboard that had been moved to its original spot and gobbled down most of the bacon.

"That's right. I'm sure you need your sustenance after last night." Eawynn giggled and started for the door.

"Eawynn, it wasn't like that."

She waved a hand. "You can deny it all you like, Princess, but before that terrible moment..." She shuddered, most likely recalling the shaking and the Matchweaver's magic.

"It was a shoulder rub, Eawynn. Don't get too excited."

The fae rolled her eyes.

"You learned that from Aury, didn't you?" Filip said as he snatched the last of the bacon and chewed it quickly.

Eawynn laughed. "I did!" She left them to their breakfast, her giggling trailing her down the corridor alongside Drago's and Stefan's deep voices.

"Did they find anything on the grounds last night? I'm embarrassed to say I fell asleep. They reported to you, yes?" Aury asked Filip.

"They did," he said. "No sign of anything amiss. I worry she'll strike during our journey."

The trip to Balaur would be cold and long, and now with the Matchweaver showing off, possibly deadly. But they had to go through with the ceremony in Filip's kingdom. Unless Aury could somehow claim the title of Magelord, she was trapped, and she wouldn't put the welfare of his people and hers in jeopardy for her freedom.

CHAPTER 45

The longest stretch of the trip to Balaur went well. One Lore guard suffered frostbite after falling asleep at his post, but aside from that...

Filip should've been feeling good about the endeavor, but he felt more like a mouse waiting for the hawk to strike. The Matchweaver was out there. Somewhere. He wished she'd come at them so they could get the battle over with.

They'd stopped at the Gryphon's Flight Inn, a crowded place that served better-than-average food. Filip trotted down the steps of the inn, then crossed the smoky main room, dodging soldiers, mages, and townsfolk. Costel, Drago, and Stefan sat drinking at a large round table in a dark corner.

Filip slid onto the bench beside Costel, and Stefan pushed a mug to him. The ale was tangy and welcome after a long day in the saddle. They weren't far from the mountains now, and thus far, the trip had been good. Aury had been unusually quiet, but it made sense. Weddings, war...there were a thousand reasons for worry in addition to the Matchweaver's threat.

"Still no word from Dorin?" Filip asked Costel.

Costel shook his head. "Our three messengers haven't returned."

Drago and Stefan exchanged glances.

Filip wished he could get some dragon help from his elder brother, but if it didn't come soon, it would be too late. "You three still good with leaving after the Balaur ceremony?"

"To sneak up on a dragon and a large band of bloodthirsty Wylfen and their trained wolves?" Drago finished his ale. "I wouldn't miss it for the world."

"How is your invention going, Costel?" Gaze flicking to the door of the upstairs room where Aury was talking with her fae ladies, Filip grabbed a slice of bread from a platter and bit into the chewy crust.

Costel removed a clay ball from his bag and set it on the table.

"Looks like a turd." Drago poked it with his eating knife.

Stefan chuckled, then whispered something into the ear of one of the serving women.

"I like elves," she whispered to him, loud enough for the table to hear.

"Glad I am of that," Stefan said. "Meet me upstairs when you're through here. Third door. I'll teach you all about our kind."

She kissed his cheek and hurried off, several of the surrounding soldiers gawking at her. It was interesting how they could celebrate his marriage to their princess but in day-to-day life, most of the humans still held a prejudiced view against elves.

Filip studied Costel's clay creation. "What's in this one?"

"Well, it's not filled. Can't have such a thing in here with this lot. It's only a mock example. But the real ones are packed with break powder encased in three smaller balls and goat's blood."

Filip raised an eyebrow. "Yum."

Costel gave him a glare. "The weak outer clay shell should explode on simple force of impact, then the blood will lure the dragon."

Stefan leaned forward, squinting. "And then the smaller balls of break powder explode?"

"Yes," Costel said. "The dragon will devour the snow where the goat's blood is spilled, then the break powder will explode and release its indigo gases, and if the Source blesses us, take the dragon into a serious stupor for a good three or four days, depending on its size."

Drago nodded. "Pretty smart, Costel. I wouldn't want to be the one carrying break powder though."

"They're packed in straw in my saddlebags."

"How many do you have?" Filip took another sip of ale. The door of Aury's room swung open, and his heart tripped. But it was only Hilda.

"Five. I set them up alongside the town mayor and his engineer right after we arrived."

Filip clapped Costel on the back. "You've done a fine job, communicating with them ahead of time with messengers and organizing this. Tough thing to accomplish on the road."

Costel grinned under the praise. "Thank you."

"We'll get a volunteer to carry them up the mountains," Filip said.

"I'll do it."

"Costel, no. You're too important to me. Not everyone can design a weapon to take down a dragon."

"They probably won't work."

Filip snorted. "Such a fine attitude."

"But really. They most likely won't, and you know it."

"I don't want you carrying them." He couldn't stand to lose Costel. "I'm pulling rank on this. I'll find a volunteer."

Drago cocked his head. "I don't want some Lore stranger on our mission."

Filip saw the wisdom in this. "No humans. They won't be able to keep up anyway. We'll be moving as fast as possible. We'll recruit someone willing once we're in Balaur. One of our own. Their family will be rewarded no matter the outcome."

"Agreed," Costel, Drago, and Stefan said in unison.

Stefan's friendly serving woman returned with a platter of cheese and cold venison.

They tucked in, and after a few more drinks, Filip made his way upstairs to find Aury sleeping in the one bed, sprawled out like she owned the place, which, in fact, as princess, she pretty much did.

Her shift had slipped off her shoulder to show smooth skin. She flexed her hands and sighed, and he snapped out of the spell she cast on him. With a quick peek at her subtly webbed fingers, he took the extra blanket from beneath the bed and unrolled it on the floor. His dreams weren't of dragons or war, but of a curtain of silver hair, his hands circling a slim waist, a velvet voice in the dark, and the feeling of being understood and loved well and truly for who and what he was, scars and all. When morning came, he stubbornly kept his eyes shut, longing for the dream to become reality.

CHAPTER 46

T he countryside, frosted and sparkling, spread out before them as they left the Gryphon's Flight Inn and rode hard toward the northeastern mountains and the kingdom of Balaur. Aury blew a strand of hair from her chapped lips as they galloped, Goldheart churning up snow just in front of Filip's mount, Avalanche, or, as he said it in the Balaur tongue, *Lavinā*.

With her staff strapped to her back securely, she smiled into the wind and welcomed the speed. The rush of cold wind and the challenge of staying a few hoofbeats ahead of Filip drove the fear of the Matchweaver from her mind. Her guard had given up their warnings a few miles back, realizing their princess would simply never listen. If the Matchweaver wanted to strike, the royal Lore guard would do little against the goddess witch.

They'd already stopped for sleep twice, and the

foothills were showing up now, sloping steeply in the near distance.

"You'll have to switch out mounts, Aury," Filip said, his voice a bit breathy from the riding. They trotted along, their words mostly snatched by the wind.

"Goldheart, he thinks you can't handle his mountain. What do you say?"

The horse tossed her yellow head and snorted, and Aury pet her neck, slowing a bit and glancing at Filip. "She disagrees, but I'm inclined to agree. I don't want to lame her with my wildness."

Filip's grin was becoming far too familiar and pleasant to her. "Incline is the correct word for it. How steep does the mountain get after just five miles in, Mage Sunniva?"

Aury had requested Sunniva posted temporarily by her side. She trusted Sunniva, and the woman was amazing with numbers and facts, not unlike Filip's man, Costel.

Sunniva's bay trotted up to them, Costel's chestnut gelding not far behind and the rest of the guard with Costel, Drago and Stefan included. Their horses were all of the mountain breed, stockier, larger, with tufts of hair at their hooves.

"What was that, Prince Filip?" Sunniva wrapped her reins around one hand in a manner that reminded Aury she was from the eastern province. Filip repeated the question, and Sunniva clicked her tongue, thinking. "I think I've read that the main route inclines around thirteen hundred feet per mile."

"That's right," Costel said, arriving with a grave look in his eye and his curly, red hair braided away from his face in the Balaur style.

Filip had done the same with his raven-wing hair, and his sharp jaw and slightly crooked nose stood out all the more. He was handsome in such an unusual way. Every time she looked at him, she expected not to be moved by his face or the way he turned his hands or twisted his torso, but every time she was taken aback by how her body responded to his appearance. The fact that he was a good man—a good elven prince—made him all the more appealing.

But loving him would mean more than just a loss of freedom. With the Matchweaver in play, such love could mean death. They were most likely doomed regardless considering the witch's response to Aury's declaration that she didn't want to wed Filip. The Matchweaver wanted to strike. Aury had no plans to encourage the violence and would do what she could to avoid it.

At the next village, a squat settlement meant more for trading than comfort or farming, Filip himself bought her a fine white mare with a mane like snowdrifts and a tail like the clouds on a stormy day. Aury forced her gaze away from the new horse to say a temporary farewell to Goldheart, who would remain in the village to await her return after the ceremony and the battle. If she lived that long.

She pressed her hands lightly against the sides of Goldheart's sweat-lathered head and set her forehead to the horse's nose, reveling in the velvet and whiskery feel. "I love you, beautiful girl. Thank you for always listening. I don't want to ruin you up there with all those vicious elves." Aury turned and gave Filip a wink. He chuckled, holding the reins of the white mare. She kissed Goldheart, then relinquished her to the stable master. "I will be back soon. Please treat her as you would me."

Filip leaned in. "She means by giving her ungodly amounts of bacon and letting her sleep in."

Aury smacked Filip, then snatched the white mare's reins.

As they made their way up the winding mountain trails, the new horse, *Călător*—which meant Wayfarer—swished her tail like she was at court rather than the side of a cliff. They stopped for camp, the last stop before Balaur, and Filip found Aury beside Călător near their fur-lined tent.

"A Balaur witch cast a spell on the tents during my great-grandfather's time on the throne." Filip found a handful of oats, and the horse lipped them from his palm.

Filip's people had brought the tents over the border and were now setting up to spend the night alongside the party. The rest of the Lore army would arrive soon, trailing Aury and Filip by a few days. After the ceremony, Filip and his men would head quickly toward the area where scouts had said the Wylfen had been seen. They would hopefully find a way to take out the dragon before the battle ensued.

Filip eyed the tents. "They'll shed snow and increase the heat of those inside three-fold."

Aury ran a gloved hand down Călător's nose. "That's incredible. I wish there were more witches who deigned to work for our court." Witches were rare, and their moods varied as much as their skill set.

Aury realized her hands were shaking. She looked at her fingers. With the heavy gloves, they were strange to her. She felt like she was in someone else's life, like she wasn't really here with Filip.

He rubbed her back and leaned close, concern pinching his lightning-touched eyes. "Costel made us a stew. Let's eat."

"You think I'm losing my nerve before the battle has even begun, don't you?" With a glare, she dared him to say it aloud.

A frown pulled at his full lips. "You're a new warrior heading into a battle with the one enemy your country has fought for ages. If you weren't showing signs of fear, I'd worry that you'd left your mind back in Lore."

A warmth filled her, and the longing to give him a quick hug nearly overwhelmed her. But she held back, following him into the tent. The ceremony was tomorrow, and she didn't want to lead him on, to make him believe there might be a chance for them. It was too dangerous.

The scent of onions, tomatoes, potatoes, and parsley filled the peaked enclosure. Costel stirred a black pot that hung over the fire built into a dip in the ground. Smoke curled up and out of a small hole in the center of the roof.

He stood and bowed. "Want me to ladle you each a bowl?"

"No," Filip said kindly, "we can handle it."

The two hugged, patting one another on the back roughly before Costel left through the heavy flap.

Aury shed her gloves and oiled outer coat, then sat on a pile of furs by the fire. "Smells fantastic."

"It's the paprika. It's smoked and makes even the worst of Costel's stews taste like glory."

They ate in companionable silence until Aury's shaking hands grew worse. She set her bowl down and fetched her staff from her things on the other side of the fire. The warmth and buzz of the magic helped her take a deep breath.

Filip finished his stew and refilled his bowl again, the firelight touching his pointed ear and the twist of his braided hair. "*A-ti lua inima în dinti.*"

"What does that mean?" she asked. His voice was alluring when he spoke in his native tongue. The sounds hit his tongue and turned, and the vowels were more pronounced, which made him bunch his lips as if he were about to kiss.

"To take your heart in your teeth."

"Perhaps the rumors of your people eating human flesh originated with that phrase."

He huffed a small laugh. "Maybe." Taking another spoonful of stew, he watched her, searching her with his eyes. "The saying means you are brave."

"I feel more like a wee rabbit worrying it's meant for that stew pot."

"What does this rabbit do? Run to the bushes? Or ride toward the villainous cook with magic in its feet?"

A thousand different strategies—drilled into her by the Master mages, Filip, and the generals of Lore—roared through her mind and set her to trembling again. She clicked her nails on her staff and wiggled her nose like a rabbit, making Filip chuckle.

"I wish I had years of experience."

A sad smile ghosted over his mouth. "It would be helpful, no doubt. But there's little use in wishing. The Masters put you in a position of power because of your magic. They know what they're doing. You won't be expected to run military moves. And I'm not telling you anything you don't already know."

"Yes, yes. But what if I freeze up? Forgive the metaphor." She laughed darkly.

"You won't. I believe in you. Even if you do for a moment, you'll snap out of it. You found your battle mindset, and from what I've seen of the mages during our time at Darkfleot, mages like you have an inborn ability to handle a fight."

They settled into the furs to sleep, Filip an arm's length away. She stared into the fire as his breathing grew regular and deep. The sound was comforting, as were the scents that always surrounded Filip—leather and sandalwood. She longed to move to the place beside him and curl against his strong, warm body, to hear the smile in his voice as he welcomed her, to enjoy the brush of his calloused fingers over hers.

He and his men would die trying to take out the Wylfen's dragon. She knew it. No scrying needed. She felt it like a fever in her blood and bones.

Shifting onto an elbow, she reached to pull his blanket higher over his shoulder. "You are a great one, Filip of Balaur," she whispered into the dim light. "I'm not sure anyone could deserve you."

CHAPTER 47

T he sound of "Hatchet!" being chanted in the streets followed the wedding party through the streets of Balaur City, capital of Filip's homeland.

"Look!" Costel shouted and pointed.

The youngling dragon soared through the skies, its lapis lazuli color bright in the late day sun. "Good friend!" Filip called above the crowd's cheering.

The dragon wheeled left and right high above, shooting a stream of fire.

"I think it's showing off for you, Filip," Aury said, her smile tinged with worry. "I can't believe it trailed you up here."

Filip laughed, unable to fret over the possibility of the dragon doing damage. It was just so lovely and majestic, with wings like dark opals and spikes that turned the light to rainbows along the city's shops and homes. He was thrilled that the creature had permitted him to ride upon its back.

"I shall call you Jewel if you allow it, dragon!" he called up.

The dragon roared and flew one more circle before disappearing into the mountains.

The people shouted joyfully, now chanting both Filip's nickname and the name of the dragon.

His men, the fae, and Aury talked excitedly all the way into the throne room at Balaur Castle, where the mood immediately quieted.

Filip bowed low as his parents, Queen Sorina and King Mihai, welcomed the wedding party.

"We loathe to know we meet you first in a time such as this," Sorina said to Aury, who gave a fine curtsey, "but know that the union between you and our son brings the greatest joy we've had since the birth of this wild child." She pushed a lock of her brown and gray hair behind her ear.

Filip's heart cracked at the pure happiness in his mother's eyes. This was all a lie.

"Thank you," Aury said, sadness showing in her blue eyes if he wasn't mistaken. It was all so terribly tangled.

Mihai was all smiles as well. He squeezed Filip's shoulder. "I hope you showed those humans a thing or two."

"They are far better off now, I'm proud to say. They have worked in advanced archery techniques, new cavalry moves attuned to the steeper fields of battle, and they are prepared with the orangebranch distraction."

"Very good. Our armies are ready to move on my order.

I heard some disturbing reports though and would like to meet with you and your men as soon as possible."

He was talking about the dragon. "Yes, of course, Father."

Sorina waved to the door, and the guards opened it to reveal a stout woman Filip remembered from his youth, a seamstress and expert in traditions. "Daria will aid your ladies, Princess Aury. She can assist them in what you will need for tonight's ceremony. And of course, you will all need to take a few hours of rest first. We can't delay long, I'm afraid, since the Wylfen are making quick progress, but you have today and tonight to care for body and soul and heart." She stepped forward, face tentative, then lunged and hugged Aury tightly.

"Oh!" Aury stiffened at first, then wrapped her arms around Sorina.

The fissure in Filip's heart widened.

Sorina pulled away. "Now, bid your bride well, and let us prepare for the wedding ceremony."

Aury turned to Filip, who took her hands in his. He tried to tell her with his eyes that he was sorry for all of this, for the fact that fate had forced her into this marriage, that none of this was her fault. He pressed a soft kiss on her wrist and heard her take a quick breath, her exhale stirring his hair. She smelled like Frostlight snow and the sage of magic.

They broke apart.

"Don't let Drago and Stefan drag you into drinking too much of that fruit brandy," Aury said to Filip.

"Oh, that's nothing to the ceremonial drinks you and I will have to imbibe," he said.

Aury grimaced.

He smiled. "A painting of that exact facial expression should be on the drink's label."

She groaned, and then Eawynn was rushing her away to meet with Hilda, Gytha, and Daria.

The next hours were filled with military meetings with Mihai and the other generals. Filip managed to grab a short sleep between a meal and a fourth talk, this one with Mihai, Sorina, and Filip's men, and involving the dragon weapon Costel had created. They managed to find a warrior willing to carry the dangerous clay projectiles. The older elven lord had lost his family in the war and wanted his chance at defeating the Wylfen once and for all. Filip considered bringing up the Matchweaver, but after a run-down on dwindling grain stores and the lack of salted meat, he knew they had to risk all for this union, for the land, for the people.

And then suddenly, it was time for the ceremony with Aury.

Filip's body heated just thinking about it.

DRAGO, STEFAN, AND COSTEL LED FILIP DOWN THE DARK corridor, past the throne room, and into the long, rectangular chamber that held the blessed bones of the god Rigel and the goddess Ursae. The black-painted doors swung open to show oil lamps hanging in a pattern mimicking the constellation that had come to represent Balaur, the same as the markings in his sigil ring. The furred cloak they'd set on his bare shoulders dragged across the floor, tugging at his neck, and he blinked away some of the black cosmetic with which they'd ringed his eyes. He adjusted his twisted iron crown. Thankfully, he was at least permitted to wear a fine pair of leather trousers, but his feet were as bare as his torso, as was custom in this holy place. The sides of his head had been freshly shaved and the top of his hair styled in waves and set away from his face.

He hoped Aury hadn't had to go through the annoyance of being painted and shaved and so forth. She was gorgeous exactly as she was.

The candles did little to light the black walls and floor, so he didn't see anyone gathered until he was nearly upon them. He knew nobles and his parents stood along the outer edges of the circle of chest-high stones where the ceremony would take place, but he had no desire to look their way.

Aury, crowned in gold and emanating regal strength, stood in the stone circle.

She pulled the very breath from his body.

Eyes painted gold, the light to his dark, she watched him approach, her river-blue gaze like that of a lioness, predatory, powerful, unafraid. A surge of desire shot through him like he'd been struck by lightning.

Under a draping, fox-fur cloak, a gauzy shift cut high over each leg, barely covering gold-laced underclothes that flattered her curves and strong build. His elven gaze picked up far more than she would realize. The thought made him grin although he silently chastised himself for it.

The ladies had painted scrolling golden symbols of fertility and power down her arms and fingers. Her stag-and-water symbol sigil ring winked from her hand, and her pink lips parted as he met her in the center of the circle. The space was purposefully small, encouraging the marrying couple to stand chest to chest, bare toe to bare toe. He splayed his hands in the Balaur custom, and she must have been instructed in the manner of this ceremony, because she did likewise and set her palms flat against his.

Her chest moved against his, a brush of fabric on skin, a swirl of sage-scented magic in the air.

His breath caught and hitched, heat flooding him.

It was all he could do not to throw her against that stone and taste every inch of her skin, to feel the pulse in her neck under his teeth, to brace his hips on hers.

How was he supposed to get through this ceremony with her looking like that and standing up against him?

Sorina brought forth a stone bowl and a knife, setting them at the barrier of the stone circle. Keeping one set of hands linked, he and Aury lifted bowl and knife. She set the knife to his collarbone, just beneath the cloak's clasp, then made a small cut. Her gaze darted from his face to the cut, the first sign of worry lighting the depths of her eyes. He nodded, encouraging her. Swallowing, she wiped a drop of his blood with her finger, then pressed the blood into the bottom of the bowl. Handing over the knife, she took the bowl from him. He cut her quickly and so shallowly the wound barely bled. With a bead of red on his finger, he did as she had, combining their blood in the stone bowl.

Mihai walked out of the shadows and placed a branch of indigostar on the circle's boundary. Indigostar was the plant they used to make break powder. Even the sap was dangerous, but when mixed with his elven blood, it would only warm the skin. He hoped Daria had told Aury that important information. With a hand still linked with Aury's, Filip set the knife on the ground and broke a stem of the indigostar. Standing—so incredibly close and feeling every breath as one—Filip dripped a fair amount of the indigostar sap into the bowl. Aury was supposed to go first, but Filip dipped his thumb into the sacred blend of their blood and the indigostar to ease any fears she might have of the plant. He lifted his hand, then began to paint the symbols of marriage on Aury's body.

CHAPTER 48

A ury held her breath as Filip drew a slow circle below the hollow in her throat, his finger dragging across her pebbled skin, shivers dancing down her body. With the thin line of black cosmetic charcoal around his eyes, they looked brighter, sharper, more dangerous. The muscles of his chest shifted with his movement.

She couldn't get enough of looking at him.

This was like a hunger of a whole new kind, and she'd been starved her entire life. She'd never be satiated if she began her feast. If she breathed him in again, took in his scent of leather and sandalwood, she'd cave and kiss him fully and without reserve.

His thumb dragged a line across her upper chest, and she had to breathe, her whole body wide, wide awake.

And then it was her turn. He handed her the bowl, and she marked him with a swirling circle below his throat as he raised his chin to give her more room to work. His throat moved in a swallow as she worked, his thighs warm against hers and the fingers that held hers tensing as if he too were holding himself back.

Costel moved to the stone circle's boundary and waited. Filip handed the bowl to him as a new face appeared, one Aury hadn't expected to see.

Werian gave her an impish grin and set a smaller bowl of some clear liquid on the boundary. He must have arrived while she was readying for the ceremony. She had known he would come for the fight. Unlike the Fae Queen, he didn't shy away from war. He nodded respectfully then disappeared into the chamber's shadows.

Everyone outside the circle called out the Balaur words of joining.

"*Doi devin unul. Doua inimi. Un suflet.*"

After picking up the bowl of clear liquid, Filip gazed into Aury's eyes. "Two become one," he translated for her. "Two hearts. One soul."

He held the small bowl to her lips, and she downed a gulp that tasted like fire. Her head felt light, and she clumsily took the bowl from Filip and gave him his portion of the drink he'd warned her about earlier. A drop stayed on his lip, and she had the wild urge to lick it off, but of course she didn't. They each drank three times, then the room chanted the sacred words once more.

Slipping a hand into his pocket, Filip retrieved two golden rings set with blackened etchings. He slid one onto her forefinger, his lightning gaze striking through her. She took the second from him and placed it on his finger. *To the ends,* the inscriptions said in Balaur. Gytha had told Aury that this morning, and the simple nature of the vow twined around her heart, pulling her closer to Filip in both body and spirit.

Filip led her out of the stone circle to raucous cheers. Aury still felt that odd hunger, that need for more of Filip. More of his touch, his skin, his breath and warmth. They walked in silence through the cheering nobles gathered in the corridors until they were on a platform that looked out on Balaur's capital city and all its brightly clothed inhabitants. A mighty shout went up from Filip's people, and the warmth of it took the sting out of the cold weather, weather in which she normally would never wear so little. Such strange customs, baring oneself almost fully to the world. There was an honesty and humility to it, but that made it no less uncomfortable.

But soon enough, Filip was finished waving to the crowd, and she was done accepting bundles of pine sprigs and braids of ribbon from noble children. They found the quiet of what she assumed was Filip's bedchamber, her ears ringing from the noise.

None of his men or her ladies were anywhere in sight. They were completely alone with only the snapping fire in the huge hearth to keep them company.

"Thank you," she said, her voice hoarse.

He filled a drinking horn with what smelled like hot, spiced wine and handed it over. "For what? It was my pleasure, even if it was not yours."

A sigh left her. She wished it could be all joy. "For translating. For taking the indigostar markings first. You're kind, Filip, and I see that. I can't believe I ever thought you were vicious and hungry only for killing." She felt like a fool though it was truly the fault of her tutors at the fae court.

His eyebrow twitched, and he flashed his sharp incisors before taking a swig from his horn of wine. "In the spirit of honesty, I can be rather vicious."

"When it's necessary. I understand that. I can be deadly too."

He set his horn in its stand and grinned. "Oh, I know that quite well."

The room tilted a bit. "That ceremony drink is something else."

"I warned you. Do you need some water? Tea?"

She took a sip of the wine. "No, it's pleasant to relax. To let loose."

Filip held out a hand. He had shed his cloak, but still wore his crown. He looked like a king who'd lost his kingdom, tragic and beautiful, the black around his eyes smeared just a bit at the edges.

"Are we dancing now?"

Unease flickered through his gaze. "Didn't they tell you about the bundling?"

Oh. Yes. The elven woman named Daria had said something quickly about how Aury must be wrapped in a long cloth, stitched with the royal family's sigil by Filip's own hand. She had to remain wrapped by Filip's side until the bells rang midnight. Then, they would be truly joined.

Aury downed the rest of her drink. "Yes. Of course."

"We can tell them we did the bundling. You don't have to go through with it. It's an age-old tradition and rather backward, in my opinion."

"But if someone finds out we didn't follow tradition,

the marriage will be voided, and our ruling houses won't uphold the deal between our kingdoms."

"True. They'll check the bundling in the morning for wrinkles and ask us to swear on Rigel's bones." He smiled bashfully.

"It's all right. I trust you." She set her drinking horn in its stand beside his, then crawled onto the fur-draped bed.

With careful fingers, Filip laced the wide ribbon beneath her back. He kept it loose as she knew he would. He cleared his throat as he began winding the ribbon across her stomach and around her hips. His knuckles grazed her navel as he drew the bundling material around her thighs, then tucked it beneath her knees. He ended by tying the ribbon neatly at her ankles in a ridiculously loose bow she could undo with one shake.

"If at any moment, you don't like this, you tell me, and this thing gets thrown into the fire, and into the fires of the galtzagorri with all of it." The ferocity in his gaze said he meant it.

"I'm fine. I could wiggle free easily. What is the thinking behind this custom?" she asked.

"It's meant to keep the non-royal partner chaste until the dawn and the sun's sealing of the union."

"Little do they know the elven prince is the one to watch."

A wicked gleam rose in his eyes, and her blood raced. "Indeed. For what if I accidentally touched you?" His voice was a caress. His hand hovered over her stomach, the heat of his palm radiating through her shift and into her skin. He brought his mouth close to her ear, his warm breath reminding her of the tangy scent of the ceremonial drink as well as that kiss on the rooftop. "Or what if one errant hand slipped beneath the ribbon?" His fingers undulated, so close to the bundling, but not quite touching. She was on fire from head to toe.

Two could play this game. She lifted her hips slowly, so slowly, until her stomach almost brushed his hand.

"Perhaps the elven tradition has its merits," she said, "and my villainy demands such precaution." The spice of the wine remained on her tongue, and she felt as if she were falling fast, like a rock dropped off a cliff or rising like a dragon to fly or perhaps both at once. What had been in that ceremonial drink?

A chuckle came from Filip's lips, and she started to reach for him. The bundling stopped her, of course. She'd forgotten it was there.

"Ah, is this what you are after, Princess Mage?" He came close, his lips a breath from hers, his gaze flitting from her head to her neck, then back again. "Would you kiss me even though you long to shatter my heart?"

"If we're going to lose this fight, we might as well go down smiling." Head swimming, she met his mouth.

He jerked like she'd surprised him, but then he pressed into the kiss, enveloping her lower lip, a sound almost like a growl rumbling in his chest. Fully set against her, he struggled to undo the bundling, one hand fighting the ribbon at her waist and the other tangling in her hair.

She freed one arm and slid it around his neck, pulling him close. Her heart beat like a thunderstorm, and her skin lit up with sensation, every touch a new joy she never knew she'd wanted. Filip had encouraged her from the moment they'd met. He'd shown his care—even love—during the

Mage Trials and in his respect for her decisions. He was the best of men, of elves, and she hungered to know his heart and every angle of his body and soul, to be the one he turned to, the one he woke to greet, the one he sought for pleasure, for comfort, for battling the struggle that was life.

With both of her hands freed, Filip laced his fingers in hers and drew her arms above her head, kissing her relentlessly, his hips pressed against her. His occasional whispers were of her courage and heart, her body and mind.

"I was ensorcelled from the moment you spoke with that sharp tongue of yours, my lioness, my princess of ice, my torture, and my salvation."

She was breathless with joy and pleasure as he kissed his way down her neck, his elven teeth grazing her skin and his hands setting her to flame. Before Filip, if anyone had asked if she would risk death for love, the answer would have been a resounding *no*. But now, with the soaring bliss of knowing she was in the arms of the one who adored her, she would risk absolutely everything for true love.

CHAPTER 49

F ilip woke, feeling as though the sun had risen in his heart, illuminating every dark corner and blessing it with warmth. He was forgiven, renewed, empowered. Aury slept soundly, mouth slightly open and eyelids the color of dusk. With the pale light of near dawn casting a ghostly light over the bed, he shifted a strand of hair away from Aury's pert chin. Even in sleep, she had a stubborn attitude. Grinning, he placed a soft kiss on her forehead, and though the true sun still hadn't chased off the night, he reluctantly slipped from their bed to prepare for the quick and quiet mission to take out the Wylfen's dragon.

In the second section of their bedchamber, servants had laid out two breakfast trays with a pot of tea and what appeared to be a scroll from Lore's archives, its case marked with the stag and river. No doubt it was something else he and Aury were required to sign to seal the union between their kingdoms. A smile pulled at his mouth. They would make history with their love and their rule of Lore. Peace would be secured once they put down this group of Wylfen, and all would be glorious, filled with Aury's wit, courage, and zest for life.

He gobbled down two bites of warm bread with butter, then picked up the scroll from Aury's tray. Usually, they each had to sign and set a seal at the bottom of the scribe's work. He'd go ahead and sign his side so the agreement could be completed while he was away, before the army traveled to Dragon Wing Pass.

Dawn was scraping the moonlight from the sky and turning the clouds red. Time was running out. He brought the scroll to his desk in the corner. After lighting a candle, he readied the wax and ink. The scroll's cracked green leather case unscrewed roughly, age marring the bronze grooves. Strange that they had an agreement in such an old case, but then again, the humans of Lore were downright obsessed with tradition.

The scroll that slid from the case was not newly scribed. A flicker of unease washed through him as he carefully unrolled the vellum and made sure not to damage the brittle edges. The ink had gone brown, and the language was difficult to decipher, some older version of the Lore tongue that used more vowels and a letter he hadn't studied. The scribe had written about a battle with scores of horses, spears, and water mages coming together in a place called the Red Meadow, if his translation was correct.

"*Wiccehlaford...*" he read quietly to himself. "What in Arc's Light is that?"

It was something about a leader in the battle, how the man had won the day for the preferred king, and another leader had knelt on the field and sacrificed a family ring, or jewel? He wasn't sure, but it seemed as if the second leader declared the first leader a wiccehlaford by way of a sacrifice after winning the battle. The wiccehlaford then could...what did that word mean? Oh, perhaps wed? The wiccehlaford could wed any they chose or divorce their partner, and they were given what seemed to be a large expanse of land holdings. Freedom. The wiccehlaford was given full *freo*—full freedom. And the captain given this title had a staff, so he was a water mage.

Filip gently returned the scroll to its case, his mind spinning over what this was and why it had been on Aury's tray. With one last longing look at the sleeping beauty in his bed, Filip gathered his hatchet and cloak and hurried to meet Costel, Drago, and Stefan.

At the stables, his men gave him a wide berth. As he tightened Avalanche's girth, they mounted up to ride the first leg of the journey toward the last place the Wylfen had been spotted. Hopefully under the dark of night, Filip and his men would reach the next place the scouts claimed the Wylfen army would rest.

Filip urged Avalanche to canter forward and catch up to Costel. "Eh, have you heard the Old Lore word *wiccehlaford?*"

Costel's face bunched as he thought. "*Wicce* is mage, I believe. *Hlaford*...hmm."

"Mage *hlaford.*"

"Sounds like lord," Drago said, joining them, snow falling from his fur hat as he shook his head.

"Ah!" Costel held up a finger. "Yes, Drago is right. *Hlaford* is lord."

Filip took a breath of sharp, cold air to calm his suddenly too quick heart. "*Wiccehlaford* means Magelord."

Stefan came up behind them, finishing a swig from a horn he kept on his baldric. "My grandfather used to tell a story about a Magelord from Lore who married and divorced ten women and farmed all the land from the Sea's Claw to the southern cliffs beyond Illumahrah."

Pulse ticking like a beetle on its back, Filip pulled the reins, stalling Avalanche so he and Stefan were side by side, Drago and Costel going on ahead through the twisting mountain path. "Yes, that's what the scroll was saying about this Magelord. The man gained what the scribe called full freedom."

"Sounds like a fine way to live." Stefan offered Filip his drink.

Filip waved him off. His stomach was sinking.

A realization crawled over his skin.

The scroll hadn't been meant for Filip's eyes. It was Aury's. Some research of hers. Delivered by a well-meaning servant or perhaps by Gytha or one of the fae. Maybe Werian. Yes. The fae prince would have access to historical scrolls such as that one, and he'd be motivated to help Aury escape her horrible, forced marriage to Filip, to the vicious mountain elf. Filip winced like Aury herself had been here to say it aloud.

The betrayal of what he'd thought they'd created last night hacked through heart and soul.

No matter what happened, the army of Balaur was now committed to die for Lore if need be. His people would have the farmlands. Now all Aury had to do to be free of Filip was to prove herself in battle and have Werian or some other captain make a sacrifice when the fighting was finished and declare her Magelord. She'd be fully free.

The thought stabbed him in the gut.

Freedom was exactly what she'd told him she wanted. She'd not hidden that desire from him. This was no surprise, so why did he feel shocked, hurt, betrayed? He had ignored everything she'd told him since that first night in Loreton Palace. And last night—what had she said? They might as well go down smiling? He was means to gaining an army and someone to kiss when the desire struck her. His jaw tightened, and his teeth ground together. He was going to be sick. The night of joining hearts with Aury had only been the product of drink and convenience. She didn't love him. She wanted freedom from their marriage, from him.

He dug his heels into Avalanche's sides and launched through his men, galloping forward, fighting the burn of tears. He wished the possibility of true love had never touched him so that he wouldn't suffer the agony of losing it. If he could, he'd cut out his own heart to stop this deep, dark pain.

CHAPTER 50

Aury woke and stretched languorously, having had the deepest night of sleep in her entire life. She was loved and she loved. And yes, they were headed for a terrible battle, but if they made it through, there would be a lifetime of joyous days and glorious nights with Filip.

She'd never forget the way he'd cradled her head and kissed her softly, then more heatedly, sending her into oblivion. Her body perfectly recalled the feel of his muscled arms circling her, the way his waist narrowed to slim hips and how he moved, the warm whispers of devotion in her ear, the elven scent of him, alluring and mysterious.

He was hers, and she was so incredibly grateful she'd decided to risk the Matchweaver's curse before making the mistake of giving him up by striving to be a Magelord. She had to see Werian and make certain he didn't try to give her the title in the coming days. She felt no need for it anymore. She had more than enough freedom, and she wanted to be tied to Filip forever. It was now her choice and his, decided last night in word and deed.

The scent of bread and butter hit her nose, and she scrambled out of bed and into the second area of Filip's bedchamber. He must have left early for his mission to take out the dragon. A shiver ran over her as she thought of him skulking around a massive creature capable of lighting a kingdom on fire. *Source, protect him,* she prayed.

She reached for the undisturbed tray. An encased scroll toppled from the table, the top rolling across the stone floor. Bending, she picked up the case and removed the scroll, an ancient one from the looks of it. Ah, the Lore sigil.

A shadow crossed her mind.

What was this?

Frowning at the Old Lore tongue, she read as quickly as she could.

Wiccehlaford. Magelord.

This was the scroll Werian had told her about at the Staff and Steel feast. He had left this for her. She'd heard knocking in the middle of the night, but they'd ignored the bother. He must have had Hilda, Eawynn, and Gytha deliver it with the breakfast trays.

She fetched the top of the case. Someone else had read this and hastily replaced the lid, not screwing it on correctly. Only one person had been here; only one person would open a Lore-marked scroll, possibly thinking it was something meant for the two of them.

Filip.

She dropped into a chair. "No."

He'd read this and remembered all that she had said about wanting to end this marriage as quickly as they thought possible depending on the good of their people. He would think she didn't want him, that she still planned on leaving by gaining the title of Magelord. And now he was gone, and she'd have no time to talk to him and explain the poor timing and tell him about her change of heart and how true it was until after the battle was won or lost.

She crumpled the scroll in her fist and hung her head. Filip was in the wilderness right now, thinking she cared no more for him than a passing fancy.

He had no idea he possessed her heart, and if he died without knowing...

She dressed as quickly as possible, then, at his desk, she used a striped quill to pen two duplicate notes, explaining the scroll and laying out a simple version of her feelings. Outside the doors, she found Hilda, Gytha, and Eawynn chatting with the Balaur guards, who used a stilted version of the Lore tongue.

"No," Gytha said, "in Lore, *barda* sounds like the word for a storyteller that usually sings and travels about."

"It is an ax. A hatchet," the guard said. "Our prince is powerful warrior. Not only a maker of tales."

Aury slammed into Hilda and thrust one of the notes into her hands.

The guards bowed low. "Your Highness."

Aury ignored them. "Find a way to get this to Filip the moment he returns from his mission. I don't know where I'll be in the fight at that point, so I can't count on having a chance to speak to him. There has been a terrible misunderstanding."

Gytha elbowed her. "Didn't sound too terrible last night."

Aury's glare shut her up. "Find my armor and help me dress. I want to be seen as the captain I am for the first meeting with the joined war council."

Gytha, Eawynn, and Hilda curtseyed. "Your Highness."

"I'll be back in a blink." Waving at the two guards who had been at her door to come along because goddess knew they would follow anyway, she hurried away to the stables, hoping against everything that for some reason Filip and his group hadn't left yet.

Armored Balaur captains and a multitude of what appeared to be nobles talked and drank steaming mugs of mulled wine in the area around Balaur Castle. Merchants hawked leather bags, gloves, and round cakes that looked to be spiced with paprika.

At the stables, the master of the place bowed low. "How may I help you, Your Highness? Do you wish to see Cālātor? She ate well this morning, and we checked her shoes."

"He's gone, isn't he?" she asked the stable master.

"Prince Filip? Yes."

Darkness flooded Aury's heart. She longed to ask the stable master if he'd heard Filip say anything about her, but that wasn't the way of a future queen. "Is there any way to get a message to him before he reaches the Wylfen's camp?"

"I doubt it, but I can send a man, if you wish it."

"No. It's too risky. Thank you." She turned, her guards at her elbows and her heart falling into her stomach. He would hate her now or, worse, love her and live broken. He didn't deserve that and all because of poor timing. It wasn't Werian's fault either. He'd only been trying to help. "Do you know where the fae prince is currently?" she asked her guards.

"He was housed in the eastern wing of the castle, but I don't know anything past that."

The other guard lifted his face. "Oh! I just remembered one of the noblewomen mentioned that Prince Werian left for the pass. She bemoaned his absence." The guard's lips twitched.

Exhaling, Aury returned to the castle and her rooms to dress for the march to the pass. She had to shove all her worry to the back of her mind. It was time for war.

CHAPTER 51

Filip's grief over Aury burned his mind, seared his chest, as he and his men traversed the peaks, recalling the scouts' information about where the Wylfen were most likely stopping for rest. He pushed his feelings down deep. He had no time for raging or weeping or begging for hope. He had to incapacitate the Wylfen's dragon and stop the enemy armies from unleashing fire onto the Lore and Balaur forces.

The stars like eyes above him, he led Costel, Drago, and Stefan down a steep incline, their elven feet gripping icy outcroppings through their thin-soled boots, using the skills passed down through the generations.

Below them, a dragon slept.

The main Wylfen force had set up tents eighty paces from the beautiful, deadly beast. A few men stood watch, but they were gathered around fires rolling dice and not as alert as they should have been.

The dragon's scales glittered against the snow as it

breathed slow and steady, sides like cottage-sized blacksmith bellows. Smooth wings tucked tightly, the dragon appeared completely at ease as it rested beside a single Wylfen soldier and his flickering campfire.

"Why isn't the dragon having him for a midnight snack?" Drago asked, his words so quiet only an elf could've picked them from the air.

Filip shrugged. He'd been wondering the same thing. This man had a relationship with this dragon, sleeping beside him as one would a trusted mount. Surely, the Wylfen weren't riding this thing as Filip had? This was no youngling dragon. This was a full-grown male with the cluster of head spikes he'd read about. Had this soldier saved this dragon during its youth? No, that would be too much of a coincidence. But what other explanation was there?

On a ledge above Filip's head, Costel held two of his explosive clay balls of break powder and goat's blood.

The break powder was made from the plant he and Aury had blended with their blood during the wedding ceremony. An image of her bright blue eyes circled in golden cosmetics and her parted lips flashed through his mind. He shoved it away, gritting his teeth.

Drago held the third clay projectile, while the rest of the small weapons remained at their own camp, a mile away, where the elder soldier who'd volunteered to carry the projectiles waited on their word.

Now was as good a moment as any to begin this mess.

Filip met Stefan's gaze. Beyond Drago, standing on the cliff's edge that overlooked the Wylfen army's camp, Stefan aimed an arrow at the tent closest to the dragon and his soldier. If things went south, he could at least give them a moment longer by taking out the men most likely to call out a warning.

Filip checked the wind, set his focus on the dragon's soldier, nocked an arrow, and let it fly. The soldier let out a grunt, then died without another sound, his death not even waking the massive beast at his side.

Drago and Costel threw their clay projectiles into the snow near the dragon's nose.

The outer shells cracked open on impact as planned. Goat's blood darkened the ice and snow.

Would the dragon take the bait?

No, he was soundly sleeping. Filip nocked another arrow. Maybe he could prick the beast and urge it to seek the scent.

As he nocked the arrow, one of the dragon's great, yellow eyes flashed open.

Filip's heart crashed against his ribs.

The dragon lifted its head and flared its nostrils. Filip and his men stepped silently away from the edges of their perches. The crystalline spikes on the dragon's back shone like silver torches under the stars as the beast stood on all fours to sniff the place where the second projectile had landed.

Whirling around, the dragon eyed its companion, who lay dead in the snow. The dragon reared back and roared, shaking snow from the cliffs and sending Filip and the rest running.

Filip's legs shook, and his throat burned as he hissed to his men, "Go, go, go!"

They were like the wind on the mountains, practically

flying in their haste to flee from the dragon and their failed plot. They had to get far enough away so their scent would die in the cold before the dragon or the scar wolves could track them.

"That went down like Costel in his first wrestling match." Drago panted as he ran beside Filip.

"Shut it, Drago." Costel's voice was pained, as if he blamed himself for the failure.

"It's not your fault that didn't work," Filip said as they rounded a peak and slid toward the crevice that would lead them to their horses and the volunteer warrior who held the rest of the projectiles. "There were a thousand things that could've gone wrong, and fate chose one of them. I probably shouldn't have killed the soldier with him, but I wasn't sure if the man would hear the clay hit."

Stefan was a step ahead of the rest of them, his long legs giving him an advantage. He glanced over his shoulder as they braced hands and feet against the sharp walls of the crevice and crawled across the top of the fissure. Filip wished there were another way to go, but the mountain had split in two and this was the only way to the other side that wouldn't take weeks of travel. The crack was as deep as the world's memory, and it yawned below them, wind howling from the darkness.

"Do you think without the dragon's companion that perhaps the beast won't be as amenable to the Wylfen?" Stefan asked. "Perhaps it won't do as they wish anymore?"

"It's possible. I will pray every moment of every day until we meet them at the pass that your guess is right. If not..." Filip didn't have to say it aloud. With that dragon and the wolves, the Wylfen were all but unbeatable.

He tried very hard not to imagine Aury bleeding to death on a battlefield, wolves at her throat, but the image bloomed in his mind all the same.

"Leave the weapons!" he shouted to the elder warrior. "Mount up and ride!"

The man, trained well all his life, did as instructed, gently tucking the remainder of the clay balls into the snow before leaping onto his saddle.

Filip found Avalanche and waited for Costel to mount before taking off at a gallop behind the group. The horses would earn their keep this night.

Howls rose far behind them, and chills ravaged Filip. If their enemies caught them...

They rode and rode, the night going pale as they took the long route to Dragon Wing Pass. The howls had faded hours ago, and there was no sign of a winged enemy from above.

At long last, Filip and Avalanche trotted into the flat land that approached the southern side of the ice-choked Dragon Wing River. The men behind him were silent with what he guessed was dread. He looked to the pass and saw the armies of Lore and Balaur assembled in the flats and along the cliffs of the pass. Atop Cālātor, at the very front of the mages, Aury held her staff, her armor blue and gold and sparkling in the rising sun.

The dragon they'd failed to kill drove through the cloud-covered dawn and opened its fiery maw.

CHAPTER 52

B lood icing in her veins, Aury rode through the last of the night toward the kings and queens assembled above Dragon Wing Pass. The enemy hadn't arrived yet, but they would soon. Very soon. She had to find Werian now and make sure he didn't declare her Magelord. If she, by some trick of the gods, fought fantastically today, he could not raise her to that title. Filip would think she wanted freedom from him, but she didn't. Not anymore. She wanted freedom *with* Filip. Forever.

"King Mihai will know where Werian is hiding." Gytha spurred her dappled mare to run past Aury, then announced Aury's arrival.

Aury spurred her horse on with a pat on the neck, then a nudge from her heels. Athellore and Gwinnith glanced her way as she approached, Mihai and Sorina deep in conversation.

Pulling Cālātor to a stop, Aury didn't bother with fancy

greetings or stupid bows of the head. There was no time. "Has anyone seen Prince Werian?"

"He's with the fae guard on the northeastern cliffs. Just there." Sorina pointed a gloved hand to indicate a dozen dark specks traversing the snow an impossible distance away.

"Will he join the units in the pass?" She would be down there, albeit protected somewhat by the royal guard and her unit of warriors and mages. She'd wanted to be at the front, but her parents had denied that request.

Athellore raised an eyebrow. "I don't believe so."

She pressed her eyes shut. If the day was filled with victory and she proved herself somehow and Werian did declare her Magelord, she could still choose Filip. All wasn't lost. Not yet. She would thank Werian and announce her feelings to the world. Yes, she could do that. They would listen, right?

She opened her eyes to see that her terrible father was by her side, staring. "You're not up to some mischief that will ruin this union between our two nations, are you?" he hissed in a quiet whisper.

Mihai and Sorina were talking to Gwinnith about the dragon and how it hadn't yet been seen over the approaching warriors. Mihai said the Wylfen had broken into two groups for some unknown reason.

"Aurora Rose," Athellore snapped.

She faced him again, anger rising.

"Because that would be catastrophic," he whispered. "A boil upon our reputation."

The incoming Wylfen and the fear of losing Filip scraped away any tiny consideration she had for being obedient or avoiding this man's wrath. "You're a boil on my life, you nasty beast. Shove off." She popped her heels against Călător's sides, then they galloped down the slope, snow in plumes around them and her guard and ladies struggling to keep up.

As dawn blossomed, the back of the Lore and Balaur forces in the pass had become the front. Aury stopped flinging ice shards into the first of the Wylfen long enough to see hundreds of the wild-eyed warriors marching forward, wolves at their sides.

A dragon soared out of the skies.

Chills swept down Aury's back.

"Aury!" Sunniva cried from the ranks behind her.

"Now!" Aury raised her staff and cut lengths of ice from the snow and sent it spiraling toward the Wylfen, magic burning through her veins and the sound of crashing waves in her ears.

"Spelled water injures dragons!" Sunniva called out, ignoring another captain's calls for the cavalry and for the mages to strike with flooding.

The river gurgled between the thick chunks of ice at its borders, and the Wylfen began to run and gallop toward them.

The dragon released a rippling wave of fire and heat that warmed Aury's head. Far too close for comfort. Ice from the surrounding cliffs turned to water, and Lore and Balaur soldiers poised there lost their arrows and bows and tumbled to their deaths on the sharp rocks that framed the pass.

"Sunniva, you had better be right." The water was rising from the mages' work, filling the pass with churning, white-capped eddies that halted the Wylfen's progress. Some of the scar wolves, driven mad by their training, swam into the magicked water and struggled to cross. Some would make it. What then?

Lore and Balaur arrows zipped past Aury's head and plunked to the icy ground, others finding their targets at the far edge of the water, taking down too few Wylfen to matter much. This was going to be a massacre. And that was if they lived long enough to let the Wylfen have their chance. In the sky, the massive dragon, a mottled green and blue, veered around the peaks, then circled back. No, they might not die from wolf teeth or Wylfen blades. They might all burn to ash right where they stood.

"Aury!"

Sunniva's voice cut through the chaos of shouted orders, sizzling magicked water, and the enemy's war cries. The Wylfen's battle shrieks sounded like screams and growls tangled into one noise, an almost inhuman sound that lifted the hairs on the back of Aury's neck.

The dragon swooped low, fire torching the unit of mages and foot soldiers next to Sunniva's. Shrieks of pain and the scent of burning flesh filled the air. The dragon tipped sideways over the Wylfen and headed straight for Aury.

She raised her staff and willed the rumbling river to rise like a hand. "Stop the dragon. Grab it. Take it."

Her staff grew hot under her fingers. The dragon was close enough that she could see its yellow eyes, the sun through its wings—at least her death would be one for the history scrolls.

"Stop the dragon," she willed the water with hissed whispers, the magic surging in her.

The river shot into the air, fifty feet high, liquid claws reaching. The dragon shrieked and slipped to the side of her spelled water, only its back leg touched and even that not damaged at all.

Roaring, the dragon flew high above the battlefield, then there was no more time for thinking of that beast because other enemies were on her.

Suddenly, wolves surrounded her, and a group of Wylfen had struck through the river and found a way to their side. The huge wolves snapped white teeth at Cālātor's shoulders and caught the hem of Aury's tunic. The bottom half of her armored tunic ripped as easily as a flower's petal, jerking her body and nearly unseating her. She stabbed at the nearest wolf with her sword, keeping her staff held high above her head as the horse bucked and pawed at another wolf.

Cuthbert threw dried orangebranch beyond her, and the wolves dived onto the food. He jammed his short sword through the neck of a wolf, which only made it angry instead of killing it as it would a normal animal. The creature whirled and bit Cuthbert's arm. Groaning in pain, Cuthbert thrust his blade into the side of the wolf next to the one with its teeth in his flesh. The third woke from his orangebranch stupor and drove Cuthbert into the snow, where the second one continued gnawing on his arm. He raised his staff and used a magical hand of snow to yank the wolf away. Standing, bleeding at the neck, shoulder, and arm, he struck the wolves again and again, but they refused to die.

"Good fighting, Cuthbert!" Aury shouted as the Wylfen fighters found her in the bloody tangle.

Shaking and swearing darkly enough to black the entire sky, she cut the air with her staff. Water careened from the river, turning to ice as it flew, then slicing across her enemies' spines, dropping them dead to the ground before they could shout. Two more Wylfen launched themselves out of the rising water, their wolves at their sides. Teeth bared, the animals latched onto Cālātor's neck. The horse screamed, and Aury fell, losing her sword but not her staff.

Teeth found her boot and bit hard. She shrieked beside her dying horse, her foot surely broken in the wolf's huge mouth.

A shout of rage punched through the cacophony, and then Filip was there, his hatchet a lightning strike, hitting men and wolves faster than her eyes could follow. His men fought nearby, their blades moving too quickly to see clearly.

Buoyed by his presence, her eyes burning with the cold and the tears of every emotion a human could experience, she found her feet. She grabbed for her muddied sword, dropped it, then took it up, finally successful.

"Jewel!" Her mind spun with ideas. "You have to call the youngling dragon and get it to take you into the skies. It's the only way to fight the other dragon."

She made a lifting motion with her staff and willed the water to rise from the mud and freeze into many-bladed weapons of ice. Then she pushed at the magic and sent the five-foot-long ice spears straight into the Wylfen. They fell, writhing.

Filip would question her madness. How could he not? But then—

He whistled louder than any human could. "*Micā bijuterie a cerului!*"

They fought on with blade and water, Filip calling for the youngling dragon over and over again. The Wylfen's dragon had yet to make another appearance.

"Did I hurt the large dragon with the spelled water? Sunniva said it would injure the dragon."

"Definitely," Filip said. "We saw it fly off with a blackened foot."

"Really?" That was amazing news. She hadn't noticed the damage.

A Lore soldier next to Drago and Stefan collapsed under a scar wolf's attack. Two other Lore warriors used their orangebranch and distracted the wolf long enough to kill it, but the shrieking Wylfen took them both to death with their broadswords.

Aury whipped a storm of ice around her, her unit, Filip, and his men. They were surrounded. Lore soldiers slumped, lifeless, in the bloodied snow and mud. Balaur elves lay dead in piles. They were losing this battle, and the Wylfen's dragon hadn't even hit them again yet.

Like she'd summoned the beast with her mind, the jade-and-lapis-lazuli-colored dragon soared out of the clouds and shot straight at them. The smell of blood swamped Aury's senses, her stomach turning. Fire exploded from the dragon's mouth, and a mighty roar hit her ears. Losing every shred of battle mindset, she dropped to the earth with a scream, her staff and sword forgotten beside her.

Hundreds and hundreds of warriors and mages battled beside pine trees that now burned freely beside charred bodies and mud. The fire had melted everything in the vicinity, but it had killed Wylfen too, their bright red clothing showing among the dead.

With the dragon attack, the mages lost their tenuous hold on the river. The flooding shrank to nothing. The walls of water dissolved. The Wylfen advanced.

Filip called for the youngling once more as he knelt beside Aury, his hatchet dripping blood.

Gytha and Filip pulled Aury to standing, and Cuthbert shoved her staff into her hand.

"What's the plan?" Sunniva shouted over the din. Then she began working on the river.

Cuthbert held his staff high to help her raise the water, but his gaze was pulled to the sky.

The Wylfen were crying for blood. Their dragon roared, and the walls of the pass shook, sending rock and ice into the narrow battlefield, pressing enemy to enemy, sword to sword, the mages back to back as they flung magicked ice and spears of frosted water.

Aury whipped her staff through the air and spun a wheel of ice at the battle-crazed Wylfen storming through the river's churning depths. The wheel knocked one across the forehead, and he slipped under the surface. More raged forward. Wolves snarled behind her, but she had to keep spinning magic, multiplying the water, trying to force a wall of ice to rise and stop them. Her body shook with fatigue, her heart beating too quickly, arms trembling so hard that she could barely hold her staff and sword.

"It's him!" Filip shouted as he cut down a Wylfen and his wolf. Blood soaked his right leg. His blood.

The youngling dragon swooped low, and Aury's mind spun a strategy as the waterfall that fed the river spilled into the bloody pass.

"Go to the waterfall!" she shouted, her throat packed with needles. "Try to bait their dragon to follow you. Be ready to turn and fly high when you see the water changing!"

Filip used his elven agility to leap onto the youngling's back, his hand snaking around a spike.

The three Wylfen crossing the river hit her at once, a sword's edge blazing across her forearm. She dropped her blade, feeling no pain yet, but blood welled frighteningly bright. With a flip of her staff, she struck the second man across the temple, and he stumbled. The third gripped her staff, but she held on, magic surging through her fingers, helping her keep a hold on her only weapon.

"Freeze," she hissed, pouring her fear and rage into the spell.

Frost crawled over the man's hand, then sped up his arm and through the rest of his body until he was frozen solid. She jerked her staff free, cracking one of his fingers clean off. Spinning, she searched the skies for the two dragons.

The deep scarlet tunics of the Wylfen swamped the pass, the Lore ruby and cerulean colors scant. The elves had moved to the high ground and were attempting to shift the tide of the battle with more arrows and throwing knives.

Rock and mud and wolves and Wylfen surrounded Aury and her mages in the painfully tight space between river and mountain. She whirled her staff, sucked the water from the river's edge, then threw shards of ice at three Wylfen slashing at Costel. They shrieked and went to hands and knees, dying as Costel turned to fight another scar wolf, his hand tossing a meager amount of orangebranch.

A dark shape shot through the air and stirred Aury's hair. Filip and the youngling soared toward the waterfall, and Aury's heart shivered hard. The greater dragon gave chase and let out a blood-curdling shriek, its scaled belly, arm-length talons, and serpentine tail turning the pass to night as it blocked out the sun.

Sunniva, Cuthbert, and the rest of the mages scattered among the battling warriors of Wylfenden, Balaur, and Lore, weaving magic through the waters, their attacks separate and uncoordinated. The fight had broken down their plans and stomped it into the mud alongside the dead and broken.

Aury raised both staff and her fisted hand and shouted. "To me!"

The mages who hadn't collapsed from fatigue wasted no time gathering around her as magic sparked inside her fingertips, crashed inside her ears, and crackled to life in her staff. The youngling flew toward the waterfall, then veered abruptly upward. Their timing was off. This wasn't going to work. She might accidentally freeze Filip and Jewel. The greater dragon blazed along the scent trail, and Aury blasted magic toward the falling water.

"Still. Capture. Reach and take and hold." Her outstretched arm shook, and her sight blurred. The massive animal was going to burn Filip and consume the ashes. It would never work.

Sunniva and Cuthbert joined in her spell; their magic snapped alongside hers, almost visible as swirling sparks of white and blue. Then the magic heaved and tugged, and ice spread like wildfire over the river, the land, the rocks, the waterfall—even the great dragon.

Every beast, all the warriors on every side—everything froze solid, save Aury and her mages. The only sound was their breathing and the wind howling through the gnarled pass.

A towering wall of blue-black ice encased the great dragon. Its wings remained stretched wide but still, hanging inside the frozen creation.

"Sunniva," Aury panted. "It will kill the warriors. Our warriors."

And where were Filip and the youngling? Had she frozen them too? They'd cleared the top of the waterfall, but they weren't flying above the battleground.

Sunniva whipped around to face the rest of the mages. "We must break this ice. Only the ice around our warriors."

"Impossible," Cuthbert said.

"No." Aury swayed on her feet. Holding the ice spell was the most difficult thing she'd ever done, and sweat was rolling down her temples. One would think with as cold as it was, the freeze would keep on its own, but the massive amounts of water flowing into the falls threatened to break her hold. "Sunniva...she has the control rune. And who else has it? Speak up!" Three other mages raised their staves. "Do it. Now. Free them!"

The mages with the control rune strong in their magic formed a small circle, pressed their staves together, then hissed spells. If they didn't break out the warriors soon, they'd all die. Every single warrior in the Pass. And then the Lore and Balaur armies would be without leadership, without their best fighters, and the Wylfen would send another army—there were so many of them—and Balaur and Lore would be lost, the fallen gone for no reason, no purpose. All the blood would be for nothing.

"You can do this," Sunniva whispered to the black-haired woman in her circle, "Ninety-seven point six percent of mages with the rune you have are successful in this spell after earning rank in the trials. You can do this."

The woman nodded and shut her eyes.

Where was Filip? Aury held to the ice spell, but the energy of the great dragon pulled at her, tugging at her staff. Pain shot through her hand like the magic itself was rebelling against this massive spellwork.

"I can't hold the dragon any longer. Sunniva!"

The crack of splintering ice broke the battlefield's silence, and Lore and Balaur warriors fell away from their ice cages to gasp for air.

"Archers! Spearmen!" Aury cried over the hushed armies, the frozen Wylfen growing pale inside their icy tombs. "Surround the great dragon! I will release it, and you must strike under the chin, the legs!"

Sunniva cupped her mouth with a hand. "And aim behind the ear, in the soft spot where head meets neck!"

The warriors assembled around the frozen waterfall and its scaled, ice-covered captive.

Aury's staff trembled violently. If Filip was in the wrong place when she released this dragon... "Now!" She could hold it no longer. Unspooling the spell, she drew her staff downward and fell back against Cuthbert and Stefan.

The great dragon roared and collapsed to the ground stunned. Glinting spearheads and arrows flew at the massive beast. It howled, standing on its back legs and flapping its wings, trying to lift into the air. One spear cut through the front membrane of its left wing, and the dragon dropped to its belly. The archers finished the dragon, and a shout of triumph went up from the Lore and Balaur armies.

The shout became a chant, the energy of the warriors and mages infectious. But Aury couldn't celebrate. Not until she found Filip.

"Princess Mage Aurora! Princess Mage Aurora!"

The chanting grew louder and cries of "Reward her!" and "Honor her!" punctuated the cheering.

Aury scanned the battleground, the cliffs, the skies.

Then Filip and the youngling topped into view, falling from a section of the sky partially blocked by jagged peaks.

Her heart crystallized. "No!"

She had frozen Jewel and Filip while they'd been out of sight, somewhere within reach of her magic. She'd been afraid of this. Pushing away from Cuthbert and Stefan, she thrust her staff forward. The ice around the Wylfen army dissolved into snowflakes, and the bodies collapsed onto the riverbanks.

The youngling dragon found its wings and flew into the

bright blue sky, but Filip, silent, careened toward the ground. Aury slammed her staff's end against the muddy earth, and snow shot through the pass. The tumbling mass of sparkling flakes spun a storm beneath Filip.

He disappeared into the twisting white.

The chanting, the rumble of the river, the crunch of ice, the warriors banging swords on shields—all noise whispered like memories under the high-pitched buzz in Aury's ears.

She formed a bridge of ice as she ran. Rushing over the creation to the far side of the river, she passed the great dragon's body and stumbled. Drago, Stefan, and Costel were there, lifting her up, then running with her, not outpacing her as they could have easily, especially in her current state.

She found Filip sleeping in a heap of snow formed of her magic. Blood leaked slowly from his leg and from a cut over his eyebrow. She stopped, standing, afraid to touch him, to speak his name, to make this moment real.

"I can't..." she whispered, tasting the salt of tears. "I tried." She had done everything she could to save him, to save them all. And she'd failed. The one who had thawed her heart and brought her the greatest joy was dead.

CHAPTER 53

Filip blinked the darkness away and opened his eyes to see tears rolling down Aury's cheeks. The armies of Lore and Balaur chanted her name, the banging of steel on shield near deafening.

"Filip?" Aury went to her knees, reaching out a tentative hand like she was afraid to touch him.

He sat up, glancing at the dead dragon she'd miraculously frozen as he'd flown high with the youngling. Then he looked to Costel, Drago, and Stefan, who smiled, their faces full of gratitude that warmed him.

"Aye," he said. "I'm all right. I assume you saved my life."

She laughed and wiped her eyes. "I did, and it was a right pain in the arse, so you had best say thank you."

He kissed her hand, grief filling him. This was the happy rush of a victory in battle. This wasn't the beginning of their life together. This was the end. The chanting of "Princess Aurora!" went on and on as he stood, Aury turning to scan the crowd, her body tense as if another enemy awaited. And of course, another did. The Matchweaver. She would strike if Filip didn't give Aury up. And Aury's scroll that spoke of becoming a Magelord had told Filip that Aury still wanted freedom from their union, to be free of him.

Aury grabbed a nearby soldier. "Where is Prince Werian?" she whispered.

Filip nodded to no one but himself. Indeed, she did want Werian to declare her Magelord. She deserved it. Truly. But the truth shredded his heart.

Swallowing against his burning throat, Filip knelt before Aury. "As Prince of Balaur and General of the Balaur Army, I declare Princess Mage Aurora a Magelord and hereby sacrifice my bride. Let it be so." He removed his black-etched, golden wedding ring and set it in the blood of the battlefield as his heart crumbled to pieces, as broken as those who had died during this terrible, victorious day. It was over.

CHAPTER 54

The crowd roared approval, shouting "Magelord! Magelord! Magelord!" as Aury snatched up Filip's ring, her fingers turning to ice.

"No," she whispered, mind whirling around Filip's words, the night they'd had, the fact that she'd thought to watch for Werian declaring her Magelord, not Filip. "You can't."

He swallowed and got to his feet. "I can and I did. You deserve the life you want. I'm sorry that I tangled your path for a while." His humble smile snapped her in two. "Our people have what they need. No one will fight this. I realize now that it's better this way. Everyone gets what they need. No need for archaic, forced marriages. We will start a new way of devising political alliances. It's a proud moment."

She couldn't think. Her heart surged inside her as she reached for him. In her hand, his ring seemed to sear her skin, so cold that it burned. *He wants this too. This is his choice, and seeing the scroll helped him understand that he didn't want to be stuck with me.* Her stomach turned.

"Filip." She extended her hand...

Athellore, Gwinnith, Sorina, and Mihai galloped toward them, then stopped, throwing mud and ice at the nearby warriors, but it did nothing to dampen their spirits as the crowd shouted for Aury.

Athellore scowled as he dismounted. "Daughter, you have saved our kingdoms." He gave her a stiff bow that further shocked her.

Gwinnith hurried over and kissed her on the cheek with cold, cold lips. "Fine work," she whispered. "Although I do wish you would have kept your vows. There will be consequences despite what Mihai and Sorina say."

No, this wasn't happening. She could undo this. Filip had to be hers. "I—"

She spun to see Filip mounting up with his men. He gave her that sad smile again, then dug his heels into his gelding's side and tore away from the battlefield.

He would never have left like that unless he truly wanted to be free of her. If he had loved her like she'd thought he did, he would've fought for her.

Gripping his ring, she steeled herself, frosted her heart so no feelings could touch her.

And she left Balaur without her groom.

CHAPTER 55

Filip dismounted at the castle and strode through the doors and to his chamber, ignoring his men's shouts of his name and calls of "Your leg, my prince. You're bleeding." They would only stop him and attempt to talk him into going after Aury or console him with jokes about more women to be had. He slammed his door before anyone could follow him inside and leaned on the solid oak, his chest heavy with the shredded remains of his heart. He wanted nothing of talk.

The servants had made his bed so that only the slightest hint of Aury's sage-like scent endured. Her laugh echoed in his memory, her sigh...

He couldn't take this. He ripped the doors open to see Costel, Drago, and Stefan, wide-eyed and worried.

"I can't stay here," he said dumbly, knowing he was a right fool.

"My rooms." Costel immediately started toward his

chambers down the corridor. "I have stitching goods, too, for that leg."

Drago gripped Filip's sleeve and hurried him along. Stefan was blathering on about something, but Filip wasn't listening.

In Costel's smaller chambers, they called the servants to gather their bloodstained clothing and deliver them trays of food and drink. Costel stitched up Filip's wounded thigh and helped him wash in a large basin. Limping a bit, Filip built up the fire himself, sending the servants away so he would have peace. He arranged a fresh log amidst the flickering heat and watched the colors of the flames dance.

Stefan rubbed his freshly washed hair with a rag, then leaned against the hearth, arms crossed over his chest. "Were you always planning that fool move?"

"Shut it, Stefan. I have no energy for arguing. Especially at your altitude." Filip tried to grin at his own teasing but failed miserably.

"Aye, sure, but did you?"

"No. I found a scroll..." And he told the three of them about the old Lore scroll and what Aury wanted. "It doesn't matter. Aury is free, as she deserves to be. And Balaur has already reaped the benefits of our short-lived marriage. The farmlands are already ours. It's written and sealed. I don't think they can undo it."

"Think?" Drago ripped a leg from the roasted chicken on the tray, then took a bite.

Filip leaned against the side of the hearth, letting the heat lick its way up his leg and arm. "They know there are more Wylfen still. They need us. And we need them. The marriage was unnecessary, and Aury didn't want it. She was honest about it, and I let my fool heart lead me away from the truth into a lie I preferred. This is how it must be." *And I must somehow survive it.*

Drago finished his chicken leg and handed Filip a horn of strong-smelling ale. The cup was cold, and he drank it down in full.

"Your parents will want to find you a new bride," Drago said, his gaze on the tray.

"They will," he said, "but not today."

Costel sat in a stool beside the fire and began organizing his stitching tools in his leather case. "But Aury could still choose you."

"She won't." The words stuck in his throat.

"How do you know?" Stefan asked.

"She was quite clear on the matter from the start. Said she would only marry me if that was the sole path to keeping our people alive and fed. Since those needs are fulfilled, our union has lost its purpose."

"Bull shite." Stefan threw a chicken bone into the fire. "She looked at you like Drago does a venison steak."

Filip raised an eyebrow. "As endearing as that image is, I'm afraid it's erroneous."

The conversation flowed around him, but he shut his eyes and let the exhaustion of battle take him into sleep. At some point, he rose, set another log in the fire, then took one of Costel's chairs to finish the night. Costel snored from the bed; Drago and Stefan were asleep on furs on the far side of the hearth. He smiled sadly. They were good friends, and he was blessed by the Source to have them. He would need them in the coming days.

She was gone. He couldn't believe it. They'd been

perfect together. Or so he'd wanted to believe. Now that he'd met her, life would be colorless without her teasing, her incredible power, the way she went head-on into every challenge like a lioness. The breath went out of him. He gripped his tunic and was surprised he found no hole in his chest.

THAT EMPTY FEELING SPREAD LIKE MELTING CANDLE WAX over the following days.

In the great hall, he dined with his parents, the court assembled on long tables below the dais. Sorina's eyes were red. She had liked Aury from the start, and he hoped she wasn't too stricken over the separation.

"Mother." Filip passed the platter of stuffed cabbages. "Are you ill?"

"Only in heart. I thought...I didn't realize what you had planned," she whispered. "Are you certain you don't want us to strike out at Lore for this situation? Was this truly your decision, to break the marriage and let her choose?"

His throat tried to close around his swallow of wine. "I don't want Balaur to fight Lore. And yes, it was my decision."

She touched his hand, eyes too wise. "I am your mother right now. Not your queen. How can I help you, my love?"

He pulled at the neck of his tunic, then ran his hands along the grain of the well-worn table. "I should consider a new marriage. It will take my mind off her."

Mihai leaned around Sorina, his nose red from the ague he often suffered. "Good choice, Son. I have a woman in mind already."

Filip imagined winding his words back into his mouth. "Already?"

Mihai wiped his mouth on a napkin. "The princess of Khem. She is far lovelier than any Lore brat, from what I've heard."

Anger surged through Filip's veins. "No one is lovelier than Magelord Aurora. No one." He dug into his plate and fought the urge to leave the feasting and find silence in his chambers. Thankfully, his parents picked up on his mood and let him be.

His mind whirled with agonizing questions that he wished he could bury like corpses. How could he even consider another wife? What would it feel like if Aury chose another to wed? To think of her clasping another's hand... He stared at his forefinger, where his wedding ring had been. Had she already removed hers? Would she melt them down to use in some other way? Or would she keep them in a jewelry box and think of him now and then?

Gods, this was going to kill him.

At the conclusion of the night, Mihai stood and raised a horn. "My son has another grand announcement."

A wild idea galloped through Filip's head. He stood and raised his drink. "I do. I am going on a Wandering."

Mihai blinked and traded glances with Sorina.

"I will walk the lands and listen to the wind as our forefathers did before us. I seek guidance for Balaur's next chapter."

Sorina's eyebrows remained near her hairline. "It's a cold time to begin a Wandering."

"The last of the winter will only sharpen my ability to listen." It was a mad plan, but he couldn't stay here. He couldn't begin more marriage negotiations so quickly. Why had he brought it up? He was a fool. Again. At least when he went Wandering, traveling the mountains and beyond, he could possibly purge his fiery love for Aury through sheer physical exhaustion. He'd walk his legs off to get the job done.

Costel, Drago, and Stefan caught his eye from the table running under the tapestry of the god Arcturus and his spheres of bright light. Costel mouthed, "What are you doing?" while Drago and Stefan traded comments that couldn't be heard above the shouts of support for the Wandering and the toasts made in Filip's name.

He bid goodnight to his parents, then left with his men trailing him and loosing questions like arrows.

"How did you know about the Magelord status?" Stefan asked. "When did this start?"

Drago frowned. "Where did the scroll come from again?"

"We're coming with you," Costel said.

Filip shook his head, too tired in heart to answer every query. "It's a Wandering. Not a holiday."

"Don't care," Drago said. "We're going."

"Seriously, my prince." There was no jesting in Stefan's voice. "Are you all right? I would be happy to take you to my family's lands far in the southeast region where no one will bother you about the princess."

Filip wasn't sure which princess he meant—Aury or the one from Khem whom Mihai had up his royal sleeve —but it didn't matter much. He wanted both out of his mind.

They walked elbow to elbow down the corridor, the oil

lamps above flickering with the cold that the castle never seemed to shed despite all the fires.

"I need to clear my head, brothers. I love you all, but this I must do alone."

They argued with him for hours that night, offering him all sorts of options, but by midnight, they'd given in and wished him well.

He embraced Costel first. "I'll miss you, friend."

"Can I ravage your library while you're gone?"

A laugh spilled from Filip despite his dead heart. "Of course. Anytime. Take simple notes for us lesser minds."

Stefan took Filip's forearm in his and set his head against Filip's. "Stay sharp out there, Filip. One stupid move and you're a mountain cat's next day turd."

"Delightful imagery as always with this crew."

Drago punched Filip in the liver, then grabbed him in a tight hug. "Don't miss the spring festival. If you do, I'll go into the mountains myself and run around screaming your name until you're found."

"I'll return before then. I wouldn't want my people to suffer such a horror as your voice at top volume."

The next day, Filip left with the dawn to find solitude and sweat, the only possible balm for his grieving soul.

CHAPTER 56

Aury and Goldheart flew over the snow-covered fields near Loreton Palace, the thundering of hooves an echo to the throbs of pain in her chest. She didn't bother worrying about how she'd evaded Hilda, Gytha, Eawynn, and the rest of her royal guard for this solo ride. This was exactly what she needed. Filip's black-lined eyes and full lips passed through her mind. The deep timbre of his voice, whispering words of support, of love, echoed in her memory, making her wince like a blade sliced toward her throat.

"Get over it. You're fine," she whispered to herself. "He thought you wanted this. He obviously wanted out too. It's over. You're a Magelord, for Nix's fiery sake. You need no one!"

She urged Goldheart to speed up, absolutely raging into the woods that lined the expansive meadow along the Silver River. Trees zipped by, too close, deadly close, but she relished the fear it shot through her and the way

Goldheart tossed her head, as reckless as Aury, enjoying beating the odds as they galloped.

Panting, Aury slowed the mare, then turned her around to head back home. Loreton didn't feel like home though. Not without a grinning, vicious elven prince at her side.

At least a dozen times, she'd struck out for Balaur, determined to convince him that she wanted him and that might be enough for them both, to win him. But she'd heard talk of the Khem princess. He'd moved on already, only waiting a matter of days before arranging a new alliance to help his people. Of course he had. He was a good prince, selfless, driven to do what he could with his position to aid his people.

In her weaker moments, Aury fervently prayed the Khem princess was a toad who snored like a woodsman.

Goldheart was fully lathered by the time they trotted over the drawbridge.

Aury studied the smooth stone and arrow slits of the gatehouse. Strange. The guards weren't at their posts. Goldheart clomped into the courtyard and Aury dismounted, expecting the eldest stable boy to run up like the kind pup he was, but no one approached.

Sharp nails of fear raked her neck.

She led Goldheart inside the stables and set to washing her down, a chore she enjoyed and rarely permitted the stable hands to perform, but the boys' absence had her jumping at every sound. Once Goldheart was clean and brushed, Aury put her in her stall safely and hurried into the palace.

An odd scent flitted through the air—sugar and rosemary—and voices poured from the great hall. It seemed as though every person who worked or lived on palace grounds had packed into the room to dance. The stable hands whirled in circles while Athellore and Gwinnith stepped formally across the end of the dais. Scribes, the blacksmith, Hilda, Gytha, and Eawynn stomped their feet, lined up in a reel formation.

Aury shivered.

This was magic.

She spun to see a haze of golden light, and her vision dimmed as if she'd put on a heavy veil. The shape of a great spinning wheel shimmered into view, and it was such a lovely piece of woodwork that she longed to step closer, to touch the spindle's sharp point, as bright as a dragon's spike. A tingling pressure built at the back of her neck. Her feet shuffled forward a step, the veil of haze thicker. She wanted so badly to press her fingertip on that shiny point.

A flicker of unease sparked inside her mind. Why did she feel like this? She wiped her sticky forehead. Wait. What had she been thinking about just now? What was she worried about?

The spindle caught her eye. So beautiful. The tingling at her neck increased. Who had given her this splendid great wheel? She had to touch it. No harm in touching it.

Smothering the ember of caution, she extended her hand and pressed her finger to the spindle's point.

The scent of old stone and moldering wood overwhelmed her senses. Bright green ivy whipped across the floor, shadowed in her veiled vision. She was numb, lost in visions of scarlet yarn and the sound of a cackling laugh as the ivy wound around her body and dragged her out of the hall.

CHAPTER 57

Filip walked southeast. Days ago, he'd used his elven speed to flee the bitter chill of his homeland. He'd crossed the border and wandered into Lore, pining and muddy and hollow and lean. He knew very well he was setting himself up for more pain, but he didn't have the will to stop his feet from striding into the very town where Aury had traded Goldheart for Cālātor.

"I need a horse. A very fast one, please."

Now that he'd given in to this mad quest to simply see her face again, he couldn't get there fast enough. She could deny him. She certainly would. But he would have given all the gold in the world simply to hear her utter his name one last time. He shook his head at himself. Pathetic.

"Your Highness," the horse master said, ignoring his odd behavior and bowing low. The man sold him a proper lowland gelding with a nice leap in its step.

After a bowl of mutton stew at the local tavern and a

fortifying cup of cinnamon and orange tea, Filip rose to leave.

Two men whispered at the next table.

"Did you hear?" the first asked.

The second man set down his mug, spilling half the contents. "About the merchants not arriving from Loreton?"

"Not just that. They say the whole palace is under some dark spell."

Filip threw coins for his meal next to his bowl, then flew from the tavern as fear reached blazing fingers inside his mind and squeezed.

He raged out of town atop his new, sleek mount. Throwing mud and snow, he rode to Loreton Palace, mind bursting with images of Aury's smile, ears ringing with the memory of her velvet voice, and the phantom sensation of her hands on his body.

A half mile out from Loreton Palace, he pulled the gelding to a halt.

Squinting, he didn't see the gnarled, outer castle walls and the shining stone of the newer palace inside its protected square. From the flatlands by the glistening river, a structure of scarlet rose like a bleeding wound.

He passed the road leading into the town below the palace. Not a single merchant's cart or a cry of a child came from the normally bustling settlement. He gripped the reins, palms sweating.

And then he faced Loreton Palace.

He inhaled sharply. "What in the name of Arcturus and Vahly is that?"

Stomach twisting, he urged the gelding onward until

the lines and slopes of the palace became clear. The walls, the drawbridge, the chains, the keep—scarlet woolen yarn covered every last inch.

Filip was suddenly as bitterly cold as he'd been on Balaur's highest peak.

The Matchweaver held the palace in her magic-heavy hands.

He dismounted before the drawbridge, then slapped the horse to get it running away from Loreton. "Find a filly and don't come back, friend."

His foot hit the first board of the drawbridge, and the wool wound around the palace began to shudder and roil like the river during a storm. He ran under the portcullis as the yarn twisted fifty feet into the air and shaped itself into thorns that lashed toward him. Leaping to avoid a length of blood-red points, he was momentarily dazed at how the witch's magic could transform yarn into something so deadly sharp. Heading for the main doors of the palace, his heart hammering and his jaw clenched to the point of pain, he ducked beneath another swing of the magicked red thorns. One caught his temple, and hot blood ran down the side of his face. His heart beat out one question.

Was Aury alive?

He kicked the doors in and rushed through the foyer. Bright ivy twined the balustrades and joists in the towering ceiling. The scarlet yarn slithered from every archway, chasing him as he burst into the great hall.

He let out an incoherent noise. The Lore folk had pushed the tables to the sides of the room for dancing, but there was no movement. Utter stillness reigned. A hundred or so bodies lay slumped on the flagstones, their sleeping faces crisscrossed with yarn and their limbs lashed together like they were deer packed out after the hunt. Were they dead? Their faces had gone pale, but Athellore's chest moved and—did Gwinnith's lips part?

Yarn wrapped Filip's boot and yanked his foot out from under him. He drew his hatchet and cut through the magicked wool.

"Aury!" His throat was raw.

Hacking at another thorny yarn branch, he fought his way to the corridor where Aury's chamber sat. She might not be trapped there. She might be dead. He murmured a dozen prayers as he ripped a length of magical thorns from his sleeve. Their tips tore at him, scratching him deeply despite his tougher elven skin.

Shoving a shoulder into her door, he powered into her chambers only to find himself tangled in a woolen web so thick that he couldn't see into the room. The strands scratched at his face and hands as he swiped his hatchet, attempting escape. Immediately, more threads replaced the ones he cut.

"Aury! Magelord Aurora! Are you here? Aury!"

The magic thorns ate through his leathers, gauntlets, the knees of his trousers...the more he struggled, the more he suffered.

A thought shone through his wild panic. Aury would mouth off to the Matchweaver right now. Originally, he thought her tongue only gave her more trouble, but who was the Magelord? Aury.

"Listen, Matchweaver!" he shouted. "We aren't together. We heeded your warnings, the bird at the chapel, the evil you spewed at Aury when she scried you. We broke our union. It's over."

A wind gusted across the chamber, and his body pulled against his bindings. The scent of rosemary and something sweet...

A face materialized, disembodied and surrounded by an undulating shadow. The face had bright green hair, the exact shade of the ivy that curled amidst the wool. The Matchweaver's eyes shone like a snake's, glittering, ready to strike.

"A marriage I did not approve occurred in this land. Not simply any marriage either. The wedding of two royal-blooded folk. Such disrespect will not be tolerated. You will live in this web forever while the rest of this castle sleeps on and on and on and..." Her voice trailed away, and her visage dissolved into nothing.

"Know what I think? You're pathetic."

The walls shook, and the wool tightened around him, taking his breath.

"Pathetic," he gasped out. "You strive for attention from the courts of men, fae, and elves and can't be content with your own abode. You long for glory like a youthful fool even after all the long years of your life. One as old as you should have gained wisdom, but you've only grown ridiculous." He tsked and shook his head a fraction, as much as he was able.

A disembodied scream filled the palace, buzzing against Filip's ears, the yarn burning his scratched and bleeding skin.

Then the threads trapping him loosened.

The second he could move his axe arm, he slashed the

threads, then leapt through the middle. The wool snarled like it lived and snapped shut behind him as he rolled out of his fall. He came up beside Aury's bed.

She lay sleeping. Eyelids dusky. Chest barely moving beneath twists of ivy and scarlet yarn. Filip couldn't breathe. Her rosy lips were a dark red, and her cheeks were milky white.

"Aury. You have to wake up." Unwilling to sheathe his hatchet, he carefully used the edge to cut the ivy and yarn, but it reformed itself faster than he could work without hurting her. "Please. I'm so sorry. I don't think you want me, but I'm here, and I'll be your knight, your friend. Whatever I can be for you. Unless you demand it, I won't leave your side. I just have to be a part of your life. I'll take any position."

He stopped fighting the Matchweaver's bonds and leaned over Aury's beautiful face.

"I love you. I tried not to, but I do."

He leaned forward and pressed a desperate kiss to her lips.

Her brilliant, sky-bright eyes flew open.

CHAPTER 58

Aury's mind rolled like storm clouds in the spelled dream state. Visions of the witch's castle in the enchanted forest of Illumahrah, not far from where Aury had lived, shimmered in her mind's eye. She saw the women who had chosen to live on the grounds, their happy faces.

"You see, I am no villain. It's only that your family has wronged me, disrespected my one role in this kingdom, in this life. I am Love, and if they ruin me, they ruin Love."

The Matchweaver showed Aury the whole of Lore as if from a dragon's back. Athellore's face rose up, his mouth a slash and the steel of his blade flashing toward the witch. The land went black like a shutter dropped over a window, immediately dark.

"I must keep the balance here. He must be mindful of my power to match, of the loom and its early witches, the founders, the three that built that magic. And so I do this to you and yours. To show them. To explain the nature of this. All will know when they hear news of Loreton. And poor Aurora Rose. True love's kiss would break you free, but you ran him off, didn't you?" The Matchweaver laughed and laughed, the sound poison. "The king, the queen, they sleep forever as does their only child. A just punishment, I think. I have been merciful. Did you know that I did indeed see you and the elven prince in the loom?"

Even through the murk and haze of the heavy magic, a shock registered with Aury, making her tremble in the bindings she could feel along her arms and legs, around her neck.

"Yes, I saw you both," the witch said. "You are meant to be. Fated. I simply wanted Athellore and Gwinnith to ask me. And they did not." Thunder pounded against Aury's mind. "They arranged the most important marriage without even knocking upon my door. Sleep forever, Princess, and suffer the wrath and the mercy of my will."

Then there was a light pressure on Aury's lips. The scent of sandalwood wove through the air. A shiver of joy ran down her body and lit her from the inside.

It was a kiss. From her true love.

Binding ivy and scarlet wool blackened and crumbled from her body, her mind clearing as she took in Filip, his bleeding face, the chamber filled with ivy and the Matchweaver's yarn, the same shade as the one dropped by her spelled blackbird at the chapel. A myriad of emotions flooded her senses. Joy. Fear. Confusion...

Meeting Filip's gaze for a breath, her questions and desires crooned a silent song between them, then she dove for her staff.

"Rise, river! Rise for me!" She whirled her staff as one

thousand scarlet threads rushed them and the Matchweaver's eerie cackle echoed off the walls.

Spinning and jumping and lunging, Filip sliced and struck with his hatchet, his sharp teeth bared as he thrashed every woolen thorn that grabbed for Aury.

Magic snapped in her veins, crackling down her arms and into her hands as the chamber's temperature dropped. With a grip on her staff, the runes pressing her pricked fingertip, she pulled a flurry of icy snow through the red web blocking the doors.

"Draw together," she whispered.

Would this even work? She hoped to turn the snow to small blades of ice to help Filip fight the witch's magicked yarn and ivy. Her chest ached from the Matchweaver's spell. Her mind tried to shake its fog.

"Come on..." Her hands shook as the magic worked, the snow spinning around them, sparkling brighter and brighter. "Cover your face!" she called to Filip.

He put one gauntlet up as the snow solidified and the sound of it flying grew higher-pitched, the air scented with river and frost. The ice severed the scarlet threads all at once, and the room went silent.

Filip stepped closer.

Aury held her breath. "She's still here. I feel her. I feel the curse." It was a panting mountain cat that stalked every beat of her heart. Death ringed her thoughts, a shadow growing longer, taller, darker.

The beams of the ceiling cracked and plummeted. Filip shoved Aury out of the way before she was crushed. The castle opened to the steely sky, stones flying and wood snapping. A massive dragon spun of scarlet wool raised its head and roared above them.

Filip grabbed her, his fingers tight on her arm. "Source save us. Or can you?" A laugh of despair fell from his lips. "This elven mage is out of tricks."

The dragon thrust its head into the chamber as Aury's legs tried to give out. Dodging the beast's teeth and its flickering, barbed tongue, she held up her staff and threw her power into it. Filip hacked at the dragon's outstretched neck, but the wool healed faster than a fae's flesh.

Magic slithering down her arms like snakes made of fire and ice, Aury willed every drop of water, snow, and ice anywhere near the palace to crash together. Her magic formed a white mass above the dragon. She envisioned a scythe.

The dragon whipped its head around and knocked Filip to his back. He didn't rise.

Fighting the urge to crumble to the ground, to give up and just let the cursed thing end this nightmare, Aury pointed her staff at the dragon's skull as it reared into the sky again, then lunged.

The Matchweaver's curse pushed at Aury's will, crushing it, burning it. She smelled death, cloying and horrible. Taking deep breaths, she straightened her back and stood protectively over Filip, magic swelling inside her like a sacred spring.

She had to shut her eyes to fight the curse's dragging sense of doom. "I will not bow to your vanity, Matchweaver. I claim my fate, my life with the one I love."

There was a noise, and she turned to see Filip leaping from the ground to slash through the dragon's talon. The wool tumbled inert to the floor, only the very tip slicing her gown, the wool magically as honed as any sword.

Hanging above the dragon, magic visibly curling off its edge like cerulean threads, the ice scythe reflected a sliver of the sun.

Aury punched the air with her staff and forced the scythe to slice the head from the witch's dragon and seal the ends of those threads with bitter frost.

An inhuman shriek reverberated through the air, so loud it seemed to be visible, shaking the very essence of the world.

And then Aury's heart lightened. The Matchweaver was gone, and the curse unspooled.

Filip laughed with delight as he grabbed her around the waist and spun her around.

"Enough with the acrobatics, elven mage, let's see this sorcery everyone thinks you have."

He cocked an eyebrow and leaned closer, his lips brushing hers and his gaze touching her cheeks, her forehead, her chin. "You still believe the old myth that elves have magic?"

"You cast a spell when you kissed me on the rooftop, and I dare you to talk me out of my fervent belief."

"I wouldn't dare," he said, a dimple showing in his cheek.

She kissed his dangerous grin, tangled her fingers in his jet-black hair, and savored the oldest magic there was in the world. True love.

CHAPTER 59

Though Aury was technically on holiday from training with Sunniva, the fully-healed Cuthbert, and the Masters, she couldn't stop trying new spellwork. Not far from Loreton, she stood on the banks and whirled her staff over the river's shimmering water. The summer sun warmed her head and Filip's quiet humming filled the air. The water shifted and heaped, then formed a sphere. If she could just get it to move over her without soaking her, then serve as a shield... This would be great for battle.

Once they'd ensured the Matchweaver was gone and everyone had awoken from the curse, Aury had put Filip's wedding ring back on his finger. She'd ordered both him and herself to stop being fools and never again doubt their fated love.

It was appalling to think the Matchweaver had seen them together in the Mageloom and still found it necessary to punish everyone involved. Athellore had tried to arrange her hanging, but Aury had told him about her vision of the land going black, all love lost when the Matchweaver was attacked.

He and Gwinnith had decided to order a border of magicked water to be placed around the Forest of Illumahrah, manned by a unit of mages. The witch wouldn't be able to leave the enchanted wood, but the folk of Lore would still be able to go to her for a love match if they so chose. It placated the people and kept the Matchweaver's power in check.

Aury still wanted to see the hag hanging from a rope someday.

But for now, the kingdom was at peace. The Wylfen would no doubt return, but Lore and Balaur folk would enjoy the calm as long as possible. The summer appeared to be leading them into a bumper crop of wheat and apples, and the Balaur people were already benefitting from the new farmland.

Werian had visited two times over the past season, congratulating the couple and quietly assuring Aury that if she ever needed to escape, he had a ship at the Sea's Claw under a false name. She had only to ask about a strange sea captain named Robin.

Holding her spelled water with her magic, Aury focused on raising it higher and drawing it over the land, little by little. It was easy to pull up a simple lump of water, but to keep the center hollow was an incredible challenge. Her magic tended to be more suited to using blunt force than fulfilling exacting standards.

Filip came up beside her and peeled off his long shirt in one languorous movement, his elven grace jaw-dropping.

His shoulder muscles rolled under his sun-browned skin, an effect courtesy of the outdoor training he kept up at Darkfleot.

Aury swallowed, enjoying the line of his back and the way his trousers hung low on his hipbones. A bead of sweat rolled down his back.

Her sphere of water splashed against the riverbank.

Filip turned a grin toward her. "Oh, I'm sorry. Was that my fault?"

She grabbed his belt and pulled him to her, savoring the feel of his body against hers. "Evil elven prince."

His smile brushed over her neck, and delicious chills spread down her body. He nipped the edge of her ear. "Scary Magelord. Why don't you order me away if you loathe me so?"

"I might if you ruin my spellwork again." She kissed his collarbone. His skin tasted like summer.

He swung her to the ground, then lay atop her among the red-hat wildflowers. The scent of him, sandalwood and leather, flooded her senses as she smoothed her hands over his chest and shoulders. His fingers ran through her hair as his lips grazed her throat. She snaked her arms around his neck and urged him closer. A rumble vibrated through his chest.

"Are you growling at me now?" she whispered.

He looked into her eyes, his bright with longing. "Ah, Aury..."

His mouth found hers, and desire thrummed across her skin, increasing the intensity of every touch, every shift of their bodies.

"Promise me we'll spend the rest of the summer like this," she said.

He kissed her. "I might have to wear a shirt if we're in the chapel." His voice was raspy and full of breath.

"Only then."

His laugh tickled her ear. "As you wish, *amant*."

"What does that mean again?" she asked.

As his hand slid over her ribs, he whispered, "Lover."

Her heart beat wildly against the drum of his. "Will you teach me the Balaur tongue?"

"I thought I already was." He nipped her bottom lip as she laughed and luxuriated in her happy ever after.

Lovely readers,

I hope you are on board for more in this world. **Next up is ENCHANTING THE FAE PRINCE**, the story of Prince Werian and the cobbler's niece, Rhianne. Some of you read an early version of their tale in a limited release I had with the amazing Juliet Marillier. I hope you'll enjoy the expanded edition. Preorder it now so you don't miss out.

For an **exclusive dragon-rider epilogue of Aury and Filip's story, join my newsletter at https://www. alishaklapheke.com/free-prequel-1.** (It says prequel because there is a library of free reads you get when you join.)

And hey, pretty **please review this book**. Reviews help everyone! It's super important. https://www.amazon.com/review/create-review? asin=B08NHZ47MW

Interested in how the gods and goddesses that Filip and Aury mention went from normal folk to amazingly powerful beings? Check out my complete series, DRAGONS RISING, today.

Thanks so much for reading!

Alisha

P.S. If you preordered, here is the link to your exclusive bonuses! https://www.alishaklapheke.com/limited-edition-character-art

Magic Reigns in Lore

Highest Power
The Source

Conduit
The Sacred Oak in the Forest of Illumahrah

The Four Elemental Powers
The goddess Vahly of Earth, Mother of Humans

The goddess Nix of Fire, Mother of Dragons

The god Arcturus of Air, Father of Fae and Forgotten Elves

The goddess Lilia of Water, Mother of Mages

Lesser Gods and Goddesses
The god Rigel, Father of Elves

The goddess Ursae, Mother of Elves

The goddess Lyra, Mother of Witches

ACKNOWLEDGMENTS

Thanks to...

my family, near and far, for putting up with me and my occasionally eccentric behavior. And to Amelia for saving the map!!!

my Goonies. Long shall you reign.

my Turtles, may you have Henries forever and a day. I couldn't do this job without you.

Melissa Wright, Elise Kova, Robin Mahle, Elle Madison, Sarah K.L. Wilson, Grace Drury, and Kelly Stepp for the amazing help shaping this beast into a beauty.

my fabulously clever editor, Laura Josephson, for the wordsmithing.

Storywrappers for the glorious cover.

my Uncommon Crew, Dragon Den, and Typo Hunters for the incredible support throughout my career. You complete me. Seriously. Sometimes you really do have to compl

;)

Love you all!
Alisha

P.S. If I forgot you, blame it on my pirate-like affinity for rum. I DO love you as well. And you know it, so hush.

CPSIA information can be obtained
at www.ICGtesting.com
Printed in the USA
LVHW101544070722
722976LV00020B/527/J